PENGUIN
The L

Katherine Fleet is a writer and author coach for The Novelry. As a journalist, she wrote for *The Guardian*, *Sunday Times*, *Red*, *Stella* and *Grazia*. She lives in a Cotswolds valley with her two rescue dogs, where she writes and coaches full-time. A trip to the small Greek island of Paxos was her inspiration for *The Liars*.

The Liars

KATHERINE FLEET

PENGUIN BOOKS

PENGUIN BOOKS

UK | USA | Canada | Ireland | Australia
India | New Zealand | South Africa

Penguin Books is part of the Penguin Random House group of companies
whose addresses can be found at global.penguinrandomhouse.com

First published by Penguin Books 2024

001

Set in 12.5/14.75pt Garamond MT
Typeset by Falcon Oast Graphic Art Ltd
Printed in Great Britain by Clays Ltd, Elcograf S.p.A.

The authorized representative in the EEA is Penguin Random House Ireland,
Morrison Chambers, 32 Nassau Street, Dublin D02 YH68

A CIP catalogue record for this book is available from the British Library

ISBN: 978–1–405–95783–0

www.greenpenguin.co.uk

In memory of my lovely dad.

'Truth had run through my fingers. Every drop
had escaped.'
Virginia Woolf, *A Room of One's Own*

The wide green eye of the Pool had been there from the beginning of everything. It knew death of old and didn't much care for human drama, which was always so fleeting. Theirs were such small lives, passing in moments, leaving no mark, signifying nothing.

Until this one.

In her, the Pool recognized a very different creature. A seam of rock at her core, dense and unyielding. Something of the ancient running through her. Something of the Ancients. It waited to see what she'd come for.

She stepped into the clearing, the edge of the water just feet away. She didn't mind the near-dark of night, her heartbeat steady and slow. Her skin gave off a dull gleam where the moonlight had lanced the canopy of trees.

The Pool understood then that she was angry, and there was something ancient about this, too. It was like the fury the gods had once felt. There was no heat or fire in it. It went beyond that. It was pitiless, and without passion or doubt, its sparks not from fire but as when metal strikes ice.

A noise in the undergrowth, clumsy footsteps blundering and breaking twigs, made her head lift. She moved silently behind a tree. Aha, thought the Pool. She's come for vengeance.

Now

I get a taxi from the island's tiny ferry port. I didn't think it would be wise to drive a hire car tonight, negotiating hairpin bends in the dark. I've been awake since before dawn because I wanted three clear hours at the airport. I'd been feeling anxious about the flight and didn't want even a hint of rush. I knew my thoughts would otherwise tend towards the catastrophic: bird strikes and black boxes.

Nightfall makes it difficult to tell but things must have altered since I was last here. Change is inevitable, especially in desirable places, and there are definitely more lights winking from the dark hills that flank the road, a star scattering of creeping development. There's a line in a song my brain is too jittery and tired to retrieve: something about losing paradise, if you call it that. I don't even know if I want it to be different or not, nostalgia and dread battling it out.

Whatever other changes might be hidden in the dark, it's still only fifteen minutes from one end of Eos to the other. Richard's house – my mother's now, I remember with a lurch – is in the far north of the island, caught between the wild west coast, where the sun goes down each evening in a blaze of ostentatious glory, and the tranquil white stone beaches of the east.

I open the window to smell the air: the foreignness of it; its warmth without edge, so different from the English night. It's headier than I recall, herbal and floral, cut with sea salt. But, then, it's spring now, everything still new. It was August when I was here before. It had already been sweltering for weeks, the air smelling mostly of baked dust and sun cream.

I tell the driver he doesn't need to take me to the top of the drive – it's steep and winding, and tricky to turn at the top – but he does it anyway. Maybe because I'm a woman. Maybe because he doesn't understand. He'll have to reverse down, taillights illuminating the shrubbery that will reach out to scratch his paintwork. There was only one taxi serving the island back in the day: a dusty saloon with pleather seats that stuck to hot legs. This man doesn't look familiar, but lots of people are unrecognizable decades later, aren't they? Probably I am too.

It's as I'm handing over some cash – euros, these days – that he mentions her. I can't think of anything to say so he assumes I haven't heard and repeats himself, his English good after all. I meet his eyes briefly in the mirror. He can't be much older than thirty. It's probably his father's taxi company: he's too young for the beaded seat-mat tied to the headrest. He's also too young to have his own memories of that summer, yet he knows what happened and its connection to this house.

'Twenty-five years this summer,' he's saying now. 'We never give up. We always hope, you know?'

And I realize that during my long absence she has passed into legend. Things have a way of doing that in Greece.

I watch the taxi retreat into the night. As the engine fades, other sounds sidle in. Insects, a dog barking, the distant thud of music – the bass too heavy to be from a taverna or

4

one of the tranquil waterside bars, at least as I remember them. Maybe there's a club somewhere in the hills, not like the one we went to once back then, but something permanent. Lex would approve of that.

Lex. Her name still catches at me, like a torn fingernail on soft wool. My sister for a single summer.

I push her away, and regard the house looming over me. Reaching out for the gate, I run my fingers over the name spelt out in iron letters. Another exotic name from that time. *Calliope*. For the muse with the beautiful voice.

I hadn't known how to pronounce it. It was Mum who said it out loud first – who got it wrong before I could. *Cally-ope*, she said, on our second evening here, the four of us heading down to the village for dinner. Lex had turned away to laugh, making me hate her a little bit, because how on earth was Mum supposed to know? That hadn't stopped me wishing she just *had*.

But if Lex had wanted her dad to be put off by Mum's lack of education, she was out of luck. He was enchanted by her. Theirs was a real love match from the start, and they both knew it. They felt they'd come home at last.

Cally-ope, Mum had said, smiling, and Richard smiled back, eyes soft and indulgent as he tucked a golden curl behind her ear. 'That's exactly what I thought at first, too,' he said, ignoring Lex's snigger. '*It's all Greek to me!* But it's pronounced cal-*eye*-oh-pee. She was a goddess.'

Mum nodded, and put her small hand through his arm. 'Oh, yes, that's much prettier. I can see why you kept that.'

Lex wasn't laughing any more. I watched her watching them, and wished I could read the thoughts inside her head. I was always wishing that.

I'm back to thinking about her. But then if I do that most days in England, all these years on, it's bound to be worse here, where I knew her.

I make it sound as though she's dead. She's not. That was another girl. Her I try not to think about at all, if I can help it.

We were all fifteen then, our ages coinciding for a few crucial weeks. It's the age girls are most dangerous, or so I've always thought. Young enough for something savage from childhood to remain but old enough to keep it hidden. It's there, though, just underneath: a dark shadow moving through clear waters. It only takes a single drop of blood to bring it to the surface.

Then

The first time I saw Lex, she was sitting in a pool of light from the big window, sun-bathed and gold-edged. She looked up as I came through the door and, in the second before she smiled, her expression was cold. No, that's not fair. It wasn't cold, not quite. Cool, then. Appraising. And in that moment before her expensive manners kicked in and she got to her bare brown feet, I guessed at the adjectives that ticked off in her brain for me. Awkward. Needy. Plain, too, probably.

It would never have occurred to me that she had run to place herself there, having heard the car pull up outside, her father delivering a brand-new family straight from the island hydrofoil. She told me about it later, and I think if I'd known about that small act of faked nonchalance from the start then things might have turned out differently. Why not, if a tiny change of course can save a planet from an asteroid? I didn't know, though, so we set hard that way: her in charge while I followed, a taut wire vibrating with the effort of not being annoying or embarrassing. Of trying to be less like me, and more like her.

'How come you're so tanned?' I said idiotically. 'You must catch the sun really easily.'

She shook back her hair, damp and mermaid-wavy from swimming. 'My school broke up a couple of weeks ago. We came straight out. We always come as soon as we can.'

We was her and Richard. She was drawing a circle around them already, in case I had any notions. And of course she went to private school, where you apparently paid good money for longer holidays.

'Dad says you live in a flat right next to Heathrow.' Her mouth twisted up on one side slightly, an almost-smirk that ruined the symmetry of her face. 'Must be convenient.'

Before I could think of a reply, Richard came in with Mum.

'Ah, here are our girls, together already.' He smiled and ushered Mum further into the room. 'Marilyn, darling, this is my daughter Lex.'

The curse of seeing things through Lex's eyes began in that moment: the make-up Mum had applied in the thin light of the English dawn, and reapplied as the hydrofoil entered the still waters of the port, where Richard was waiting for us with the car. It looked garish now, in the spill of late-afternoon light, her cheeks flushed from her need for this meeting to be successful, and from the mini bottles of wine drunk on the plane. She was always so easy to read – the sort of openness that made people love her if they were kind, and take advantage of her if they were not. I didn't know which Richard was yet. I had an idea about Lex.

I watched Mum cross the room, arms open, offering herself up in the guileless, girlish way she always did, and felt the usual push-pull: protectiveness and scorn, and the after-burn of guilt.

'Aren't you a pretty girl?' Mum said, her hand going out to touch Lex's hair and then pulling back as she lost her nerve. 'I'm always trying to persuade Zoë to grow hers.'

I shoved my hands into my jeans pockets so they didn't go up to fiddle with my boring brown bob, the ends that always curled up wrong on one side. As if merely not cutting my hair would ever have made it like Lex's. The unfairness of this and the stupidity of Mum for suggesting it made my cheeks burn.

'Darling, why don't you show Zoë around?' said Richard to Lex. 'While there's still plenty of light.'

'You don't have to,' I said, once I'd followed her outside and we were on our own. 'It's fine, honestly.'

She cast me an arch look over her shoulder. 'If I show you now, you'll know and won't need to ask again.'

'Right,' I said, pulling at my hair, deciding there and then to grow it long, and feeling cross about the predictability of that.

I thought she'd take me round the garden for a bit and then we'd go back inside, the ordeal over, but she led me instead down a path that wove towards the road through bushes of tiny blue flowers. I wanted to ask what they were called but obviously that was out of the question.

The light had done something peculiar since we'd been inside, ramping up from honey to an almost-neon pink, the same shade as the streetlamp outside my bedroom window when it first stuttered on at dusk. A spasm of homesickness for everything that was familiar went through me like hunger, even though home was so mundane it generally made me want to scream. I stopped to take in the view – the amazing colours, the sea rolling out in all directions, the big old stone house behind us, now an unreal pink itself – and though it was only for a second, Lex whipped round.

'Are you coming or what?'

Like everything else, her face was bright pink. But rather than look hot and sweaty, as I no doubt did, Lex looked like she'd been picked up by the gods and dipped in rose-gold.

'Sorry,' I said, hurrying down the steps to catch her up. 'It's just strange. This morning I woke up in London and now I'm here.'

'Well, yes.' She shook her head minutely. 'The wonder of air travel. Maybe when you grow up you can be an air hostess too.'

I flinched. Her second dig about Mum's job. The job that had thrown her into the path of Richard.

'No, thanks,' I said, as airily as I could. 'I'm probably going to be an artist.' I lunged to catch the wrought-iron gate Lex had left to swing shut in my face.

The road down the hill towards the village was really just a strip of bumpy tarmac flanked by loose earth and stones. Dark skinny trees rose up to block the late sun in places, and I wished again I could ask the names for things. I scanned my memory for books I'd read that were set in hot places and thought they might be cypresses, or maybe parasol pines.

I caught up with Lex, matching my stride to hers, but careful to leave enough space so we didn't touch. We were exactly the same height, I realized, and felt pathetically gratified.

'What sort of artist?' She asked it reluctantly, as though being tested on her manners.

'Mixed media,' I said, hoping she'd leave it there. I'd made it up on the spot. 'Are you nervous about your results?' I continued, before she could press me further. We were both fifteen, but Lex was a school year ahead and had just done her GCSEs. I had only been fifteen for two weeks while she would turn sixteen later in the month. A fiery Leo to my easily wounded Cancer.

She gave me a pitying look. 'Nervous? No. What's the point of worrying about exams once they're done? I leave all that to Dad.'

As we wound down towards the sea, the buildings became more numerous: villas with the same blue bushes and balconies hung with washing. Tumbledown sheds that looked about a thousand years old. There were sleeping cats everywhere, once your eye was tuned in to them, slung across walls and hanging off corrugated-iron roofs, stretched out in depressions in the dry earth and even one in the middle of the road, which I tried to shoo away to safety. Surely a car would be along eventually.

'Don't bother,' said Lex. 'They're strays. They know what they're doing.'

Despite our identical heights, we'd fallen out of step again, me scuttling along in her wake, the dust from her flip-flops coating my repellent-sprayed shins. A man walking uphill on the other side of the road said something as he passed us. He had a round loaf of bread tucked under his arm and was smiling broadly. I was already smiling back when Lex replied to him in Greek, the words spat out like olive stones.

I ran to catch her up. 'What did he say?'

'Nothing.'

'Well, what did you say, then?'

'I told him to fuck off.'

'Why won't you tell me what he said?'

'He was just a disgusting bloke. Aren't you supposed to be from the big city? You're like a weird kid.'

I dropped back, stung, and we walked the rest of the way in silence.

The tavernas were just opening as Lex marched us through the narrow lanes that led to the sea. Their signs were hand-painted and, although I could guess at some of the words, and the sounds they'd make read aloud, others I didn't have a clue about. It was like code. My eye kept going to all the Zs. They were so rare in English that I'd always thought of that letter as mine.

The sea, when we got to it, seemed more like a huge lake. There was so little swell they hadn't even had to build a wall to keep it out. Jutting over it was a bar with an ice-cream counter and glass-topped tables. Lex chose one so close to the water that, when I sat down, I had to double-check all four chair legs were on solid ground. I could imagine toppling in all too easily, embarrassing Lex, who would stare down at me, appalled.

When the waitress came over, a sullen girl who looked about our age, Lex ordered something in Greek without asking what I wanted. I didn't have any money on me anyway. Mum had all our cash back at the villa, an impressive wedge of notes covered with zeros because it was about eight million drachmas to the pound.

While we waited, I plucked at the homemade bracelets my friend Nira had given me last Christmas and which were tatty now, their colours washed out, the ends fluffed and frayed. Twice I managed to bang my leg against the table, making it rock. The first time Lex gave me a look but the second she seemed not to notice. She was frowning, her gaze fixed on the far side of the bay, which curved round so you could only see a chink of open sea, and beyond it the bulky shadow that was Corfu, or maybe the mainland, I wasn't sure. Perhaps I would be able to ask Richard for the answers to all these questions.

There were only a few other tables occupied so the girl brought the order quickly, and it turned out Lex had ordered me a Coke and herself a beer. Her glass said *Mythos* on it in gold and green, and was frosted with cold.

'Why couldn't I have a beer?'

'Do you *like* beer?'

'No. I don't know.'

'Exactly.'

The Coke was actually delicious. We never had the proper stuff at home, only cheap cola from the convenience shop on the corner. As for alcohol, Mum bought German white wine in narrow bottles, which I had somehow gleaned weren't what you drank if you were sophisticated. I quite liked it. She let me have a bit sometimes, at the weekend, though only after she'd had a few glasses herself, her face slackening as it worked through her, making her look more like my nan. For years after, the smell of sweet wine would transport me to the days before that summer: Saturday night TV, *Blind Date* and *Baywatch*, the heating up too high, a whole other day as a buffer between me and school. The claustrophobic comfort of it all.

I watched Lex as she drank her beer. She was so apparently uninterested in me that it was easy to take in all the details without her thinking I was creepy.

She wore denim cut-offs I suspected she'd made herself because I'd seen the tiny red flag sewn into the back pocket. Levi's 501s. I couldn't conceive of taking a fifty-pound pair of jeans and cutting the legs off. Underneath her little white vest she was wearing a black bikini top. The curled ends of the halter-neck tie were tangled through her hair. The black showing through the white would have made me self-conscious, especially around men like the one with the bread, but it was already clear to me that Lex didn't care about things like that. She had said whatever she said to him without even breaking stride, like it happened every day, which it probably did to her.

We might have been nearly the same age, but while I still looked like a child to adults, Lex had passed over the invisible threshold I half dreaded and half yearned for. She actually had something to push out her bikini, but it wasn't really about that, I knew. Or not just that, anyway.

I didn't want to stare at her chest so I looked instead at her silver rings, five on the hand around the beer glass and three on the other, lunar-bright against her smooth brown skin. Her bitten nails, with their torn cuticles, were the only part of her that wasn't beautiful.

I took a breath. 'Look, I won't bother you while we're here. Just because our parents are together, it doesn't mean you have to look after me. I can do my own thing. I'm totally used to it.' I swallowed. 'I'd prefer it, in fact.'

If she knew the last was a lie, she didn't let on. She merely stretched out long in her seat to pull a battered packet of cigarettes out of her shorts pocket. Some Greek brand, with a purple plastic Bic lighter tucked inside. She offered me one, eyebrow raised to show she knew I'd refuse. I nearly took one to prove her wrong, but knew I'd mess it up. It wasn't worth the humiliation.

'Has this happened before?' she said, after a couple of expert puffs, smoke exhaled prettily into the rosy air.

I looked at her blankly.

'The rich-man thing. Is this what your mum does? *Marilyn.*' She drew it out in a cutesy Mr President voice. 'Does she always make sure she's looking after First Class?'

I went hot all over. 'No, not at all. Actually, she hasn't gone out with anyone for years. So don't act like she's some sort of gold-digger. Your dad asked *her* out and she said no to begin with.'

'Yeah?'

'Yeah. And anyway, he wasn't in First Class, only Business.'

'All right, all right. Keep your hair on.'

She stubbed out her cigarette, though it was only half smoked. Out beyond the embracing arms of the harbour, the sun finally slipped into the sea.

'So, it's just you?' I said, after a while. 'I mean, you're an only child, like me?'

She turned her head towards me and I thought for a crushing second that she wasn't going to answer. I felt like I could see the wheels turning in her mind, weighing up which would be more amusing: ignoring me, or doling out a withering put-down. Instead she shrugged.

'I'm Dad's only one. On Mum's side I've got a half-brother. He's three.'

'Oh, sweet.'

'He's a little shit.'

I meant to make a commiserating sound but the combination of the fizzy drink and my strange situation, sitting in a bar on the edge of the darkening sea with this terrifying girl, the harbour lights flickering on with the stars, and the whole of August ahead, had me making some kind of awful snort. I clapped my hand over my mouth but hysteria rose and bubbled over.

'Sorry,' I spluttered, shoulders starting to shake.

I spotted it then, the twitch of her mouth as she nearly laughed, too.

'You're so totally weird,' she said, but she was smiling now. She looked different when she did it, more goofy, less perfect. I admired her for not covering her mouth, as I always did.

She raised her hand for the waitress and when she came ordered two more drinks, this time beers for both of us.

Now

I hesitate at Calliope's front door, not quite ready to go in, and it's then that I notice the lemons – dozens of them rotting where they've fallen, their scent sharp and boozy. It reminds me of the citrus alcopops Lex and I begged for from the mini-market because they were new then, and because the adults didn't seem to count them as alcohol.

No one has picked up the lemons because it was Richard who made things run smoothly here, and Richard is dead. My lovely step-dad – the only father I ever knew – is gone, and Mum is a widow. I can't really absorb these facts yet, but not even I could avoid coming back to Eos under these circumstances. The funeral will be held here, in the place he and Mum moved to full-time a decade ago.

I hope she's still sober, as she has been for so long, but I've spoken to her on the phone from London, detected the tell-tale slide of her words. I've got a horrible suspicion she's been drinking every day since she woke up and found Richard cold beside her in the bed.

I try the door and of course it's unlocked. It still feels careless to me, ever the city girl, but it's how they do things here. There's something heart-in-mouth about it for me, though, especially with death hovering so close.

Mum must have heard me because she's waiting in the dimly lit hall, barefoot like a teenager. I'm used to seeing her in the airport arrivals hall in England, the smartest-dressed person off the flight in her skirt suit and three-inch courts, as though she never retired as cabin crew at all.

'Hello, love,' she says, and the tremor in her voice makes my eyes fill with tears.

'Mum, I'm sorry.' I've said it so many times already, but it's different here, in their home, in real life.

When she doesn't come to me, as she usually would, I go to her. She feels diminished, bird-boned and brittle.

'Come into the living room so I can have a look at you,' she says, and this feels more normal except that now I can see her properly too, and she looks ten years older than when she came to stay at Christmas. Too much alcohol and not enough food have given her a pouchy jaw and hollow eyes. She'll be seventy next year and, for the first time, she looks like an old lady.

'Are you eating anything?' I say, and the transition from daughter to parent feels horribly complete.

'Oh, I know I look awful.' Her hands flutter at her face. 'I can't stop crying. It's all I do. You should see the state of me in the morning.'

'You don't look awful. But even if you did, it's fair enough, isn't it?'

She reaches out to squeeze my hand.

'Where's my little Jess?' She looks behind me, as though a twelve-year-old might be hiding behind my legs like a shy toddler.

'I did tell you. She's coming out later so she doesn't miss too much school. Ben will drop her off at the airport. She'll be here in good time for the . . . for the funeral.'

She forgets to offer me a drink when she goes to get one for herself. Back before she stopped, she was someone who pressed drinks upon people. A generous host, but also one looking for accomplices. She'd always liked a drink, but it was during that summer that it began to seem more than that. Richard never drew attention to it, but maybe he just felt comfortable with it. His own mother had been a drinker so the association wasn't a bad one for him, both of them benign drunks, blurry and sweet rather than belligerent.

I mention the taxi driver asking me about *her* then. I can't seem to help it, being here. Of course, I'm also aware Mum is unlikely to remember in the morning. 'He was saying it was twenty-five years. That they never give up hope. I wasn't expecting it. He was only a young guy.'

She turns to look blearily at me from the open fridge door, hand clasping the neck of an open wine bottle.

'I'll have a glass of that too, if it's okay.'

'Oh.' She looks at the bottle, confused. 'Yes. Of course.'

It seems to take a while, the finding of another glass and the pouring. I resist getting up to help her, and I don't know why. Actually I do. I don't like seeing her drunk. If asked, I would say I'm worried about her falling or damaging her liver, but there's more than a vestige of teenage embarrassment in it, too. In the corners the lamps can't reach, Lex is there, smirking in the shadows. *Does your mum always drink like this?*

'I can't believe it's been so long,' I try again, when she's settled back in her chair. I take a sip of my wine. It's good, cold and crisp. One of Richard's.

'What's that, love?'

'Since she went missing. Since I was last here. It all feels quite . . . I don't know, surreal.'

'Surreal?'

'I can't get my head round where the time's gone. I've been so anxious about coming back. I barely slept last night and obviously the funeral is not for a week yet, and I –'

'There are things I need to organize,' she interrupts. 'People will want to pay their respects but they can't all fly out here at the drop of a hat.'

'No, I know. Of course. I wasn't criticizing.'

'I know you don't want to be here, but I told you not to come and you have anyway.'

'Well, of course I had to come. How could I –'

She cuts across me. 'Although God knows there are worse places to be stuck.'

'I didn't mean –'

'It's not about you, is what I'm saying,' she interrupts again, sitting forward in her chair. 'It's about Richard. My Richard has died.' Her voice cracks, but when I go to stand, she puts up her hand. 'That's why you've come. It's not *surreal* for me to be here. This has been my home all these years. Our home. Mine and Richard's.'

I had said it to myself on the plane, and on the hydrofoil, over and over: be kind to her, don't be sharp, don't *revert*. I breathe out slowly. 'Look, you're right, I'm sorry. Let's not . . . We always . . .'

She nods. She knows the old ruts we slide into as well as I do.

'I think it's just that I can't take it in. Richard being gone, I mean. I don't want to take it in. We got lucky with him, didn't we?'

She softens then, almost smiles. I know she appreciates the *we* especially. 'Oh, we really did.'

The two of us sit quietly for a while, drinking the good wine, the atmosphere between us easing. I take in the room properly and everything looks just the same, to an unnerving degree. Mum and Richard came to live here full-time when he retired and I suppose I'd thought things would change once Calliope became more than just a holiday home. They didn't. Memories stir and shift around me. All of it feels like yesterday and a hundred years ago.

'Do you think you'll sell up?' I dare to ask, as we head up to bed, both slightly unsteady. We'd finished the wine and opened another bottle, red this time. I had put one of Richard's old LPs on – Crosby, Stills & Nash – and when it finished, the turntable still going round because neither of us could be bothered to get up, I thought I could hear the old ghosts whispering in the static from the speakers. Or maybe it was just the house, lulling herself to sleep.

She turns at my question, hand gripping her bedroom door. Her mouth is dark from the wine. 'Sell Calliope?'

'I'm not saying you should.'

'Well, it might not be mine to sell.'

'Oh, but surely . . .'

She sighs and reaches up to pat her hair into place. It's an old tic, which only draws attention to the fact it needs a wash, and that the bright blonde has iron-grey roots. I've never been allowed to see it like this before. I doubt anyone has.

'We didn't discuss the specifics,' she says. 'I didn't like to. He tried a few times, but I thought it was morbid. Anyway, I knew he'd take good care of me. He always did.'

'Mum?'

She's halfway inside the big bedroom in which she now sleeps alone. 'What, love?'

'Is she coming?'

'Well, of course she is.' She says it gently. 'He was her father. They might not have seen eye to eye all the time, but he was more of a parent to her than that mother of hers ever was.'

'When?'

'Oh, come on. This is Lex we're talking about. You never know what she'll do from one minute to the next. She'll show up when she shows up.'

It takes me a long time to fall asleep, despite the early start. The window is wide and I wonder if I'll hear the strange beeping cry of the little scops owl, but the silence of the night is complete. When I do drift off, my dreams are of girls. Three of them, heads bent together, lies and secrets rising off them like mist.

Then

I wasn't sure what the next morning would bring, whether the fragile bond forged between Lex and me at the bar would have survived the night. I was the first to wake in the house and it was a relief to be able to explore without her cool gaze on me.

I hadn't been expecting the house to be old. I'd never stayed anywhere like it. Our maisonette at home was built in the 1950s and always felt makeshift, like the temporary huts at school they'd slung up after the war, and which were still there. I'd assumed Richard would own a sleek modern villa: a white sugar cube balancing on jagged cliffs, looking like it might at any moment tumble into the sea and dissolve in the salt. I'd seen it so clearly in my mind as the plane climbed out of the cloud hunkering over London and nosed into the blue.

Instead, Calliope must have been there for a couple of centuries at least, her stone soft with the years, her shutters painted dark green. They perfectly matched the cypresses that encircled her like a queen's private guard, as dark and dense as yews in an English churchyard. They were cypresses; it was the first of many questions I asked Richard.

Honeyed beams of light fell across me as I moved around the downstairs rooms, picking things up and putting them back carefully, all of them lovely and interesting.

It was the sort of house I knew from old children's books. I'd long dreamt of living in such a place, just as I'd wondered what it would be like to have a sister, someone like Lizzy Bennet, or one of the Fossils, or Katy Carr.

The sun soon lured me outside. Without the shade of the house for protection, the light was blinding, like nothing I'd ever experienced. I felt stunned by it, and the way it made all the colours brochure-bright and vivid. I'd always assumed that nowhere really looked like that, that they doctored the photos so they were more tantalizing to people booking their holidays abroad. Apparently it did look exactly like that, at least in this place.

I went back in for my new sunglasses and a wide-brimmed old hat I'd noticed hanging on a peg, spotted with damp. Even then, I had to squint. The hat couldn't have belonged to Lex – it was too old-fashioned, too stiff and proper – and I wondered if it was a cast-off of her mother's, or left behind by some other girlfriend of Richard's. Someone posher than Mum, who knew about hats.

Lex had told me the previous night that around the headland to the west the coast was completely different from the east, with cliffs that rose straight up out of pounding waves. There was a lighthouse she'd take me to see, although I wondered now if she'd meant it, or whether it had just been something she'd said when she was tipsy. After the beer, we had drunk two daiquiris each, freshly made with liquidized peaches to sweeten the rum. Lex had paid for them all with a credit card she'd produced from the back pocket of her cut-offs.

All I could remember of the walk back up to the villa was the warm dark night pressing in like soft hands and the din of the cicadas. I kept my eyes on Lex's feet ahead of me in the gloom, placing mine exactly where hers had trodden. Calliope was quiet when we got there, just a single lamp left burning. The only other sign we weren't alone was the empty champagne bottle in the kitchen. Though Mum had been seeing Richard for months, it was at that moment I finally understood that everything had changed, the realization cutting through the cocktail blur like iced water. It wasn't just me and Mum any more. I would no longer be her whole world. It was a precarious sort of feeling, but it was also a relief. Being Mum's everything had sometimes felt like a lot.

In the sun-drenched kitchen, I was halfway down a tepid glass of water from the tap when Lex came in, features still blurred with sleep. She looked younger without eyeliner.

'You know you're only supposed to drink the bottled stuff, don't you?'

I looked at the glass as though it contained cyanide and tipped it down the sink. As she poured herself a glass of chilled mineral water, the plastic bottle cracking as she gripped it, my hand went to my stomach as though I might be able to feel the bugs already raging inside, green and spiked.

'You'll probably only vomit for forty-eight hours,' she said. 'It's good for losing a few pounds.'

She caught sight of my face and laughed. 'Christ, I'm joking. You'll be fine. You're just hung-over. A walk will sort you out.'

I took my hand away. 'A walk?'

'To the lighthouse. Remember?'

'Sort of.'

'That's my mother's hat you're wearing.'

I snatched it off.

'No, have it. She's hardly coming back for it, is she?'

I couldn't think what to say so I watched her drizzle honey straight into a large tub of yoghurt and eat it with the tip of an enormous, battered serving spoon.

'How long do you need to get ready?' She shoved the yoghurt back in the fridge with the spoon in it.

'Five minutes?'

She stopped at the kitchen door. 'Wear trainers rather than flip-flops. The paths are rocky. And your bikini under your clothes in case we stop off for a swim on the way back.'

'I haven't got a bikini.'

She rolled her eyes. 'Swimsuit, then. Has it got your ten-metre badge sewn on it?'

'Twenty, actually,' I shot back.

She snorted. 'Excellent. See you back here in five.'

'What's the big rush?' I called after her.

She hesitated in the doorway. 'Dad wants to talk about something. One of our "family meetings"' – she did inverted commas in the air – 'even though there's only two of us. I think it's to do with something that happened last term and I . . . Well, if I'm not here, we can't discuss it, so chop-chop.'

Only two of us. It was silly, but for a second, when she said 'family', I thought she'd meant me and Mum, too.

I was expecting an English sort of lighthouse, tall and white, shaped like a salt cellar, but Lex's lighthouse was squat and square and made of yellow stone. The view was incredible, though: a vastness of deep Hellenic blue from the sky and the sea that reflected it. The breeze was strong enough to push at us as we stood there, drying the sweat from the steep walk and tugging strands of Lex's hair out of its ponytail. I was gratified that she kept glancing at me to gauge my reaction.

'This is amazing,' I said truthfully, and she offered me a stick of her Juicy Fruit.

'What happened at school, then?' I said later. We were sitting on a big flat rock close to the edge. In the near distance was a huge stone arch, the sea shoving back and forth through the hole at the bottom. Lex had claimed you could walk the narrow path over it quite safely, which I was now dreading she would decide we should do.

She sighed. 'Oh, God, it's so boring.'

'I highly doubt that. What's boring is me having a hundred per cent attendance record this year.'

'You didn't have a single day off sick?'

'Nope. I got a certificate in assembly and everything.'

She laughed, less reluctantly than she had the evening before. 'I had loads of time off – mainly because I kept getting suspended but also there were weeks when I didn't go back after an exeat. My mother wasn't there so I just stayed at home. Strangely, I didn't get a certificate in assembly.'

'Don't you like it at school? I mean, don't you have a swimming-pool and lacrosse and stuff?'

'Yes, because I do actually go to Malory Towers.'

'I always wanted to go to boarding-school but Mum thinks they're cruel.'

'Well, you couldn't have affor–. . .' She tailed off.

'No, but there are scholarships and stuff.'

'Actually my school does play lacrosse. It's brutal. See this?' She held back her hair and pointed out a faint, inch-long line just above her temple. 'Got it in practice, during second year. Dad wouldn't let me play after that.'

I smiled, knowing she'd given me that to make up for what she'd said about money.

'Do you miss it?'

'No, but my teachers think doing sport kept me on the straight and narrow. They reckon it's all been downhill ever since.'

'What are the other girls like?'

'Awful. I hate them, and the feeling is mutual.'

I digested this. My thoughts felt clearer here, away from London's clutter. After I'd met Richard back in June – me, him and Mum going out for dinner in the West End, Lex's absence never sufficiently explained – I had often tried to picture the daughter he'd told me about. I imagined her at her posh school, the undisputed queen of the popular group, the ones who were pretty and clever *and* did no work. Meeting her hadn't dispelled this image: I still had a vivid image of her sashaying through sunlit corridors, gaggles of younger girls nursing crushes on her from a distance, sighing about her hair before they went to sleep in their fuggy dorms. But perhaps it was a little more complicated than that.

'I don't hate anyone at my school,' I said. 'Not really. I mean, maybe some of the more disgusting boys. I don't think anyone hates me either. It's just . . . nothingy. I've got this friend, Nira. She made me these.' I slid a finger between the inside of my wrist and the friendship bands and pulled them taut. 'But I don't think we're that close.

Like, we don't see each other outside school much. We hardly ever speak on the phone. Mainly, we're just the two cleverest girls in the year.'

'If you do say so yourself.'

I shrugged. 'It's true.'

The thing was, Nira and I hadn't chosen each other. It had made perfect sense to everyone that we had paired up as the most academic in a school where even the teachers were suspicious of brains. One of us came top in everything, and we were called boffins as a matter of course. It ended up making perfect sense to us too.

The phone thing had bothered me for a while. I knew other girls in our class were straight on to the phone to each other as soon as they got home from school. They did stuff at the weekend, too. I did none of the social stuff that went on in the *Sweet Valley High* books I borrowed by the half-dozen from the library. I found the blonde twins in them much more foreign than the Victorian heroines I'd come across in Hardy and the Brontës, with the little red sports car they shared, and the boys they dated, who carried their books for them from locker to home room. No one seemed to own a bag.

'I've got a not-quite-friend like that too,' said Lex. 'Not that we're winning any prizes. We mainly just sneak out to smoke together.'

'It's not what I thought it would be like at our age,' I said. 'With friends, I mean.'

'No.' She spat her chewing-gum into its foil paper and rolled it into a small ball.

'Was it the smoking you got suspended for?'

'One of the times. Then it was because some of us

skived off to meet the boys from St Patrick's and were seen together *in our uniforms*!' She did an outraged posh voice. 'Then there was this rave I sneaked out to.' She glanced at me to see if I was impressed so I kept my face carefully neutral. 'The third was something else.'

I waited. People found silences awkward. I found everything awkward, which meant I could withstand them quite well.

'It was actually really unfair.' Her voice had dropped and I leant in so the breeze didn't snatch away the words. 'I got the blame for something because the other girl went crying to her parents. It should have been between us but once she'd involved them and they went to the headmistress, it all got out of hand. They made out like I'd been bullying her.'

'And had you?'

'No. She got nothing she didn't deserve. She . . . she was saying stuff about me. We'd been at this party and afterwards she spread all these stories.'

'What stories?'

Lex shook her head. 'Just a load of bullshit.'

'She was probably jealous of you.'

That won me a rueful smile. 'Yeah, maybe,' she said. She went to say more but stopped, then said it anyway. 'That only just happened actually. I got thrown out a week before the end of term. I was already on my last warning because of the rave thing.'

'Oh. But you're going back in September?'

She shrugged. 'Dad's talking about trying somewhere else. He never wanted me to go there anyway. It was Cassandra's old school.'

'Cassandra?'

'My mother. They got divorced when I was eight and, frankly, it was a miracle they lasted that long. I think Dad stuck it out as long as he could, which is probably why he was sworn off women for so long. Until your mum, really. I started calling her Cassandra to wind her up but I think she actually prefers it. She'll play Mummy to Archie, but not me. Anyway, all the suspension did was buy me extra time on holiday here, with Dad.'

'No regrets, then, eh?'

'No regrets.'

I couldn't tell whether she was genuinely unbothered about the whole thing or just acting tough. I wanted to know more about the suspensions, too, whether she'd really been to a rave, which I'd only seen on the news, and what had happened between her and the girl she'd fallen out with. Either way, she seemed unreachable again now, her eyes on the navy-blue line of the horizon while her hair whipped around her head. The line of her jaw was hard and set.

Now

I wake early, unsure where I am for a second, the pillow-case under my cheek smoother than usual, the light angling in from the wrong side. When it clicks, an old excitement crackles through me before the sadness for Richard and the anxiety of having dared return here kick in. I always need more sleep at home – the first thing I do each morning is calculate how many minutes I can get away with hiding in bed. Here, I get up instantly, not just the jitters but the pull of the place too strong to resist. It was the same back then.

When I remember that first week it stretches out in my memory, long and blissful. Or mainly blissful. Lex was disdainful of Mum at times, even as she effortlessly charmed her in the next moment, asking if she would plait her hair or offering to fetch her a drink.

As for me and Lex, it was surprisingly easy at the start – particularly when we were on our own, when our parents weren't watching us to check we were getting on, and before the dynamics started to get complicated. I couldn't quite believe my luck, hanging around with this golden girl who seemed to think I was quite funny, and chose to spend time with me when she could have just blanked me.

Still, even at the beginning I knew instinctively when I was getting on her nerves. When that happened, I tried to make myself scarce and Calliope was my refuge. Lex was never inside during the day – like Mum, she craved the sun; it was something they unexpectedly had in common. Neither of them could get enough of it, their skin another shade browner each evening, their hair even paler, the pair of them like photographic negatives of me.

I liked the heat too – the way it made my muscles loosen and my thoughts spread and drift – but I couldn't be out in it for long. When it got too much, I liked to retreat to the quiet rooms the sun was only admitted into by degree: a slanted beam here, a bright splash there. It was in those hours, searing outside and cool within, that I got to know every corner of Calliope.

Inside, the past's echoes turned and shimmered like dust motes in the sun, and were especially obvious in the attic. I hid up there not just to give Lex a break but for my own sake, too, when I was tired from looking at things through her eyes as well as my own, and from being the most appealing version of myself.

The attic was one big room with huge wooden beams and round windows pushing out through the roofline. There were no rugs on the floor but the boards had been beeswaxed and their dusty smell rose up when the sun was strongest. I liked to lie across those bars of gold, broad bands heating my skin. Beyond the high-up windows there was nothing but sky: perfect circles of fathomless blue.

I found that if I lay there quietly for a while, eyes un-focused, the old days of the house would start to flicker on the lime-washed walls, as though someone had set a zoe-trope spinning in the corner. The whispers that went with them were in Greek so there wasn't much point in trying to catch them. I only knew 'thank you', 'good morning' and 'good afternoon'. *Efcharistó. Kali mera. Kali spera.* Often, I fell asleep.

Calliope was an anomaly on the island – a relic of the last days of Venetian rule, before Napoleon turned up at the end of the eighteenth century. She should have been built in the middle of a town, so people could have paused to admire her fine stonework. As it was, she was appreciated mainly by Richard and me, and the swallows that nested in the crannies where fragments of stone had slipped, worried at by the sun and the passing years, and occasionally by a shift in the earth's plates, miles underground. My favourite time of day was just as it began to wane, when they came out to swoop and circle around Calliope while she blushed at the sinking sun.

'She was my sleeping beauty,' Richard told me, on our first full day. It was just the two of us out there in that unreal pink light, him in a Panama hat and sipping from a glass of Sancerre, like a poster-boy for sixties grammar-school upward mobility. He'd been born in a council flat in West Ham, just a mile or so east of where Mum had grown up in Bethnal Green.

'The cypresses had completely surrounded her. She was like a rumour, or a ghost. No one had seen her properly for years.'

He told me he had fallen in love with the crumbling bits, seeing what the place had once been, and what he could make it again. Make *her* again. Lex was just a baby then, but already his marriage to Cassandra was falling apart. I think part of the reason he'd saved Calliope was because he couldn't save that. I get that now, as an adult – an adult whose marriage has also foundered lately.

Richard had had to go over to Corfu to find a proper architect – Eos was too small. Spiros was a huge bearded man who'd made a name for himself celebrating the old and decrepit when that was still quite unfashionable. He had a way of shoring up in subtle ways, making a virtue of the falling apart, doing just enough to make it safe without diminishing its character.

He'd got particularly excited about the well that was discovered in the slightly chilly corner of what was now the kitchen.

'He reckoned it was hundreds of years old,' said Richard, leading me back inside and switching on the spotlights that illuminated the long drop. 'Maybe even a thousand. Much older than the house. I thought it ought to be made a virtue of, hence the glass top and the lights inside.'

He smiled at me, checking I was still interested, and I smiled back sheepishly – wanting to please him but also aware of Lex's sudden arrival in the kitchen, to root noisily in the fridge.

'Not really Lex's thing, history,' said Richard, with a wink, loud enough for her to hear. 'She prefers to forge onward, never looking back. Isn't that right, darling?'

'When are we going for dinner and when is Eleni coming next?' Lex said. 'There's literally nothing to eat in this house.'

'Literally nothing?' He gave me another conspiratorial look. 'She'll be here tomorrow morning. She needs to sweep your floor so make sure there are at least one or two small gaps between the mountains of clothes.'

The glass disc that topped the well was thick enough to walk over, anchored in place only by its weight. Richard stood on it to demonstrate as Lex rolled her eyes and headed back outside. I never dared stand on it, certain it would crack and fissure, like a thawing lake, but Lex took to lying across it on the days when the sun's ferocity defeated even her, bare belly down, suntan oil smearing the glass, annoyingly nonchalant about the drop – which was so far down the spotlights couldn't find the bottom.

I loved that a house could be a she – like a ship or a nation. Calliope quickly felt more intimate than that, though: a beloved family member known to all by a single name. I realize now that I was as desperate for a family as I was for a friend. Of course I had Mum – had always had Mum – who constantly juggled her work schedule so someone was there when I got home from school. After Nan died, it was Auntie Ann from up the road, who wasn't a relation at all, but often it was Mum. She'd gone part-time because of me, and always did short-haul after I was born, even though she'd loved the longer routes, chasing the sun to Hong Kong or outrunning it all the way to San Francisco.

It was the night that Mum pronounced 'Calliope' wrongly. It was also the night when the waiter at the taverna thought I was Richard's daughter. It was probably just our colouring, but I was so pleased, and Richard saw that and was pleased too, his eyes misting, while Mum beamed at us both. He was such a soft-hearted man, and he didn't get much softness from Lex. I'm sure it seemed like I was sucking up to him, when really I just wanted both of them to *keep* me and Mum. The thought of going back to Hounslow, of never coming here again, of never seeing Lex again, was already terrible to me. I made myself picture it every night in those early days in the hope I'd be inured to it when it happened.

I was more eccentric then than I am now – or perhaps I've only buried that part of myself, along with so much else. Perhaps we all do as adults, afraid of being thought odd – but I remember, even as I was playing out worst-case scenarios in my bed at night, being sure I could sense the house shift and breathe, settling down like an animal for sleep. Once that idea took hold, I flinched whenever Lex slammed a door, as though it might bruise Calliope's old bones.

'I've just had a message.' Mum's voice makes me jump. She's standing in the doorway, holding a cup of coffee, eyes bloodshot from a night of crying. It comes at me again, like a hard shove: Richard has gone, and the years with him.

Her hand trembles as she sets down the coffee on the bedside table.

I watch as she opens the shutters, movements both stiff and wavering.

'Was it from Lex?' I say, though I hardly need ask.

Mum straightens up wearily. I can't read her expression with the light behind her. 'She's arriving tonight.'

My heart dips and flutters at the thought of seeing her again. I wonder if it's like Mum and the drink: the dreading it and the wanting it swirling together so that you can't tell what's true and what's a trick.

Then

It took a week from when we'd arrived, but I was finally beginning to tan. My nails were growing faster, I was sure of it, and hoped the same applied to my hair, though that was harder to judge. Lex had been sulking in her room all morning, only perking up when Richard said he'd drop the two of us at a beach bar that was too far to walk to in the heat. The cause of the sulk was to do with her school, which Richard and Cassandra had decided she would go back to in September, either to start A levels or, if her GCSE results – only a few weeks away – were bad, to retake. Richard had apparently promised Lex he would talk to her mother about alternatives, and I think she'd secretly hoped she could start again somewhere new. Still, I knew by now that her sulks didn't last long, her natural energy and low boredom threshold winning out soon enough. I was already so attuned to her patterns, you'd have thought we'd known each other for years rather than weeks.

The beach bar was at the bottom of a steep path shaded by pine trees, through which you could glimpse the ridiculous blue of the sea. I had expected something more English: family units separated by windbreaks and coolbags full of clingfilmed sandwiches. This was a much more sophisticated affair. The bar was built around a huge tree whose dense canopy served as a roof, tiny lights woven through it, like the night sky. It also serviced a long line of loungers that snaked down the beach, a thatched umbrella shading each pair. There was only one left when we got there. Lex took casual possession of it by overtaking an elderly couple. They went off grumbling about our lack of manners, which was thrilling and shaming in equal measure for me. I'm not sure Lex even noticed. The shade was such a relief after a morning spent cooking by the pool that I fell asleep almost immediately.

When I woke, the white noise of the beach pulling me up and out of grey dreams of home, Lex had ordered a big bottle of water. It had been sweating in its plastic for a while but was still deliciously cold and we drank the whole thing. The fact that there was waiter service felt impossibly glamorous, and now I was awake, she ordered a lunch of calamari and salad topped with a huge slab of peppered feta. I poked around it, not really eating anything, until she sighed extravagantly, called the boy over again and got me a bowl of chips covered with vinegary ketchup.

'I've just realized,' I said, licking sauce off my finger. 'Both our names are Greek.'

'Are they?' Lex was frowning, half off in her own thoughts.

'Yes.' I rolled my eyes. 'You're so oblivious. Alexandra and Zoë.'

'How do you know I'm an Alexandra?'

'Well, aren't you?'

She tutted. 'Yes, all right. But no one calls me that except my parents if I've been awful. And Penny sometimes. Zoë doesn't really go with you, somehow.'

'Who's Penny? And what do you mean, Zoë doesn't go with me?'

'I dunno. It's just not very you. You should be called something Victorian and eccentric.'

'Thanks very much.' I said it sarcastically but I was smiling. She'd given this some thought. She'd given *me* some thought. 'I think I'll take that as a compliment.'

'Weirdly, I think I actually meant it as one.'

'It was Mum who came up with Zoë. I think she thought I'd turn out more like her, good at stuff like . . . dancing.'

Lex smirked. 'You do actually look quite alike, though.'

I turned to her in astonishment. 'No, we don't. She's all blonde and . . . *done*. We're total opposites.'

'No, you're not, actually. Yeah, she wears make-up and dresses up, but you've got the same face. You're the same shape, or you're going to be.'

I put my arms round myself and Lex laughed, reaching over to pull them away.

'What's about to happen to you happened to me last year. I was straight up and down like an ironing board and then, boom, tits and hips. I hated it. At first.'

'But I . . .' I stopped. I knew she was right. Something had started to happen this year. Silvery marks had appeared across my hips, three on each, like the stripes of a fairy tiger. I finally needed my bra. The quality of the boys' teasing at school had subtly changed in a way it hadn't for Nira, though I generally avoided thinking about it.

They touched me now, when they called me a boffin. That was new. Hard fingers reached out as they passed to dig under my white bra straps, hatefully visible under my regulation polyester blouse. Sometimes they barged into me in the hectic corridors between lessons, close enough for me to catch their boy-stink, breath sour from school-dinner gravy, sweat overlaid with Lynx. I didn't want it, any of it. Not yet.

When we finally got back to Calliope, the dusk was thickening, deepening the blue of the sky until it was violet. I felt drunk on sun and sea air and knew I'd sleep like the dead.

Mum and Richard were sitting on the terrace. There was music on in the sitting room, floating out through the open doors. Round lights like moons were strung through the trees and staked at either side of the paths that twisted through the garden. Desperate moths batted at them, though they couldn't have got any closer to the light. It was like they wanted to be inside it.

Richard got to his feet the second he saw us. 'Here you are,' he said. 'We've been waiting hours.'

'Why?' said Lex. 'You knew we were at the beach.'

'I gave you money for a taxi so you'd come back in good time. We said five, remember?'

Lex shrugged. 'Why does it even matter? It's supposed to be a holiday, isn't it?'

I glanced at Mum but she was gazing at Richard adoringly. She hadn't looked my way in days. There were bowls of olives on the table and she didn't even like olives. She liked cheese and onion crisps. Both of us were being steadily seduced by everything around us. I wanted that and I knew she did too, but I was still afraid of it — afraid of what would happen to us if it was snatched away, just as we'd allowed ourselves to be seduced.

'Well, never mind,' Richard was saying. 'You're here now. Sit down and join us, if you can stand it. We wanted to take you out for a special dinner, to that sunset place on the cliffs, but we'll never get a table now, so we'll have to make do here, have a barbecue instead. Maybe that'll be nicer anyway, a family dinner for just the four of us.'

As I glowed from Richard's reference — Mum and I definitely part of the *family* this time — I felt rather than saw Lex's inevitable eye-roll as he went inside. In some ways, I wished the two of us had stayed out, maybe ordered more chips and an ice-cream at one of the tavernas in the village. I would gladly have played happy families with Richard and Mum all day long but in many ways it was simpler when it was just me and Lex — when our differences made it fun, rather than something to be competitive about: Mum so impressed by Lex's confidence and looks, and Richard approving of my bookishness and good manners.

He came back out with a bottle of champagne and four glasses. I turned to Lex in confusion to see if she knew what this was about. But she was frowning too.

'Oh, Richard, maybe we should . . .' Mum didn't finish her sentence because he popped the cork with practised ease. She was still smiling anyway. He handed her the first flute and her hand wasn't quite steady. She was clumsy when she'd drunk too much, but not shaky. I realized she was nervous.

Richard looked meaningfully at her but she seemed too uncertain to take any sort of cue, sipping instead at the champagne, her eyes cast down to the table, even though we hadn't even done a toast yet.

He covered her hand with his and raised his glass with the other. 'We've got a little announcement to make. Well, a big one actually. I'm very proud to say that Marilyn has agreed to be my wife. We know it's quick — not quite six months since we met – but we're sure. Actually, we've been sure for a while, but we wanted to know that you two girls got on.'

A stream of thoughts whipped through my mind but the first was the loudest. *I might never have to stop coming here.* It wasn't just about the island, or Calliope, or having a sort of sister, although I felt as though I was pretty besotted with all those things already. No, it wasn't so much about the particulars, although they were all wonderful. It was the window into a whole other life. I had been looking through it hungrily for a week, and now Richard had lifted the sash as high as it would go. A new family and, yes, the freedom that wealth brings. The liberation and luxury of not having to think about money is something rich people never appreciate.

As all these thoughts fell over each other inside my head, Lex got to her feet, shoved her chair back with a screech and ran inside. Her glass rocked dangerously and I reached out to steady it, even as I absorbed her reaction like a punch – a winding hurt I could see reflected precisely in Mum's face. I understood then why she'd been nervous. She knew I'd be fine with it, but Lex would need winning over.

As Lex's dance music began thumping from upstairs, Richard squeezed Mum's hand and smiled encouragingly at me. 'She just needs some time. I said she would. Lex is not one for half-measures.' He leant towards me across the table. 'Zoë, I hope you don't mind the thought of me spending a lot more time with you and your mum. I'd never muscle in and try to be your dad, of course. Your mum has been both your parents all these years, and she's done a tremendous job as far as I'm concerned.'

I wanted to ask more questions – when they'd known and why, and what they'd have done if Lex and I had hated each other on sight – but it was intoxicating to be the easygoing one, the one Richard was so obviously grateful to for not making a fuss. Part of me felt treacherous, glancing up to check Lex wasn't watching me from an upstairs window, but then I remembered what she had said, and what that meant about how she viewed Mum and me, and raised my glass instead.

'Congratulations,' I said. 'When's the wedding?'

I said it almost as a joke, expecting a laugh. People were engaged for a couple of years, or so I'd observed. And, like Lex, Richard did seem to find me funny in an offbeat way – I'd noticed it. Now, though, he and Mum looked at each other like excited children.

'At the end of the month,' Mum said, smiling. 'We didn't see much point in waiting. We know in our bones it's the right thing. I thought you and Lex could be bridesmaids.'

I refused a second glass, not because I was sulking – far from it – but because I was increasingly aware of Lex's absence, the bass of her music a constant reminder, though I was hardly likely to forget. I felt I needed to face it head on, or we'd never get past it.

'Leave her,' said Richard, when I got to my feet. 'She'll come round.'

'I just need something from my room.'

It was a poor excuse but they let me go, so entranced by each other that they didn't even notice me swiping Lex's glass.

Her bedroom was the second largest but the nicest by far, with two windows she would keep wide open that whole summer. The lemon trees were just outside, close enough that you could lean out and pick the fruit. The branches were silhouetted now, gnarled fingers against the violet sky.

I hovered nervously in the doorway until she caught sight of me, which made her jump. She hadn't heard me coming over the music. She hesitated and then, with performative bad grace, reached over to turn down the volume.

'What?' she said.

'I was just wondering if . . . Can I sit?'

She didn't say no, so I took it as a yes. I handed her the glass of champagne I'd brought up with me and went to the window seat while she drank it in one.

It was nearly eight but the air was still so warm, as warm as mid-afternoon in England. There was a slight breeze, soft as breath on my sun-sore skin. The lemon tree's leaves rustled softly. Down in the garden, Richard had lit the brick barbecue. I could smell the charcoal smoke curling through the night, grey-blue. It made my stomach fizz.

Lex stretched out her legs on the rug, pointing her toes, fingers plucking at the pile. 'God, champagne always gives me a headache.'

'Oh, me too, darling,' I said, in a silly voice. 'But I find I can never resist.'

She laughed. 'Dickhead.'

We lapsed into an easy silence. She'd turned the music down even lower, so I could only hear the beat now, faintly. Leaning back on the cushions, I let my eyes close.

'You'll get to spend more time with him than I do,' she said, after a while.

'What?' I was already half asleep.

'With my dad. Once I'm back at boarding-school, you'll

be with him and your mum all the time. It's me who'll be shoved out again, just like it was with Cassandra when bloody Archie came along.'

I sat up straighter. I'd barely thought beyond the summer or the island. In the twenty minutes since the announcement that had changed everything, my mind hadn't ventured further than the incredible concept that Calliope might be, in a small and circuitous way, mine. I realized I didn't even know precisely where they lived in England. Somewhere in the Home Counties was all I'd absorbed. Surrey, maybe, with a flat in London for the week? I wasn't sure.

'Maybe we'll go to the same school,' I said.

'There's no way your mum would let you board.'

'She might.'

'She won't, and Dad's against it anyway. He wanted me to go to a grammar school like him but Cassandra wouldn't have it. *Won't* have it, even now, when I've been in all that trouble. Apparently she's saying it was part of the divorce settlement.'

'Is that another reason you're upset?'

'What?'

'Your parents' divorce. I mean, if your dad gets married again, then . . .'

'What — it will ruin any chance of him and Cassandra ever getting back together? Oh, my God.' She laughed. It sounded brittle.

'It's just I think I'd feel weird too, if I'd known my dad. I know you don't get on with her very well but . . .'

Lex snorted. 'You have no idea how much they hate each other. What do you mean anyway, about your dad? Why don't you know him?'

47

'Mum and he were never married. He didn't . . . he didn't want to know.' I looked away, out of the window.

'Let me guess, a womanizer pilot with a wife in another city.'

I stood up without making a conscious decision to do so, the threat of tears filling my throat.

Lex clapped a hand over her mouth. 'I'm right, aren't I? Shit, sorry. I only meant it as a joke.'

I stood there for a moment, hovering with indecision again, then sat down. It *was* a cliché, and she was right. She obviously hadn't known about it so it wasn't like Richard had been talking about me and Mum behind our backs. I would never have chosen to tell Lex but I was no good at hiding the truth when someone guessed it outright. *You're like an open book*, Mum said sometimes. *Just like me.* I didn't like it and always made a face, but it was true.

'Is the idea of being in a family with me and Mum that bad?' I said, in the lull. I hated how needy I sounded but the champagne on my empty stomach meant I wasn't able to bite the words back.

'No, not really.'

'Brilliant.'

'Oh, God, you did ask. It's just a shock, that's all. It's so quick. You can't deny that.'

'No, it is. But they seem happy, don't they? I mean, they seem really sure.'

She picked at a loose splinter of wood on one of the floorboards. 'I guess.'

'We can ask for matching bridesmaids' dresses. I was thinking peach chiffon.'

She shot me a look of pure contempt, then saw my face and burst out laughing.

'Imagine.'

'I'm not even joking about the chiffon, if Mum has any-thing to do with it.'

She laughed again. It was a cheap shot at Mum, and I was a bit ashamed, but it also seemed like it was worth it. It wasn't just Calliope I wanted a small piece of for myself, it was Lex too. I wanted her to be my sister and best friend rolled into one. I had never had either, and now both were in reach. Of the two of us, people would have said that Lex was the strong one but it wasn't as simple as that. She was bolder, sure, but I was tenacious in my own quiet way. I already knew I wouldn't let her go easily.

Now

I notice it as soon as I step outside into the brilliant morning, low down in the pit of myself: the old unease I had forgotten until now, a nagging sensation I had come to attribute to Eos back then. As though the place had a real, tangible power over me, some weird magical phenomenon deep in the earth, pulsing at too low a frequency for anyone but me – and maybe Lex – to hear. As though the island itself didn't want to let us forget what we'd done.

It's still early – I hadn't closed the shutters properly, too dozy from wine and exhaustion – but it wasn't just the light that had woken me before Mum came in. I'd dreamt of Lex, which was nothing new, except that today I'm actually going to see her. She might already be on her way, every hour bringing her closer. Behind me, Calliope's whispers are rising in pitch as though she senses it too.

Last night, Mum had only said she was arriving tonight. That could be six or midnight. Knowing Lex, it could be another day entirely, but I have a feeling it won't be. As a little girl without siblings, I was obsessed by the idea of twins having a psychic link – one feeling the other's pain even if they were miles apart. After that summer, a part of me thought the reverse had happened for Lex and me: that our shared trauma had forged a connection which, despite the fraying of the years, couldn't entirely be severed.

I had trained as a teacher but that life wasn't for me. I

didn't know how to navigate the power balance with the students, particularly the girls. Most particularly the girls of fifteen or sixteen. I wanted them to like me too much; my cheeks were always hot under their arch scrutiny. I'm a genealogist now, and the work – mainly online, mainly solitary – suits me better. I am well aware of the irony in this choice, of course, threading families back together when my own is unravelled.

Anyway, the point is that it's made me adept at tracking people online – the live ones as well as the long dead. Over the years, whenever I've felt a tug on the rope that snakes through the ether, I've checked on Lex. For those occasions when I couldn't, no digital footprint yet to find, I've given in and rung Mum. The long night when Lex gave birth to her daughter, three weeks early, I waited until six before I made the call. Mum didn't ask how I knew. She no longer asks questions when the answers might disturb her.

My phone vibrates in my pocket, making me jump. I get it out and see that Ben has texted again. I know exactly what he's messaged about but haven't got the wherewithal for that conversation yet, so I leave it unread for now. I need to stave him off, just for a little bit longer.

Hangover and the brutal light have given me a headache so I go back into the relative shade of the kitchen to root around in the cupboard where the medicines are kept. There used to be a single Tupperware box with paracetamol, plasters and a load of half-empty anti-mosquito sprays. One box has become three over the years, spilling over with mysterious drugs and supplements, and even one of those pill boxes with the days of the weeks on. 'Pick me up and I rattle,' my nan used to say about her angina pills.

It strikes me that Mum is older now than Nan was then. I'll be forty next month. Only a few years younger than Mum was that summer. It seems unbelievable.

I find some Greek pills I assume are painkillers from the illustration on the packet of a red target on a forehead and take two with water from the fridge, not bothering to get a glass. I would never do this if Richard was still around — it seems I've already regressed slightly to the days when it was just me and Mum. I don't know how Lex's arrival will alter that dynamic — three when it was once four, a parent for each of us. I won't think about that yet.

'I might go for a walk,' I say, when Mum comes in. She's washed and dried her hair and put on some make-up, and seems much more together for it. She's never understood those women who didn't bother with any of that. Penny Rutherford never wore a scrap of make-up, of course. Probably Lex's mother, whose old schoolfriend Penny was Lex's godmother, didn't either. 'I don't know why they think they're above it,' Mum would say, and although I adopted the opposite view when I was young, for the sake of teenage contrariness, I agreed with her on the quiet, and still do. I would never leave the house without mascara.

'Will you go and see Rob?' she says to me now. 'He was asking when you were arriving.'

I close my eyes briefly. I had been pushing away the fact that he's here now, on the island. 'Maybe tomorrow,' I say. 'When I've found my feet.'

Mum nods. She knows what I mean. 'I'll have to draw you a map. You'll never find him otherwise. It's a funny little place that he's rented. Just a couple of rooms, really. I don't think they get much light.'

'Will Penny fly out, do you think? And . . .' I pause, then say it anyway '. . . Lex's mother?'

She actually shudders. I see the tremor pass through her, and feel awful.

'Lex told *Cassandra*, of course. But who knows if she'll come? She wouldn't deign to tell me either way.'

A masochistic part of me would be fascinated to see the woman who gave birth to mercurial Lex. She'd never looked much like Richard.

He and Mum knew Lex was slightly out of control that summer, had been going that way even before what happened at the end of it. I think they secretly worried the engagement would make her worse, but told themselves she was already in trouble at school, that she had always had a wild streak.

I think it was lots of things, all converging, but there's no doubt that the arrival of Mum and me was part of it. Richard couldn't hide his approval of me, and didn't try to. He loved that I worked hard at school and had never got into any trouble. The very opposite of his own daughter, who'd *had every advantage*, as I heard him saying once, even though I was downstairs and they were up. Calliope's wooden floors offered almost no soundproofing, but it was more than that: the acoustics were peculiar, so that even slightly raised voices could always be heard in other rooms with ease. I wasn't sure if it was peacekeeping on the house's part, an attempt to bring us together, or trouble-making.

A spoilt child. It's a phrase so often trotted out that it has ceased to have any real impact. But if you think about it, *really* think about it, it's such a damning judgement to level at a child because it's a one-way road. I've never said it to

Jess, even when I've thought it. There's no coming back from being *spoilt*, is there? I think of the lemons turning to mush and mould outside, good for nothing but the compost heap. Richard loved Lex so much, but he shouldn't have used that word about her so often. It did damage.

Mum notices the pill packet on the counter. 'Have you got a bad head?'

I nod. 'Too much wine.'

She glances away, though I wasn't going to say anything.

'That's why I thought I'd go for a walk. Some fresh air might help clear it.'

'Where will you go?' She's frowning. Mum doesn't walk unless there's purpose to it. Walking for leisure is one of the many things she puts in the box labelled *posh*. But there's more to this today, I know. I don't think she's left Calliope in a while.

'Are you sure you won't go and see Rob?' she says now. 'He's got some plans under way for August, I think.'

'August?' I know what she's getting at, but parroting the word back at her is all I can think to say.

'The anniversary, of course. *Her* anniversary. Strange it being this year, so soon after Richard.' She shakes her head. 'Didn't you say the taxi driver mentioned it? Twenty-five years. God, where did the time go?'

'I'll text him soon. I just want to nip down to the village quickly, get some bits to eat.' I gesture towards the fridge, which is almost empty except for wine. 'I won't be long.' I'm suddenly desperate to be outside.

'I know you don't want to talk about it, love,' she says, as I shove my phone into my bag. 'Neither do I. But I've been thinking about that lately and, well, it's everything to Rob.'

I turn to leave. 'I'll go. Just not today.'

She nods. 'Put a hat on, then. That old scruffy one you used to wear is still there, on the pegs in the hall.'

The winding walk down the hill is so much the same that I feel as if I'm dreaming: cats sprawled everywhere, thin fingers of shade from the cypresses, that hot earth smell. I shunt in and out of time, jolting as I catch sight of my adult body – neatly painted toenails and waxed legs, feet in their metallic sandals, when I'm expecting to see scuffed plimsolls and skinny shins. I shaved my legs for the first time that summer, sneaking into Mum and Richard's en suite to steal a pink disposable razor.

It's not until the road flattens at the outskirts of the village that time is grounded again. I don't think there even were outskirts before. New villas have been built; others are still mid-construction, raw concrete and metal rebars exposed to the sky. There are cars parked everywhere, though I'm oddly relieved to see that they haven't changed except in number, all of them scruffy little hatchbacks with dings, and dusty windows wound halfway down, the doors unlocked. Just like before.

A chained-up dog in a yard barks as I pass, making me jump and the nerves in my stomach flare. I pick up the pace, suddenly desperate for a cold drink in the shade. I buy a bottle of water in the mini-market, which I'm sure is in the same place, though it feels distinctly classier than I remember it: bottles of Greek rosé costing twenty euros outnumber the exotically foreign sweets and biscuits Lex and I used to eat cross-legged on the oil-stained slipway, watching the boats come in. We used to mark the yachties out of ten for how neatly they moored up, then disembarked down the wooden gangplanks. When someone tripped or nearly went in, it would render us hysterical. Not that it took much when we were high as kites on E-numbers and sun.

I can't remember the three of us ever doing that, so it must have been early on, before she arrived on the island. It's strange how the weeks of that summer – a mere five – have expanded in my memory. I suppose I learnt to eke them out in the years that followed, like rations over a long winter.

I wander along the front as I sip my water, wishing I'd bought something with sugar in it. I can't remember there being any tourist shops here before, unless you counted the hardware store that had baskets of black rubber snorkel masks and sea shoes for the pebble beaches set out as afterthoughts.

Now there are boutiques selling jewellery, olive-wood ornaments and cotton sarongs. I wander into one, empty and deliciously air-conditioned, smelling of expensive candles. There are cases of resin bead necklaces, and sandals like mine, but mostly it's patterned beachwear. There's one rail of pure white and I go over, the dresses and cover-ups of bleached cotton so sheer and fine that I can hardly feel them between my fingers. I pull out a sundress and hold it against me in the mirror propped against the wall. It's pretty, simple and not too young. Definitely not too middle-aged cruise-ship either. I turn over the thick card price-tag: 110 euros.

'You want to try on?'

I look up to see a smiling assistant approaching but before I can answer my attention is pulled to the figure behind her, lifting a scarf from the display outside. Her hair is chestnut, red lights glinting as she bends her head and it falls over her shoulder, holding the sun in its waves.

'Madam?'

An old synapse is starting to fire but the assistant is in the way and by the time I get to the doorway she has gone. I look left and right, but there's no one in sight except an ancient man, who turns to smile gummily at me. Shouts go up on a yacht gliding away from its mooring, bound for another island, but she couldn't possibly have boarded it in time.

A gentle touch on my shoulder makes me whirl round. The assistant, still smiling patiently, gestures at the dress balled in my hands, crumpled and sweaty. I hold it out to her, knowing I'll have to buy it now, knowing also that Lex would have handed it back with a thousand-watt smile and no compunction to pay for it if she hadn't wanted to. But of course I'm not Lex, and never could be. Will I say anything about it to her later? The thought of that possibility – of being in the same room as her at all – makes me catch my breath.

I thought I saw her today, you know. Down by the water. It was her hair I noticed. Do you ever see her, Lex? Does she haunt you too?

He's waiting for me as I leave the shop, tall and impossibly tanned. His eyes are still a beautiful shade of aqua but there's an emptiness in them that I've always found difficult to look at. I didn't need Mum's map after all: Robin has found me first.

'Hello, Zoë. I heard you were back. I didn't want to rush over to Calliope, intrude on you and your mother, but here you are.' He smiles and, for a second, the shadows in his face retreat and he's a boy again, golden and lovely. We hug quickly and I become aware as we separate that the shop assistant is watching us with frank interest from the doorway of her shop. Robin seems not to register this, gesturing instead to a bar right on the edge of the water. It's where Lex and I went that first night, though it's smartened up almost out of recognition.

I sit down, already braced for him to mention her but, to his credit, we manage to order coffee and talk about how Mum's coping for a good fifteen minutes. In the end, it's me who brings the conversation round to his sister, just to get it over with. I've endured many conversations like this over the years but it's totally different here, on the island.

'How's it going then, living out here permanently?' I make myself say, surprised at how natural my voice sounds. 'Do you think it will make a difference?'

He sips his coffee. He's drinking the Greek stuff, as though total assimilation will make up for something in the past. 'I think it's been good to be on the ground, yes,' he says. 'And obviously with the anniversary this summer . . .' He shrugs. 'I've had a new flyer made. Colour photo this time. There are stacks of them in the flat. Hardly any room for me.' A quick smile, which dims immediately.

But then he brightens again. 'I've also been in touch with one of the old policemen who worked on the case. He's retired now, of course, but he remembered it straight away.'

'Papagiorgiou,' I say, hearing the crack in my voice. An image of him rises in my mind as I say it, as vivid as if I'd seen him yesterday. Such a soft, twinkly sort of name, which belied his nature completely.

'Yes, that's right. Christ, you've got a good memory.'

'He was pretty memorable.'

'Of course, he interviewed you and Lex, didn't he? I'd forgotten that. He must be seventy now but he's no less formidable. I got the impression he'd never got over the whole thing.' He looks down, smiles ruefully. 'Something we have in common. Anyway, a good person to have onside, I think.'

I don't reply. I can't think of anything to say, my head full of that name – one I never expected to hear from Robin, even in my most doom-laden imaginings of the last few days. Under the table, my legs have started to shake.

'I'll have to go in a minute, Robin. I'm feeling a bit rough this morning.'

'Oh, I'm sorry. You should have said. I'd love to talk to you more about the campaign, about whether you'd be willing to lend a hand while you're here, but that can wait, of course.'

'It's just that I've only been back a night. And I'm still getting used to the idea of Richard being . . .'

He looks pained. 'Yes, of course you are, and here I am going on. Look, shall I call a cab to take you up the hill? Let me walk you back at least.'

'No, it's fine, honestly.' I get unsteadily to my feet and allow myself to be hugged again. His hair needs washing, I notice. He's thinner than when he still lived in London, too. There was a period when he came over to have dinner with Ben and me quite often, having got back in touch via Facebook. Of course he always wanted to talk about her so I found those nights exhausting, but could never say no – just as I could never have ignored his friend request. It was the least I could do, wasn't it?

Ben found the whole thing bizarre at the time. 'I know he's your friend and he doesn't have many, but he can't talk about anything else,' he said once, when we were stacking the dishwasher after Robin had left. 'It's not healthy for him and it totally drains you.'

In truth, it was a relief for both of us when he moved to Eos. Not now, though, not now I'm here myself.

'I know it's a big year,' I say, as we reach the small village square where we'll separate. 'But I worry. What about *you*? We're in our forties now.' I don't add, *And you haven't even asked after your goddaughter yet*, because I know he can't help what has long been an obsession for him, obscuring everything and everyone else. He loves Jess, but no one living will ever be as important to him as his long-absent sister, even though no one has seen her for a quarter of a century.

He shrugs, squinting against the sun. 'I was her big brother. It happened on my watch.'

I shake my head but don't object. There's no point. We've been having variations of this conversation forever.

'I thought I saw her earlier,' I say, wishing immediately I hadn't.

For the first time, his face comes alive. 'Did you? Where?'

'It wasn't her. It was just someone with hair like hers. She had beautiful hair.'

His hand goes through his own, which was the same hair once, but like the rest of him is now thinner and beginning to fade.

'I used to see her all the time in London,' he says, dropping his voice. 'All the time. It wasn't getting any better either. It was actually getting worse. This might sound ridiculous – I wouldn't admit it to many people – but I realized one day it was a sign that I needed to come back to Eos, to find an answer once and for all. I felt as though Abigail herself was asking me to do it.'

Abigail.

Her name hangs in the air like old smoke. I haven't said it aloud for a long time.

'Really, the anniversary was just the final push for me to sell up in England and focus on it full-time.'

'And have you seen her here?' I manage to ask.

He smiles and it's slightly manic. 'No, not once. But that's a good thing, you see. It's because she knows I'm getting closer.'

Then

I had been on the island for nine days when I met the Rutherfords for the first time. It seems obvious now that this is the point when things began to go awry, though there was no sense of it that morning, Lex and I sitting at a waterside bar in the small port in the south of the island that acted as its capital. I can picture the scene so clearly: our hired mopeds next to us so we could keep an eye on them, propped on their stands, engines ticking as they cooled. The scrunched-up paper from our straws, a length of which I was winding round my finger again and again. The coral-coloured church across the square against the hot-blue sky and the sound of its off-key chime as it turned eleven. This is the precise moment I would return to, if I could.

By now, Lex and I had fallen into a rhythm I hadn't dared comment on, for fear I'd ruin it. We did everything together. We were our own unit, capable of both companionable silences and in-jokes. Each night over dinner with Richard and Mum, I willed them not to comment on it, and have Lex dump me just to make a point. She was perfectly capable of doing that, I knew.

Each day, we had been doing more or less the same thing: morning at the beach – either the narrow one near the village, or further round the headland below the lighthouse, then lunch at the beach bar or the one we'd gone to on the first night, which did club sandwiches with cocktail sticks skewering them together – they were impossible to fit in our mouths so had to be eaten in layers – then back up to Calliope to flop out by the pool until dusk, Lex in the sun with her headphones on and me reading in the shade.

In truth, I would have been happy to do this every afternoon, but Mum had started making noises about wedding preparations and Lex said she would go round the bend if she had to listen to discussions about who they should invite, how much Eleni might be offered to do the food, and what colour scheme would work with everyone's skin tones. On my ninth island morning Lex announced over breakfast that we'd be out for the whole day. They were so pleased we were getting on that they didn't even ask where we were going.

Down in the village, Lex attempted to hire us a couple of battered mopeds, imperiously waving away any suggestion of checking our passports to see if we were old enough, which we were not. She got her way when a man of about twenty wandered in and greeted her with a double kiss and a lazy smile, his thick silver chain bright against his neck. He must have vouched for us, because within a minute the forms were signed and Lex was blowing him a kiss as we wheeled our mopeds outside.

'Let me know if you need anything else, *koukla mou*,' he said, with a wink.

'Who was that?' I said, when we were out of earshot.

She gave me a funny little smile. 'Ah, that's Panikos. Eleni's son. Bit of a legend on the island these days. It's weird because I remember him as a boy when Dad first bought Calliope. I was five and he was nine and Dad let him swim in the pool while Eleni was cleaning. Obviously he took no notice of me at all.'

I wanted to ask what she meant about him being a legend but she was already starting her moped and I didn't want to be left behind. After the first minutes of over-steering and over-revving, it was actually quite exhilarating – when I didn't think about losing the skin off my bare legs if I lost control on one of the bends.

It was Lex's idea to go to the port. I had thought we might go to the haunted pool she'd mentioned a couple of times, a secret, impossible-to-find place, which she'd said she'd never breathed a word of to anyone else – the privilege made me glow. It had taken me a while to understand that this wasn't some man-made chlorinated pool but the very opposite, something ancient and unknown: a strange silent place that had been there forever, sunk into a rocky cleft beneath the ruins of a Byzantine temple, or an Orthodox church, she wasn't sure.

'The point is, it's not a pool-pool,' she'd said impatiently. 'This is *Circe*'s Pool.' She was hamming it up, I knew, but it seemed like the perfect place to go to on our mopeds. When I suggested it, though, she gave me a long, considering look and shook her head. 'You're not ready for it yet.'

What she meant was that she wasn't ready to share it with me. I hadn't passed whatever test was required. I wish I never had.

But that was all to come. That day we were at the port where Mum and I had arrived by hydrofoil what seemed like months before. The bar Lex had chosen was apparently famous for its fresh lemonade, so we'd ordered a couple of tall glasses. The citrus was so sharp it was catching in my throat, making breathing slightly difficult, but I didn't want to say anything because it would sound like a criticism and Lex had been going on all morning about how delicious they were.

We heard them first, or rather her, the English sharp and querulous compared to the easy Greek rumbling around us from the old men drinking their tiny cups of coffee. There were five of them: a mother and father, two boys – one tall, the other small – and a girl of about our age at the very back. She wasn't fat but stolid and strangely pale compared to the rest of them. While the mother talked on and on, the others plodded along in silence, the girl almost tripping as a corner of her case clipped her ankle. It sounds cruel to say it but, apart from her hair, she was unremarkable in every way.

'I can't be expected to do absolutely everything,' the woman was saying, as she came into earshot. 'It would be nice if someone else took on some of the bloody arrangements occasionally. Even once would be nice.'

Her husband said something inaudible out of the corner of his mouth and she pressed her lips into a thin line.

I was so engrossed by her particular kind of Englishness – not least her skin, which was burnt to a deep brick-red in the open V of her pink polo shirt – that I didn't really register the brothers' good looks until they were virtually upon us. They moved with the same easy grace, utterly comfortable in their own skins. I knew in a glance that they would be good at games and effortlessly popular.

The little one looked about ten. The other was older than me and Lex, maybe even eighteen. Like the girl, he had gold-tipped red-brown hair, long enough at the front to flop over one eye. Every five seconds he flicked it away with casual expertise. It was already a boiling hot day, but he wore a long-sleeved rugby shirt as though it was April in Surrey, the white-white collar dazzling against his skin. It was half turned up and half turned in, which would have looked hapless on anyone else, but on him just added to the air of gorgeous nonchalance.

'Seventeen,' Lex breathed into my ear, her lemony breath hot. 'And a half.'

I looked at her quizzically.

'I know them. She' – she nodded towards the woman – 'is my godmother. Penny.'

'Oh.' I remembered the name. 'Well, hadn't you better say hello?'

I don't know if she would have done or not, because in that moment she was spotted anyway. It was the girl who pointed and said something to her mother, who barked at her to repeat it, irritation marking a deep cleft between her eyebrows. It cleared instantly when she spotted Lex.

'Darling, it's you! Thank God. Are you here with Richard?' Her gaze passed over me without settling. 'We're having boat trouble. Had to get the hydrofoil over with the hordes, would you believe? It was even more ghastly than I imagined, everyone shoving their way on and not enough space for the luggage.'

Ridiculously, I found myself blushing. I suppose because I was the hordes, and so was Mum. I hardly ever thought about this stuff when it was just me and Lex, and I wished then that we'd never bumped into these people, however good-looking the boy was. I think Lex must have sensed my discomfort because she poked me under the table

67

where it tickled the most, just above my waist, trying to make me laugh.

There followed a lengthy conversation about the broken yacht, which had had to be abandoned on the mainland. Something about a cleat. It was going to be mended and brought to them in two or three days. At some point, the husband went inside the bar – I heard him asking where the facilities were in a voice that carried as effectively as his wife's.

'This is Zoë,' Lex eventually interjected, just when I'd thought I'd got away with the embarrassment of introductions. 'We came down here for the lemonade.'

'Can we get some, Ma?' said the small boy. 'I'm amazingly thirsty.'

'Name's Penny,' the woman finally said, in my vague direction. 'Pal from school, Lex?'

'No, she's Marilyn's daughter. Dad's new . . .' She trailed off.

'Oh, God, right.' She looked me over more carefully, and I tried not to squirm.

'This is Tom,' Lex said to me, gesturing towards the little boy who'd by now pulled up a chair next to hers. 'And that's Robin.' She left a significant pause while the older one leant over to shake my hand, which was excruciating. He had perfect white lines fanning out from the corners of each aquamarine eye, which must have come from squinting at the sunlit sea from deck.

'Oh, and that's Abigail.' Lex gestured at the girl as an afterthought.

She had been staring pensively at her feet, one leg crossed awkwardly over the other, which did nothing for her thighs in their khaki shorts, but she looked up sharply at Lex's words. Her hair really was beautiful. I always noticed hair because I didn't like my own and Abigail had crowning-glory hair of the same warm golden-brown as her brothers', tied in a loose plait that reached almost to her waist.

'Pabs, aren't you going to reply to Lex?'

She blushed, and not prettily, the colour creeping up from her neck to turn her whole face red. 'Sorry.' Her voice was only just audible over the bustle of the café. 'Hi, Zoë.'

I smiled at her but she'd already transferred her gaze back to Lex. She really was pale, even paler than me, despite being on a boat for weeks already.

As though Penny had read my mind, she shook her head at Lex. 'She's hardly stirred herself from the cabin. Burnt her shoulders on the first day and that was that. Does nothing but write in her diary. What she has to report at such length is anyone's guess.'

Robin took the chair next to me, which seemed to be a cue for Penny to sit down too. I noticed she addressed everything she said to him or Lex, as though the rest of our opinions were of no consequence. That suited me. I was keeping myself as still as possible so my bare thigh didn't accidentally brush Robin's. It was tricky because he'd opened his legs wide, as though they were too long and muscular to be accommodated under the table.

They all ordered lemonade except the father, who had come sauntering back from the toilet, ordered a coffee with a raised forefinger and introduced himself to me as Alastair Rutherford, as though I might say, 'Now, are your people the Hounslow Rutherfords or the ones from Feltham?' He looked like a beaky, balding version of his sons.

'Are you enjoying the island?' Robin said, in a conversational tone, once the drinks had arrived.

I was observing the girl, Abigail, who hadn't yet taken her eyes off Lex, when the latter nudged me under the table. 'Earth to Zoë.'

When I turned to him, astonished he could be talking to me, he raised an enquiring eyebrow. 'I think it's my favourite island,' he continued. 'We've been coming here since I was Tom's age.'

He spoke like an adult would. I didn't know any boys who did that. None of the ones I knew at school had anything like the self-possession.

'Y-yes,' I said. 'It's amazing. I can't get over how turquoise the sea is. And how clear. The little fishing boats in the harbour look like they're floating in mid-air, it's so transparent and . . .' I stopped, suddenly hearing myself so eager, but Robin was nodding.

'Yes, they do, exactly. The island's known for it, actually. It's because the beaches are pebbles rather than sand that it's so clear. The Greeks think rocky beaches are superior for that reason.'

His mother was watching him as he talked, leaning forward in her seat as though the table between them was too big a gulf. When she turned to Lex, she looked hungry in just the same way as her daughter did. I wondered if I did too.

'You fancy him, don't you?'

We were wheeling our scooters back towards the main road out of the port, having left the Rutherfords at the bar, Penny and Alastair squabbling languidly about where

70

to have lunch. Abigail had watched us go – I had felt her eyes on my back.

'No,' I said, too quickly. 'I mean, he's good-looking and everything, but I don't even know him.'

'Yeah, like that matters.'

'Don't you, then?'

'Don't I what?'

'Fancy him.'

'Nah. I've known him forever. It would be like doing stuff with my cousin.'

I wondered what stuff she meant, specifically, and again what she'd done at that party to make the other girl spread stories about her.

'Besides,' continued Lex, 'he's too young for me.'

'But he's older than us.'

'He's still a boy.'

'And I suppose you've graduated to men.'

When she didn't immediately answer, I looked over and she was smiling secretively. It made me uneasy, a faint tang of danger souring the air.

'Have you?' As I said it, I realized I didn't really want to know.

She shrugged. 'All I'm saying is that most of the boys I know seem like kids. You can't talk to them properly about anything because they're too worried about what their friends will say if they didn't get far enough with you.'

The idea of her knowing how far I hadn't got with anyone, man or boy, made me die a little inside.

'Well,' I said, 'it's a shame you don't like Robin because Penny would totally love it if you did. If she let anyone get

71

near him, it would be you. She acts like she prefers you to her own daughter.'

'Pabs and Penny are basically different species. Do you know why she's called Pabs?' She pulled a face and then laughed. 'It's short for "Poor Abigail".'

It had never occurred to me that being part of a normal family unit could be anything other than enviable. But maybe it was worse to have a family and be the odd one out in it, like a changeling in a fairy tale.

'Are you two close, or what?' I said, keeping my voice light.

Lex screwed up her nose. 'Not really. I mean, I see her every summer. She's just always kind of . . . been there.'

'She watches you the whole time.'

'Does she? Pabs is kind of intense. It's just how she is.'

'She seems totally miserable.'

'Yeah, well, they're horrible to her sometimes,' said Lex. She swung her leg over the scooter's saddle and turned the key, the engine spluttering into life. The men smoking in the café opposite were watching her intently, though she hadn't noticed. 'Especially Penny. But I get it too.'

'What do you mean?'

'She's such a victim. She expects you to be mean to her so sometimes it's impossible not to be.'

She revved the moped and took off towards the hill that wound out of the port, hair billowing out behind her because she'd refused a helmet. The men watched her go before turning their gaze on me, as I scrambled to catch up. Before I took off, I looked back one last time. In the distance, too far off to make out if I hadn't known what to look for, Abigail was still watching.

Now

I know Lex is there before I push open Calliope's front door. There's no outward sign, but I know it just the same. My skin prickles with her presence, just as the band of tension around my head tightens a little more.

When I find her, she's in front of the sun that floods into the room, just as she was that first time. For a moment she seems unscathed by the years, her hair still long and swinging, too silky to stay in a hairband when it had just been washed.

But then she comes towards me and I see there are lines on her face, more lines than I have. They fan out around her eyes and above her upper lip, tiny tissue-paper fissures. Still smoking, then. That and too much sun, although she looks pale today – paler than I've ever seen her.

We stand there looking at each other, and it's so surreal to be in the same room as her, breathing the same air, that it's not even that awkward. She always set the agenda back then, and it's no different now. I wait for her cue, just as I did as a girl.

Still, when her arms go round me, pull me close, it's physically shocking. Her smell almost stops my heart, because that hasn't changed at all. Sun-hot skin, tobacco and oranges. It's almost overwhelming. I pull away because I feel that if I don't something inside me will burst.

'It's you,' she says, voice hardly more than a whisper. 'It's really you, here.' She steps towards me again, hands going up to grip my shoulders, hard enough to leave marks. 'Let me look at you properly. Christ, you look about twenty-five. I hate you.'

The last words land hard and we both wince at the off note, a fork on chipped crystal.

'I'm old now, look,' she says, rushing past it, lifting a hank of pale hair and pointing out the grey roots. I can see them now: coarse little hairs a sparse halo against the sun.

I wonder if this is how it's going to be. If we're going to act like old friends who've bumped into each other at a school reunion. As though our separation of actual decades was down to *life getting in the way* and *time flying*, rather than the secret that should have bonded us forever but actually tore us apart. A rift that felt necessary in the aftermath but set like that for good.

The weight of all those years swings between us, a heavy pendulum that threatens to knock one of us down.

'Come on,' she says, when she releases me, nodding towards the kitchen. 'I don't know about you, but I need a drink.'

If Mum is slow and unsteady, Lex moves around the kitchen as though she's been speeded up. She pours us both a large glass of wine before I have a chance to say no.

'It's just that I'm feeling a bit fragile.' I realize I'm being apologetic already and make myself stop. 'Too much last night with Mum, when I got here.'

We sit down opposite each other at the table, the bottle of wine between us.

'So she's drinking again?' she says.

I feel the old defensiveness. 'A bit. It's fair enough, isn't it, given everything?'

'She stopped dead, didn't she? After . . .'

'Yep.'

'I always wondered how much she knew. Guessed.'

'She only ever asked me once.' I reach for my glass after all.

'And did you . . .?'

'Of course not.'

She waits for me to say more but I don't want to talk about it, not with Lex or Robin or anyone else. Back then, it was me trying to discuss it and Lex not wanting anything to do with it. The thought of Lex opening it all up again now, on top of the funeral, makes my stomach tip over.

'I'm so sorry about Richard,' I say. 'About your dad. He was always so good to Mum, and to me. I . . . I loved him.'

I absolutely mean it, but I'm also using him to change the subject and I despise myself for that.

'Oh, and he adored you,' says Lex. The emphasis on *you* has real heft. She's looking right at me, and her blue eyes have turned harder. She pours herself some more wine – I've barely touched mine – and when she looks up again, the coldness has gone.

'Do you remember we used to drink those bloody alco-pops? Christ. I haven't had any refined sugar for years but I can still feel them coating my teeth.' She flicks her tongue across them, then reaches over to one of those slouchy brown handbags that cost a grand and pulls out a packet of cigarettes. She holds them up, triumphant: her old brand, Karelia Slims – the skinny ones she said were more elegant and which the mini-market in the village always ran out of. I can't help smiling at her glee.

'I got them at the airport. They're ridiculously strong.'

'So sugar's banned, but you still smoke?'

'Sugar is worse.'

'Smells better.'

She's about to light up, but rolls her eyes and gets to her feet. 'Come on, then. Let's go outside so I don't pollute the kitchen. Anyway, it's just about time for the Pinkening, isn't it?'

I'd named it that, but had forgotten: Lex's and my personal witching hour, when the whole island was splashed that gorgeous, almost gaudy pink. It was so different from the subtle English twilight that I'd thought it deserved its own name.

I watch her smoke, just like the old days, and the smell of it is intoxicating, bound up as it is with all that youth and possibility. I wish I wasn't so pleased she remembered the Pinkening. My eyes fill with tears and I blink rather than brush them away so she's less likely to notice.

'When are Ben and Jess coming out?' she says, after a while.

I look closely at her to see if she's being cruel but her expression is clear. Tears threaten again, but I manage to swallow them.

'I'm not sure they are.'

'What do you mean?'

'I think Jess is a bit young. She has school and –'

'She's twelve. Doesn't she want to come? She loved him, or so I heard. She called him "Granddad", didn't she?'

'Ben and I have separated.' I assumed she knew.

'What – recently?'

'After Christmas. It's just a trial.'

'Divorce lawyers love January.' She rubs her fingers together but then catches my expression. 'Shit, sorry. I'm a horrible old cynic. It's only that you're talking to an expert.'

'Well, maybe the next one will be third time lucky.' It's a risk, and maybe she deserves it after what she's said, but there's a part of me that's simply falling back into our old patterns. Her in charge, but occasionally – just occasionally – me shooting something back, just when she least expected it.

Now, she turns to me, eyes narrowed, and I'm just thinking I've misjudged it when she bursts out laughing, which turns into a cough from the cigarette, which sets me off. And even though I'm laughing, the tears edge in again, hysteria fizzing inside me in a way that it never has with anyone since her.

'I'm sorry about you and Ben,' she says, when we've calmed down. 'You sounded like a really solid couple.'

'How do you know?'

She rolls her eyes again, in the way she always did, a vestige of irritable teenager rising. 'From Dad, obviously. I always asked after you.'

That shuts me up. I had only very rarely asked after her. I couldn't. Lex became a banned subject.

'Do you think Liam will come?' she says now. She's lighting a second cigarette, though the first is still glowing on the ground. Her voice quavers slightly on his name.

'I hope not. But Robin will. You know he lives here now?' I pause, wondering whether to tell her about earlier, about Robin's new-found determination and the fact that he's seen Papagiorgiou. I don't know whether it'll make me feel less alone to see my own fear reflected in Lex's face, or whether it will make it more horribly real. But before I can decide, a noise from the house behind us makes me turn, expecting to see Mum.

It's not Mum. For a split second, it's Lex as she was then: a golden girl who is almost but not quite a woman, supremely confident in her own skin. But the light shifts, a cloud passing over the sun, and of course it's not Lex at all. She's not just taller than Lex, but built on a larger scale altogether. Her eyes are different, too. Colder.

'Darling,' Lex addresses her, head on one side, mouth wry, 'before you say anything, I know I'm smoking, but I've decided I'm allowed. Extenuating circumstances. My father is dead, after all.' She glances at me, perhaps to see if I'm shocked. She always loved shocking me. Then she smiles, and gestures towards the girl-woman. 'Zoë, this is my daughter, Cleo.'

Then

We were tramping up the hill having returned the mopeds. Lex had paid for twenty-four hours but we couldn't possibly take them back to Calliope or Richard would hit the roof that we'd managed to hire them illegally in the first place. We'd faffed about in the village for a while, buying sweets in the mini-market and debating whether to go to a bar high on the cliffs of the west coast, but Lex suddenly seemed to run out of steam, her face closing down. This happened sometimes. It was as though she'd been punctured. I couldn't get much out of her after that, and it seemed easiest just to drop off the mopeds early.

Whenever this happened, I was afraid it was me, that she was desperate to shake me off but was reluctant to say so outright – possibly because she didn't want to hurt my feelings or, more likely, because she thought her dad would find out and tell her off for being rude. Despite the days we'd spent together, I still didn't feel I knew Lex very well, not deep down. It hadn't yet occurred to me that the weather of her moods wasn't related directly to my presence. No wonder it's so confusing being a teenager: you're convinced of your total, agonizing insignificance even as you believe yourself to be the centre of the whole universe.

The walk up the hill, even without the mopeds to push, seemed longer than ever. Sweat inched down my spine as I replayed the last hour, wondering what I'd said wrong. It had to have been me, surely: nothing else had happened. The muscles of my legs were trembling from lack of food but also from going faster on the windy roads back than I had wanted to. It hadn't seemed to occur to Lex that I might be scared to go so fast, or that if I fell behind and lost her, I wouldn't know where I was. A rush of anger went hotly through me that I was now worrying about her being cross with me when I had every right to be cross with her. I tamped this down immediately: I didn't want to dislike Lex, even for a moment. I wanted everything to be fine. The alternatives made me feel sick.

The hot dry air of the roads had made me thirsty. I hadn't finished my lemonade in the end, for fear of my throat closing over. I licked my lips, tasting salt, and tried to picture the cold drinks waiting in Calliope's fridge to take my mind off the gnawing worry of Lex going off me.

'So, do you think we'll see them again soon?' I pushed out, slightly breathless. 'The Rutherfords, I mean.'

'Ha. I knew you fancied him.'

My heart lifted to get a reply. 'Well, maybe a bit.' It was more than I wanted to say but it was worth it. 'Perhaps your dad will invite them round.'

'They'll invite themselves round, don't worry about that. Apart from anything else, Penny will want to get a look at your mum.'

I tried to picture the two of them making small-talk but it was too painful. Mum couldn't be herself around people she deemed posh. It was all right when she was flying because she was acting a role. But in normal life she hated it. I'd seen her do it with some of my teachers. She would either be fawning with Penny, tugging on an ancestral forelock, or she would retreat into herself entirely, for fear of giving herself away as common whatever she did. Penny was so awful it would probably be the latter. But something else was still niggling at me too.

'Will Abigail hang around with us now, do you think?'

Lex threw me a look. 'Maybe a bit. Why?'

'I dunno. I just wondered. Because she's our age and you know her family.'

'She's a drip. Do you want her to hang around with us or something?'

'No.' I didn't want to share Lex with anyone. I think I was just trying to keep her talking. 'I just felt a bit sorry for her.'

'Christ, how many waifs and strays am I meant to look after this summer?'

Foolishness flooded in. I'd been trying to make things better and had only made them worse, pushing her into the rejection I'd been fearing. Now she'd redrawn the lines and we weren't really on the same side after all, not in her mind. I was over there, in Siberia with Poor Abigail. I felt it then: a bolt of pure certainty that the easy, lazy days we'd shared were over. Everything would be complicated now, I knew.

There was another car in Calliope's drive when we got there, parked behind Richard's at a vertiginous angle. It was a shiny black convertible when every other car on the island seemed to be small and battered and caked in dust. If I had needed a sign to confirm my fears, this was surely it.

Lex had stopped dead in front of it, a strange expression on her face. 'I didn't think he was coming out,' she said.

'Who?'

She didn't answer, already pushing open the front door. I watched her dart up the stairs without a backward glance.

Mum would be anxious about this person turning up, whoever he was. I think we'd both assumed it would just be the four of us all month. Now this car had brought a stranger, and the Rutherfords wouldn't be too far behind. She had been nervous enough about meeting Lex. 'We come from the same place, me and Richard,' she'd said to me on the flight over. 'It's just that he's travelled a lot further than me.'

She'd smiled then, at the play on words given how many miles her job had taken her, but I knew what she was getting at once I'd met him. Richard hadn't been working-class for a long, long time – not in terms of money and status – but at heart he was still a boy from West Ham. He was one of those lucky people who was easy in himself, whoever you put him with, just like Lex. His London accent had softened naturally with the years spent in boardrooms. I don't think it would ever have occurred to him to lose it.

But, still, if you had money like he did, and contacts like he'd been required to make in his kind of business, other people were always around. People dropping in for lunch or supper; people flying out on a whim for a few days. People doing the same social networking they always did but in a different place, with better weather. I always seemed to know things like this, when Mum didn't. It was probably all the reading.

They were having lunch out on the terrace; I could hear their voices beyond the empty rooms of Calliope. It felt like Lex and I had been out for hours and hours, but it was only half past one according to the clock in the hall.

I was tempted to disappear upstairs like Lex but curiosity won out. I suppose I wanted to check that Mum was okay, too – to see how fast she'd been drinking to cope with whoever had turned up, and whether that had already tipped over into too much.

It had. It took me about two seconds to work that out. Her face was flushed and there were mascara smudges under her eyes. I was so intent on her – wondering if I should signal with my finger that she needed to wipe away the black – that it was a beat before I took in the new addition. I suppose I'd assumed it would be another Alastair Rutherford type but the man sitting opposite her, in a pressed white shirt with the top three buttons undone, was much younger. Much better-looking too.

He noticed my arrival in the same instant, checking me over with a practised up and down, lightning fast, then away. Unlike the boys at school, there was no performance in it, just cool appraisal followed by dismissal. *Too young*, or so I assumed, but then Lex appeared in the kitchen doorway. She'd changed out of her shorts and T-shirt into a pale pink sundress that showed off her tan. There was no sign of her messy ponytail either. She'd brushed it out, long and loose, and it shone a burnished gold.

When he saw her there, a second behind me, his whole body tensed. It wasn't obvious but I caught it. I watched him watch her as she walked towards the table in her lazy, loose-limbed way. I knew then that my invisibility to him wasn't about age. That wouldn't have precluded me, if I'd had whatever Lex had.

Richard seemed oblivious to all this as he got to his feet, smiling. 'Ah, the wanderers return at last! Where on earth

83

did you two get to? Lex, you know Liam, of course. Go and fetch a couple of plates. There's plenty left.'

He gestured towards me as Lex sauntered back inside. 'Liam, this is Marilyn's girl, Zoë. Thankfully she and Lex seem to have hit it off. Zoë, this is Liam, my right-hand man. I'd be lost without him.' He clapped him on the back.

'Zo, love, go and change,' said Mum, as though I was ten. 'You look like you've been dragged through a hedge backwards. Put on that nice dress I bought you. You've been wearing that old T-shirt for days.'

I went, cheeks burning, and almost collided with Lex carrying the plates.

'Thanks a lot,' I muttered at her, which was stupid but I couldn't help it. She gave me a look and carried on past, hips swaying.

I was tempted to go upstairs and stay there, let Lex charm everyone at the table, which she was perfectly capable of if she felt like it. But I was too hungry to resist – and not really for food either, but whatever it was I'd scented about the new arrival.

As Richard had said, there was plenty of food, and all the adults were still picking at the bread and olives. I piled my plate with salad, bread and slices of grilled halloumi. I'd never come across it in England and I liked the way it squeaked against my teeth. Lex was hardly eating, I noted.

On first glance, I'd thought Liam was a bit of a Hugh Grant type. Me and Mum had been to see *Four Weddings and a Funeral* at the cinema a couple of months earlier, and I wondered now if Liam had too: he had exactly the same haircut as Hugh Grant, though his was blond, streaked with gold, like Lex's. He had mastered the self-deprecation bit as well, waving away Richard's compliments and recounting the hapless things he'd done on the journey from England that morning, even down to sleeping through his dawn alarm. Belying the bumbling schtick was his habit of looking right at you as he was speaking, just for a few seconds, before he moved on to the next person. For that brief moment, it was like he could see right inside you. It felt unnervingly intimate, and seeing him do the same thing to everyone didn't diminish it.

As the meal meandered on, another bottle of wine opened and drunk, and then another, his accent began to slide. It wasn't that he was slurring, though he was drunk — they all were by now, even Richard. It was that his vowels flattened and opened up. I noticed it because he started to sound like Mum.

'This is amazing news,' said Liam, raising his glass, after Richard announced over a collapsing tiramisu that he and Mum had got engaged. 'Huge congratulations to you both.' He shook back his fringe and twisted the signet ring on his left little finger. Only I, whose curse was to notice everything, heard the slight softening of the *th* of the last word into *f*.

After another round of toasting was complete, and Richard had gone inside to put on some music, I caught Liam studying Mum. He'd mainly been looking at Lex until then so it was noticeable, though she was oblivious, smiling down into her wine glass. He wasn't looking at her in the same way at all, obviously. With Mum, it was more like a reassessment. Now that she was marrying in, or perhaps marrying *up*, her stock had risen dramatically.

As the phone inside started ringing and Richard shouted

that he'd get it, Lex began collecting the pudding bowls, which confused me until I saw how she leant across Liam to get his and realized that of course she wasn't just being helpful. She wanted the full focus of his attention back on her.

When Richard came back outside, he was frowning. 'That was Penny Rutherford,' he said to Mum, who looked up at him blearily. 'Apparently these two hired mopeds today. No, don't set your jaw at me, Alexandra. You know it's illegal at your age. They're supposed to check your ID but presumably you talked them into getting your own way.'

Lex, still holding the piles of bowls, shook her hair out of her eyes, mouth sulky. 'Well, so what if I did? Nothing happened. We're still in one piece.'

'You didn't have helmets on either, apparently.'

'Thanks, Penny,' she muttered.

'Oh, don't blame her. Your adoring godmother didn't mean to drop you in it. She was too busy inviting herself and the rest of them over tomorrow to do that.'

'Dad, can we just leave it now? We're sorry, okay? We won't do it again.' Lex was darting little looks at Liam. Richard was ruining her street cred. As for Liam, he was drawing shapes in the spilt wine on the table, a funny little smile on his face.

'It's too late for that,' Richard was saying. 'No, you've got to start understanding that there are occasionally consequences for your actions. You're grounded for a couple of days.'

Lex cried out in dramatic frustration and flounced back inside the house, clattering the bowls and spoons into the sink. I imagined Calliope bracing as she thundered up the stairs and slammed her bedroom door. I didn't believe in this performance for a second: she would be perfectly happy to hang around the house if Liam was going to be there. What was it she'd said about men versus boys when we were talking about Robin? Was it Liam she had been referring to? Surely not. Lex, as my nan would have said, was all mouth. Wasn't she? I remembered the way she'd stopped dead at the sight of his swanky black car.

I was glum at the thought that the delicate dynamic had been upended, first with the Rutherfords and now with Liam. I didn't blame Richard – he was just being a good father, a concept I had never known and couldn't help but covet. I didn't even blame Lex, who was naturally inclined to rebellion and couldn't wait to grow up, when I felt the very opposite.

No, I mainly blamed *him*, even as I was apparently unable to stop studying his perfectly symmetrical face. Liam, with his gold signet ring and expensive slip-on shoes. I looked up to find his eyes on me, like they'd been on Mum, sizing me up as though he could smell the animosity coming off me, like pheromones. When our eyes met, he smirked and I had a sudden urge to stick out my tongue. Partly out of frustration because I couldn't say anything in front of Mum and Richard, but also, I think, to demonstrate that I was just a kid. And that, by association, Lex was too. I wished he wasn't so good-looking. I wished he didn't know it so obviously, too. There's such misplaced power in beauty. And even misplaced power is still power.

'You're grounded as well, Zoë,' Mum said belatedly, trying and failing to look stern across the table. 'It's only fair.'

'Fine,' I said. 'It's not exactly Alcatraz, is it? I think I'll survive a couple of days by the pool.'

Richard turned away to hide his smile, which made me feel a bit better. Until I glanced back and saw Liam, still appraising me, as though weighing up his options.

Now

It takes me a while to tune into Lex's brittle state. It's a side I don't think I ever saw back then. She covers it well with the preparation of food and drink, finding bowls and a particular set of pretty blue glasses she remembers that she says will be perfect for the salmon-coloured Greek wine she found in the mini-market. After dinner has been cleared away, and we stay on at the table outside, the solar lights flickering into life, it's more obvious. She smokes one of her thin white cigarettes after another. She's drinking a lot, too. While it makes Mum slide and blur, alcohol always made Lex go faster and louder.

All of this seems to incense Cleo, though she doesn't say anything. She glowers silently. She doesn't drink, apparently, let alone smoke. She hasn't eaten much either, picking at the salad Lex made, and not taking any bread.

'Did Cleo mention she's eating raw at the moment, Zoë?' Lex says, as though she's read my mind. 'I can't imagine she didn't. It's like that old joke: how do you know someone's a vegan? They'll tell you.'

Cleo shoots her a pitying look, picks up her enormous phone, so big Jess would have had to hold it with both hands, and heads for the stairs, though it's still early. She doesn't bother to say goodnight to any of us. The atmosphere lightens as soon as she's gone, up two flights to the attic I still think of as mine. I doubt the old ghosts will show up for Cleo, though. I doubt they'd dare.

'Isn't she something?' Lex says, when she's gone. She's stage-whispering, as though play-acting the idea that she's scared of her daughter, when I think she actually might be.

'She certainly is,' says Mum. She seems oddly galvanized tonight at the sight of me and Lex in the same room together, like she's fulfilled Richard's dying wish for him. Maybe it was his dying wish. The thought fills me with a terrible grief. We always think we'll have more time and it's true that we all thought Richard was fine. Yes, he had elevated blood pressure, but he'd had that for years, despite his lean frame. 'He can't turn off, that's his trouble,' Mum would say. But, still, death seemed to come for him out of nowhere. 'Such a good way to go,' she'd said to me on the phone.

'Not for you,' I'd replied.

I look at her now. She's still shaky, yet she's had only a single glass of wine, which I think has taken some willpower. Being here with Lex is the least I can do, isn't it? I say that like I don't want to be in the same room as her when in fact, and in a strange way I hadn't predicted, I feel more right with her here than I have in a long time.

Over the years, when I've searched online for some trace of her, opening up a private tab if I'm on my phone as though she's illicit, I've stumbled upon her work. She's an artist, of a sort, and sometimes there'll be a painting on a gallery website. *Of a sort.* It's a spiteful way to put it, but I genuinely don't like her abstracts in clashing colours. Of course there's jealousy too, though I didn't pursue art beyond A level. I can't deny that I haven't wondered though: did Lex gravitate towards art because I'd said I wanted to be an artist all those years ago? I suppose I can ask her now. I look back at her, jolt internally again that she's here with me, just a couple of feet away.

'She was always a serious little girl, your Cleo,' Mum is saying, 'but she's suddenly grown up. She towers over me.' She shakes her head admiringly. 'Must get that from her father.'

At that moment, Cleo reappears with an empty glass, startling us. For such a big person, she's silent on her feet. We listen to the fridge opening, the sound of liquid being poured deftly.

'Allowed water from a plastic bottle, are you?' says Lex, seemingly unable to resist, as Cleo passes through.

She stops, her feet broad and firmly planted, a silver ring on the long right second toe that she apparently picked up while backpacking in Laos. I haven't seen her in shoes yet. Her hair has been braided into a fat plait that sits on her broad shoulder and she's wearing an oversized T-shirt straight out of the nineties, which still only reaches mid-thigh. She must be almost six foot. The T-shirt has a woman's face on it, a Cyclops eye in the middle of her forehead.

'Have you taken your meds today?' she says to Lex, in a neutral tone. 'You seem a little manic.'

'Yes, thank you, dear.' Lex waves her away as Mum and I exchange a glance. 'What would I do without you?'

I watch Cleo turn and leave and can only marvel that she is not quite nineteen. She's the sort of direct that women like me say we'll be when we're seventy, and old enough not to care what anyone thinks any more. Somehow she has already achieved this. I'm not sure if it's a generational thing, or a Cleo thing.

91

It can't all be down to progress because my own Jess is like another species entirely, with her tiny frame and quick, tentative movements, her fine dark hair, bird-bright eyes and skin that can look sallow under white winter skies. Cleo's upper-crust grandmother and absent Dutch father very obviously rule her gene pool. She's a Valkyrie, raw-boned and thick-haired, the strands a different blonde and texture from Lex's. Cleo's plait makes me think of the word *flaxen*: hair that would weave into strong ropes from which great weights could be suspended.

'Size eights, can you believe it?' says Lex, when she's gone. She must have seen me looking at Cleo's feet. 'She was in adult shoes by the time she turned twelve. Cost me a bloody fortune.'

'Are you all right, Lex, love?' Mum blinks fast a few times as soon as she's said it, suddenly nervous that she's prying.

'I'm fine. Well, apart from the obvious. Why?'

'Just what Cleo said.'

Lex smiles. 'Oh, the *meds*. It's fine. As long as I take them every day, I'm relatively sane. It's probably wise to lock your doors tonight, though, in case I have another of my psychotic breaks.'

'I think she was just being concerned,' I say. My voice sounds surprisingly firm.

'I'm not sure concerned is the right word. She looks at me sometimes and there's not just pity in her eyes but contempt. More of that than the other, really. And it's not just a teenager thing, before you say it. She's been like this since she was seven.'

'I meant Mum.'

'Oh.' Lex laughs and finishes off her glass of wine.

'Sorry, Marilyn. I'm fine, honestly. So I'm on something to even me out a bit. Who isn't? And whoever isn't, should be, frankly. I think we all need a bit of a muffler on the world. Something to knock off the edges.'

'I've got these pills to help me sleep,' says Mum. 'I don't know what they are – the doctor gave them to me after Richard, but they're wonderful. It's like falling into a black hole. A lovely cushioned one.'

Lex smiles at her, and I remember that Mum could disarm her like this sometimes – a light touch that Richard could never manage.

'The difficult bit is waking up from them.'

'Because you remember.'

'Yes.' Mum swipes underneath her eyes so she doesn't ruin her mascara.

'It hasn't sunk in yet,' Lex says, her face closing. 'And that suits me just fine.'

'I remember when Zoë's nan died. My mum. I didn't believe it until I saw the coffin in the church. It's funny: she insisted she had a church service though she never went.'

'What did Richard want?' I say.

Mum smiles tremulously. 'Oh, you know Richard. Something simple, classy. He wants us – wanted us – to come here afterwards, champagne in the garden, with a service in the chapel first. Nothing religious, and I did ask because you know his mother was Catholic. But, no, he said he'd like it to be casual. Just people saying a few words, but only if they want to.'

'I don't know if I can,' says Lex, her face suddenly stricken.

'That's okay, love. There's no pressure.'

'I – I'd like to, I think,' I say. 'If that's all right.'

Lex nods. 'Of course. You and he hit it off from the start, didn't you? Do you remember that waiter who was convinced you were his daughter? People always thought it was that way round. It made me so jealous. To be honest, it made me hate you a little bit.'

'I never knew what to do about it.'

'It wasn't your fault. It's just that you were so . . . *good*. It shone out of you.' She laughs quietly. 'I couldn't compete.'

I don't want to get into this now. We're skirting dangerous territory. It was me who wanted to confess everything back then, while Lex practically went around with her hands over her ears. I've got a horrible feeling that it's going to be the other way round now. I realize I haven't been in a room with someone who knows the worst thing about me for a quarter of a century. The thought makes my stomach turn over. There was always a reckless streak running through Lex, but it was focused elsewhere then. It'll still be there, though, darting through her blood, looking for a different route out into the open. Perhaps this time it'll be me. I take a breath and attempt to focus on Mum.

'Do you need me to do some ringing around tomorrow, make sure everyone who might want to come knows about it? It's only five days away now.'

Lex looks as though she's going to say something about my obvious change of subject but reaches for the wine bottle instead.

'Oh, I told you, I've done all that,' says Mum. 'I used the Christmas-card list.' She starts to laugh and bursts into tears.

I go and squeeze into the chair next to her, pull her to

me, and it's as though the contact transmits the huge welter of her emotion directly inside me. The enormous absence Richard's death has created, of course, but also the profound sense of their era together ending. No more 'Love from Richard and Marilyn' at the bottom of a card. Small things that are actually seismic: aftershocks that will go on for years, the ground never quite certain again.

Lex is watching us, squashed up together while she sits alone. I have spent a lot more time with Mum and Richard over the years than she has. They always came to me for Christmas, rather than to wherever Lex and Cleo were living that year. I never asked why, in case it prompted Richard to suggest it was high time we all got together – high time we all got over what happened that summer. That although we weren't blood sisters, it would be really nice for him if we could be a family again, especially now he and Mum were getting older.

He never did say anything like that, though, and I've suspected for a while that that was down to Mum. Women see so much more than men and I've always wondered if the estrangement would have held for so long without Mum facilitating it in the background. Back then she knew instinctively that Lex and I weren't telling the truth. Or, as I think she viewed it, *Lex* was lying and I wouldn't tell tales on the stepsister whose spell I had fallen under.

At the top of Calliope, I hear a floorboard creak. It's Cleo, of course, moving around in the still uncarpeted attic, going down to the bathroom to brush her teeth, perhaps. But for a split second I have the unwavering thought it's *her* up there: our third wheel, ever on the periphery, even now listening in on the stairs.

Then

If Lex thought our grounding would mean plenty of time sashaying around in her acid yellow bikini with Liam for an audience, her oblivious father was there to thwart her. The next morning, Richard took over the table on the shaded terrace and covered it with their work papers. The phone, at the full extent of its long flex, was taken out too, for calls back to London. I'm not sure Liam had anticipated this either, his mouth sulky when the boss wasn't looking.

Lex had tried hanging around them at first, offering drinks and asking interested questions. She was so transparent I cringed for her and went off to the pool with my book so I didn't have to witness any more. It wasn't long before she joined me, Richard having shooed her away, as mystified as he was irritated because Lex never helped with anything. He was totally obtuse about what seemed blatantly obvious to me. Perhaps it was denial. What father wants to acknowledge his daughter's sexual awakening? Especially when it involved his ladies' man employee, who was fourteen years her senior.

'So what is it, anyway?' I said.

Lex was arranging her beach towel on the lounger, velvety side up. She paused to look at me. Her face was fully made-up in a way she didn't normally bother with, foundation and everything. In the diamond-hard midday light, it made her skin look chalky, and highlighted a couple of small spots on her jaw.

'What's what?'

'What is it about him?'

'About who? Is this something to do with you sulking? Everyone's being so boring today.'

'I'm not sulking. For your information, I'm actually worried.'

She tutted but wouldn't look me in the eye, which told me she knew exactly what I was thinking. She knelt to adjust the rake of the lounger, yanking at it when it stuck, then plonking herself down.

'What?' she said, after a minute, face belligerent, though I hadn't said anything. She pulled her legs in towards her and started chipping away at the hot pink varnish she'd painted on her toenails, which she'd nicked from Mum. Tiny flakes settled on her towel.

'You know exactly what,' I said. 'So let's not pretend you don't.'

She rolled her eyes. 'Do you know how prissy you sound?' She reached over to poke me and I shoved her hand away.

'You're just jealous anyway,' she said, turning her face up to the sun. 'You think you're disapproving because an older man likes me, but actually you're pissed off because you're jealous.'

'I am definitely not jealous. He's good-looking, but . . .'

'What?'

'I'm not sure.' I didn't know how to put it that wouldn't make Lex say something scathing. *He makes my hackles go up*? It sounded ridiculous.

'So maybe you're actually jealous of *him*, then.'

I gave her a baffled look.

'You're jealous of him because you don't want to share me with anyone else. Especially now the Rutherfords are here. You've got to share me with other people just when you'd got used to having me all to yourself. And it's not just that.' She turned on her side so she was facing me again, seemingly so she could get at me more effectively. 'You're scared too.'

She poked at me once more, making me wriggle away. I couldn't think of anything to say.

'See? I'm right.' She tossed her hair over her shoulder, triumphant, and extended a slim brown leg to the sky. 'I know I am. If Liam did show you some attention you'd be terrified. You were like a rabbit in the headlights at the café in the port, and all Robin did was ask you if you liked the island. Literally the most innocuous question ever.' She laughed. 'Poor little Zoë. Maybe you've got more in common with Pabs than we thought. Maybe you should hang around with her instead of me. You could compare all your woes and worries. We could get you a diary, too.'

'Shut up, Lex.'

'Ooh, I've hit a nerve. Tell me, honestly, have you even kissed a boy before? I bet you haven't. I bet you secretly think all that stuff is totally *disgusting*.'

I was on my feet and heading up the garden before she could say anything else, suddenly wanting to be back inside Calliope, the heat too intense, and Lex way too much. I heard her calling after me and hesitated because part of me wanted her to come after me and say sorry. To make things nice and easy again. I would've forgiven her straight away.

But she didn't follow and I felt stupid hovering there, the sun bearing down on me, like a physical weight, and something biting my ankle, so I carried on towards the house, speeding up as I passed Richard and Liam in case they noticed my face, which probably looked upset because I was such an open book, like a child.

I could hear Mum moving around in her room as I went upstairs. She was humming to herself, and I thought about going in, allowing her to extract everything I was worried about. But there was a risk she would look at me like Lex had – like I was an overreacting killjoy, a strait-laced prig. So I carried on up the stairs to the attic as silently as I could, where the ghosts were too busy with their own concerns to bother with me.

I don't know how long I'd been up there – I'd fallen asleep on the rug, a cushion tucked under my head and the usual wide bands of sunlight making my limbs liquid and heavy – but I woke instantly when she came in. She'd changed into an old T-shirt and shorts. The foundation had been scrubbed off.

'Come on, let's go,' she said, propping one grubby foot flat against the door jamb. 'Just you and me.'

I knew this was an apology so I got up without another word, stifling my smile. It was all I'd wanted really, to spend time with her, on our own. Then I stopped. 'Aren't we supposed to be grounded?'

'Dad and Liam aren't going anywhere for a while yet. Your mum is fast asleep by the pool. I reckon we've got two hours.'

I hesitated at the top of the stairs.

'They can't ground us again, can they?' Lex looked back

at me with a sly smile. 'What else do they have? They can't not feed us. They can't have us arrested.'

I laughed. 'They can't send us home. Or . . . sell us. But shouldn't we wait? Just until your dad . . .'

Her face closed. 'Fine. I'll go on my own.'

'Hang on.' I ran down the stairs to catch up with her. 'Where are we going?'

She grinned broadly enough to show her twisted tooth. 'I'm going to take you to Circe's Pool. It'll freak you out at first. It did me. And then you'll love it. But, look, I've never shown it to anyone before so if you breathe a word . . .'

'I won't.'

She smiled again. 'I know. Come on.'

Even after what she'd said, I didn't really think the pool would be scary. I was from London. The fine hairs on the back of my neck were raised by the urban night, shadowy men looking for lone girls and open windows, the clang of bins that might just be a fox or might be something more. A pond by a cave underneath a church sounded pretty tame.

'It's not a pond, it's a pool. And it's not a church either,' she said. We were walking in single file along a twisting stony path, feet dusty because in our hurry to leave Calliope we still had our flip-flops on. 'I mean, there is a church here but it's abandoned and the point is that it was built on the site of a Byzantine *temple*. I got all this from a book of Dad's. There was this freak summer when it did nothing but rain and I was so bored I thought I was going to die. But I read about this place and the next time we came I followed the map and found it. I don't think anyone else ever comes here.'

'Hang on a minute,' I said, out of breath. Lex was like a mountain goat on the paths that dipped and wove down into a valley dense with trees that looked unEnglish for reasons I couldn't pinpoint. The wall to our left was so tumbledown that I understood what Lex meant. The place felt utterly forgotten by everyone except her.

To save time, we had cycled the mile or so to a turn-off I would never have spotted, the journey on an old bike of Richard's harder than I'd expected, thanks to the hills. Lex had balanced on the handlebars while I did all the work because I didn't trust her not to kill us. My hair was sweaty, strands sticking to my face and getting into my mouth, and the back of my T-shirt was wet through. My calves were streaked with oil. In many ways I'd rather have stayed at the house but I kept reminding myself that this was a special place to Lex, and that while we were here, she wasn't with Liam.

I saw the bell-tower first, its pointed roof reaching up incongruously out of the canopy of trees, some of its terracotta tiles missing, others looking as if they might slide off at any moment. As we got closer I could make out the hulk of the old bell in the shadows and, suddenly, the air felt as still as a long-shuttered room. Along the path we'd come, I'd got used to the birdsong and the slap of our flip-flops, the rustlings of creatures out of sight, maybe even snakes. Distant cars combed the hills and a plane flew so high it was probably closer to space than it was to us. But down there? It was like I'd gone deaf. And then something shifted, and just as I knew the bell hadn't rung in decades, I was sure its mechanism was about to grind slowly into life, the great metal skirt tilting and tilting until the heavy clapper fell, like an iron tongue. The certainty of it, which came and went in a second, made my hot skin goosebump with cold.

At the base of the bell-tower there was a wooden door whose planks had slipped out of alignment, like bad teeth. I glanced at Lex, hoping she wouldn't want to go up there. The air tingled still, waiting for the first clang. But she was already making off down an overgrown path, which descended even more steeply than those we'd been on so far.

I looked back at the tower and saw that the light had played its early-evening trick.

'The Pinkening,' I said, under my breath, so low it was practically a whisper, but Lex, twenty feet ahead of me, turned and smiled.

'Yes, I like that. The Pinkening. When the magic happens.' Her voice bounced around me, the acoustics all wrong. She was waggling her fingers, eyes comically wide in a parody of fear, but it seemed like tempting Fate to talk out loud about magic there. It already felt like something was about to happen. I didn't realize, then, that it always felt like that: a teetering on the edge, the split-second tip into oblivion at the top of the rollercoaster.

In truth, I was afraid of it from my first moment there, though it didn't stop me going back.

The pool itself was a large oval in a shade of green that was somewhere between ripe lime and snooker baize, and behind it, the dark void of a cave as tall as a house. Directly above that, the rusted cross on its decaying roof, just visible through complicated layers of branches and vegetation, I could see the bell-tower rising up to the sky, the blue turning lilac by the Pinkening that couldn't reach us in the shadows by the pool.

It wasn't just sound that had stopped behaving in the normal way, our voices playing tricks and everything else swallowed, but the air was bending the rules too, its texture wrong: it was thicker than was usual, as though it had a meniscus, like water. Moving through it felt closer to wading. It wasn't hot any more, not there, yet I was sweating where I stood, even as I felt chilled to the bone.

'See? I told you,' Lex breathed. 'I *told* you.'

I nodded, unable to speak.

A fat pipe of bright blue plastic snaked incongruously through the undergrowth, carrying water down to the coast, I supposed. It was comforting to see it, like a neon sign in the dark of night. I'd always thought certain places had an atmosphere. It was like the air was thinner, or more porous, or something. In physics, we'd had a lesson on Einstein's theory that time is only another dimension. Mr Summers had got sick of us messing around with the Newton meters, and we'd done the Van de Graaff static hair trick the year before. It was the only thing I remember from a whole year of lessons, and though I didn't really understand it – one of those ridiculous, brain-imploding concepts, like everything to do with space – it still captured me, so that for once I stopped making lists about boys in the back of my exercise book.

From what I could gather, time wasn't a straight line, the past behind us and the future ahead, with no way of getting to the future any faster and no chance of getting to the past. All of it was there, the whole of forever, if only we knew how to access it. Anyway, when I heard that, I thought of those places where it felt like it would be easier to break through, that all it would take was a little shove and you might just stumble into two hundred years ago. It was like that here, where the air felt thicker precisely so you could rip a hole in it to somewhere else. Some*when* else. Except here it was much more ancient than anywhere I'd been before. If you did tear a hole through it, the other side would be more like two thousand years ago.

Lex pressed her mouth close to my ear. 'I told you it was cool.'

She pulled away and spun in a slow circle, knowing I was watching.

'Do you know about Circe?' she said. 'I don't expect you do classics at your comprehensive.' She strung out the syllables and rolled the *r*, then laughed to show she was joking. Or mostly joking.

I shook my head. 'What do you think?'

'She lured men here. To seduce them. But if they refused to fall in love with her, she turned.' Lex widened her eyes.

'Turned?'

'Turned vengeful. And also turned them into swine.'

'Handy.'

'Or wolves or lions. There are different versions. But I like the idea of the pigs best. More humiliating.'

'There's a lot of turning things into other things in Greek mythology, isn't there? I looked up Calliope in that book your dad lent me.' I was trying to sound casual, interested, but really I just wanted to drown any other voices that might be about to start speaking.

Lex raised her eyebrows. 'Such a little scholar.'

I ignored that. 'It said she turned people into magpies.'

'I didn't even know Greece had magpies.'

'There were these sisters who thought they could sing as well as her. She turned them into magpies for being so presumptuous.'

'Seems fair enough. It would have been useful last term if I'd been able to turn Caroline fucking Cunliffe into a magpie. Or a pig.'

'What did she say about you? Was it about boys?'

'Why do you say that?'

I shrugged. 'We should take an oath or something.'

I said it to change the subject more than anything. I didn't really want to talk about boys, or Liam, or any of that. Lex looked at me quizzically, her nose scrunched up, and I thought she would dismiss it or make fun. But she only looked thoughtful. 'What kind of oath?'

'I dunno.' And I didn't. I hadn't even planned to suggest it until it came out of my mouth. 'Maybe like a blood oath.'

She did laugh at that. 'We can mingle our blood and make potions. Dance around our cauldron like blood-sister witches, stirring our toxic brew.' She started to spin on the spot again.

'We can do incantations,' I said, thrilled at her reference to sisters. I stood up and almost wobbled over, my balance off. 'Make curses against our enemies. Invoke the ancient goddesses.'

She stopped spinning and stumbled off to the side, down on one knee, laughing as she did.

Then she looked up and squinted at the sky. It looked bruised now, yellow mixed with the lilac. 'What time do you think it is?'

The film that was holding up the air snapped.

'We should go,' I said. 'They're bound to notice soon, if they haven't already.'

We started up the path, passing the abandoned church. Still the bell hadn't tolled. Still it felt as if it definitely would.

It was hard going on the way back, harder than it had been before, and steep enough that we were both panting. The old dry-stone walls on one side of the path were painted at intervals with a red letter A I hadn't noticed on the way. There wasn't enough breath in my body to ask Lex what they meant.

At some point, we speeded up without needing to confer that we should, me leading the way for once. We went faster and faster until we were running at full pelt, the stone path jarring our heels, the blood pounding in our ears. We didn't say a word to each other until we were back at the bike, sweat streaming off us. Even then we didn't really talk about it. We didn't need to. We both felt the same: that we had pushed our luck as far as we should.

For that day anyway. We'd be back soon enough.

Now

The sun is even brighter than it was yesterday. You forget, living in the city, how clear the light can be outside it. You get used to brick and concrete obscuring the sky, the air as dingy as old net curtains with traffic fumes. Exhaust is the right word. Here, though, once the shutters are open, I have to put on my sunglasses to make the bed. Not that it's unwelcome after my dreams. I'd been at the Pool, unable to get back up to the stone path and away, my feet rooted to the ground, everything around me shadowed and humming with weird intent, the green eye of the water blinking behind me.

I check my phone to shake off the strangeness. It's after eleven but, then, I was still awake at three, lying there thinking, thinking. Another couple of messages from Ben are waiting for me. I've been reading them – making sure that Jess is fine – but not giving him any straight answers in my replies. She hasn't got her own phone yet. I arbitrarily said thirteen a couple of years back, when some of the other kids in her class got them, and she started badgering us, but I wish I'd pushed it even further now her birthday is approaching.

I'm intrigued by Cleo's obsession with hers. It seems not to fit the rest of her, but then that generation have never known anything else. Their phone is an extension of themselves – no more of a cultural signifier than their ear or elbow. I wonder if she's posted pictures of Calliope on Instagram yet. She must have an account. I don't like the thought of it, a little piece of the old house's soul taken without permission.

The others must have been up for a while.

'We're having brunch,' Mum says, when I get out to the terrace, sunlight filtering down through the vines to the scrubbed oak of the old table, dancing on the cutlery. 'I hope you don't mind that we didn't wait.'

I shake my head and sit down, wondering whether I can be bothered to make fresh coffee. Cleo and Lex are engaged in some sort of debate that I only half tune into, my mind still on Ben, who is now losing patience. *If you don't let me know soon, I'm just going to book her on the next flight.* He won't do this, would never use Jess in that way, but I need to ring him. Behaving like I am is going completely against the decision I'd made, in the grief-sharpened hours after Mum told me Richard had died, to save my marriage.

'You literally have no idea what it's like,' Cleo is saying, pointing at Lex with her spoon. 'What we go through now. There was a girl in my year who got her first one when she was, like, ten.'

Lex is sitting at the far end of the table, smoking instead of eating, blowing the smoke over her shoulder. 'It's a bizarre thing to do. I don't understand the impulse.' I notice that she's got a glass of wine, and so has Mum. I glance at the time surreptitiously. It's not that far off midday. Besides, I can't worry about everything.

'You don't need to understand it,' Cleo says. 'It's not about *you* understanding it. You probably can't, at your age. What it is is patriarchal control, starting before puberty, conditioning girls into being submissive before they even understand what's happening.'

Mum is looking at me, her eyes slightly glazed and signalling something with her eyebrows that I'm too distracted to decipher. 'Cleo's telling us about how men send pictures of their . . . of their privates,' she says.

I have a terrible urge to laugh.

'Not just men, Marilyn,' says Cleo. 'Boys, too.'

'And how old were you when you first got one?' says Lex. 'You didn't tell me. I would have complained to the school. I'm not that useless a mother.'

'I can't possibly remember. It was a long time ago. But it's not just the sending, it's what's expected in return. The bullying into it, even when you don't want to. When you never asked for anything at all.'

I would never say it, the thought so out-of-touch, so *problematic*, that I feel like a relic. After all, I know this stuff goes on, often before they leave primary school. I feel sick at the thought of Jess going through it, and obviously it's a large part of the reason she hasn't got a phone yet, though she claims it makes her a pariah among her peers. Yet the notion of some idiot boy sending Cleo an unsolicited dick pic seems ludicrous.

I catch Mum's eye again and know she's thinking something similar. I will her not to say it. *But you'd have them for breakfast, Cleo, if they tried it.* And she would, too, square white teeth grinding them up with her oat-milk porridge. I think I admire Lex's daughter, but I'm not sure I like her. She's fast becoming another reason I don't really want Jess here, Jess who is an observer like I am, who might sense the elephant in the room, who might be old enough now to think of asking some questions of her own. I remember how embarrassingly swiftly I was ensnared by Lex's charms back then, and though Cleo is a very different proposition, who knows what kind of girl Jess might be drawn to? Certainly not me, her mother. This is why people talk about boys being easier. Girls are mysterious, inscrutable, especially to the people who gave birth to them.

'It was ever thus, though,' Mum is saying, and for a second I think she's tuned into my thoughts, when in fact she's talking about boys. As pronouncements from the older generation go, it's better than it might have been. 'Men have always behaved like this,' she continues, finishing her wine. 'Some men.'

But Cleo shakes her head implacably. 'It's not the same. Children didn't watch hardcore porn as a matter of course. It brutalizes them. Their impression of what sex should be is totally warped.'

'A girl's gone missing,' Mum says to me. 'That's how we got on to this. She was walking home after going out for a drink. It was only half past eight.'

I go cold. 'Here? On the island?'

Cleo gives me a funny look. 'In London. They have her on CCTV most of the way, but then she cuts down this path and never comes out. Her phone has been turned off.' She's scrolling on her own phone, eyes scanning fast as she reads, back and forth.

'It's a terrible thing,' says Mum. 'It'll have been her boyfriend, I bet. Or an ex-boyfriend. It's always someone they know.'

'Not always,' says Cleo. 'Sometimes it's just someone

who hates women, and then any woman will do. Sometimes it's a policeman who hates women.'

'God, yes, that was awful. But at least these days you don't have people saying, "Why was she out on her own?" or "Why did she drink so much?"'

'Actually some politician has said that people need to tell their daughters and girlfriends to be careful, to avoid walking about on their own at night. Why shouldn't we walk on our own? Why should we have to change *our* behaviour?'

'Well, it's just common sense, isn't it?' says Mum. 'Until they catch him. It's not as though they're talking about what she was wearing, like they used to.'

Cleo sighs, puts her spoon down very deliberately. 'It's not just a case of catching *him*. It's an epidemic.' She picks up her phone again. I catch sight of the screen and see she's on Twitter, rather than a news site. All of this awaits Jess.

I'm about to go and fetch my own phone from where I've left it upstairs – to call Ben, to speak to my daughter, who is in the same city as this other girl who has been taken – when Mum says it.

'They don't always find them, though, do they? I mean, look at what happened here.'

I see Lex freeze and then, very carefully, shake out the last cigarette from her packet and light it with a long kitchen match. I can smell the phosphorus.

'Of course they don't always find the perpetrator,' says Cleo. 'Particularly if his victim is poor or from a minority background. Especially if they're a sex worker. I don't think they even try when it comes to them.'

'Sometimes even when they're none of those things.'

Mum is looking dolefully into her empty wine glass. 'But what I meant was that they don't always find the girls.'

'Mum.'

'What?' She's querulous this morning. I wonder what's hangover and what's today's drinking, started so early. '*You* mentioned it yourself as soon as you got here.' She looks over at Lex. 'Zoë saw Robin yesterday. It can't possibly be good for him, living out here.'

Cleo is sitting up straighter in her chair, a neat frown line between her eyebrows. Her phone screen has been allowed to go dark for once. 'What are you talking about? Who's Robin? Who wasn't found?'

'Oh, it's just something that happened a long time ago,' I say, as lightly as I can.

Cleo looks at each of us in turn. 'Tell me what happened.'

Lex and I meet eyes and I don't know what she reads in mine but she seems to make a decision. 'There was a girl who went missing on the island,' she says. 'But, like Zoë said, it was years and years ago.'

'She was younger than you are now, Cleo,' says Mum, eyes far away. There's more wine in her glass; I didn't see her pour it. 'That's a strange thought, isn't it?'

'And they didn't catch the man who did it?' Cleo is a picture of concentration, leaning forward in her seat, expression avid.

'Well, there might not have been anyone to catch,' says Mum. 'No crime committed at all.'

'What do you mean?' says Cleo. 'That it could have been an accident?'

Mum gets stiffly to her feet. 'Well, that's what the police and the authorities concluded was most likely.'

Cleo makes a contemptuous sound.

Mum is almost inside but then she turns back. 'The trouble is, when there's no body, there's never any certainty. Never any closure for the family. That's poor Robin's trouble.'

'And what – she just vanished? There were no leads at all?'

'Not really.' She glances briefly at Lex. 'There was a theory that she might have left the island altogether, but that never rang true to me. And, well, she wasn't the sort of girl to do something bold like that.' She looks towards me now, perhaps hoping I'll rescue her, but it was her who lit this fuse, apparently on a whim. I can feel Lex's eyes on me, but I don't meet them this time. I know what she's thinking anyway. It's the same as me. *What the hell is she going to say next?*

'So, on the basis of having nothing else to go on, they assumed she simply vanished into thin air?' Cleo doesn't like uncertainty.

'There was a diary,' says Mum, vaguely. She starts gathering up the brunch things, though her own plate is hardly touched. 'She was always writing in it, apparently, and they never found it, so it must have gone with her. But I don't think there can have been anything very specific in it, or else . . . And of course they didn't want to make things even worse for the family, for Penny and Alastair and the boys, so—'

'You knew the whole family?' Cleo interrupts.

Mum hovers awkwardly, as do I. Lex is looking determinedly out to sea, the ash of her cigarette precariously long.

'Well, yes. Her mum was Lex's godmother. Still is. Haven't you ever met her?'

Cleo shakes her head.

'No, well, I suppose you might at the . . . on Saturday. She's coming out for it and, of course, Robin – he was the eldest – lives here now.' She points her glass towards Lex and then me. 'The girls spent some time with Abigail, didn't you? They were the same age. All of them were fifteen that summer.'

'Abigail.' Cleo sounds the name with a strange reverence. 'You never told me.' She's looking at Lex again, her tone accusing. 'Why did you never mention any of this? It's a huge thing to have happened and you were obviously pretty close to it. I think it's totally weird that you never said anything to me about it. You must have been questioned by the police and everything.'

'The girls were,' says Mum, and it's all I can do not to pull her inside and out of this conversation. 'There was this policeman – not one of the mainland ones, someone from the island – who wouldn't let it go. I still see him around sometimes. I . . .' She glances at me and then away. 'Well, I always avoid him.'

Lex finally turns back to the table. 'I never thought to tell you,' she says to Cleo. 'Why would I? It was so long ago.' But the hand holding the cigarette betrays her. It isn't quite steady. The ash finally falls to the ground.

'And yet Abigail's brother is still here, still hasn't given up, by the sound of it. That's right, isn't it, Marilyn? You just said it couldn't be good for him. He lives here because of her, doesn't he?'

Mum shrugs. 'He's given his life to it, really. Never got

married, or had his own family. And he was such a star when he was a boy, too, everything ahead of him. It was like part of him died with her. It's twenty-five years this summer, but what can he do, really? Stick up some more posters?' She shakes her head and turns to go, almost stumbling on the step up from the terrace.

I follow her in, to make sure she doesn't fall with all that glass and china, and maybe to ask about her drinking if it means she's going to dredge up the past like this. Still, I find myself looking back at Cleo and Lex. They're sitting silently together, both staring out to sea, each as unreadable as the other. But then, as though she feels the weight of my gaze, Lex turns. She looks as deeply uneasy as I feel.

Then

After Circe's Pool, we stayed close to Calliope for a few days. Neither of us acknowledged we were doing that, but we were. Somehow we'd got away with sneaking out: Richard and Mum hadn't noticed, too distracted by Liam's presence and Richard's work, and much too wrapped up in each other to seek us out while we were gone. This seemed unbelievable to Lex and me – we felt as though we'd been gone for a long time when it was only a couple of hours. But time had seemed to operate strangely in that place, just as it did in a more subtle way everywhere on the island and inside the walls of Calliope, bending and stretching when it suited.

Richard had managed to hold off the Rutherfords during these relatively peaceful days, using our grounding and a crisis in the London office as excuses.

'Wouldn't it be more of a punishment if you let Penny come as soon as possible?' Lex said, when this was mentioned.

'Now, now,' said Richard, but his eyes were bright with amusement. Lex was forgiven again.

So, it was just the five of us for a while, and though there were little tensions and jealousies that arose between us, they were inconsequential, nothing leaving a mark. Richard kept Liam busy and Lex didn't seem so keen to seek him out. We didn't know it then, of course, but we were approaching the end of what would become *before*. *After* was bearing down fast.

Penny turned up the following Monday, still uninvited as far as I knew, though I don't think she would have thought she needed to be asked. It was a small but insistent way in which Lex's mother still held some sway at Calliope, over Mum.

I didn't hear her arrive. I'd been up in the attic, reading. Late morning was my favourite time to be there, the thick beams of light in just the right place so that they lay across my middle and didn't get in my eyes. I had nearly finished the book Richard had found for me about Greek mythology, which I had dutifully continued with despite the confusion of deities, the complex hierarchies, the overlapping of their grisly fates. Most of them seemed vengeful and cold, without mercy, and though I loved the music of the names, and the fact that I was in the place where these stories had begun, I couldn't warm to them. In fact, since Circe's Pool, it was more than that: I found them disquieting. I preferred Calliope's benign ghosts, who went on with their gentle bickering while I turned the pages.

I wasn't wearing a watch, but hunger eventually took me downstairs in search of some lunch. There was no one in the kitchen and both Richard and Liam's cars had gone but all the windows and doors were open. Lex had to be around somewhere, probably sunning herself by the pool, headphones on and hair spread out to catch the sun's lightening fingers.

I fetched a bottle of cold water and two plastic picnic glasses, then made my way down the garden, yellow butterflies scattering around me, bright against the blues. I stopped at the top of the steps down to the pool, next to the plumbago bushes, shading my eyes to look out over the Ionian Sea towards Corfu. I'd just been reading about the god Pan, how his death had been shouted across those waters by a passing captain, a great lamentation going up on the island as news spread. I didn't understand why everyone was so bothered. He'd seemed sly and sinister, deeply creepy. It was he who'd given us the word *panic*, coming from the unnameable fear that stole over people in lonely places when he was close, his strange music not quite in range of human hearing, but sensed in other ways, making their skin prickle.

I started down the steps, wondering whether Lex would be interested in hearing about Pan or whether she'd do her bored face. I was always trying to think of things to tell her that would spark her interest or make her laugh. I suddenly wanted to be with her, feel her live-wire crackle and smell her Juicy Fruit gum. But then I heard her laugh. It stopped me in my tracks, the silvery peal dancing over the low hum of the pool's filter.

I kicked off my flip-flops and tiptoed silently down the last steps, trying to work out who she could be with if both cars had gone. As if in answer, the other person spoke, voice low-pitched and gravelly compared to Lex's. It clicked then: Penny. She'd been bound to show up in the end. Now I knew it was her, I could smell her perfume, too light and floral for her, too girlish.

'I said to Cass on the phone this morning that it's quite absurd. They've only known each other five minutes.'

Blood rushed to my cheeks. I almost dropped the water bottle, sweat and condensation making it slip. I crouched, putting it down silently as I tried to slow my breathing so I didn't miss Lex's reply, even though I was afraid to hear it in case it was unkind. But Penny was talking again.

'Pass me that, would you, darling? Christ, I'm stiff today. Pabs was no help yesterday, as per usual. It was our first day back on the water and she just skulked below deck all day, scribbling in that bloody diary of hers. Did I tell you about that? She wears the key to it round her neck, you know. Terrified her mother is going to read it, as though she has any secrets I need to know about. Chance would be a fine thing.'

There was a pause and then cigarette smoke curled into the air, acrid against the garden's fresh green scent. I pictured Lex lying on her favourite lounger, the wooden one with wheels that squeaked when she pulled it into the full glare of the sun. She'd be stretched out like a cat under the sun's searing eye – perhaps surreptitiously listening to her music, headphones pulled down round the back of her neck, her mane of hair covering her ears so Penny didn't realize. The thought made me smile briefly.

'I don't expect Marilyn is much of a sailor,' Penny continued in her relentless way. 'Sticks to package flights she gets a discount on, no doubt. Alicante and Tenerife. But listen to me rattling on and I haven't asked how you feel about it.'

'Cassandra didn't do that either, when I spoke to her.' Lex's tone was world-weary. I wasn't sure if she was putting it on.

'Oh, you know Cass. She was never cut out to be anyone's mother, darling. You can tell me, though. I'm here. Look, have a cheeky fag while Richard and his paramour are still out.' She laughed at her own joke.

'Actually Marilyn's okay.'

I held my breath again.

'I mean, she's a bit of a ditz sometimes, but she means well.'

'Does she? You don't think she's marrying him for his money? For all this?'

'I dunno. I don't think so actually.'

I crept closer, without intending to, only four or five feet from them now. Through the foliage I could see Penny's little gold diving watch sparking in the sun. Next to it, her tanned arms looked dry and parched, like the earth in need of rain.

'Cass said it's hilarious. Only honourable Richard would marry the trolley dolly instead of merely shagging her. What about the daughter? Zoë, is it? She didn't have much to say for herself at the port.'

She sounded hungry. She was disappointed in what Lex had given her so far.

'Dad loves her already,' said Lex. 'She's clever. She's always reading. He's been lending her his books.'

My stomach roiled coldly.

'I wouldn't worry,' said Penny. 'No one likes a smart Alec.'

'No, but . . .' Lex trailed off '. . . Dad does.'

There was a lull and I was about to return miserably to the sanctuary of the attic, when Penny spoke again. 'Look, Lex, I've got a boring favour to ask. Robin made me promise.'

'What is it?'

'Pabs is getting worse. She's turning into a bloody recluse and we're all worried. Alastair said she's like the proverbial albatross around our necks when we're on the boat, but Robin thinks she just needs some female company. I don't count, apparently, but we've never seen eye to eye. I don't go in for all that hand-wringing. Anyway, his idea is that being with other girls her age might bring her out of herself. You know what a saint he is. I can't think where he gets it. So, look, it's a total bloody bore and I hate to ask, especially when you're already having to play happy families with Duty Free's girl, but will you take her under your wing?'

'Sure.' Lex's voice was neutral. I couldn't tell if she minded or not.

'You're a treasure. In return, I'll try to persuade Richard to cancel your grounding. I'll do it tonight. Did he say we're all eating together at the Three Sisters? I've booked it for the nine of us. We'll be on the big table in the garden.'

A sixth sense suddenly had me whirling round. Liam was standing there, just a few feet away, wearing a pair of shorts and nothing else, his chest hairier than I would have guessed at, making him seem even older. He was smirking down at me, half crouching in the undergrowth with my water. I had just straightened, pulling at my top where it had rucked up, when Lex spoke again, her voice as clear as a bell in the hot, still air.

'You need to make it ten,' she said. 'Liam will be coming too.'

'Oh, him, really?' Penny replied. Her voice seemed even louder. She'd got up, I realized, was gathering her things. 'Does he have to? Bit of a wide-boy, isn't he?'

'He's fun.'

'If you say so, darling. I assumed he was another on the make.'

I watched Liam's satisfied smile slip and felt embarrassed for him but a bit triumphant too, unsure whom I disliked more: him or the odious Penny.

Now

I head down to the pool to call Ben. It's the place I'm least likely to be overheard. My phone beeps with another message as I get there, but it's Robin's name on the screen this time. I know it'll be about his campaign and, though it makes me feel heartless, I leave it unread.

The water is perfectly still and clear of debris. Calliope's pool is built of stone, like the house itself, which Richard insisted on when everyone else was still opting for those blue plastic liners that turned the water a blinding turquoise. The result when it's filled is a subtle, enigmatic blue, more like the sea. It always reminded me of Lex's eyes. Perhaps it did Richard, too.

I squat on my haunches to dip my hand in, see how cold it is, but I almost misjudge it, the water's surface coming up too fast as I rock forward. I've just steadied myself when a dark mass in the depths seems to shift and rise towards me. I rear back, almost dropping my phone in, grazing my hand on the rough stone as I twist away from the edge to save it, and myself. When I dare look again, I realize it was only my shadow and feel ridiculous.

Still, it takes a few minutes for my heart rate to return to normal. It occurs to me that, having more or less avoided him for a couple of days, I really want to hear Ben's voice at the end of the line. It's not just the near tumble into the pool, but the conversation with Cleo. It's all of it. He was my safe place for so long, my bulwark against the world. I'd worked hard to try to forget that during the five months since he moved out but since hearing about Richard, I can't seem to keep up those defences any more.

Before Ben, I managed to go through the rest of school, university and multiple flat-shares with friends I told myself I was close to, without ever mentioning it. In some cases, I didn't even tell them I had a stepsister. As we never saw each other – Lex in Scotland with Cassandra until she left home – it was surprisingly easy to omit all mention of her and what happened with Abigail as though neither had ever existed.

The closest I came to telling Ben was at the very beginning of us, during our third or maybe fourth date. We were in one of those London pubs that was early to gentrify, the fruit machines and swirly carpets ripped out, replaced with reclaimed church pews and carefully mismatched chairs, the menu written up on a chalkboard behind the bar.

It was packed and noisy that night, a post-work Friday full of twenty-somethings like us, spending more money than we were earning, busy convincing ourselves we were having the time of our lives. And then she came in.

It was the hair my eyes went to, just as they had done at the harbour: undulating waves of shining chestnut-brown. Without making the conscious decision to do so, I stood up. She had been looking in the opposite direction but then she turned, finding her friends a couple of tables away from us, and of course it wasn't her face, wasn't her at all. I caught sight of my own as I sat down again, in the foxed glass of an overmantel mirror, and it was stark: white and rigid with shock.

Ben, alarmed, took my hand across a table too small for the big white plates. 'What's going on, Zo? You look . . .' He tailed off and I knew he was about to voice the cliché that was so close to the truth. *You look like you've seen a ghost.* I don't know why he stopped because he would have been right. That was exactly what I'd seen.

'Sorry, I just . . . I just thought I recognized someone, that's all.'

He squeezed my hand. 'Come on, you can trust me. That's not *all*, is it?'

So I told him I'd known a girl the summer I was fifteen, on the Greek island where my stepdad had a holiday home. The daughter of a friend of the family, she'd mysteriously vanished on the night of Mum and Richard's wedding. I think I already knew Ben was a serious prospect by then – that some of this stuff would come out anyway.

'Oh, God. No wonder. That must have been traumatic.'

I knew my hand was clammy in his and had to fight the urge to pull it away. Instead of answering, I nodded, hoping he'd leave it there, suddenly feeling like I might be sick: three large glasses of red and an oily steak sandwich beginning to churn ominously inside me.

'I can see why you looked so spooked,' he said, rubbing my hand with his thumb. 'For something like that to happen to you when you were only a kid.'

'I was fifteen.'

'Yes, and fifteen is still a child.'

Which was exactly what Richard said to Papagiorgiou, after Abigail went missing. Not about her, but us – me and Lex.

Ben was in his first year of teaching when we met.

Unlike me, he was a natural and rose quickly through the ranks, getting his first headship when Jess was five. He's in charge of a big, challenging, all-girls comprehensive now, the absence of boys down to some historical connection to the Catholic Church. When he was still a simple class-room teacher, he used to share student horror stories with colleagues in the staffroom, but once he was a head, he offloaded them on me instead.

I came to dread those stories of girls growing up too fast, of the bullying that mobile phones and the internet had made ever more insidious and hard to police, of com-plex female dynamics and hierarchies I couldn't imagine he – as a man – had the first idea about, despite all his training and experience, not really.

They frighten him sometimes, I know – though he's only ever expressed it like that once, when he'd drunk too much. I don't blame him for not wanting to analyse it, a grown man in charge of nearly two thousand of them. They do, though. They scare me, too. It's why I catch myself wishing Jess could skip her teenage years altogether.

He admitted to that fear on the day a particular girl had finally been excluded, after many months of trouble. Ben took it as a personal failing. He came home and opened a bottle of wine before he'd even taken off his tie.

We were halfway down the second bottle, when he said it: 'We think of men as the angry ones, and they are, mainly. But her face on that video they pulled off one of her little acolytes' phones.' He shook his head, filled his glass again. 'She'd just finished kicking another girl in the head for a whole minute and she turned to the camera and there was just this . . . blankness in her face, in her eyes. She's five foot one, seven stone something, right? And we sat there watching it over and over, me, the police, this educational psychologist who's been in the job since the eighties, seen everything, and we were all terrified of this child waiting in the corridor outside.'

Since her, he's made anti-bullying his mission. The school is now considered a leading light on the handling of this issue. What would he have thought about Abigail, if he'd known her, about us, if he'd seen us together? Of course we were nothing like that girl. *Nothing.* And yet . . . 'Threes are always a bloody nightmare with girls,' he has said, more times than I can count.

He answers on the second ring, and his voice performs its old trick, separation or not: my shoulders drop. We were never a couple who fought their way into splitting up, both of us conflict-averse, neither of us shouters. Some of it was a gradual turning away – or, rather, a turning towards Jess, so that we poured all we had into her, rather than leaving anything over for each other. Which is common enough.

But that wasn't the whole story. It was also about how closed off I can be, how little I let him in. And, crucially, how that seemed to be worsening with the years. I wonder if not properly telling him about Abigail that night in the pub set a dangerous precedent, the years of our marriage spent honing secret-keeping to a fine art. Or, rather, my secret-keeping.

'What's going on?' he says now, without accusation, his voice weary rather than angry. 'It's not like you to ignore messages.'

I cover my mouth with my hand because I'm suddenly so close to tears that I can't speak.

'I've been thinking about you,' he says, working out immediately what my silence means, 'about how it's going with you and your mum together.' I close my eyes because he knows me so well, knows how it all works. 'How's she coping? You sent her my love, didn't you?'

'Yep.' It's all I can get out. I swallow and swallow, trying to clear my throat of tears.

'Jess is fine,' he continues, easing into the gap again. 'She's been making our dinners. She thinks I never cook for myself, or have any proper food. We had to go shopping for all this stuff, fish sauce and coriander. Nowhere had any bloody lime leaves, whatever they are.'

I manage a laugh.

'Look, I know it's hard for you out there, for all sorts of reasons I've never really understood.' He pauses, maybe aware of how easily this could tip into accusation. 'I sometimes think I should have made us all go there for a nice, straightforward holiday. Overwritten the ghosts once and for all, you know? But, look, Jess really wants to be there. Not just because of Richard, but *for you*. You know what she's been like since I moved out, always trying to take care of everything, or make up for things, or whatever it is.'

'Yes.'

'I think she has a right to go, to be honest. She's old enough. He was her granddad, as far as she was concerned. I think you'll regret it if you don't let her.'

'She won't forgive me, you mean.'

He sighs. 'She's not like that. You know she isn't.'

I hang my head. 'No, she's not.' I take a deep breath. 'Okay, you're right. She needs to come.'

'Good.' I can hear the smile in his voice, the relief.

'There's a flight on Thursday morning, so she'll only miss a couple of days of school. I'll take her to the airport and you'll meet her at the other end, yes?'

'No, I thought I'd let her get the boat over to the island on her own.' I pause, rub my eyes, turn away from the direct glare of the sun. 'Sorry, bit of a headache. Of course I'll meet her.'

'Your head hurts because you're stressed.'

'I guess so. It's strange being here. And, well, Cleo is . . . pretty formidable.'

'Lex's daughter Cleo? Does that mean . . .?'

'Yes, they arrived yesterday. Didn't I say?'

'You know you didn't. You never do.' He says the last gently, but I deserve the dig.

I need to give Ben something, precisely because I've so often said nothing. I've done my best to avoid him for the last couple of days but it suddenly hits me with a clarity that feels like the truth: this might be the only way we'll find our way back to each other, and I want that more than anything.

'It's not just because of Richard,' I say in a rush, 'that I'm stressed, I mean. It's because of Abigail, too.'

'Abigail?'

'I bumped into Robin yesterday, down at the harbour.'

'God, I'd forgotten he'd be there. Of course, he's always there now, though I still don't really get that, to be honest. It seems so . . . morbid. He was obsessed enough in London.'

'It's twenty-five years this summer. He said he's had new posters printed. He's been in touch with a policeman who worked on the case. I know it doesn't sound like much but . . .' I stop, tears threatening again.

Ben sighs. 'Poor Rob. I always thought he was a lovely guy. But I'm confused. Why is that making you stressed?'

I take a breath, think about the unread message. 'Being here brings it all back. About his sister, I mean.'

'Yes, I see. And with Lex there too –'

I cut across him, desperate to get it out, get *something* out: 'Look, there are things I haven't told you about what happened with Abigail.'

He doesn't say anything. He's leaving space for me to expand into, like all good counsellors. The pastoral side of teaching has always been Ben's strongest suit. As he waits, I listen to the static and then, faintly, a siren in the London streets, some fifteen hundred miles away.

'There's stuff I didn't want to tell you,' I finally say. 'Stuff that looks bad. But I know that me keeping so much to myself is what's been killing us. I know that.'

'Okay.' He draws it out slowly. 'I appreciate you saying that. You know you can tell me anything.'

'I do,' I say, though I don't.

'Well, look, I did wonder if . . .' He tails off.

'What?'

'No, it's all right. I think it'll be too much. It was just a thought I had yesterday.'

'Ben, say.'

'Well, I was wondering if it made sense for me to come out there too. Jess loves the idea of flying on her own – she's been telling her friends about it like she's some sort of jetsetter. But I thought if I came too, you wouldn't need to worry about her, and you wouldn't have to come over to the mainland when you should be with your mum, and now you've said that about Abigail –'

'Yes, come.' I cut across him again, a tear finally spilling over to roll down my cheek. 'That would be good. Thank you.'

'Great.' He laughs softly. 'That's not the answer I was expecting.'

'I wasn't expecting you to suggest it. What about school?'

'It's two days and then half-term starts. I can take it as compassionate leave. I don't think anyone's going to complain. As you know only too well, I've been doing ten-, twelve-hour days for years.'

I don't move for a while after we hang up. The relief of knowing Ben will be here in three days is profound. It almost cancels out my misgivings about telling him the whole truth, about Jess coming here at all.

Then

We were assembled at the Three Sisters by eight o'clock, all ten of us, Lex getting her way. At home, Mum and I ate at six, straight after *Neighbours*, and I still hadn't got used to this late continental way of doing things. My stomach fizzed with emptiness, but also felt pleasingly concave. In the flattering light of the restaurant's garden lamps, I looked almost tanned. Nothing compared to Lex and Mum, of course, but better than before.

We were the biggest party in the restaurant and, thanks chiefly to Penny and Alastair, we were also the loudest. Mum looked strained, sipping regularly from her wine glass as evidence of her discomfort, but Richard was holding her hand under the table as though they were closer to my age than their own. He seemed happy and relaxed, totally unfazed by the presence of the others and their penetrating voices. One day, there would be many more like them but the island was still quite undiscovered then, and most of the other families were wholesome Germans or affluent Greeks who had fled the polluted furnace of Athens to their summer villas in the island's lush hills.

After a fairly excruciating group photo in front of the garden's bougainvillaea, Lex made sure I was sitting opposite Robin, which involved some very obvious manoeuvring when we first took our seats. Her own angling to be opposite Liam had also come off and I could see, if I sat back, that one of her gleaming legs was resting against his. On my other side, at the end of the table, was Abigail. She was wearing a dress in a strange flesh colour, a bit like one of my nan's old girdles. It made her look jaundiced, and she was supremely uncomfortable in it, pulling at the narrow straps, which didn't seem equal to the task of keeping her chest contained.

'Stop fiddling, Pabs,' Penny hissed at her from the other end of the table, which made her still immediately, hands clasped in her lap. She leaked misery into the soft evening air, and it surrounded her like an aura of the same insipid colour as her dress. Mum felt sorry for her: I'd caught her looks, could hear her thoughts in my head as though they were my own: *Why would her mother let her go out looking like that, poor thing?* And I felt sorry for her too, of course I did. But I was also afraid that whatever she had might be catching. If Lex was at one end of some unidentifiable girl spectrum and Abigail at the other, where was I? Maybe the spectrum would tip and I would slide down to join Pabs.

'What are you going to have?' I said, feeling guilty, and rather at a loss after five minutes of silently staring at our menus while everyone else seemed to be chatting easily. I couldn't catch Lex's eye because she was too busy showing off to Liam, and Robin was conspicuous by his absence, having been dragged off by his little brother to the water's edge to inspect some creature or other.

'Tom's our own little Durrell,' Alastair had said. 'Couldn't give two hoots for humans.'

'Probably just a salad,' said Abigail now, so quietly I almost missed it. 'I'm on a diet.'

'Yeah, me too,' I said, with an attempt at solidarity.

She gave me a look, which was fair enough: if there was one thing I wasn't, it was fat. We went back to silence.

'Dad, can I smoke?' Lex sing-songed, though her eyes were on Liam as she said it, a coy little smile playing on her lips that made me want to look away, though I didn't.

'Of course you can't, you awful girl,' he said, but he was smiling. 'Don't make me change my mind.'

Penny had done as she'd promised and our grounding had been lifted as of that night. It was another reason I was dutifully trying to talk to Abigail: Lex had told me about the favour Penny had asked of her, me having to act as though I hadn't heard it already.

Plates began to arrive before we'd even ordered our main courses: what must have been octopus, judging by the tiny round suckers, wafer-thin curls of something green in a light batter, and bowls of pale pink taramasalata, which I had judged revolting even before Lex told me with great glee what it was.

I took two pieces of bread and spooned out some tza-tziki, which I was slowly coming round to. Abigail shook her head when I offered her the bread basket and I saw that the only other person on the table eating nothing was her mother, who had instead ordered a large gin and tonic, its heavy tumbler in one hand and a cigarette in the other. She was oblivious to the fact that her smoke was settling over the family behind.

'So, your boat's mended, then?' I said, feeling like an idiot for not knowing any of the correct terms. Needless to say, I had never met anyone who owned a boat – or who had ever even been on a boat, barring a cross-Channel ferry to Calais. Lex secretly scorned the posh sailing set, with their wraparound sunglasses and windburn, but she still knew how it all worked. I didn't know how anything worked, or so it felt.

Abigail nodded, her expression grim. 'It's hellish. I'm scared of deep water, which is pathetic really, but I can't seem to get over it. Something happened when I was eleven. I got caught in a riptide and I thought that was it, but Robin rescued me, swam out to be with me, and stayed until it spat us out. I was never a very strong swimmer, though. To be honest, I dread us being on the yacht. It's not like it's just the summer, either. We go to the Caribbean at Easter.' She gave me a baleful look. 'It sounds amazing, doesn't it? Mummy calls me the ingrate. But I absolutely detest every minute of it. I can't seem to help it – being useless, I mean. It drives them,' she nodded towards her parents, 'completely round the bend.'

I looked at my plate. I couldn't think of anything to say. All my brain came up with was that Penny was a truly awful person. Alastair, too, if they made her spend all that time on the water when she was so frightened of it.

'Anyway, let's not talk about stupid sailing,' Abigail said, and attempted to smile. 'Tell me about Lex.'

'What about her?'

'Well, anything. Everything. I haven't seen her since last summer. What's it like to live with her? To be a sort of sister to her? She's so cool. I know if Mummy could, she'd swap her for me in a heartbeat.'

'Oh, I'm sure that's not true. I mean, she gave birth to you.'

'It absolutely is true, and I wouldn't really blame her either. Lex is so . . . so much more than me.'

Her face had taken on a strange intensity. Her eyes were on Lex as she spoke, following her every gesture. As a test, I didn't reply and it took her half a minute to notice because she was so entranced.

It was at this juncture that Penny raised her voice to the point at which everyone else was forced into silence. 'I know what I wanted to ask Lex this afternoon!' She slurred slightly on the last word. 'Darling, tell us all about your latest adventures at school, you little rebel. Cassandra reckons you're in the last-chance saloon this time. Are they finally going to kick you out?'

I could read Lex well enough by now to know that she was uncomfortable about this line of questioning but trying not to show it. I was beginning to suspect that part of her didn't want to be the little rebel, not really, and not in front of her dad especially. As for him, Penny's grating presence had finally impinged on his serene mood. He'd gone thin-lipped, turning his wine glass very slowly between finger and thumb, as if checking for smears. Lex was shooting little glances at him but he didn't look her way.

'Actually, Lex is going back next term,' I piped up. The words seemed to exit my mouth of their own volition. 'It's all sorted out.'

Penny looked irritated. 'Really? Is that right, Lex?'

'Didn't Zoë just say so, Ma?' Robin said, in his easy way. He was back, Tom in tow, the latter's bare feet leaving wet footprints on the ground, his trousers rolled up. I couldn't help grinning.

'They *have* said I can go back for A levels,' said Lex slowly. She'd given up on her father and was back to sneaking glances at Liam. 'But I don't know if I will. I haven't decided yet. I might go to art college.' She said it carelessly, her hands going to her hair and piling it on top of her head, exposing her neck. I tried to catch her eye because she'd never mentioned art college: it was me who'd talked about art. But she was too busy preening.

'She *will* be doing her A levels,' said Richard quietly, though we heard him well enough. 'After the many discussions I've had with the school, and with her mother, she will definitely be going.'

Lex let her hair fall around her shoulders, all trace of nonchalance gone in an instant. 'Oh, and never mind that it's my life, and that I fucking hate that place.'

Tom let out a delighted whoop but Richard's face darkened. 'Whatever my thoughts about the public-school system,' he said, 'you're extremely lucky to go to a school like that, with its stables and its Olympic-sized swimming-pool and the kind of contacts you'll be able to make use of for life. Do you know how many kids would give their right arm for the kind of privileges you enjoy without so much as a thank-you?'

'*Thank you*,' she said, and it was so heavy with sarcasm I winced. Robin did too. Liam was smirking at his plate.

'I mean, take Zoë as an example,' Richard continued, gesturing towards me. I had been dreading something like this. Mum and I exchanged a look as she reached for her wine glass. 'Think of her in that library I doubt you've ever set foot in unless you're on detention. It's such a waste.'

'I'm a waste?' Lex pushed back her chair so abruptly it fell over.

'That's not what I said. Stop being so spoilt and sit down.'

'You did say it. You think I'm a waste of your precious money. Well, don't spend any more of it on me, then. Spend it on my perfect new stepsister instead.' She jerked her head at me. 'Send her to my school and see how much she likes it. She wouldn't last five minutes.'

As she stalked out of the garden, no one seemed quite sure what to do. For a horrible second, I thought I might burst into tears, but I pushed my longest nail into my palm until the urge passed. Penny was the first to move, swaying as she got laboriously to her feet before Alastair pulled her back down.

Abigail nudged me. 'Shall we go and check she's all right?'

She was flushed and trembling slightly, I could only assume from the impact of Lex's histrionics. A sort of deep empathy with the subject of her obsession. I didn't want to go. I had unwillingly become the competition when it came to Richard, which was the last thing I wanted to be. If it was between being in Lex's favour or her father's, Lex would win every time. I couldn't bear the thought of her telling me to piss off now, especially in front of Abigail, who would obviously side with Lex whatever happened. She had the look even then of someone who would jump off the nearest cliff if it won her a scrap of approval from Lex.

But I let myself be pulled out of the restaurant, our waitress pointing out the direction in which Lex had fled. She was heading towards the quieter side of the harbour, where the buzz of the evening's crowd straggled into nothing. We weren't that far behind and Abigail called her name but she didn't look round, hair bouncing on her shoulders as she flounced away. I had an idea of where she was going, and it wasn't to sit on the hard white pebbles of the deserted beach. Lex always needed an audience and there was one last taverna in this direction. It never seemed to do much tourist business, but the locals went there to play cards and drink ouzo. With its pile of lager crates full of empties and a noisy generator that made the whole place smell vaguely of petrol, it wasn't somewhere Richard would have chosen. Lex had already told me she thought it was cool.

We found her sitting at a rickety table with her feet up. She snapped her fingers at a man twice her age, who raised an eyebrow but came over slowly.

'I'll have an ouzo,' she said.

He puffed out his cheeks and looked questioningly at me and Abigail.

'Oh, yes, good idea. Me too,' she said.

'A lemonade, please,' I said.

Lex snorted. 'No alcohol for the sainted Zoë.'

Abigail giggled and I glared at her.

'It wasn't my fault, any of that,' I said to Lex. 'I was trying to help.'

She sighed, then lifted her feet, kicked the cheap plastic chair towards me. 'I know.'

Abigail dragged up another chair, and when the drinks came, I asked for my own shot of ouzo, which earned me a smile from Lex at last.

'I hate my school too,' Abigail said, after our second round. Lex had asked the man to leave the bottle. 'I don't honestly know which is worse, there or home.'

'Oh, Jesus,' said Lex, laughing. 'Pabs, you don't have to live up to your name all the time, you know.'

Abigail laughed in a forced sort of way.

'Tell us about this diary of yours, then,' said Lex. Her bad mood had melted away entirely.

'What?' Abigail looked wide-eyed at Lex. She wrenched at her dress straps again.

'Penny said you do nothing but write in some diary. She's worried you're turning into a weird hermit.'

'Did she ask you to be nice to me? Is that why she said she was going to talk to Richard about you being grounded? I thought that was because she'd dropped you in it about the mopeds.' Her lower lip was beginning to tremble.

'No, it was nothing to do with that, was it, Lex?' I tried to pour Abigail another shot but she covered the glass.

'Was it, Lex?' Abigail echoed me.

'Well, it sort of was. But it doesn't matter, does it? It was your brother's idea anyway. He thought you needed some company.'

'It was Robin?' She looked tearful and confused. 'It's none of anyone's business if I keep a diary. I don't know why they can't just leave me alone.'

'But, seriously, what do you write in it?' Lex threw back her shot. 'I mean, I'm not being funny but doesn't it just say "Mummy is being a bitch" over and over again?'

That got a small smile. 'Yeah, basically.'

At that moment Robin and Liam arrived. They were such an unlikely pair that we all did a double-take.

'The parents have made their excuses,' Robin said. 'And poor old Tom had to be put to bed. He fell asleep at the table. He's been secretly staying up late all week, listening out for scops owls.'

'And I wasn't ready to call it a day yet,' said Liam,

143

shrugging. 'So I thought I'd come for one more. You'll never guess who I've just bumped into, Lex. Our old friend Panikos.'

'Yay,' said Lex, face alight. 'What did he say? Come and sit by me.'

'Ouzo, is it?' he said, picking up the bottle as he took his seat. 'Where's my glass, then?'

'I'll just have one,' said Robin. 'I've really come to round up Abs. We've got an early start tomorrow.'

Abigail hung her head.

'Pani said he's started up this club night,' Liam said to Lex, as more glasses were brought and another round poured. Robin sipped his, as I had been doing with mine before I got used to the burn and it started to make me feel warm inside.

'Oh, my God, amazing,' said Lex. 'Where?'

'Up in the hills somewhere. He said we should go.'

'When? Tonight?'

Liam shrugged, all casual, but his eyes were bright. 'Yeah, if we like. He can get us a lift.'

Robin got to his feet and tipped the rest of his shot into his mouth in one go, eyes watering as he swallowed. 'Christ, I think I'll stick to beer in future.' He gestured at his sister to do the same. She hadn't said a word since he'd announced the family plan for the next day but now her face crumpled.

'Do I have to go? I want to stay with Lex.'

'Yes, do you have to?' I said – not for Abigail's sake but because I wanted Robin to stay, especially if we were going to this club thing.

'Mother's orders, I'm afraid.' He gave me a quick salute

and began to steer Abigail away, the protest gone out of her now she'd stood and the ouzo had hit her. 'See you soon, though, okay?' Robin smiled at me. 'We'll call up to the house when we're back.'

'Lex, I'll ring as soon as I'm back, okay?' Abigail said, but Lex was whispering in Liam's ear. Her face fell again.

I watched the two Rutherfords as they walked back towards the bustle and lights of the village, Abigail leaning heavily on her brother, her lovely hair draped over his shoulder.

I wanted to go back to Calliope and think about the evening, analyse various things that had been said, but when I turned back to Lex to ask if we could go, she'd gone. Liam had too.

Now

I feel stronger as I go back to the house after speaking to Ben. He always did have this effect on me, something I'd probably taken too much for granted.

'Was that home?' Mum says, when I come across her washing up in the kitchen, ignoring the existence of the dishwasher just as she had during that summer.

'Well, it was Ben,' I say, but she's exactly right. He is still home to me, him and Jess. 'He's going to come out with her on Thursday.'

Mum lets the plate she's washing slide back under the water. 'Oh, love, I'm so glad. I didn't want to go on about it but I was so hoping she'd come. And Ben. I still don't understand why you two . . .'

'Mum.'

'I know, I know. It's none of my business. But you always seemed so right together. I said to Lex . . .'

'You've been discussing my separation with Lex?'

'No. Well, not like that. She asked, that's all. I said I didn't understand it because I don't. Richard didn't either. Ben adores you.'

I take a breath, wondering whether to say what's been on my mind, but worried I'm likely to be too abrasive.

'What is it?' she says. 'Come on, whatever it is.'

'It's just what you were saying earlier, about Abigail.' I can't help dropping my voice when I say her name. 'It . . .

well, it surprised me. That you would talk about it like that, so openly.'

'Cleo's family.' Her chin lifts. 'She's Richard's granddaughter.'

'Yes, but we don't talk about that stuff. We never have.'

'Well, maybe we should.' She jabs too hard with the plastic brush at a wine glass.

'What do you mean?'

'I mean, that between you, me and Lex, we've kept the family split in two all these years. It made Richard very sad. He always hoped it would be all right one day, but it never was, and now it's too late.' She begins to cry, the tears running unchecked down her cheeks because she's wearing rubber gloves.

I tear off some kitchen roll and dab at them carefully. 'He never said anything to me.'

'Of course he didn't. He thought you had your reasons, he thought I had mine. He left it at that because he trusted my judgement.'

'Your judgement?' I feel stupid. I can't quite get to what she's saying.

'After Papagiorgiou came that second time, I said to him that Lex had to go to her mother's in Scotland. I said it wasn't good for you two to be together, not at that age, not when you were so besotted with Lex. She –' she glances round to check we're still alone '– she's not a bad person. I've come to love her like a daughter. Not like you, but she *is* family. And Richard adored her, of course. But he knew she was out of control. He thought what I was saying was right. I'm not stupid, Zoë. I know you think Richard and I were so wrapped up in each other that summer that we didn't see anything else, but I'm your mother. I'm a woman. I saw, and I don't regret what I did then. I did it for you. But I do regret getting in the way of things being mended later on. It would have made Richard so happy for you two to be sisters again, to have come out here and been a family again. We only had a few weeks like that in all these years.' Her voice cracks.

It's confirmation of what I've suspected. The rift wasn't only down to me and Lex but Mum too. Maybe without her shoring it up, we would have come back together years ago.

'I thought I had more time,' she says, so quietly I have to lean towards her. 'If I'd known . . . And now we're back together, but only because he's gone.'

I turn her to face me and put my arms around her. She cries into my shoulder, twisted awkwardly because her hands are still in the sink.

'I knew you had nothing to do with it,' she says, voice muffled. 'But I also knew there was something you weren't saying – something to do with Lex. I felt like I'd put you in danger by bringing you here, like it could have been you who went missing instead of that poor girl. I just wanted you to be safe. But I went too far with it, let it go on for much too long. I look back now and I can see that I was probably being paranoid. Lex was a bit wild but she wasn't violent or cruel. I should have had more faith. We could have been a proper family all these years.'

I don't say anything. I don't know what to say. It's not like it would help to say she was right the first time, or at least half right. Her absolute conviction that, whatever happened, I had no part in it makes me die a little inside. But I do get it now: this urge to talk about what's been kept in the dark for so long. It stems from guilt. I just wish it wasn't in front of someone like Cleo.

Mum pulls gently away, strips off the gloves and blows her nose. She's about to say something else when the door is pushed open.

'I think I'll go out for a bit.'

It's Lex and I wonder if she heard any of that. She's changed into a voluminous caftan in hot colours that would look awful on most people. The bright oranges and pinks only emphasize the jittery energy that surrounds her like static, and is only getting more pronounced as I relearn her, tuning back into the complicated weather of the moods I once knew so well.

'Where are you going?'

'For a drive, maybe to the port. I need some things. And I wanted to get out for a while. Why don't you come?'

I hesitate. I feel like a child who has been paired by adults with another child she doesn't know, and is wary of. It would be so much easier to be on my own. I was half waiting for Cleo to vacate the attic so I could go up there and lie on the bare boards, have the sun stripe me until I fell asleep. And now, after all Mum has said, I need to think.

'You go, love,' says Mum, and despite the endearment her voice is firm. 'It'll do you both good. It's time you sorted everything out. It's just a shame it had to take Richard to be gone, that's all.' She gives me a pointed look. She's not going to let this go.

I open my mouth but I can't think of anything to say. I glance at Lex and she widens her eyes as though we've been ticked off for leaving wet towels on the floor, when there's so much more going on here, bubbling under the surface. Still, I find myself nodding. It's not just because of Mum, it's Lex. I can feel the tug of her, exerted so effort-lessly. Just like before.

When we get outside, I can see she's hired what must be the worst car in the island's small fleet, which is saying some-thing. It has a dented door, broken air-con and a strange smell emanating from the back seat, like sour yoghurt.

As she reverses at speed down towards the road I real-ize I've never seen her drive. I don't know when she took lessons, or – and this seems unlikely – whether she passed her test the first time. All these gaps in our knowledge of each other. Still, once we get on the proper road, it doesn't feel surprising that she drives like the Greek cliché: with a cheerful disregard for both safety and rules.

'Lex, put your seatbelt on or I'm getting out.'

She tuts but the alarm has started beeping anyway. She clicks it in. 'You were always such a goody-goody.'

'And you were always such a bloody show-off.'

She laughs and reaches round with one hand to the back seat, blindly scrabbling for her bag as we round a bend.

'I'll get it, for God's sake. Just concentrate on the road. Think of my poor mother if you kill us both. Think of Jess and Cleo.' I'm only half joking.

'Cleo would be fine.'

'Yes, that's probably true.' I hold up the bag I've retrieved. 'What do you need?'

'Light me a cig, would you? There's a packet of Marlboros in there. I'll get some more Karelias today. There are men-thol ones I want to try. You know you can't get menthols in the UK any more, the nanny-state killjoys? Something about the mint numbing the throat and making it more pleasant, which is no good for getting people to give up. Plus the mint makes them seem healthy. As though we're idiots when actually we just like smoking.'

I put a cigarette between her lips and push the car's lighter in to heat up. Holding it there, waiting for the glow as she pulls on the filter, feels strangely intimate. I wind down the window.

'Bit pass agg,' she says, with a smirk. 'I was about to put mine down.'

We go on in a silence that is as easy as the bickering, despite the oceans of time since we were last alone together. I start thinking back to when it might have been and stop. It's better not to think of those last days.

I wonder how long we can go on like this, both of us skirting round the shadow looming into our peripheral vision. Maybe we could maintain it until we both go our separate ways again, after the funeral. The possibility of that should feel like a relief but it doesn't convince. Instinctively, I don't believe we'll be allowed to do that.

I think of opening my mouth and starting the conversation right now, facing it head on, but the thought goes through me as a cold shiver. Back in London, I persuaded myself that it would feel different when I was here, that I *had* to come back for Mum whatever, so I should just get on with it. That no one would remember anyway. That I had needlessly turned the island into a phobia through long absence and avoidance. That I would step off the hydrofoil and feel . . . nothing.

That was wishful thinking. Twenty-five years is nothing here, as it turns out. It's as though Eos has been frozen all this time, waiting for Lex and me to return. Now we have, the enchantment has lifted, blood rushing through its veins again.

We're on the road that will take us to the heart of the island, where all routes converge. Lex slows to let an old dog cross where a restaurant I remember is just opening for the lunchtime trade. It looks exactly the same, tables on both sides of the tarmac so that the waiters have to negotiate the traffic as well as their orders.

I expect Lex to turn right for the port but she suddenly wrenches the wheel to the left. She takes another left soon after, this second road little more than a track, peppered with huge stones that the little car struggles over, axles and undercarriage complaining. Round a sharp bend it gets abruptly steeper and I can see in the wing mirror the clutch beginning to smoke just as the smell of burnt rubber curls in through the open windows.

'What gear are you in, and where the hell is this?' But even as I'm saying it, voice shaky, the memory slides with a heavy *thunk* into place. I know exactly where we are, my eye caught by the letter daubed on the old dry-stone wall in dark red paint. Like the stray cats, once I see one I see them all: a series of As, put there by a farmer marking his boundaries God knows how long ago, but doomed to stand for something else now, at least for me.

Lex has brought us to the beginning of the path to Circe's Pool.

We come to a stop and she takes a last drag of her cigarette, dropping the end out of the window as though there is no such thing as wildfires. We stare ahead, eyes fixed on the path that snakes away into a blur of green. The trees overhanging it are denser and more tangled now, but the sun makes it through in places, copper-bright speckles that throw the shadows. I see the two of us flicker there, not as we are now but then. Two girls in shorts and flip-flops, stone dust rising in their wake as they shimmer in and out of time.

'Why are we here?' I say – a last attempt at avoidance.

Her profile is lined in the glare that angles in through the window. I look back but the girls have gone.

'Lex?'

She picks at the steering wheel's rubber with her thumb-nail. 'I don't know. I didn't plan it. I just turned down here, like I was compelled to.'

'That's total am-dram bullshit,' I say, though this place had always made anything seem possible. 'Please don't play mind-games with me. I don't think I can cope with it, after Mum earlier, going on and on in front of Cleo.'

'I'm not. But if you think we can come here after all this time and pretend nothing ever happened, then you're nuts.'

'But you were the one who made us swear never to talk about it back then,' I say, knowing I sound desperate. 'You made us take a blood oath, for God's sake.' I hold my left hand up in front of her face so she has to look at it: the hair's breadth scar that crosses through my heart and life lines.

She lets out a long sigh. 'I know that. I know you would have handled it completely differently and I wouldn't let you. But I think now that I might have been wrong. Maybe Dad dying is a wake-up call to us.'

'You sound like Mum. What are you saying? That we need to confess everything now?' My heart is thumping and skipping in my chest.

'No, of course not. Not yet anyway. I just mean you and me. I want *us* to talk about it. But, look, we don't even have to do that right now. Part of me just wants to *be* with you for the moment. It feels like such . . . such a relief. We only had that summer, I know, but I've really felt the lack of you all these years. I thought of you literally every day.'

'And I thought about you, too. Of course I did. But what do you mean "not yet"? Lex, I need to know if you're planning something. If you're going to blow everything up on a whim.'

She turns to me. 'A whim? It's been with me my whole adult life.'

I cover my face with my hands, and after a moment she lays a hand on my knee.

'I'm not going to blow anything up.'

'We swore it,' I manage to get out, tears veering in as they did when I spoke to Ben. 'You made me and I meant it. I can't just . . . I can't.'

'I know.'

We sit quietly for a time, the silence pressing in from outside, nothing but the sound of my own constricted throat inside the car, as I battle not to cry.

'I don't think I realized that would be it,' she says eventually. 'When I went to live with Cassandra. I did try but you never returned my calls.'

'There was only one.'

'No, there were four over the next couple of years. A letter too, which was hardly my style. Ridiculous, isn't it, that I remember it all so precisely? I know it's not much, but it was way more than you.'

I'm about to say that I never knew about the other calls, the letter, but then I grasp what must have happened. Mum.

'You were so angry with me about Edinburgh,' I say instead. 'For being the one who got to live with your dad instead of you.'

'And you were so angry with me for forcing you to lie.'

'Sure, but it wasn't just that. It wasn't even mainly that. It was the association thing.'

'What do you mean?'

'I couldn't think about you without thinking about her. And I couldn't bear to think about her.'

'Yeah, I get that. But I keep thinking we should have done it for Dad. I've been thinking it ever since your mum rang and told me he'd gone. It was such a clear thought: *Zoë and I should have made up*. He would have loved to see us together again.' It's her voice that breaks now and I place my hand over hers, just quickly, feeling the heat of her skin, and the bulky hardness of her silver rings, between us.

'I never saw enough of him, never gave him enough of a chance to be a grandfather to Cleo. I was always such a fucking brat. But I loved him. I hope he knew that.'

'Of course he did.'

'He's left you Calliope, you know.'

I take a second to absorb what she's said and then my heart is speeding all over again. Lex is smiling at what my face must be doing, and it's the goofy one I haven't seen yet.

'In his will,' she says. 'We talked about it quite recently. He rang me, like he knew what was going to happen. I think he wanted to talk to someone about the end and your mum didn't like to. I think she thought it would tempt

Fate. Anyway, that was what he said. Your mum can stay at Calliope as long as she wants to. But after that –' she briefly squeezes my arm before putting her hand back on the wheel '– it's yours.'

'Oh, Lex. I don't know what to say. I had no idea. I can't . . .'

'You can't, what? Accept it? Don't be proud. He wanted you to have it. He knew how much you loved it.'

'Loved her,' I say softly.

'Well, exactly. I used to come across the two of you together, discussing some arcane architectural feature, Dad parroting whatever Spiros had told him, you drinking it all in.'

'But I haven't even been here, not once, since then. I abandoned it all.'

'So did I. But maybe this was Dad's way of forcing your hand, *our* hands. It's not a bad kind of manipulation, is it? As manipulation goes. And you know what they say. Don't look a gift house in the mouth.'

I snort with laughter. 'Idiot.'

She's still grinning. 'Anyway, I'm not bitter. I get the Surrey house. It's got tenants in it who've been there for years. I'll probably just let that run. I don't put down roots – just ask Cleo, who despises me for it. And, of course, there's also the flat in London, which your mum can live in if she doesn't want to stay on here, but I think she will, won't she? For a while anyway. The island ended up being home to them.'

I think of arriving back at Calliope the other night, and how I'd felt when I got into bed and felt her settle around me. *Ah, it's you,* she seemed to say. *You neglect us all these years*

157

and now you decide to waltz back in. But she didn't really mean it. She knew how much I'd missed her. Her arms were open again.

And one day she would be mine. I didn't deserve her. But, also, Calliope is *here*, on Eos. And being here feels risky. Again I have that sense of pushing my luck.

'Do you ever see her?' It comes out as a whisper. It seems dangerous to talk about it, especially so near the Pool. Ahead of us in the lane, the sunlight flickers strangely again. Leaves flutter in the windless air.

Lex doesn't pause for a second to wonder who I'm refer-ring to, of course she doesn't. 'Never at home. I've always been grateful to my subconscious for that. But here . . .' She takes a shaky breath. 'I went downstairs for a glass of water in the night. I say water. I was picking through the fridge – it doesn't count if you don't sit down, if you don't get a plate, blah-blah – and suddenly I knew she was there, in the corner by the well, where it's always cold. I could smell her.'

The fine hairs on my arms rise.

'What was that lip balm she used? It was in a little round pot from the Body Shop.'

'Kiwi.'

Lex lets out a strangled laugh. 'God, that was it. She was always putting it on. I can see her now.'

I can too: the shine on her lips and her fingertip with its bitten-down nail; the outline of the pot in her shorts because they were too tight across the hips, designed for a sporty girl without curves.

'We keep saying "she". We're not going to summon her up if we say her name.'

'You're sure about that, here?' My voice has risen but Lex's warm hand is on my arm again.

We drive back the way we came, much slower now, I notice. Neither of us suggests going on to the port and I suspect Lex feels as drained as I do. At the crossroads, the restaurant is beginning to fill. Someone is crossing as we approach, taking his time, large hand raised as a greeting is called. Lex leaves it slightly late to apply the brakes, which squeal horribly in response, and I'm just thinking it's a good thing she wasn't going at her earlier pace when the man turns at the noise. We recognize him instantly.

Papagiorgiou. He's been in my thoughts since I saw Robin and now he's here, in the flesh. He's slower than he was, thicker around the belly and the jowls, but the eyes are the same. He fixes us with them through the windscreen, then continues unhurriedly to my open window.

'I heard you were back,' he says.

'Yes, for my father's funeral,' says Lex across me, when I don't say anything. Her voice is only slightly wobbly. You'd have to know her.

'I'm sorry for your loss. People say he was a good man.'

We nod our thanks. I can't look away from his hand, which he's clamped around the top of the door, thick fingers just inside. It's surely our cue to say goodbye and drive away but nothing happens. It comes back to me in a rush, how good he was at this. Letting the silence yawn, not in the reassuring way that Ben does but so you fall into it and drown. While I sit frozen, Lex fidgets – with her hair, and the broken air-con, twisting the dials pointlessly – till it's all I can do not to slap her hand away.

'You've seen your friend Robin,' he says eventually. He's

159

looking at me and it's not a question. 'A big summer for him, for all of us. He has funds now.'

'Funds?'

'I've just heard.' He gestures to the restaurant. 'Some money to . . .' he stops again, taking his time to think of the word '. . . revive the investigation.'

'The police are reopening the case?' Lex's voice is obviously shaky now.

Papagiorgiou shrugs and smiles. 'I tell my wife I retire, but good policemen don't retire. Especially when something is unfinished. In the city, girls go missing every week. Not here. Not ever on Eos. We don't forget her. I never forget her.' He presses his other hand to his chest, 'The case never closes. Not for this island. And now I hear a journalist is coming. They say there could be enough for a re—' He clicks his fingers but can't locate this word. 'To make the memories come.'

It comes to me cleanly, and it's out before I can stop myself. 'A reconstruction.'

'A *reconstruction*,' he says, dark eyes lighting. 'Correct. Maybe you can advise, yes? So we do it right. So people remember this time.'

Then

I couldn't find Lex and Liam in the village. It had got late while we'd been drinking ouzo, and everywhere had emptied out. The tourists had gone, and anyone who was left was male: old men outside the tavernas, whose eyes swivelled as I hurried past, and young men clustered in groups next to their mopeds, whose notice I was beneath. I thought of finding the Rutherfords' boat and enlisting the help of Robin, then remembered that Penny would be there too.

I was paralysed in the middle of the small square, apprehension for Lex and self-pity warring inside me. At least she had Liam. I was alone, and she knew that. She had sneaked off without bothering to tell me, like I was some sort of repressive Victorian chaperone they couldn't wait to be rid of.

I spotted him as he peeled himself away from the huddle by the mopeds, his loose, lazy gait matching his smile. Eleni's son. The one Liam had seen, who was running the club night in the hills.

I approached him before embarrassment took hold of me. 'Have you seen Lex?'

A few of his friends glanced over at the sound of English and then, seeing it was only me, turned away again.

Panikos – the name came back to me – tipped his head on one side. 'She goes with Liam to my club. I get them cab.' He smiled. 'You want to go? I go there now. I take you, if you want.'

I didn't want, and I did at the same time. As I followed him, nerves burning through the ouzo, I told myself it was because I wanted to check Lex was okay, but it wasn't really that. Lex could take care of herself. It was that I didn't want to be excluded, just like Abigail hadn't.

He had a car a bit like Liam's hired one, long and low-slung, dusty black from the dirt roads. I put my seatbelt on but he didn't wear his, which was no surprise. He drove fast and with total confidence, dance music thudding out of a sound system even I could tell was expensive. I tried to take comfort in the deep dark around us: at least we'd see another car's headlights coming a mile off. Despite the nerves, the alcohol in my blood meant I cared way less than I would have done sober, just as I didn't mind much that neither of us had spoken since the village. He seemed lost in the music anyway, head nodding, thumb tapping hard against the steering wheel.

Eventually the tree-cover thinned into nothing and I could see the stars again. We started to pass the odd building, all of them dark. It took me a moment to work out what else seemed odd: there were no parked cars. Lights glimmered ahead, though, and Panikos turned to me with a smile as he switched off the music and put the windows down. Now I could hear the same heavy bass outside, just like the hypnotic pulsing Lex always had on when she was getting ready, making Calliope's floors shake and Richard tut.

When I got out, it took me a moment to understand what I was looking at. Strung along the hillside was a series of gutted houses – simple dwellings of a single floor and a couple of rooms, roofs gone. Each was lit from inside, like a Halloween lantern, with more lights strung between them in long curving lines. Clusters of people, maybe fifty altogether, were dancing in and around them.

As we drew closer, I half shouted my lantern observation to Panikos. When he understood, he seemed delighted. 'Yes, yes, I like this.'

'But where are the people?' I said. 'From the houses?'

'They go. Many years ago. No work, no water. They go down,' he pointed vaguely in the direction from which we'd come, 'to the sea.'

He squeezed my shoulder lightly. 'You go. Find Lex. Have drink, dance, yes?' And then he was gone.

She was sitting on his lap when I found them. She and Liam were holding court with a group who looked nineteen or twenty. From their dreadlocks and deep tans I thought they must be backpackers. Next to them, Liam looked even more like a city stockbroker. I was hovering, suddenly uncertain, when Lex spotted me.

'Zoë, where the fuck did you come from?' She was grinning, and relief washed through me.

Liam glanced my way but didn't smile. He also didn't help Lex as she heaved herself off his lap and rushed over to hug me. She smelt of cigarettes, oranges and fresh sweat.

'Panikos gave me a lift,' I said, into her hair.

'You're so bloody . . . *resourceful*,' she said, pulling back and cupping my face in her hands. 'Like this brilliant Girl Guide.' Her eyes glittered and I felt my hurt melt into nothing as she kissed my forehead. 'Everyone,' she announced, 'this is my new sister, Zoë. Isn't she adorable?'

The next hour or two swept past in a blur of dancing and getting drinks and going to the loo. Lex couldn't keep still for a second, grabbing my hand and pulling me after her to a different part of the abandoned village, or to say hello to someone else.

'How do you know all these people?' I said at one point.

She laughed and kissed me somewhere near my ear. 'I don't.'

By three, I was so exhausted I couldn't stop my eyes drooping.

'Can we go soon?' I said to Lex, pulling on her arm like a little kid.

'Now?' She seemed incredulous.

At that moment, Liam appeared at her shoulder. 'Is it past baby's bedtime?' he said.

'It's hardly early,' I shot back. What I really wanted to ask him was why he was even there, when he was so old. Why he wasn't back at Calliope with the other adults. I wished I had the guts to tell him he was pathetic, at least ten years older than everyone else there. I had seen the backpackers looking at him quizzically, not quite able to compute his presence, in his pressed chinos and shirt, his big gold watch glinting.

'You know what she needs,' said Liam, smirking at Lex in the secret way that made my skin prickle.

Lex laughed, showing her sharp incisors. 'Oh, shush.'

'Why not? Might chill her out a bit.'

'What's he even talking about?' I said to Lex. 'I don't want any more shots.'

As I said it, I realized how drunk I was. We'd been drinking vodka and some peach thing that had coated my teeth. When I shut my eyes, everything spun. Even when I blinked a bit too long, my vision lurched. The distance to my clean white bed back at Calliope seemed vast and impossible.

'I'm not talking about shots,' said Liam.

I leant over to whisper right in Lex's ear. 'Please, Lex. I don't feel very well.'

She rubbed my arm. 'Okay, baby sis. Just one more dance and then we'll go and find Pani. Get a lift from someone.'

Liam leant in, angling himself so he was between us again. He was holding something out on his fingertip, so close to my face that I couldn't focus on it. I pulled back slightly and saw it was a tiny red heart. 'What's that?'

He laughed, glancing at Lex as if he expected her to join in, but she was frowning.

'Stop it, Liam.' She brushed his hand away so that he nearly dropped it.

'Oi, careful. And stop what?' His smile had twisted into a scowl. 'She hasn't got a fucking clue anyway.'

'I know it's drugs,' I said, because what else could it have been? 'I'm not a complete idiot.' But then I found I was going to cry and, in understanding that, tears spilt down my cheeks.

'Oh, Zoë!' Lex's face fell. She tried to pull me into her but I'd had enough. I couldn't bear it any more: not the club, or the proximity of Liam, or my own immaturity for not understanding before. I shook her off and stumbled away, out of the ruined little dwelling we were in and towards the Portaloos, where I was horribly sick, my throat burning as the alcohol came up, my bare knees going down on the filthy, sodden floor.

Panikos happened to be passing as I stumbled out, tear-streaked and shaky. 'Hey, hey,' he said, coming over. 'Where's Lex?'

I shook my head, unable to speak because I knew I'd sob. Tears were already rising again.

'You want to go home now, yes?' He squeezed my shoulder as he had before, and steered me towards a man sitting on a chair smoking.

'Christos will take you in my car, okay? He knows your house.' I must have looked alarmed because he smiled. 'He's my cousin. Eleni and his mum are sisters, yes? You will be safe. I tell Lex.' He paused, laid his hand briefly on my head. 'You're different. Good, young. She's older but also . . .' he frowned, looking for the word '. . . wild.'

He shouted something unintelligible to Christos and threw him the car keys. This time I got into the back and lay down, the journey over in seconds because I passed out as soon as Panikos softly shut the door.

'*Efcharistó*,' I said to Christos, as I got out at the bottom of Calliope's drive. He gave me a nod. I watched him drive smoothly away and took some deep breaths. I could smell the sea and the garden, and Calliope, her old stones. I felt sober now, older too. Sadder, somehow.

Back inside Calliope, Mum and Richard's bedroom door was shut, the house quiet. I knew Mum would think I was with Lex but it still felt strange that she wasn't waiting up. I could see along the corridor that Liam's door was wide open while Lex's was closed, a thin line of light visible under it. I pressed my ear to the wood, even though I knew full well that no one was inside.

I pushed open the door. Lex, in her careless way, had left

166

the lamp on. Without her in it, that lovely room seemed even messier than usual, smelling of burnt hairspray and something faintly yeasty, probably from the half-eaten plates of food she let pile up until Richard got fed up and told her off.

One of my T-shirts, which, to my astonishment, she'd asked to borrow the day before, was on the floor, a dribble of Coke from an upended can staining it. It was new – one of three tops Mum had bought me before we left. I picked it up, tears of fury and all sorts of other things I was too tired to poke at prickling my eyes. Before I left, I went to her wardrobe, which was standing open as usual. I started pulling things off hangers – silky slip dresses and designer tops piling up in a heap at the bottom. I knew Eleni would have to pick them up and smooth them out – she had probably hung them up in the first place – but somehow it helped a little.

Now

When Lex and I return from our drive – from our unnerving little reunion with Papagiorgiou – Mum and Cleo are outside on the terrace; I can see their heads moving as they talk. I feel a rush of guilt for having more or less disliked Lex's daughter on sight: she's keeping my mother company in her grief when it should be me. Instead I've been allowing myself to be dragged back into the past.

Lex heads upstairs, saying she needs a lie-down, so I fetch myself a cold drink and go outside to join the others. It's then I see what they're doing. Not just chatting innocuously after all. Photo albums are spread over the table, the old-fashioned kind with a sticky film layer that anchors the photos in place. There are two albums from that summer, I know, though the second was never filled. My eyes search for their covers, cream with a narrow pink stripe, different from the burgundy leatherette ones of previous years, the years before Mum and me.

'What's all this?' I try to say it brightly.

I spot one of the albums as I say it, and the other is already open in front of Cleo, her broad hand splayed over it. Only fragments are visible but I know those photos so well that it's all I need. Two of the six on that double-page spread are of the night all ten of us had had dinner together at the Three Sisters restaurant – the same night I ended up trailing Lex and Liam to the surreal ruined village in the hills. I think that dinner must have been the only time we were all together, except for the wedding day and the evening that followed it. Doomy clichés jostle in my head at the thought.

That fateful night.

The night after which nothing was ever the same.

The night my childhood ended.

Of course, like most clichés, they're true. It was after this that the lies began.

The waiter had taken the first shot and then asked permission before taking the second. *Different times*, we say now, feeling reproachfully ancient. But it's true: finite rolls of twenty-four or thirty-six shots meant you captured images carefully then. Film wasn't cheap, and neither was development afterwards. I think of how many pictures Lex, Abigail and I would have taken then if we'd had phones. What clues and signs I would have tried to decipher in them now.

I remember clearly that in the first restaurant photo Lex had deliberately moved at the last second, turning her head so her hair swung round to cover her face. The memory of it is sharp, dominated by my annoyance because we would have to pose again: I found the proximity of everyone squashed together horribly uncomfortable – the strain of smiling facial muscles, the sour smell of Alastair Rutherford's mouth-breathing over my shoulder, and then Lex's hair whipping me across the eyes.

Now, Mum gives me a complicated look only I would be able to decipher. Apologetic but also defiant. It's been so long that I'd forgotten but she gets like this when she drinks – and I suspect she's been pouring little half-glasses for herself all day. First the things she said in front of

Cleo, then practically making me and Lex spend time alone together, and now she's decided to unearth that summer in photographic form.

'I wanted to go through them,' she says, chin raised, answering my thoughts because — wine or not — she can read me as well as I can her. 'I'm putting together something for the service. Cleo says she can do something on her phone that will . . . What did you call it?'

'A slideshow.'

I see then that various photos have been removed. Cleo has been scanning them into her phone.

'The quality is not great, obviously,' she says. 'Especially the ones taken at night. But actually, looked at in another way, the graininess is atmospheric, kind of *period*. They look authentic.'

'They're speaking their truth,' I say.

'Huh?' She looks up from a photo of Lex in her white bridesmaid's dress and fixes me with her blue eyes, paler than Lex's, the lashes sandy. 'What did you say about truth?'

'It doesn't matter.'

I don't really want to pick up the photos, study them at close quarters — and I do. The wanting wins out. My fingers scrabble towards the two taken in the restaurant, peeling them from the page. I'm drawn first to Lex, of course, and then her. Abigail.

I don't think I've ever looked at these photos outside, in such bright light, but Abigail has her diary's little key around her neck, hung on a silver chain. I'd forgotten about it. Cleo would probably feast on this detail but I'm not going to give it to her. She has her eyes closed in both, which seems inevitable because she was always so awkward. Lex once said that she was like that cartoon character who went around with his own personal raincloud above him. I can hear Penny's irritable reaction in my head as if she were at my shoulder – *Oh, for God's sake, Pabs, only you could ruin both shots.*

Finally, I study my younger self: cheeks flushed with sun and excitement; the bob that would be grown out but was at that point still slightly too short for the curly ends that made it spring up; my total lack of guile. Still a little girl, really.

'This Abigail,' Cleo says, breaking into my thoughts as she places a finger over my face in the photo to point her out, as though I don't know who she is. 'I've been thinking a lot about her today, and what happened. Why there wasn't much fuss. Why people didn't seem to care that much.'

'There was a fuss,' I say. I think of Papagiorgiou; the questions he'd asked us about her, again and again. The answers he's still coming for – the dark, searching gaze that hasn't dimmed with the years.

'Not enough to find her. Not enough to send over detectives from Scotland Yard, like they have with other missing-girl cases abroad. But now I've seen these pictures, I can't help wondering if it was because she wasn't photogenic enough. You know, there's lots of evidence to show that pretty girls who go missing get way more press coverage than anyone else. Well, pretty white girls.'

'That's not true,' I say, and put up my hand when she opens her mouth to start reeling off statistics. 'No, not the pretty white thing. I'm sure you're right about that. I mean you're wrong that no one really cared about Abigail. They did. We did.'

Cleo shrugs, as if to refute it — as if she knows better but understands it's pointless to engage any further with me about it, when she actually knows almost nothing. A surge of frustration at her, and Mum, if I'm honest, rolls through me. Cleo doesn't know any better, but Mum does. She knows something of how stressful that time was, even if she can't know the level of pressure those interviews put me under. The sheer terror of saying the wrong thing and, in a single breath, ruining my own life.

I gulp down the rest of my water and go back in to get a cold beer. I feel like I need something to blur the edges.

'There's another bottle of wine in there,' Mum calls after me. I think of pretending I haven't heard but I feel too mean. I get myself a wine glass instead, and head back outside with that and the bottle.

Cleo has made neat piles of the photos she's scanned. On top are the restaurant photos she must have scanned for herself; I can't think Mum wants them for Richard's slideshow.

'Right then,' Cleo says, tightening the elastic around her thick plait. 'I'm going down to the village now.'

'Send him my love, won't you?' says Mum.

Cleo nods and then she's gone. I think it again: for such a tall, solid person, she's light on her feet. She moves around the place almost noiselessly.

'What was that about?' I say, when Calliope's door has closed behind her.

Mum turns to me with an enquiring look. She's lost among the photos again, this time the wedding portraits in their larger format. They're upside-down but my eye goes straight to Lex and me in our white dresses, one dark head, one blonde.

'Who is Cleo sending love to? She doesn't know anyone here.'

She pauses, picks up her glass and turns it in her hands before draining it.

'Mum?'

'She's going to see Rob.'

'Rob?' Lex says it just before I can. She's standing by the open doorway with an empty wine glass, her hair messy, her face a little smudged. 'I couldn't sleep.'

'*Robin*.' Mum's tone is verging on facetious. 'She's gone to see Robin. She said she'd take a casserole down to him for me. I need to free up space in the freezer before the service and so many people brought me food when Richard . . . Anyway, I don't expect Robin ever has a square meal.'

'I would have taken it for you,' I say.

'Well, it's not just that, is it? She wants to see if she can give him a hand with his campaign. She says she can help with his reach.' As if she's got no more to say on it, she turns to fix her gaze on the view.

Lex and I exchange a look, our expressions mirrored: half outrage, half something like hysteria.

'What do you know about *reach*?' I say. 'I get what you were saying earlier about Richard, but why are you encouraging her to dig all this up, as though Abigail is some sort of . . . treasure hunt?'

'I'm not encouraging her to do anything. Cleo has always done exactly what she likes. Ever since she was a little girl.' She flicks a wary glance towards her stepdaughter, wondering if she'll be told off for criticizing, but Lex only pushes her glass towards me for wine. The shadows under her eyes are deep.

Mum goes up for a nap soon after that little bombshell. When her shutters close above us, Lex pours more wine into my glass and then goes inside, coming back with a huge bag of Greece's answer to Wotsits.

'I think we bloody deserve them,' she says, chucking them onto the table. 'Don't you?'

'It's not funny, Lex.'

'No, I know.' She pauses and then, so suddenly it makes me almost cry out, she starts swiping at her neck.

'What? What is it?'

She tries to laugh it off, but her pupils are huge. 'Nothing. It's nothing. Just . . .' She shudders. 'I thought I felt something touch me. Fuck, I'm so jittery here. Every time I shut my eyes . . .'

She doesn't finish the sentence but I know what she was going to say. I push her cigarettes and an ashtray towards her, wishing I smoked.

'The trouble is, she's like a dog with a bone,' she says, after she's smoked a whole cigarette and immediately lit another.

Abigail rises again in my mind, the pale round of her face, the indeterminately coloured eyes that were so quick to register hurt. The hungry look she always wore around Lex.

'I mean Cleo.' She hisses it, glancing behind her again, then up to the closed shutters.

'Mum won't hear us. She's taking sleeping pills at the moment. And you saw the wine. I'm getting more and more worried about it, actually.'

Lex doesn't seem to hear me. 'Cleo's always been like this. She gets obsessions and she won't let them go. You know she's going to do law? She's got it all mapped out. She could never do defence, she said, when she informed me of her plans. She wouldn't be able to live with the doubt, apparently. She wants to prosecute.'

I make myself blow out a slow breath because the references to the law are making my stomach twist. My anxiety is becoming less and less abstract. The guilt I've lived with all my adult life is morphing into proper fear. For the first time, I wonder about the possibility of not being allowed to go home. 'I can totally see her doing that,' I say, because if I tell Lex what I'm thinking she might agree and that will be much worse.

Lex raises an eyebrow. 'Yep. I remember when she was tiny. She spent all her time in the garden, even in winter. We were up in Scotland then but she never seemed to notice the cold. Not like me. Do you know what she loved doing out there?'

I shake my head, fearing insects having their wings pulled off. Lex traces a line around the rim of her glass. 'She'd be out there in the muddy patch at the back, turning over stones. I'd go out and watch her work through them methodically, one by one. It was quite mesmerizing. I realized after a while that it wasn't about seeing what was underneath. I mean, it was always the same things – woodlice, worms and millipedes, waving their legs. What she liked was the exposing. Nothing allowed to lurk in the dark.'

Cleo returns to the house a couple of hours later, just as the Pinkening is stealing in. It's gentler than I remember, more pastel than neon, but that's probably because it's not yet summer-proper. That I can note this, even as Cleo passes us on her way to the pool without a word, is because I'm now mildly drunk. Not very – just enough for a soft veil to have fallen between me and the rest of the world. No wonder it's so irresistible to Mum.

'I don't know what I'm more afraid of,' I say.

Lex turns to me, her eyes slightly unfocused. She's had more than me, as well as all the cigarettes.

'Robin's obsession, Papagiorgiou, who always hated us, or your own daughter.' It doesn't come out as lightly as I intend.

Then

I woke up already sweating, the sheet damp and twisted around my legs. I'd slept later than I usually did, and felt disoriented, unable to grasp why I was already so uneasy until I saw my Coke-stained T-shirt. Everything else fell into place: the restaurant, the ghost village up in the hills, Liam holding out the tiny heart on his finger while the bass of the music thudded, a sneer spoiling his handsome face.

I ran to Lex's room, afraid that it would be just as it was, that she had never come back. It was still empty and looked much the same as the night before, but the lamp was turned off and Lex's dress was puddled by the bed. My panic felt instantly outlandish and misplaced, shown up by the sun-drenched morning.

In the attic, because I didn't want to face anyone down-stairs yet, I dragged the leather armchair over to one of the round windows. They were set high enough to provide a view over the lemon trees to the poolside and, sure enough, I could see Lex down there as though she'd never been gone at all, or if not Lex herself then at least the circle of her floppy sunhat.

I went the long way to the pool, down the stairs, out of the front door and round the side, frustration growing with every step but still keen to avoid the terrace where Mum and Richard were sure to be lingering over breakfast as they had taken to doing every morning.

Lex was reading a magazine in a bikini I hadn't seen before, black with shiny gold fish all over it. On the lounger next to her, out of sight from the attic window, was Abigail, looking flushed in a T-shirt and the same unflattering shorts she'd worn the day I met her. She was pretending to read a battered Jilly Cooper but her eyes were on Lex.

'What time did you get back, then?'

Abigail started at the sound of my voice but Lex didn't react. I thought for a second she hadn't heard. Then she looked up and gave me a mischievous smile.

'Good morning to you too, little stepsis.' She put down the magazine and threw me a bottle of suntan lotion, which I lunged sideways to catch even though I was smarting at the 'step'. 'Do my back, will you?'

'No.' I threw the bottle back, slightly too hard. It skittered under her lounger.

'I'll do it,' Abigail said. 'Why didn't you just ask me?'

'Cos your hands are always clammy.'

I winced. Abigail looked as though she'd been struck physically. I thought she was going to cry but then she saw me watching, and her face hardened instead.

'Please, Zo.' Lex pulled a little-girl sad face at me, and my own resentment bubbled up again.

'What was all that about last night?' I said, ignoring the bottle she was still holding out. 'First you left me completely on my own in the village, and then . . .' I glanced at Abigail, who had recovered and was now making no effort to hide her interest.

'Why are we going over this again?' Lex sighed. 'You were absolutely fine flirting with Robin at the taverna. I didn't want to interrupt.'

I coloured, glancing towards Abigail. 'I wasn't flirting. And *she* was right there anyway. You knew they were about to go back to their boat so don't pretend you didn't do anything wrong.'

'Well, clearly you survived long enough on an island with zero crime to get a lift to the club with Panikos. If you were that scared you could have rung Dad, come back here. He would've picked you up.'

'It depends what kind of crime you're talking about, I suppose.' I knew I sounded prissy but couldn't stop. 'And, anyway, don't you think he would have wondered where *you* were? I'm sure it would have gone down really well if I'd rung up and said, "Oh, hi, Richard, I'm all on my own because Lex has gone off to some druggy club place with your thirty-year-old accountant who she's been all over all night."'

'He's twenty-nine and I wasn't all over him.' Her eyes had narrowed. 'Anyway, I don't know why you're being so disapproving when you went there yourself. *And* left without telling me.'

Abigail sat up straighter, her book falling to the ground. 'You went to Panikos's club? Both of you?' Her injured expression was back. 'I can't believe you went without me.'

'Fuck's sake, Pabs. Don't you start. I don't know why everyone is having a go at me this morning. It's way too hot for this kind of hassle.'

I watched Abigail wrestle her face into something like casual interest. 'Was it amazing, then? Did you. . .' she flicked a look at me '. . . did you . . . score anything?'

Lex rolled her eyes. 'Just leave it, will you?'

What I really wanted to do was go back inside Calliope, back to bed. But I couldn't leave. Probably because Abigail was there. Instead, I went over to the lounger on the other side of the pool, as far away as I could get from them, and pretended I was looking out at the view.

'Don't be moody, Zoë,' Lex called, after a while.

'I'm not,' I said.

'It's obvious you are.'

I didn't reply.

The three of us sat there in silence for the next ten minutes in that beautiful place, all of us fractious about different things, blinding us to its loveliness. For the first time since I'd arrived, I wished it was overcast and cool. My sunglasses were inside somewhere and I couldn't go and find them without appearing to storm off. For the same reason I couldn't go and get any water, though my head had begun to throb.

Without Liam there, my bottled-up anger locked on Abigail. Why was she here, now, when it wasn't even eleven o'clock? Wasn't she supposed to be at bloody sea? I studied her surreptitiously across the pool, taking some grim pleasure in despising her blotchy face and stocky white legs. It was easier than being angry with Lex.

Finally, just when I thought I'd have to give in and go inside for Cassandra's hat, or maybe just lie down somewhere dark, Abigail got laboriously to her feet and went off to the loo.

'Bring drinks,' shouted Lex, after her.

When it was just the two of us, she padded round the pool and held out her hand. Even as I thought about not taking it, I was already reaching out.

'You're cold,' she said, and leant down to put her other hand on my forehead. 'But your head's hot. Must be a bad one.'

She took off her sunhat and put it carefully on my head before perching on the edge of my lounger. I moved up a few inches to give her more room.

'I'm sorry,' she said. 'I was pissed. I wouldn't have left you otherwise.'

'It was a shitty thing to do.'

'Yeah, it was. I won't do it again, okay?'

'What about . . .?'

'What?'

'You know what. The pills.'

She shook back her hair, eyes on the sea. 'I only had one. It's not like I haven't done it before.'

'Oh. I didn't know. I thought it was all Liam.'

'Liam's a bit of a coke-head when he's in London, I think. I don't like it, though. I've seen people do it at parties and it makes them really boring. I did my first pill with him here last summer and it was completely different. You just feel . . . happy. Like you love everyone and everyone loves you.'

I thought of her calling me her sister, how she'd lit up when she'd seen me. The thought of that being in some way fake made me want to cry.

'I couldn't believe it when you turned up last night. Little Girl Guide.' She nudged me.

'You remember that?'

'Yeah, course. We had the best time, didn't we? Before you disappeared.'

I shrugged. 'I guess so. But I don't . . . Aren't you scared?'

'Of what?'

'Of something bad happening? Like that girl who died after taking one pill.'

She picked up my hand again, put her other on top. 'That wasn't the pill. It was all the water she drank afterwards. I know what I'm doing. Panikos knows what he's doing.'

'Panikos?'

She smiled but it was a soft one. It also made me feel about six.

'Don't laugh at me,' I said. 'I don't like drugs. They frighten me.'

She scooted round so that our legs were stretched out along the lounger together, then dropped her head onto my shoulder, her cheek hot against my skin, her hair tickling me.

'It's sweet you were worried about me, but you don't need to be. I honestly think alcohol does way worse to people.'

She paused and I thought of saying something about Liam, but then she sat up. 'You're not going to tell Dad, are you?'

'Of course not.'

'Phew. He would completely do his nut. You know the suspension when I was smoking? That was weed, not cigarettes.'

'Oh,' I said again. I felt like I needed some time to think about all of this properly, in the tranquillity of Calliope's attic. About how my idea of Lex had shifted and warped. I hated the thought that my knowledge of all this would spoil things somehow, that she would be spoilt for me. I decided not to dwell on it while my head was pounding.

'Okay, so how about I promise I won't go off ever again?' Lex was saying. 'Will you forgive me then?'

'I'll forgive you if you don't do any more drugs this holiday.'

She twisted around so she could look at me properly. I held her gaze.

'Okay,' she said eventually. 'For you, I promise I'll stick to the demon drink from now on. Forgiven?'

I made a cross on her forehead. 'You are forgiven, my child. Except . . .'

Lex rolled her eyes. 'Fucking hell, now what?'

'You got Coke all over my new top.'

She burst out laughing, then covered her mouth, pulled a serious face, eyes wide. 'You're such a funny one. Look, I'll buy it off you, how's that? It's too cool for you anyway.'

My face must've fallen because she got hold of my hand again. 'I'm joking. I do think you're cool. Weird-cool. Clever-cool. You know that really. And I'll get the stain out, okay?'

'You mean, you'll tell Eleni to.'

'No, I'll do it myself. I'll scrub it until my poor hands are raw and you can watch me.' She held out the little finger of her other hand. 'Make friends, make friends, never never break friends?'

'If I must.' We joined our fingers and shook.

'What's all this, then? Some secret girly pact?' Liam's shadow fell across us.

Behind him, Abigail was holding a stack of cold cans from the fridge. 'I said we were down here and he should join us,' she said brightly, looking to see if Lex approved.

Liam was staring at me. 'So how was baby's first trip to the club, then?'

'It was fine,' I said shortly.

We all watched as he went over to the lounger where Abigail had been sitting and shook out one of the pure white towels that were supposed to stay inside the house.

Abigail opened her mouth to say something, then shut it again. She looked at him in the same hungry way she looked at Lex, her eyes flicking over his arms, brown and muscled against his pale pink polo shirt.

When he was settled, hands crossed behind his head, he gave me another mocking smile. 'Fine, was it? I was thinking it was a shame you made all that effort to track us down and then ended up with your head down the bog.'

'What's this?' Abigail was handing round the cans. She smiled down at him as she gave him his, but he was still looking at me and Lex.

'Zoë had a bit more than she could handle,' said Liam. 'You were right, Lex, when you said we should lose the kids for a bit.'

'Is that what you said?'

'I did not say that. Look, let's not go over the whole bloody night *again*,' said Lex. 'Zo and I have sorted everything out.' She got up and went back to her own lounger, lying down and stretching out, long and lean. She knew Liam was watching her.

'Oh, no! Did you throw up, Zoë?' said Abigail, with a smirk and a glance towards Lex, as she held out the last Coke to me.

I snatched it from her. 'You weren't even there. You'd already been put to bed by your brother.'

'Blimey, someone's time of the month,' said Liam.

For a moment, I couldn't believe he'd said it. It was the sort of pathetic comment the boys at school made. I glared at him and then at Abigail, who was smiling as though Liam was some kind of wit.

'Don't be so vulgar,' Lex said, in the exaggerated posh

voice she and I did with each other sometimes. I didn't want her to use it in front of other people but the immediate disappearance of Abigail's smile helped a bit.

'I'll say what I like,' Liam said, going round to where she was and lowering his freezing-cold can to her stomach.

She leapt up, screaming, and threw some Coke over him.

She screamed again when he grabbed her wrists and pulled her to her feet. She was laughing but he wasn't. The Coke had splashed up his top in a long stream.

There was a strange kind of struggle that, as they play-fought their way round the pool, I ended up too close to, almost tangled in their limbs. I couldn't honestly tell whether Liam was angry or not. He looked it but then again he was letting it go on much longer than he needed to, when he was obviously so much stronger than Lex.

Slowly but surely, he got her over to the very edge of the pool, where her scream-laughing rose in pitch. She was still damp from her last swim; she was in a bikini. There was no reason she should have protested about going into the water, but they carried on grappling. I wanted to look away but I couldn't – it was so peculiarly close to actual violence. Abigail was the same, completely transfixed, her mouth slightly open.

In the end, they both went in, him tumbling after her because she'd managed to grab hold of his wrist as she wheeled round trying to save herself. I didn't think he'd actually meant it to go that far. The polo shirt was already stained but his shorts looked new, too, and were freshly ironed. He wouldn't have wanted to get them dunked in chlorine. Lex would never have thought of that, but I did.

They had gone in at the deep end, and Lex had only just

187

surfaced, spluttering and pushing her hair out of her eyes, when he got hold of her again, grabbing at her legs and hips and pulling her down. I saw his fingers close around the ties that kept her bikini bottoms on and yank. She came up again, kicking him off, and made it to the side in a couple of strokes. He came up, briefly, still thrashing around, then went under again.

'What the fuck?' She was angry now. 'That hurt,' she yelled, as he surfaced and went down again.

I went over to the side. 'Lex, I don't think . . . Can he swim?'

'What?' She twisted round as Abigail also got to her feet, hand covering her mouth, her face draining of colour as Liam went under once more. Lex dived down, got hold of him under his elbow and pulled him to the surface. He panted hard as he gulped air, then started coughing, water streaming from his nose. His hands, when they managed to grip the side, were white and trembling. He stayed there for a long minute.

All three of us watched in terrible silence as he pulled himself along to the steps in the shallow end and climbed out, clothes plastered to his skin.

'Are you okay?' Lex said. 'I didn't know . . . I wouldn't have . . .'

'What?' He rounded on her. 'Didn't know what?'

She put her hands up. 'It doesn't matter.'

The next morning he left, apparently heading back to London to sort out something in the office for Richard. I didn't care what the real reason was. I was just glad he'd gone.

Now

We go out for dinner, despite all the meals supposedly taking up room in the freezer. Lex and I walk at the back, trailing Cleo and Mum. The sky above us is clear of cloud and haze, the clarity of the blue almost too much to look at.

'Is it me, or has this been the longest day of all time?'

Lex was always like this, making jokes when she was nervous. She's right, though. It's felt endless, like another day I know we both remember. I was hoping to get away with a quick sandwich and an early night, but Mum had insisted we go out and neither Lex nor I had had the heart or the nerve to refuse her.

I see the first poster on a telegraph pole next to what was once the moped place. It's now a shop that sells organic skincare. I don't remember what the old posters were like — there are more than a few blank patches in that last week before I went back to England to start a new school — but this one is in glossy colour, so that the richness of her hair colour hooks and holds the eye. The text is in Greek, but the numbers are the same: *25* jumps out at me. I clutch at Lex's arm and nod towards it. Up ahead, Mum and Cleo are threading through small clumps of tourists, Cleo almost two heads taller, her hair in French plaits running down either side of her skull, making her look even more Valkyrie-like.

'Christ,' says Lex. 'Do you think that's what they were

189

doing this afternoon? Cleo and Robin? At least we can't read it.'

But the next one we can. Above a picture of a cat, presumably also missing, is the same poster in English. Phrases jump out at me: *25 years ago this summer. Never forgotten. Our beloved girl.* Guilt rises off the words, like a physical smell. Like the thick damp at the back of a cave, or the shallows of a stagnant pool.

'Beloved,' I repeat, the three syllables rolling slowly off my tongue. It's not a word that sits easily with my memories of her family. Except Robin, of course.

The third, just a few metres on, pinned to a notice-board full of cards from taxi and boat-hire companies, is in German. Three identical Abigails, smiling warily out of the past, mouths slightly twisted because she hated her teeth but thought braces would be worse. Remembering that detail I hadn't known I still knew makes me wonder how I'll manage to eat anything at all. Lex looks just how I feel. *This is not how it's supposed to be.* The thought comes to me clearly. I've returned for Mum, for Richard. Not this. Not *her.* I remember something else I'd forgotten then: the precise texture and taste of the resentment Abigail made me feel. It's sour in my mouth, and takes the last of my appetite.

The taverna at which Mum has reserved a table isn't one I remember. It's tucked down a lane I don't think I've ever ventured along. While those next to the water cater to the richer set, and the big tavernas off the central square sweep up the package-tour guests, who stay in the only hotel, this one is tiny and obviously family-run, with just six tables outside and three within, squeezed around the kitchen.

Ours is the only table left, right in the centre of the tiny courtyard, and the hubbub of Greek conversation drops away to nothing as we take our seats.

Mum doesn't notice. 'It's had really good reviews,' she says, slightly too loudly. 'Richard wanted to come but we didn't get round to it.' She gives us a wobbly smile.

I try to concentrate on the menu, reading and rereading it, the words not going in because I can feel eyes on me, on our table. I still feel queasy after the shock of seeing the posters and wonder where the toilet is if I need it. Despite that, and the wine I've already had today, with Lex, I nod when Mum suggests we order a large carafe of red. Maybe it'll make me feel more detached, and dull the temptation to stand up and run back to the relative sanctuary of Calliope.

Despite the clear sky, or perhaps because of it, I'm dimly aware that it's chillier tonight. A breeze has got up, making the awning above the tables swell and creak. I can hear the whine of the rigging from the harbour a couple of roads away, too. I copy the others in ordering warming comfort food: beef stifado for three, and a vegetarian moussaka for Cleo.

With a queasy inevitability, the subject of Abigail returns even before the food arrives – though, in fairness to Cleo, it's Mum who goes there first.

'Those posters are so much better than the ones the police put up at the time,' she says, small hands clasped around her huge wine glass.

Next to me, Lex stiffens. I hate to think it of my own mother but I've discovered over the last day or so that a part of her enjoys picking over something like this: a tragedy at just the right distance.

'Maybe I shouldn't say it, especially after all this time, but I never thought she looked happy in that photograph. But, then, I suppose she wasn't a happy girl altogether.'

Cleo pours herself some more water. I've not yet seen her drink. I admire it, even as it grates, even as Mum's drinking at the other end of the spectrum riles and worries me. It's none of my business if she doesn't drink, and yet, coming from her, it feels pious. Slightly smug.

'You said there was a diary this morning.' Cleo is looking at Mum. 'That Abigail was always writing in it. But you also said there was nothing much in it. How could anyone know that if it went missing with her?'

'Well, apparently her mother read it sometimes,' says Mum. 'She said it was to keep an eye on Abigail because she was worried about her.' She makes a sceptical noise.

'Why are you doing that?' says Cleo.

'Because Penny was horrible to Abigail,' I say shortly. I can't wait for this conversation to end but Cleo's eyes narrow as she thinks.

'Okay, so if she seemed unhappy – to the degree that her mother read her private diary – they must have wondered about the possibility that she took her own life.'

Mum visibly jolts. 'I never said she was suicidal. There's a world of difference between being a bit down and that.'

'Yes, although Robin said something earlier.'

'What did he say?' Lex tries and fails to light a cigarette, the wind blowing out the lighter's flame twice before it catches and glows.

'Just that she'd been getting quieter and quieter over that summer. More withdrawn. He said he should have made

192

more effort to talk to her about it — really talk to her. But that they weren't that kind of family.' Cleo shrugs.

'Pabs wouldn't have killed herself.' Lex's voice is so sharp I have to stop myself wincing.

'Pabs?'

There's a pause. Cleo looks at each of us in turn.

'It was nothing,' I say, breaking first. 'Just a family nickname.'

'But what does it mean? It must mean something.'

'It wasn't very nice,' says Mum. 'I always thought it was mean-spirited. I said so to Richard and he agreed but said they'd been calling her Pabs for so long that it didn't register any more. It was short for Poor Abigail. She wasn't like the boys, you see. They were gorgeous, sunny. Everything came easily to them, at school, with friends.

'She was the awkward one in the middle but they never made any allowance for her. Like she hated the water. *Hated* it. Some near miss in the sea when she was little. But it didn't stop them dragging her onto that bloody boat every chance they got. I remember Penny saying once, "She'll never get over it unless she faces it head-on, understands there's risk in everything."' She shakes her head. 'Anyway, it was what she'd seen in the diary that led them to look by the Arch.'

'So she'd read it just before Abigail went missing?' Cleo sits forward in her seat.

'Well, I think it was something she did quite regularly. They were a mystery to each other, those two. Chalk and cheese. Anyway, apparently,' she glances at Lex, 'apparently Abigail had talked about the Arch and how, walking over it, she'd felt tempted to jump. You can see why the police centred their searches there for a while, why some people thought she'd done . . . *that*, but they didn't find anything there, and there were no other specifics in the diary to follow up, really.'

Cleo sniffs. 'Well, anyway, just talking about something is hardly conclusive. It's actually pretty well known that people get an urge to jump when they're up somewhere high. It doesn't mean they're suicidal. Quite the opposite, in fact. They think it might be a lightning-fast recoil from danger that we misread as an urge to do it. It's called high-place phenomenon. It's surprisingly common.'

'The French have a phrase for it that sounds a bit more poetic,' I cut in quietly, mainly to stop Cleo talking. Her voice carries and a couple of people are looking around. It seems entirely obvious to me who is being discussed. '*L'appel du vide*. The call of the void.'

Mum visibly shudders, even though she's the one who brought it up in the first place. I try to push down my resentment again as she gets to her feet and heads for the loo. Cleo doesn't notice. Her phone is out, her eyes scanning the screen, relentlessly back and forth, like a mechanical loom, a deep cleft between her brows as she focuses.

'So this Arch . . .' she holds up the phone and there it is: a rainbow-shaped rock set against a blue wedge of sea '. . . is this it? The Triton Arch? And it's safe to walk across?'

'It's just around the headland,' I say, when Lex remains quiet, her hands spread, silver rings shining, eyes cast down to the table. 'It's wider than it looks. So, yes, if you're careful. It makes a nice photo.'

'Have you been there?'

'Once.'

'With my mum?' She glances at Lex.

I nod briefly. I've never heard her refer to Lex like that. It sounds odd coming from her, so much her own person.

My own mum comes back at that moment. She's met someone inside who wanted to say how sorry they were about Richard, and check if there was going to be a service. She's tremulous and flushed and we fuss over her, Lex pouring her another glass of wine while I find her a tissue. One table watches us openly before resuming their conversation in whispers.

Even as all this is going on, another part of my brain is thinking about the Arch – how I'd been there once with Abigail and how I wouldn't tell Cleo about this for the world. How it was just the three of us: an uneasy trio vying for affection and attention in a place that was too close to the edge in ways other than just the literal, all of us infected by the peculiar wind that was blowing that day – all of us in our own kind of dangerous mood, but especially Lex.

'We should have asked Robin to join us tonight,' Mum says, when she's recovered herself, apparently oblivious to the attention we've been receiving as she reaches over to take some bread. I've already shredded a piece into crumbs on my side plate. 'It's a shame. I didn't think of it.' She turns to Cleo. 'How did he seem?'

Cleo pauses. She doesn't mind a silence while she ponders something, I've noted. Even this small act – making everyone wait – feels like a way of establishing power. I think it again: she'll be a superb barrister.

'He seems determined,' she says eventually. 'He's had some money through from his family, hence the new posters. He was going to wait until August to put them up but I said, Why wait? The season's gearing up already – especially with the sailing types. Why not just put them up now? So he started with the centre of the village this afternoon. As you saw.'

I watch her eat a thick wedge of bread in two neat bites, her jaws strong. My gaze was always drawn to Lex and her beauty, some of which was due to her special brand of quicksilver charisma. Now it keeps returning to Cleo, who is no less magnetic a presence, though in a completely different way. Lex draws you in with all that light and spark. Cleo pulls you in against your will, until you smash yourself against her hard smooth walls.

'And did you help him with his . . . social media?' Mum's pleased she's recalled the term.

'He doesn't have any. Well, only a personal Facebook with fifty-odd family and friends who already know. But I've set him up with a few accounts on different platforms and I'll put something on mine. And then, obviously, there's the filming. The reconstruction.'

At that moment the food arrives. An interminable minute of fuss ensues: warnings that the plates are hot, whether we need more bread, and also a fresh carafe of wine because the first is somehow already empty. By the time all this is done, the corners of the paper tablecloth have started to rise and snap against our plates, the wind becoming steadily more irritable. The waiter brings plastic clips, spends another long minute anchoring them fastidiously into place.

'A reconstruction?' It's the first time Lex has spoken and it's impressively casual. You'd never think she'd already heard it from Papagiorgiou.

'There's this cold-case series. The production company is in Athens but someone Robin knows has a niece who works there. Or did work there, maybe. Anyway, they might be interested. I said to Robin I'd be happy to help if they needed a British girl. To act the part of Abigail, I mean.'

'You don't look anything like her,' I say.

'Zoë,' says Mum, reprovingly.

'Well, she doesn't.'

Out of sight, under the table, Lex lays her hand on my leg, just above the knee. It's warm. I've been cold for a while, my fingers numb.

'It wouldn't work,' she says calmly. 'What would they reconstruct? The wedding party? Everyone there was accounted for at the time. No one knows where she went after Calliope. There weren't any cameras. This wasn't *London*. And besides all that, you will not take part in any reconstruction.'

'Why not?' Cleo's fork clatters to the plate. It's the first time I've seen her ruffled.

'Because I say so.'

'What an intelligent response.'

'Okay, I'll tell you. For one thing, Zoë is right. You look nothing like her. But that's not the problem here. The problem is that we knew Abigail and it's extremely upsetting to drag all this up. It's beyond extremely upsetting to drag this up when we're about to say goodbye to my father, your grandfather. You seem to have forgotten that in this little quest, which has nothing to do with you.'

Cleo's thick creamy skin has begun to blotch, ironically in the same way Abigail's used to. 'I just want to help Robin.'

197

'No, you don't. You only met him five minutes ago. This is for you, for your social media. For your CV.'

'Come on now, Lex,' says Mum. 'Let's leave it. Cleo didn't mean to upset anyone, did you, love?'

Cleo doesn't answer. The blotches are spreading down her neck as she picks up her fork and begins to eat again. The action is methodical, measured, but the blotches give her away. She's furious.

Then

From the very start, there was something irritable about the day we went to the Arch.

'It's like it's got out of bed the wrong side,' Mum said, after she and Richard had been forced inside to finish their breakfast. Richard's two-day-old *Times* had been plucked from the table and separated into single sheets, which now littered the garden. 'It had better not be like this on the twenty-fourth.'

That was the day that had now been set for the wedding, which would be *simple* and *unpretentious*. It was also the day before Lex's sixteenth birthday and two days after her GCSE results. 'Oh, my God, literally no one is going to give a shit about my birthday after all that,' said Lex, when she realized.

'Quite the week,' I said, with raised eyebrows, after she'd stomped upstairs, making Richard laugh.

Mum refused on any account to wear white – some antiquated notion about virgin brides and my existence being irrefutable proof that she was not one. At least I think that's what she was getting at. Mum had always been coy about sex. I'd had Lex in hysterics telling her the various euphemistic names she had come up with for intimate body parts when I was small. My nan had been even worse. What Mum called a 'minnie', Nan would only refer to as 'down there', which was always silently mouthed.

'Stop,' Lex had said, clutching her stomach. 'Or I'll piss myself.'

'You mean your minnie will have a little accident?'

Mum did want me and Lex in white, though, if we didn't mind. She meant if Lex didn't mind. 'Just nice simple sheath dresses, I thought, but it's up to you.' She was still wary of Lex sometimes, just as I was.

I was actually looking forward to the wedding. It felt as though Mum's and my lives were suddenly full when they had been quiet and sparsely populated for a long time. The only drawback as far as I could see was that Liam would be returning for it. He'd supposedly gone back to London for work reasons and, although I suspected that was an excuse because he'd felt humiliated about being unable to swim, he was definitely coming back in time for the 'big day', as he'd referred to it, slightly patronizingly, or so I thought.

While he was gone, I felt I'd got Lex back for a little while, although there wasn't much I could do about Abigail's rather dismal presence, which became more of a regular event. She'd even stayed over for a few nights, when the rest of the Rutherfords were off island-hopping.

I would have picked her over Liam any day, though. Unlike him, she didn't appear to present any danger. That was wrong, of course, but no one could have guessed it then. And maybe it was wishful thinking on my part, but I think Lex seemed lighter once he'd left. She seemed happier mooning about him, recounting stupid things he'd said, than when he was actually there, with his sly watchfulness . . . his bad energy, as the hippies would have called it.

That day – the day when the weather was out of

sorts – Lex and I had originally had a vague plan of taking a picnic up to the lighthouse.

'Isn't it a bit blustery?' I said.

'Only you would say blustery.'

'If you like, I can teach you something your expensive education didn't provide every day.'

'Piss off. I thought we could go up there *because* it's windy. It'll be exhilarating.'

'Until we get blown off.'

Abigail appeared just as we were putting together a bag of odds and ends from the fridge.

'Oh, it's you,' I said, when I opened the door to her feeble knock. I didn't feel so sorry for her any more. The sense I'd had early on – that whatever she had might be contagious – had only grown. Standing there in the doorway while she waited sullenly for me to move, I had a flash of premonition. For a split second I understood that the three of us in our different ways were as fractious as the weather, and that it would be wiser if we all went our separate ways for the day, doing our own thing until tomorrow, when no doubt the weather would be sunny and serene once more. But I dismissed it, that little sizzle in the air, the brief whiff of cordite. At least, my own fractiousness dismissed it, the part of me that craved conflict, that wanted a bit of a spat.

It began on the walk. We were all baking under a sky that was not just overcast and strangely coloured but weighted, grubby and hotter than ever – like being swaddled in an itchy blanket. The wind didn't alleviate anything. It was hotter than the air itself, hairdryer hot, making breathing difficult.

'I think it's the sirocco,' Richard had said, just before we set off. He was inside with his reassembled paper, doing the crossword. He thought we were going down to the village beach, Lex having lied to him in her casual way, born of long habit. 'It comes down from North Africa and is full of sand. Sometimes it blows for days and days and sends people mad.'

'Do you want us to slow down, Pabs?' Lex said. We'd been traipsing along a jagged path for a while, stone walls on either side, nettles stinging and small stones rolling under tender soles, the wind buffeting us without warning.

Objectively it was a reasonable question, even a considerate one. Abigail was breathing hard, her face the sort of ominous raw-mince colour you would expect in an old man with a bad heart. But Lex didn't say it in a concerned way.

'No. I'm. Fine.' She puffed out the words.

'I want a rest,' I said, though I didn't need one, was actually quite enjoying the battle against the hot-breath wind, which forced you to drop your head so it couldn't fling grit into your eyes. There was something elemental about it; almost romantic if you were determined enough, which I was. After all, this was sand from the Sahara, which had been carried all the way to us here: three specks of nothing on a tiny green island no one had heard of.

'I think we should walk the Arch today,' said Lex, and I knew immediately this was to get me back for protecting Abigail.

'Sure, why not?' I said, some devilment in me wanting to rile her. A couple of cats with their coats being stroked the wrong way.

We went on for another ten minutes until suddenly the path widened and the sea rolled out before us. Its blue had darkened and turned fretful, and the wind, now we were fully exposed to it, shoved and barged at us as though it had hands. We found an overhang of rock, which protected us from the worst of it, and got out the picnic. Lex handed me a can of Sprite and opened her own.

'Shit, sorry, Pabs, there's only two.'

Abigail shrugged. Lex was smirking at me, wanting complicity, but I ignored it.

'Anyway, what's in the bag?' she said, trying again. 'You did bring something for you, didn't you? We've only got stuff for us but you probably need some sugar after that walk. Ooh, and have you brought the infamous diary, in case inspiration strikes?'

I knew immediately that she'd hit on the truth. It was the way Abigail jerked the bag towards her. A shiver of contempt went through me that she should be so obvious.

'Let me see,' said Lex.

'No.'

'Why not?'

'It's private.'

'But it's only us, isn't it? Just read out one thing, then.'

Abigail considered this. The wheels were almost visibly turning, which set off the shiver again.

'It's the perfect place for truth or dare up here, isn't it?' I said.

Lex looked questioningly at me.

'Truth, she reads from the diary, or dare, she walks over the Arch.'

Lex clapped her hands. 'You're a genius. It's perfect.

So, what's it to be, Pabs? Hand over the book or brave the drop? Let's go and look at it, shall we, before any decisions are made?'

It was a steep walk down, limestone crumbling as we tried to find footholds. The sea was always going to be choppy beneath it, all that water funnelling through such a narrow channel. That day it looked furious, biblical. Not so much water as boiling white spume. It was still vaguely turquoise in the shallower parts, which it was famous for, but a dulled and milky approximation in the swell, as though someone had mixed sky with heavy clay.

'No way am I going over that.' She shook her head for longer than seemed normal, like a child who hasn't learnt to speak and has no other way to make her feelings clear.

'Read, then,' said Lex. 'Or let me.'

She snatched the bag and whisked it out of reach when Abigail lunged to get it back, slipping and almost going down on one knee. She only tried once, then seemed to deflate. Lex pulled out the diary and held it up triumphantly. It was address-book-sized with a small brass lock. Its cover had a picture of a rabbit on it. The sight of it clutched at me. Abigail's hand had gone to the little key around her neck. She was so stupid it made me feel like crying or screaming.

'Hand it over,' said Lex. 'For God's sake, stop making such a fuss. I just want to see what you've said about all of us. Zoë, get it.'

'No.' I sat down heavily on a patch of scrubby grass. My knees already felt weak from the drop. Now I couldn't stand. More than anything, I wanted to shut my eyes and go to sleep.

'It was your idea.'

'No, it wasn't.'

'Fine.' Lex knelt down, hair whipping back and forth in the wind as she bent her head over the book. It only took her a minute with the post of her earring to spring the little lock open. 'I bet you anything Penny's done this already.'

She started flicking through the pages. 'Okay, early July, July, July. God, how can you come up with so much stuff every day? Ah, here we go, August.' She cleared her throat dramatically. Abigail was the only one of us still standing. She just stood there, impassive as a tree, swaying slightly, letting her hair blow into her eyes. It looked redder in the weird light, like embers.

'"I'm not sure if I can face a whole summer on the water. I cried myself to sleep thinking about it last night. I do that all the time, these days. I didn't think things could get any harder than last year, when all that stuff happened in Drama and Mrs B made it so much worse, but it really is harder. I don't know why people always talk about these being the best years of your life when they're obviously the worst. I hope they are anyway, because if it carries on like this, I don't know what I'll do."' She pulled a sad face. 'Oh, Pabs. It's not that bad, is it? What happened in Drama?'

Abigail didn't move. She looked as though she'd willed herself miles away.

'Right, that'll do,' I said. 'Give it back now. Let's go down to the village, get an ice-cream. This wind is doing my head in.'

'In a minute,' said Lex. She was skipping over the pages again. 'Aha! This is more like it. I should've gone to the latest to start with. "Just got back to the boat with Robin.

205

Mummy asleep and snoring, thank God. She made me wear the dress tonight even though I told her I hated it and looked fat. I think that's why she made me. She's such a fucking bitch and if you're reading this, Mummy, I mean it."' Lex was delighted. 'Go, Pabs, you tell her.' She was having to shout louder now, as the wind ramped up. '"We went out for dinner with everyone tonight. Lex was there, looking amazing as usual, but I hardly talked to her because she was all over that guy who works with Richard. He came out last summer too. He's gorgeous and everything but he totally knows it. Anyway, it's weird that he's always touching her when he's literally twice her age. It's way worse than last time."' Lex's face had begun to harden.

Abigail, who had been so still, suddenly dived for the book and almost got it.

'No, you don't,' said Lex, snatching her hand away. 'This is just getting interesting. "I might have to say something to Richard if it carries on. Lex never listens to me but he would, if I said I thought she and Liam were involved in a sexual way. I used to think I was in love with her last summer. I was always trying to look at her when—"'

'Stop.' The word came out of her strangled, almost a screech. 'I'll do the Arch.' Without waiting for a reply, she started descending towards it. It was like she didn't care about the diary itself any more. It was hearing it read aloud that was unbearable.

I scrambled to my feet and went after her. The wind whined around us, pushing this way and that. 'You don't have to do the dare as well,' I cried. I sounded ridiculous.

The Arch had been formed when a sea cave collapsed, leaving a narrow slice of rock standing alone and uncertain in the open sea, joined to the land at one end only. The hole in the Arch had once been the cave's mouth. Its top was uneven: it widened and narrowed like badly torn bread. Close to the middle, the path seemed to taper almost to nothing and, though I knew this was an optical illusion, the sight of Abigail walking towards it made me want to be sick. I bent over, hands on my knees.

'Lex, stop her,' I managed to push out past the nausea, but Lex was transfixed and didn't hear me.

When Abigail got to the middle, she stopped and turned forty-five degrees so she was facing the open sea. Even from where I was standing, I could see her body being pushed by the wind. She raised her arms until she formed a bulky cross and the wind stung my cheeks because tears were running down them. I was so sure she would let the wind nudge her over the edge that it was as though it had already happened. In a single second, I saw everything that would follow: Lex's and my screams of disbelief, the nightmarish run back to the village to alert someone, the emergency radio call to the Rutherfords' yacht.

But she didn't fall. She didn't jump. Her arms lowered slowly and she turned and walked back the way she'd come.

Lex whooped and scrambled down the last crumbling steps of earth and limestone. They met right where the land held tightly to the Arch, Lex's arms going around her. Abigail's face was blank, splotched grey and pink, her hair tangled and dull with salt. I watched as she started to smile, her arms going up to hug Lex back. They jumped and screamed together while I stood there, my heart juddering inside me.

If it had happened that day, my certainty that she would

die even as she still stood there, would things have been so different? Would I have felt better than I did, or about the same? I don't know. What I do know is that that day was our warning, Lex's and mine. A bitter, heady taste of the damage we could do when we flexed our muscles in the way that maybe only girls of that age can, for a little while.

Now

Cleo corners me in the living room the day after the meal in the taverna. She's wearing a red T-shirt with a cartoon pink snout in the middle, *men are pigs* written inside it in Comic Sans. As she approaches the window seat where I'm curled up in the afternoon sun, trying to get some sleep because I had so little last night, her heavy plait bounces on her shoulder.

It's the same place I saw Lex for the very first time. When everything was new and fresh and unspoilt. I must have come here looking for some sort of comfort. That's probably why I messaged Ben a few minutes ago, too. *I'm looking forward to seeing you both tomorrow.* He hasn't read it yet and I feel oddly nervous about the reply, as though this is not the man I've known since I was twenty-two but some-one else – who might spring surprises.

'Circe's Pool,' Cleo states, without preamble.

I freeze and see Cleo absorb this.

'What?'

'Circe's Pool. It's on the island somewhere. Mum said you used to go to a haunted place called that. You two and her. Abigail. That's right, isn't it?'

'What?' I say again, stupidly, even though it's obvious I heard her. I just need to buy some time, but I'm tired, my thoughts muddled, muddy. I can't think what possessed Lex to mention the Pool. A spurt of pure white anger burns through me at the thought.

Cleo's breath hitches with impatience. 'It sounds like they only really thoroughly searched the area around the Triton Arch, but what about the Pool? She didn't like water, did she? She was afraid of it.'

'They didn't search just the Arch. I was here, remember.' I sound too defensive. I make myself take a breath. 'They looked everywhere. It's not a big island. The first couple of nights she was missing you could see all the lights.'

'Lights?'

'Lights in the hills. Moving lights from the search parties. They combed the place.'

'Including Circe's Pool?'

'I'm sure they did.'

'You're sure. Well, I suspect things were missed. Rural police in a place like this would have been completely out of their depth. Robin doesn't want to say it, I can tell. I think he's friends with one of them. But was there a single proper detective on the island back then? Everyone knows the first forty-eight hours are crucial in a missing-person case.'

'Isn't it seventy-two hours?' I have no idea why I say this. I study her, Lex's girl, the broad lowland planes of her face, the implacable expression, and I have no idea what I can say to her that won't pique her interest further and make things worse. She's on her phone again now, thumbs flying. My mind slides back to my dreams from last night, though really it was just the same one, over and over: blinding lights and cameras on me as I stumble down the path towards the Pool. The total silence, except for the bell in the tower, tolling in time with my footsteps. The long chestnut wig I'm wearing, so hot and so heavy that my neck bows from the weight of it.

'I might go down to the station today. It looks like it's near where the hydrofoils come in.'

'Station?' I refocus on Cleo, picturing trains, tracks, red signals.

'The island's police station.' She says it slowly, as though to someone very dull-witted. 'No doubt it'll be like the ones you get in backwoods America. The sheriff and his sidekick deputy who've never dealt with anything more serious than a stolen car.'

'I wouldn't say anything like that to them if I were you. They weren't stupid then and I doubt they are now.'

Papagiorgiou always knew there was more to it. He wouldn't let it go, ignoring Richard's objections. 'They're fifteen,' Richard said, at Calliope's door, as he was showing the policeman out, Lex and I eavesdropping from behind the dining-room door. 'Just children.'

'Fifteen is not children,' Papagiorgiou had replied, in his unflinching way.

'Or maybe I'll try to find the Pool,' Cleo is saying. 'And there's always the Arch to see with my own eyes. Do you think there's a reference library?' Her thumbs are moving again. 'I can't tell if the one in the port has any newspaper collections. There's obviously nothing online.'

'I think you might struggle with the Cyrillic anyway.'

She glances up. 'It's Euclidean actually. The Cyrillic alphabet came later. It's the Slavic languages that use Cyrillic.'

Soon after, she departs on her mission. I'm already regretting not having challenged her more, fetched Lex, perhaps, or just reiterated what she'd said to Cleo last night – that it's in bad taste to dig all this up when people are grieving for her own grandfather. She has a particular way about her, though. You only think of things you might have said after she's left the room. When she's there, she's like a signal-blocker, scrambling your brain.

It's just past the hottest time of the day and Mum is upstairs sleeping. She's doing a lot of that. Some of it is the medication, and the wine, of course, but I think it's also because having us all here has made her relax into her sorrow a little. She's lost some of her pinched look.

The window seat no longer feels peaceful and I go upstairs. I find Lex in her old room, which has long since become the main guest room because of its en suite. Not that many people come to stay. Mum never felt very comfortable with Richard's posher friends so he'd let those relationships fade away, secretly not minding it just being the two of them. As for family, there wasn't much. It was basically Lex and me, and while I had never come back, Lex wasn't much better. It had always fallen to Mum and Richard to come to us.

Despite the intervening years, the room is still absolutely Lex's. Perhaps it's just because my senses were always heightened inside Calliope, but I even think it smells like it did then. Not the stale food, thankfully, but a girlish stickiness undercut by the lemons outside the window and old cigarette smoke. The bittersweet orange scent of Lex.

She's sitting on the floor, leaning up against the bed, arms wrapped round her knees. It takes me a beat to realize she's crying. I've only seen her do this once before; it's not a component of the Lex in my memory. Any anger I'd felt towards her melts away.

Before I can second-guess myself, or become too English about it, I sit down next to her and rest my head against her shoulder. It's the sort of thing she would have done to me once. She feels hot through her cotton top, feverishly so, as if her body is trying to purge something, which perhaps it is.

'Have you cried much for him yet?' I say softly.

She shakes her head. 'I didn't want to get all upset in front of Cleo.'

'I think she can probably handle it.'

'Not for her sake. For mine. I'm a certain way with her. We're a certain way with each other. Tough. I have to keep my end up.'

'Lex, I'm sorry to ask this now, when you're upset.'

'What is it?' She cuts across me, turning her face to mine. We're so close I can see every pore, and the perfect navy-blue rims of her irises.

'Cleo's been quizzing me again. I think she might have gone off to do more digging, to the Arch or to the police station in the port, though God knows what she thinks they're going to tell her.'

'I told you what she's like, didn't I? Christ, she'll probably bump into Papagiorgiou down there. Can you imagine if those two joined forces? We'd be locked up by nightfall.'

She stops and we look at each other.

'Don't even joke about it,' I say.

'I'm not sure I was. It seems . . . very real here, doesn't it? Very close. I was just thinking about Dad when I got on the plane. Obviously I think about her, all that, but it's been like a distant nightmare until now.'

I rub my temples as she blots her face with the hem

of her top. She's grim-faced but becalmed from her tears. 'What were you going to ask me?'

'Why did you tell Cleo about Circe's Pool?'

She looks at me, totally nonplussed. 'I didn't.' She opens her mouth to say something else, then shakes her head in disbelief. 'God, that girl never forgets anything. I told her about it once, years ago. And I mean years ago – she must have been ten or eleven. There was a craze at school for telling ghost stories and one of the other girls had got the rest of them all wound up about it. Cleo, being Cleo, wasn't afraid, said there was no such thing and the others were idiots. I don't know why I said it – I should have been glad to have such a sensible, rational, un-neurotic child – but she was so sure, so convinced she was right and everyone else was wrong. God, I would probably only say this to you, even after all these years, but she had this arrogance about her, you know?'

I knew exactly and I had known her only days.

Lex covers her face. 'Argh, such a bad mother. But, anyway, I said I had once known a place that was haunted. That I had never believed in ghosts before I went there, but that it had changed my mind. That afterwards I felt there was definitely *something*. I shouldn't have said it, not to a child, but I had this urge. I never could talk about it because only you would have understood, and we weren't speaking.'

'What did she say?'

'Nothing much. Cleo doesn't change her mind. She just took it in and stored it away, and probably never gave it another thought until today, when her infallible filing system spat it out for you.'

'But you said you were there with me and Abigail, presumably. She knew that.'

'Not Abigail, no way. I never mentioned Abigail to Cleo until this week. Remember, she definitely hadn't heard of her until the other night when she was cross with me for never telling her I'd known the missing girl. I would have mentioned you, though. I always mentioned you to people if there was a chance. Your mum noticed I did it. We met up for this awkward lunch in Edinburgh once – me, her and Dad, Cleo still in a highchair – and she said it then. "You always bring my Zoë up. I know you miss her. She misses you too." "Does she?" I said. "Did she tell you that?" So pathetically hopeful. And she shook her head, all sad and almost guilty, weirdly. "No, but I'm sure she does."'

We sat quietly, our positions mirrored, my left knee touching her right. The breeze is strengthening again and the shutters creak on their hinges, like old joints. It's been so long that I'd forgotten something crucial: how right it feels to be with her. We fitted back then somehow. Separated from all the bad associations, we still do.

'I missed you,' I say.

She gives me a sad look.

'No, Lex. I did.'

'But, then, why . . .'

'You know why. There were reasons on both sides. But, also, if I didn't see you, I didn't have to think about it. I could lock the door on it.'

'I don't think it works like that.'

'It can. It did, I think. For a long time, anyway.'

'You kept it from Ben, didn't you?'

'Why do you say that?'

'When I heard you'd separated I wondered if it was something to do with the secrets.'

I shake my head, unable to reply because she's right. I think of her own failed relationships, the strained dynamic with Cleo. Secrets fester but they also isolate.

I'm still thinking about this, about whether it's too late to talk to Ben properly, when Lex's head snaps up. 'What exactly did she say about Abigail?'

I blink. 'Just that we'd been to Circe's Pool with her.'

'Jesus, she really will make an excellent barrister.'

I sigh. 'I keep thinking the same thing.'

'No – what I mean is that I think she *tricked* you into confirming that. Like when they say in court, "What made you stab her twice?" And the defendant shouts, "But I only did it once!" She took a punt, threw it out there, and you went for it.'

'Oh, shit. I'm so stupid. I didn't even –'

'She must have dredged up the haunted-pool thing, seen how edgy we are about all mention of Abigail, and started fitting it together. Unless . . .'

'What?'

'No.'

I lean away so I can see her face properly. 'Tell me.'

She gets up in one fluid movement, pulls me to my feet, nods towards the ceiling. 'Come on. While she's not here.'

I'd forgotten how warm it got in the attic when the windows were closed. The round ones didn't open but the ones the other side did and it was always the first thing I did when I went up there to read or nap. I hesitate on the threshold, reluctant for my adult self to intrude on my teenage sanctuary, but Lex goes straight to the long, low bookcase that fits neatly under the eaves. Calliope feels as alert as a wild animal suddenly, ears pricked, nose twitching.

'What are you looking for?'

Lex doesn't answer. I cross the floor towards her, hear the familiar creaks I didn't know my body had recalled. I feel oddly charitable towards Cleo for being so tidy that there's no evidence of her up here at all, nothing to break the spell.

I'd sampled a strange mixture of reading matter from the shelves in here, which Richard had grouped together away from the books downstairs because they were connected in some way to Greece. Guidebooks sat higgledy-piggledy alongside the Durrells – Lawrence and Gerald – and big old tomes on Ancient Greece and its mythology. *Captain Corelli's Mandolin* is there too, I see, its pages swollen and wavy, and I remember that Richard was reading it that summer, when it was new. I can picture it splayed, spine up, next to the pool.

Lex is pulling out books, checking behind them and pushing them back in. She's doing it faster and faster as she apparently fails to find what she's looking for.

'Lex, what is it?' But as soon as the words leave my mouth, I know. It's so obvious I can't believe I didn't realize as soon as she led me towards the stairs. 'You took her diary, didn't you? It's here somewhere.'

'It was.'

I slump into the leather armchair, its old springs groaning. I'd always assumed what everyone else had: that the diary was in the same place as Abigail. The difference was that I knew where that place was. It had never occurred to me that Lex might have taken it.

'I didn't know you took it. How didn't I notice you do that? I thought you threw it in with the bag.'

'You were in a state. Besides, it wasn't very big, was it? I tucked it into my knickers.'

'I'd changed out of my dress.' I remember now. 'You still had yours on. You looked like a ghost, glowing out of the dark.'

Lex is almost through the last run of books when she stops dead and lets out her breath in a rush. 'It's still here.'

She turns and holds it up for me. It's smaller than I remembered. Even from where I'm sitting, I can see the pages are as rippled as Richard's *Captain Corelli*. Its plasticky rabbit cover has gone a strange greenish colour.

'Have you –'

'Ever read it?'

She shakes her head, holds it up again to show that it's still locked. It had taken her half a minute with an earring once but I think I understand what she means now. We'd invaded Abigail's privacy before. Lex hadn't wanted to do it again.

'She wore the key, didn't she?' I say. 'I think she'd hidden it somewhere until she discovered Penny was reading it. After that she wore it on a silver chain around her neck. I saw it on that photo of us at the Three Sisters.'

We fall silent. I wonder if Lex is thinking about where that chain and its little key are now. Calliope shifts, or so it seems to my sleep-deprived brain. I feel the floors tilt, just a little. The thick yellow ribbons of sunlight that cut across the bare boards stutter, like a tiny glitch.

'Why did you take it?' I say.

She looks down at the little book in her hands. 'I don't know.' She puts it down carefully on the floor and reaches up to pull the band out of her hair. It catches the light as it falls loose, dust motes spinning off it like the finest glitter. She winces as she rubs her scalp. 'I think maybe it was just instinct not to leave it there to be found by someone else.'

I would have done the same thing if I'd thought of it. But what I would never have done was hide it inside Calliope, much less on Richard's bookshelves where it could have been found at any point over the last two and a half decades. I would have destroyed it, burnt it, or if that had seemed too unbearable, too cruel somehow – or too likely to provoke whatever we'd sensed at the Pool – I'd have taken it back to England, out of reach of the Greek authorities. Temper rises in me, quick and hot, like a lit match thrown on oil.

'I can't believe you just left it here. It's physical evidence. What the hell were you thinking?'

Lex shakes her head, fingertips going to her mouth. Her nails had always been as bitten down as Abigail's, a similarity I thought so unlikely at first. What on earth could someone like Lex have to be anxious about? But that was until I got to know her better. Her bravado cost her a lot. I noticed she'd given up the habit the other night but now the middle and ring fingernails of her left hand are down to the quick. I'm still furious with her.

'Don't just shake your head. You left it here without telling me, where Richard or Eleni or Mum could have found it. And now Cleo.'

'I wasn't thinking straight. Anyway, none of them did.'

'You don't know that. Cleo could have picked the lock, like you did, then put it back.'

She looks at me and I know she's still not telling me something.

'What? And you'd better be honest. I don't think you understand how serious this is getting. I didn't, or I would never have come, not even for Mum, but I can *feel* it now, getting closer, like something's hunting us down.'

She nods, takes a shaky breath. 'There was something in the diary.'

'About that night? But there can't have been. She, well, she died that night. She can't have written that up.' It sounds so blunt that I shut my eyes briefly.

'I don't mean anything she wrote,' says Lex. 'I mean something she *read*. The note was in the diary. It was tucked inside. It was on squared paper, remember? It stuck out of the top. It's gone.'

I must go pale, or my eyes turn wild, because Lex takes my hands and makes soothing noises, as if I'm a child. 'It's okay. Nothing's going to happen, I promise. I really don't think she's found it. You're just feeling like this because you're here after so long. It's a lot. Dad. Seeing me. Cleo being like she is. *Him* rearing his ugly head.'

She doesn't want to say Papagiorgiou's name aloud, and I know then that she's as frightened as I am.

'Please don't be angry with me, Zo. I don't think I can bear it.'

I don't answer. I yank one of my earrings out so hard that the back bounces away and goes down between two floorboards. Just like Lex before me, I've sprung the diary's flimsy lock in less than a minute.

'Zoë, we shouldn't . . .' She kneels down next to me. 'We have to.'

I flip through the pages and it's impossible but they feel damp, as if the little book was pulled from the water only days ago when it never went into the Pool. The edges are dusted with chlorophyll green, which streaks my hands. I go through it twice but there's definitely no notepaper. I could close it now but I turn instead to the last entry, my fingers operating separately from my brain, which doesn't want to see.

It was written on the day of the wedding, although that date ended up with a very different association. Mum and Richard never wanted to count it as their anniversary, taking the day before instead.

I've got to be super-quick as we're leaving soon for the chapel. Lex said last night that she wants to show me the Pool later — so amazing!! — though you could tell that Zoë was really pissed off about it. She doesn't seem to get that Lex and I have been close since we were actual children. That we're basically family. She always gives me this look when I'm at Calliope as if to say, 'Oh, you again.' Which is ridiculous when I've been going there forever and she's literally just come out of nowhere. She'd so love to get me out of the way. Then she could have Lex all to herself.

The looping writing in pink biro, tiny circles over the *i*s, is like a tiny haunting, making me shiver in the stuffy attic. Written on her very last day, the time left to her counting down not in decades but in hours.

I'm too afraid to be angry with Lex now. For the first time, my mind goes where I've refused to let it since I arrived back on Eos. I can't help it, stop-start images flooding into my head: the back seat of a police car, a lawyer with halting English, Ben silent at the end of the payphone call, Jess pale and unreachable on the other side of a courtroom.

Lex grasps my hand between hers. They're clammy and so is mine. 'It'll be all right,' she says.

Once, when she said that, I believed her. Now I'm not sure I can.

Then

'Why are you in such a mood?' Lex called after me.

For once, I was ahead of her on the hill while she tried to catch me up. My leg muscles were burning but I didn't slow down.

She grabbed my arm. 'For God's sake, stop a minute.'

I swung round and wrenched my arm free. 'Get off me. I've had enough today.'

We stood staring at each other. It was totally quiet – one of those strange Greek silences, like the one by Circe's Pool. The sirocco had entirely died away. I felt as if it had sent me a bit mad. I turned and started up the hill again. Now that I'd noticed the lack of wind it felt even hotter. My head throbbed. A bright light like a flashbulb went off in my left eye and I rubbed it. It pulsed again, the colour of the sea at my back.

'I didn't make her walk it,' Lex said, breathing hard. She'd run to catch up with me again.

'You did. You basically did.'

'Well, she was fine, wasn't she? When I hugged her and we were screaming? I swear she looked happier then than I've ever seen her.'

A drop of rain landed on my arm, as heavy as a small stone, making me jump. The wet splotch showed up how dusty my skin was. As soon as I had the thought, my throat felt so dry I could hardly swallow. Another drop hit me

223

and then another. I rubbed at my arms, creating a reddish swirl.

'The Sicilians call it a blood rain,' Lex said, turning her face up to it as it came down harder. She shot me a quick look. 'It's only sand that makes it red, before you get any more het-up.'

'You shouldn't have read that stuff out,' I said. The rain was falling steadily now, as we took the last crumbling set of steps up to the villa, slower because I'd run out of steam.

'I know,' she said.

I looked at her in surprise. 'Was it the Liam stuff that made you carry on?'

'Not really. The trouble with Pabs is that she brings out the bad in me,' she said. 'She always has, even when we were tiny. And the worst thing is that it makes no difference. She always comes back. She always wants to be with me, spend time with me, whatever I say. I feel like I could push and push and push. It's hard to . . . stop.'

It would have been easy to shake my head, to disapprove, but I didn't because I knew exactly what she meant. I'd felt sick on the Arch, but after it was over, and nothing terrible had come of it, no one physically hurt, I'd felt something go out of me – a lowering feeling that felt perilously close to anticlimax. It was as though everything had burnt brighter in those few minutes, life bleached back to its bones, with nothing remaining that wasn't true.

When we reached Calliope, it was clear Mum had been waiting for us, leaping up out of her chair as soon as we appeared. It was lucky she was so distracted all the time or I think she would have read something in my face that I didn't want her to see.

Richard was exactly where we had left him, the completed crossword folded on the table. It seemed unbelievable to me that it was the same day. He got up and stretched. 'She's been up and down like a yo-yo looking out for you two,' he said, smiling as he took us in properly. 'Oh dear, I see the blood rain got you.'

I looked at Lex. She was as grubby as I was. Outside, the shower had abruptly stopped, and the sun was starting to burn through the haze for the first time all day. My skin felt tight and itchy.

'I'm going to have a shower,' I said.

'Be quick then,' said Mum. 'We're taking you both to the port to get your bridesmaids' dresses.'

'Do we have to?' Lex said, before I could. Mum's face fell.

'Yes, you do have to, you ungrateful baggage,' said Richard. He was still smiling but his tone was firm. 'Go and get cleaned up, both of you. I'll drive. We're picking Liam up when we're down there. I've told him we won't have room on the drive for his ridiculous hire car this time.'

I stopped dead. 'Liam?'

Lex had halted too, but didn't say anything. I could feel her alertness, though, crackling in the air.

'He's coming back for the wedding.'

'Yes, but that's not till Saturday.'

'What's it got to do with you anyway, Zo?' said Mum. 'Come on, go and get ready. I said we'd be there by four.'

Lex was smiling to herself on the stairs as we climbed them. It was a secretive smile that utterly excluded me.

*

The place where the hydrofoil landed was the least green part of famously lush Eos. Dust was shifting around in the air, the last gasps of the sirocco before it swept on. The expanse of hot tarmac looked just as it had when we'd arrived: waiting relatives and expats, a couple of hotel mini-buses idling, backpackers sprawled about, waiting for the return crossing.

'There it is,' said Lex.

The hydrofoil was making good progress. Conditions were perfect now the wind had died away.

'Like a millpond,' Richard said, as though he'd heard me. He was in a good mood, pleased that Lex wasn't being difficult about the bridesmaids' dresses any more. I couldn't believe he didn't see it: her mood had switched so dramatically when Liam's imminent return was announced.

I could smell her standing next to me, over the whiff of the old fishing nets and the fumes of a tourist day boat, which had just chugged away from the dock. She smelt like hot sugar and promise in her short pink dress, hair up in a high ponytail that swung. *Jailbait*, I thought, the word coming to me from nowhere – probably some old American film I must have seen late on a Saturday night when Mum had nodded off in her chair. One of the back-packer boys was watching her from his prone position on the dusty ground, head propped on a camping roll, eyes following her. And she knew it, too – I could tell by the way she was holding herself and kept reaching up to tighten her ponytail, which raised her hemline and pushed out her chest. It struck me that I'd disliked her for most of the day.

'What's up with you?' Mum said, nudging me gently. The

hydrofoil was mooring now. Lex had moved forward with Richard and wouldn't have heard.

'Nothing,' I said. 'Just –'

'What?'

I shook my head.

'Is Lex getting to you?' She smiled when I turned to her in astonishment. 'I know she only turns on the charm when she feels like it and it's not always easy for you, love. All this.'

She squeezed my hand and I squeezed hers back. Something hard inside me loosened a little.

'It'll be nice to have Liam back, won't it?' she said then. 'He reminds me of the boys I grew up with.' She smiled fondly and I pulled my hand away. She didn't notice, already reaching forward to slip her hand through Richard's arm. I watched the two of them and Lex as they moved towards the line of people now streaming off the hydrofoil. I saw Liam before he saw us and smiled the smooth smile that transformed him. For a moment his face was hard and hungry.

He looked the same when Lex and I came out of the changing rooms in the dressmaker's shop, which wasn't a changing room at all, but a dusty corner behind a sagging velvet curtain I was worried would expose parts of me to the men waiting outside. When Lex pulled it back with a flourish, no one was looking at Liam because they were admiring us in our white dresses, the silk so fine it felt transparent even though it wasn't. But I saw him and the way he looked at her – a wolf in a Jermyn Street shirt – and under Lex's sweet scent I could smell a bitter kind of danger now. I hate him, I thought, quite clearly. I hate him.

Now

Ben and Jess are coming in on the late-afternoon hydrofoil. There are white horses out there in the channel between the island and the mainland, which tend to make for a choppy crossing, and a longer one. I hope he remembered to buy the sea-sickness gum.

I'd planned to borrow Mum and Richard's car to pick them up but Lex offers me a lift in her little run-around. 'Are you sure?' I say. We're tentative around each other, almost stiff, after yesterday's emotionally charged episodes in her old room and up in the attic. The diary is now zipped into the lining of Lex's suitcase, which I'm not happy about, but I couldn't bear to have it in mine, and neither of us dared destroy it, not yet. It felt too much like provocation. Of what or who, we hadn't discussed.

'What do you think Cleo believes happened?' I say, as we take the road out of the village, the old, collapsing terraces of stone rising on each side, dotted now with purple and yellow wildflowers. Their scent through the wound-down window is pungent. It seems to be getting stronger every day, as though the island's plants and trees are cramming all their growing into a few weeks, before the parching summer begins in earnest. 'If she did find and take the note, I mean. Like I said yesterday, she could have done that and put it back – read the diary itself, too. If I'm trying to be logical about it, I feel like she hasn't seen either and the note is just lost, or she pulled that out and kept it without trying to get into the diary. Although why would anyone do that, when they'd got that far? Especially Cleo.' I'm talking too fast. I make myself stop.

Lex doesn't answer immediately. Her fingers drum on the steering wheel while we wait for an ancient flat-nosed cement mixer to turn in the road ahead, her rings clicking together.

'Lex? What now?'

She lets out a long sigh. 'I saw something earlier. I didn't know whether to tell you or not. I didn't know if it would freak you out even more.'

'Is it the note? Has she got it?'

'No, nothing to do with any of that. It's something on social media.'

'What is it? Tell me.'

'I'll show you when we stop. There's no reception here anyway.'

We drive on in silence, past churches with locked gates and a taverna painted saffron yellow, a man with long hair sitting at the front turning to watch us pass, a harmonica in his mouth. I'm already feeling anxious about seeing Ben. I know I want us to get back together and I'd thought that his idea to fly out here with Jess meant he felt the same. But now, this morning? I don't know anything any more. I'd woken with my adrenaline already pumping, as though I'd hardly dived down into sleep at all. Though I must have, because I dreamt of Abigail, following her down a narrow lane flanked by walls painted with crude As and Zs, a whiff of something rotten in the air. It was now – I was sure of that in my shallow dream – but she

230

was from then, still fifteen. She kept turning to smile at me, and it was the same smile from the posters. It never reached her eyes.

'We're early,' Lex says, as we come down into the port. 'Why don't we get a drink?'

As in the village, some of the tavernas are not yet open for the season. Timber and tools litter the ground outside the waterfront bars, and the sound of drills replaces the voices and music I remember. Despite the wind, which is even stiffer today, and the scudding clouds way overhead, it still feels quite warm to me, but most of the Greeks are wearing jumpers or light coats. A few look at us curiously and I don't know if it's because Lex has always drawn attention, or because they know who we are, our connection to back then.

We walk past the café that made the famous fresh lemonade, its chairs still stacked as though it's thinking about opening but can't be bothered yet.

'Do you think it still . . .?' I say, knowing she'll understand instantly. 'To be honest, I didn't really like them.'

She laughs, and the sound of it makes my muscles loosen a little. 'Let's go and find a Mythos. I want a cigarette too.'

We sit down at a new place that is much more sophisticated than anything that was here in the old days: everything white and grey, Ibiza chill-out-style music playing from an invisible sound system. Even this doesn't look quite ready: a man unloading plastic raffia sofas from a flat-bed truck even as we sit down at a small table sheltered from the breeze. The view, at least, is unchanged, overlooking the wooded island that protects the harbour from the worst of winter storms, with its ruined fort and colony of undisturbed birds, which circle slowly on the thermals high above.

'Are you going to put me out of my misery?'

Lex opens her mouth to explain, then hands over her phone. It's TikTok, which I know even less about than the rest. Jess teases me about my complete lack of interest in social media, when she isn't wheedling to get a phone. It's like the cigarettes Lex has apparently never quite kicked but I never got into: an addiction I'm simply not wired for.

I suppose I'm expecting something written and static: Cleo posting in a similar vein to the things she said back at Calliope to me and Mum. But it's a video, Cleo filming herself by the waterfront in the village, where the yachts and catamarans moor. The sound is too low to hear, Lex's volume button in a different place from mine so I can't work it, and the music in the café more insistent than I'd realized.

'What's she saying?' I ask, but just as I do, it cuts to the Arch. I haven't been back there – I'd had no plans to go ever again – but there it is, and it looks entirely the same as it did back then, the same as it would have done at the beginning of everything. The sight of it, even on the small phone screen, makes me instantly nauseous.

'So that's where she ended up. But how on earth did she get there? It's so difficult to find on foot.'

It's true. The island is not like the UK, with its public-footpath signs and Ordnance Survey maps. The Arch is almost always seen – and photographed – from the sea by people on the daytrip cruisers from the mainland, or their own yachts.

Lex shrugs. 'It's Cleo,' she says. 'I told you, she doesn't give up.'

I look up and the sun has gone. The high clouds have spread and slowed, joining up with the ones that always cling to the mainland mountains. I've barely ever seen this place ungilded by sun. The whole port is rendered sadder and scruffier suddenly: peeling paint and rust stains. A fat raindrop lands on Lex's phone screen, then another.

'Let's get inside,' says Lex. 'You've probably never been out in it at full tilt, have you?'

We watch it from behind the bar's plastic sheeting: rain so hard it hisses, drowning the music with ease.

'God, I hope they're all right.' I think of Ben and Jess out there in the channel. The hydrofoils can't ride over high waves when the weather turns, which slows them down and makes them liable to rock.

'It's just a shower. It probably isn't even raining out there.'

But then there's a distant growl of thunder and the rain notches up in intensity, streams of water boiling into the drains and creeping under the plastic sheeting, wet fingers reaching out for our feet. Our beers arrive, cold with condensation. I'm chilly myself now, arms goosebumped in my thin T-shirt. Still, I take a long drink.

'So what's Cleo saying? In the video.'

'She's talking about Abigail, saying that police centred their searches for her here at the Arch, when she went missing, but nothing was ever found so they decided she had taken her own life or fallen in when there was no evidence for either. That the whole thing seems bizarrely careless. And . . .'

'What?'

'That she suspects someone else was involved.'

I throw up my hands, almost knocking over my glass. 'How can she know that? It's just bullshit. She's making this into entertainment for *likes*, Lex. You need to do something.'

'You've met her, haven't you?' She sounds bitter, and looks older as she pulls hard on her cigarette.

'Do you think it's the note?'

'What do you mean?'

'If she found the note, she'll assume it was meant for Abigail. That might be what she's getting at when she says she thinks someone else might have been involved.'

Lex sighs. 'I've got no fucking clue. I hardly slept. I keep going over what I could say to her – something definitive to get her to stop. But I'm afraid of making it worse.'

'Who can see this?' I point at the video still up on the screen. 'Her friends?'

'Her followers. But the algorithm can bring it up randomly for anyone. I think that must have happened with this, or maybe it got traction because someone with a big following liked it.'

'What do you mean, "must have happened with this"?'

'It's been viewed nearly five thousand times.' She squints at her phone screen. 'Actually, eleven thousand now.'

I slump back in my chair. 'It'll go viral.'

'Well, those sorts of numbers are nothing really, are they? In the grand scheme, I mean. They might be a load of random kids who don't speak English. Or Russian bots.'

'Lex, none of us needs this right now. You and Mum least of all. I know it's a risk but I think you've got to put your foot down.'

'She'll just claim it's got nothing to do with the funeral.

That Abigail's life mattered too. She's had an answer for everything since the day she learnt to talk.'

'But even apart from the funeral, it seems distasteful. Like a sort of grief tourism.'

My eyes are on the phone screen, where the video is playing through again. It cuts to one of the new posters, then zooms right in on the photo of Abigail at the restaurant. At such close quarters, she's even more smudge-faced and indistinct than I remember from going through the albums, but this only seems to add to her haunted air, as I'm sure Cleo understands only too well.

I think of all the images out there of doomed girls smiling, oblivious not only to what will befall them, but how many strangers will study their faces afterwards, and wonder about them in a way that no one did when they were alive. I'm beginning to dread Cleo – there's no other word for it – but on this much, in some complicated way, we agree. I think of how uncomfortable Abigail felt in that tight dress, and how much I hated being looked at, shoulders rounding so no one would notice my breasts were finally growing. And how Lex loved it, or at least loved it sometimes, and sometimes didn't.

'I think they must be nearly here,' Lex says. She points to my more basic phone, which has lit up with a text from Ben. They're in range again, ten minutes from docking. We walk back towards the car, leaving our beers half finished. The rain has almost stopped, though the sky remains overcast, low-ceilinged with thick cloud, the sea a dull gunmetal beneath it.

For the first time today it occurs to me that Jess will meet Cleo soon. In a few hours, we'll all be at Calliope together. The dread of that mingles with my excitement about seeing Jess and Ben, making me jittery even before I spot *him* across the car park next to the huge iron mooring rings, smoking with a couple of taxi drivers. I grab for Lex's hand but she's already seen him, the colour draining from her face and turning her eye make-up stark, almost Halloweenish.

His face lights up when he sees us, and I think very clearly that I despise him – that if a freak wave came along now and took him I'd be nothing but glad. For all his sanctimony about never forgetting Abigail, hand pressed to his heart, this is sport to him. He was always relentless, but as Richard reminded him at the time, we were only girls. Now we're adults, I'm afraid that the gloves have come off.

The hydrofoil is close to docking, the door open and a man ready with a rope. But it's not close enough for the flood of disembarking passengers to cut off the path between Papagiorgiou and us. I see him nod in our direction and say something to the other men, who turn and crane to get a better look.

'Fuck's sake,' Lex mutters. 'That bastard. He's going to come over, isn't he?'

He already is, covering the distance surprisingly swiftly for a heavy man in his sixties.

'*Yassas*,' he says, the implied friendliness of the informal greeting somehow sinister. 'Who do you collect?' He gestures at the hydrofoil, from which the first passengers are now emerging.

'My husband and daughter,' I say, unable to keep silent, politeness so ingrained, especially in the English.

'Ah, another daughter,' he says. 'I met yours yesterday.'

He's looking at Lex now. 'Very sharp, I think. She will go far. She says she is helping Robin, which is so interesting to me.'

'And why's that?' Lex's tone is insolent, a flash of the girl she'd been rising up irresistibly.

He shrugs, smiles again. 'I think yesterday she reminds me of someone. Her determination. Her focus. Then I realize. Me. She reminds me of me.'

Lex takes hold of my arm and pulls me with surprising strength towards the swelling crowd next to the hydrofoil, where people are waiting for their suitcases to be unloaded.

'I'll see you again,' Papagiorgiou calls after us, and I see Lex swallow the urge to snap back with some insult. It makes me think of my first day on Eos, when she told off the man with the bread, and I could cry for that moment, and how wonderful it would be to return to it now, everything wiped clean.

But then I spot Jess in the throng, just as the men lift her over the gap between boat and land, and I know I wouldn't go back, even if I could. Despite what's just happened, my heart still lifts, and not just for Jess, but for Ben, too.

He's thinner than he is in my head, though I saw him only last week, when I dropped Jess off. It seems like years ago. He's slimmer around the middle and in his face than when we still lived together and ordered too many take-aways. But it's not just that he's lost some weight: out of context, he looks different in some more intangible way too. A new person. I have the same anticipatory feeling I had waiting for his text.

'Oh, look at lovely Jess,' says Lex, as we go towards them. 'I'd know she was yours anywhere. Look, try and forget about bloody Papagiorgiou for now, okay? He's just a wind-up merchant.'

We both know he's more than that but I smile at her for the attempted reassurance. I look back to where Ben and Jess are, and it's then that I glimpse another face I'd hoped never to see again, just a few commuting locals separating him from my family.

Lex grabs for my hand as I'd grabbed for hers, not five minutes ago. 'Zo, is that . . .?'

I can't bring myself to answer. He's greying now, and slightly stiff in his movements as he shakes off one of the crew to jump the gap between the hydrofoil and the dock unassisted, but it's definitely him.

Another ghost from that summer.

Liam.

Then

It was the hottest day yet. The hottest day I'd ever known. It was also the day Lex was getting her GCSE results and everyone was nervous about it except her, allegedly — although I had my doubts about that. She was too spiky, too quick with little barbs over breakfast. She wasn't even putting on a show for Liam.

There was an arrangement in place for Richard to ring a teacher at eleven o'clock to get the results — if they had been posted to Greece they would have taken ages to arrive.

'I have zero clue why you asked *her* of all of them,' said Lex. She'd just dropped a butter dish and was supposed to be helping Mum sweep up the remnants. 'She'll probably read them out wrong on purpose. She always thought I was a massive pain in the arse.'

'Imagine that,' I muttered into my cereal, but fortunately Lex didn't catch it.

While the clock ticked on, Richard and I consulted the European weather forecast in the newspaper and, though the closest we could get to Eos was Athens, it looked as if the temperature would keep climbing over the coming weekend, the whole of Greece simmering under a bell jar of high pressure.

I was in the pool by ten, though I couldn't even find any relief there, the sun pressing down on my head and prickling my shoulders where I kept burning them. Besides, Lex and Liam had come down too, and I couldn't bear to be near them. I couldn't bear to be seen in just my swimsuit either, though it wasn't as if anyone was looking at me. My body felt uncharacteristically puffy that day, my stomach a slight curve where normally it was taut and flat, and I resolved to eat nothing so that I felt better the next day in my white dress. That lasted half an hour after which, shaky and nauseous from hunger, I ended up cramming the heel of yesterday's bread into my mouth without even fetching a plate.

'You seem out of sorts today, love,' said Mum. She had come in to fetch some water from where she was writing to-do lists on the terrace, which showed how sweltering it was: she never normally drank anything in the day but endless cups of tea.

'Just hot,' I said shortly.

'Yes, it's defeated even me today. And I don't want to look burnt in the photos.'

I looked at her blankly.

She tutted. 'The *wedding* photos. Look, why don't you make yourself useful —and help me do the name cards for tomorrow? You've got much nicer handwriting than me anyway.'

The phone rang at five past eleven. Lex had refused to come up from the pool as the hour approached so I ended up sitting next to Richard and Mum, as he wrote the grades in a neat list. When he put the phone down, Mum and I exchanged glances. I knew we were both thinking the same thing: that if I got those results in a year's time, there would be tears.

'Getting a C in art is really good,' I said. 'People think it's an easy subject, but you have to demonstrate all the prep you've done, like showing your working in maths.'

Richard smiled. 'You're a kind girl, aren't you? Isn't she?' He looked at Mum, who took his hand. 'Will you go and fetch her for me?'

I shook my head. 'No way.'

Mum stood. 'I'll get her.'

I shot her a grateful look. She understood that however I'd gone down there – whatever my face had been doing, or whatever words I picked – Lex would have thought I was being condescending or smug or the Favourite Child. Because Lex cared about her results, though she'd rather have died than admit it. I knew without her telling me that it had to be effortless straight As or blanket failure, which at least had a rebellious sort of cachet. The row of Ds and Cs with a random B for maths wasn't cool. It betrayed effort without brilliance. Mum got that, like I did, while Richard didn't. Maybe it was a female thing.

It suited me to give her some space. It meant I could avoid Liam, too. Abigail had had the sense to stay away, which was also a relief. I spent the rest of the day with Mum and sometimes Richard too, doing little jobs in preparation for the following night's pre-wedding gathering – a sort of rehearsal dinner without the rehearsal – and the big day itself. I wouldn't have told Mum but it was comforting being there with her, and pretending the laughter that floated up from the pool was nothing to do with Calliope – that it was just some noisy neighbour who would soon be packing up to fly home without me ever catching a glimpse of them. I loved being with Lex, and it was exhausting sometimes, too – especially with *him* around.

The Pinkening, when it came, was even more garish than usual. Mum's platinum hair turned the colour of candy floss and the greens of the garden were made strange, almost purple. The cicadas, whose ceaseless buzzing had turned into white noise, upped their game so that we noticed them all over again, the buzzing elongating into clicks. As the dusk deepened, the sun descending fast, the swallows joined in the racket, swooping around the house and through the cypresses, missing both by millimetres, more frenzied than ever. Lex and Liam still hadn't returned from the village, where they had supposedly gone for ice-cream three hours earlier.

Mum found me sitting on the floor in the corner of the kitchen by the old well, my legs stretched out across its frigid glass lid and a picnic ice-pack from the freezer wrapped in a tea-towel and pressed to my forehead. She was already dressed for the evening. We were going out to dinner to celebrate Lex's success. 'Nine passes is more than I got,' Richard had said philosophically to me and Mum earlier, making me glad Lex was still out.

'They'll be back soon,' she said, bending down to stroke my cheek. 'Why don't you go up and have a shower before Liam gets in there?'

I nodded, not opening my eyes or moving.

Her knees creaking, she lowered herself down next to me, stretching out her legs next to mine and seemingly not minding about her new dress. 'You've got the right idea here. It's lovely and cool.'

We sat quietly for a while. Upstairs, I could hear the water running for Richard's shower. He was humming something I couldn't quite grasp, out of tune. Mum laughed quietly and turned to me. 'You do like him, don't you?'

'Course.'

'He adores you, you know. He's so pleased that you've

been borrowing his books and that you like this place so much.'

'I love it.' I pushed out the words, embarrassed but feeling it was important to say them. 'I love Calliope.'

'I know you do.' She patted my leg. 'Thank you for your help today. I appreciate it, Richard too. I've barely seen Lex all day.'

'She's proud.'

'I know. Whatever Richard's saying, we all know she ought to have done much better at that school.'

'Will you make sure he doesn't do toasts and stuff at dinner? She'd hate that.'

Mum patted my hand and glanced at her watch. 'They'd better get back soon or we'll be late for our table.'

Images of where they were and what they might be doing circled in my mind, not for the first time. I wondered if Lex was going to break her promise and meet up with Panikos to buy something. Or maybe she and Liam just wanted to find somewhere to be alone, some tucked-away cove where no one would see them. I didn't know which possibility I hated more.

'I wish it was just the four of us tonight,' I said.

'What – no Liam?'

At that moment, Richard came into the kitchen, dressed for dinner and smelling of aftershave. He did a double-take when he saw us there on the floor.

'What's all this? A sit-in? Are you protesting about being taken out for dinner? Why don't I get you both a nice cold drink while we wait for the police?'

Mum laughed. 'Ooh, I'll have a G and T, please.' She held up her hands so he could pull her up. 'Zoë was saying she wishes it was just the four of us tonight.'

'Mum!' I scrabbled to get up.

'You mean go without Liam?' Richard said, pausing at the fridge, a bottle of Gordon's in his hand.

'I didn't say that. It doesn't matter.' I tried to edge past him and out of the room but he stopped me.

'Zoë, sweetheart, if there's a problem you should tell me. Has he been teasing you?'

I shook my head. I knew if I was going to say something, now would be the perfect time: no one else around, Richard and Mum not so distracted. But I didn't know what to say. I couldn't work out if I was just being hopelessly uptight and immature, if I was sensing danger where there was none. If I was simply jealous of Liam because Lex sometimes seemed to prefer spending time with him over me, a silly little girl she'd been lumbered with, hardly better than Abigail. Besides, I didn't want to tell on Lex. I *couldn't*. It was the greatest crime at school to grass someone up. It made you despised forever, and I couldn't bear to see that in Lex's eyes when she looked at me.

When I continued to say nothing, Richard patted my shoulder. 'I know he can be a bit . . . brash. But all young men are like that.'

'I was saying to Zoë at the port, he reminds me of the boys I grew up with,' said Mum. 'All swagger and nothing much to back it up.'

Richard laughs. 'Yep, and I'm afraid I was one of those boys too, once – to a T. I went from market stall to three shops in a year, and suddenly I had all this disposable income. I bought my first car straight off the forecourt, cash.' He shakes his head ruefully as he hands Mum her drink. 'I thought I was something pretty special. On the day Liam came in for an interview, I saw a piece of myself. Rough round the edges, and much too cocksure, but *bright*. There were all these posh boys and then him. In the actual interview, he was arrogant to the point of rudeness, but I saw right through it. You need that bravado where he comes from. Sometimes it's the only thing that'll get you out.'

I didn't go straight to the shower. I hovered on the landing, then found myself drawn inexorably up another floor to the sanctuary of my attic, where Calliope's power felt most potent, and Liam like a bad memory from another time.

It had never occurred to me to get up on the high bed before. It seemed impolite, disrespectful to Richard and, of course, Eleni, who had made it so neatly. But when I saw it then, heavy-limbed and slightly defeated as I felt, I couldn't resist those cool, crisp sheets. I lay back, floppy as a doll, and wondered fleetingly if I had glandular fever, like people at school talked about. But then I remembered you caught it from kissing and I had kissed no one since a school trip two years before. It had been so fleeting I didn't believe it could have transmitted infection to anyone.

The window behind the bed was flung wide and the air that drifted in smelt of thyme and sun and something mysterious and mineral. It was probably just Calliope's old stones, but I liked imagining it was one of the Ancients veering in close, drawn by the promise of tomorrow's party.

I was half in dreams when footsteps sounded on the stairs, getting louder. I sat up, ears straining, and heard whispering between the thuds of their feet. I knew I had to move immediately or be discovered. At the last second, I rolled off and under the bed, which was high enough off the floor that there was a whole two feet gap between me and the wooden slats. I felt completely exposed but it was too late to do anything else.

What if it was Richard and Mum? The thought made me clap my hand over my mouth. It would be terrible to go through but what a story to relate to Lex. The urge to laugh shuddered through me but then someone giggled and I froze.

It wasn't Mum. It was Lex. She was back.

And, of course, the person with her was Liam. It felt like punishment for being too cowardly to talk to Richard.

'Why are we up here?' he said, as their feet came into view and moved towards the long bookcase under the round windows. Hers were bare and dusty, his were in those shiny slip-ons I couldn't stand. 'I've been trying to get you on your own all afternoon and now you change your mind, just when your dad wants us to go out.' There was a pause and then, 'A book?' His voice was mocking, an edge to it. 'An *actual* book? I thought you just said that as an excuse.'

'No, but look.' Her words slid into each other. She sounded drunk. They'd probably gone back to the bar where they'd left me on my own. They were least likely to bump into anyone they knew there.

'Liam, look. Zoë showed me. Come on, it's cool.'

I thought I knew what it was. An old photograph I'd found in the plates section of a book about the island at the turn of the century. Two girls photographed in the same intense sunlight that had made my head pound all day, their hair long and their white dresses luminous froth cinched at the waist. What I'd seen when I looked closer was that they were standing in front of Calliope's front door, while the mass of shadow to the left was the cypresses, which had since grown as tall as the roofline.

'She said it could be us. Me and Zoë. One dark and one fair.'

'You're total opposites, you two.' He pushed himself briefly up onto the bed, making the slats creak and my heart race, but got up almost immediately, maybe because his feet dangled off the edge and ruined his seduction act. 'You'd never think you were the same age.'

'Well, I'm nearly a year older. She's July, I'm August.'

'Almost sweet sixteen. And you know what that means.'

Lex didn't answer. Instead, she spun away, pivoting on one foot and dancing along the length of the long bookcase. I couldn't tell if she was showing off or restless or something else. Her gold anklet, new from the shop in the port, caught the light as she shifted about. I had an identical one – Mum had bought us one each – but it didn't look the same on me.

'Hey, come here,' he said. 'Why are you being such a fidget? Changed your mind?'

'About what?'

'You know what.'

'No.' She was trying to sound playful, but I knew Lex by then. I could hear the strain in her voice.

'I think you have. I think you've changed your mind now you're running out of time. I had a feeling you'd do this.'

'I haven't *done* anything.'

'We were getting on really well before you started hanging out with the *kids*. It was you who said about your

247

birthday in the first place, not me. I thought we had an understanding. But now you're being cold. Off with me.'

'Oh, hardly. We've been together all day.'

'Nah, you are. I can tell.' He moved towards the door.

'Don't go,' she said. I could see more of them on that side of the room. I watched her reach out to grab his arm, pull him back towards her. He shook her off.

'You just want to play games. One of your Lexy games. All that bullshit about being legal.'

'Why would I bring you up here if I was just playing games?'

He shrugged. 'Apparently to show me some boring old book. You've got little Zoë and Pabs for playing make-believe, if that's what you like. I must have read it all wrong, thinking you was sophisticated, mature.'

'Please don't be in a mood,' she said. She had both his hands in hers now. It seemed painfully obvious to me what he was doing, yet I was apparently the pathetic child. 'I don't want you to go. And I'm glad you came back. I missed you when you were in London.'

'Yeah?'

'*Yes*. All the time.'

'You weren't doing your sexy Lexy act for anyone else?'

'No, of course not.'

'What about that Robin? I bet you were flirting with him as soon as I'd gone. I don't know if you can help yourself being like that. I think it's in your nature. Is that what's going on here?'

'No! Stop being like this. Why are you spoiling things?'

He paused, hung his head. 'I just don't want to get hurt.'

'I'm not going to hurt you.'

'I just feel like if you really cared about me, about us, you wouldn't hold back so much.'

'I'm not.'

'You are. It hurts every time you pull away. It's not fair to do that to men. We can't turn it on and off like you can.'

My contempt for him grew so loud in my head, humming angrily like the cicadas outside, that it seemed unfeasible they couldn't hear it. I didn't know then that it's only the males that make the noise, and that they do it to attract a female.

While they were talking, he had slowly backed her towards the bookcase. She was now hard up against it, with nowhere to go.

'I do want to,' she said, in a low voice. But she was shifting from foot to foot as he put his hands on her waist. 'I just want to wait until the day. We talked about this.'

I suddenly understood what they had been alluding to. Lex's birthday. She turned sixteen the day after the wedding. Sixteen was the legal age of consent. She must have promised herself to him then. The thought of it made me sick. *Your sexy Lexy act.* My stomach turned over.

'Yeah? I hope so,' Liam was saying. 'I think we have something special. A connection.'

'We do. We have.'

'So still the wedding night, then, yeah? What was it you said about it?'

'After the stroke of midnight.' Lex's voice was so low I almost didn't catch it.

Liam laughed. 'That's it. Like Cinderella. Maybe you could take me to that place you keep going on about, the *magical* one. The pond or whatever.'

'Pool. Circe's Pool. Yeah, maybe.'

'Or is that just a special place for you and Zoë to play your little-girly princess games?'

'No. We could go. There's a map in that old book. I'll show you.'

'Okay, that's better. You gonna give me a proper kiss, then? So I know you mean it?'

She went up on tiptoe and I knew she was giving in to him. They had only been kissing for a second when, in one fluid movement, he lifted her onto the bookcase, pushing his body between her bare thighs. I heard her make an abrupt noise of surprise but then there were sounds of them kissing again, wetly, and he groaned.

Suddenly I couldn't bear it any longer. I didn't care if they caught me there, worked out I must've been there the whole time. I had to get out.

I rolled out from under the bed on the far side of the room to them, too het-up and claustrophobic to be silent. I didn't know if they heard me as I hurtled across the boards to the door and down the stairs, but I didn't look back and no one called out. I ran into my room, closed the door, and flung myself onto my own bed, closing my eyes and wishing time would rewind a couple of minutes so I could do it all differently.

If I had stayed put, letting them find me, they wouldn't be up there together now, doing whatever they were doing. I could have made something up so that Lex had to come away with me, and away from him.

But even if I could have done that, I couldn't undo what she'd promised him. Herself, on her sixteenth birthday. After the stroke of midnight.

Now

Ben sees my raised hand and bends to tell Jess, pointing me out. To my surprise, she runs towards me, smiling, and I break into a run, too. We meet in the middle of the tarmac and, as I hold her close, I raise my eyebrows at Ben over her head. He smiles because he knows exactly what I mean. Jess, once extravagantly affectionate, has been withdrawing physically over the last year or so. These outbursts are getting fewer and further between, so it's a rare honour.

She's already pulling away, disentangling herself. 'Too hot,' she says, but she's still smiling.

'Did you get rained on?' I say quickly to Ben, because I'm not sure whether I should embrace him or not.

'I don't think so.'

'It was biblical here briefly. Lex and I had to shelter.'

He and Jess look up. The sky is almost clear again, the last of the clouds sweeping away, back towards the mainland.

'Lex, eh?' Ben says softly. Jess has bent to get something out of her pink backpack.

'Yep. You'll finally get to meet her.' I look around to see where she is and she's talking to Liam, or rather Liam is talking to her. Papagiorgiou is nowhere to be seen. She catches my eye and looks away so I can't read her. I experience the old frustration of wanting to read the thoughts inside her head, like ticker-tape.

'Who's that?' Ben has followed my gaze.

'Liam.'

'Oh.'

He knows Liam was there that summer, and who he was to Richard, but that's it. I suddenly feel the danger of Ben being here with these people who know so much more. With everything else that's been going on, I hadn't properly considered this. I'd thought it would be comforting to have him here, and I think it will be, mainly. But I know he'll want to talk about then. I've more or less promised him that. If things are going to be okay between us, we can't go back to our old patterns. And when I say 'our', I mean my peculiar brand of emotional self-sufficiency that, over the years he has spent as my husband, my supposed *other half*, has made him feel obsolete. Before coming here, it felt as though there were other problems – stuff that could be laid at his door, like the hours he works – but I don't know now. It's as though the rest of it has fallen away.

I reach out and squeeze his arm, and he smiles at me. Jess catches the exchange and I know she's pleased, though her face scarcely changes. 'I'm so glad you're both here,' I say.

'Us too,' says Jess. 'Where's Grandma?'

'She's waiting for you back at Calliope.'

'Can I go in the pool?'

My insides lurch. But of course she means the swimming-pool.

'Sure. Wait till you see the view from up there.'

But she's not listening because she's seen something else, hand up to shield her eyes from the sun and the puddles reflecting it. 'Is that Lex talking to the man?'

'Yes, that's right.'

'And she's your half-sister?'

'Stepsister.'

'What's the difference again?'

'We don't share a parent.'

'Oh, yeah. So why have I never met her?'

She imagines she must have been told at some stage, and forgotten. In fact, I've never explained and she's never asked. Young children have a small radius of interest but Jess is growing up. She's becoming aware of a hinterland she never knew her mother had. An intriguing one.

'Oh, lots of reasons,' I say weakly. 'She lives a long way away.'

'Let's get the cases into the car, shall we?' says Ben. 'I want to have a swim in the pool too.'

I shoot him a grateful look.

Lex's little car is unlocked and we load the boot. She's still talking to Liam and I beckon her over. Maybe it's rude, but I don't care when it comes to that man. Thank God there's no room in the car for him.

He saunters over, just behind Lex, wheeling a flashy metal suitcase. 'All right, Zoë,' he says. The smile is the same, but his teeth are a little greyer. 'Long time.'

'Shall we head off?' I say to Lex. 'Mum will be dying to see Jess.' My heart thuds because I'm never rude to people.

He shakes his head, still smiling, and lights a cigarette. 'I guess I'll go and see about a cab, then,' he says to Lex. 'I'll speak to you soon.'

'What's he doing here?' I hiss at her, when he's gone. Jess is buckling up in the back seat, saying something to Ben.

'That was a bit off,' Lex says.

'No, it wasn't. It was the least he deserves. Why has he come?'

'Why do you think? He loved Dad. He used to say he was more of a father than his own dad was.'

'Did you know he was coming?'

'No. I thought they'd lost touch.'

'Really?'

She flings out her arms. 'Yes, really. I didn't bloody know. You saw my face when he appeared. I haven't spoken to him in decades.'

Ben and Jess have stopped talking, Jess peering up through the window at us.

Lex drops her voice. 'Look, I'm sorry. I know I haven't even properly said hello yet. I just didn't expect to see him. I didn't know how to be.'

'It's fine. Let's just get back,' I say. 'Mum will be wondering where we've got to. But I want us to talk about this – about him – later.'

Neither of us moves, though. We stand there staring at each other, and I feel I have access to her thoughts now, and they're the same as mine. First Robin and his bad-cop sidekick Papagiorgiou, then Cleo's obsessive digging, and now Liam. The past seems to be rearing up like a wave, gathering height and speed as it approaches dry land, Lex and me directly in its path.

As Lex finally goes round to the driver's side, eyes shadowed with exhaustion, I glance over my shoulder. Liam is still there, sun glancing off his case. Our eyes meet and now it's just the two of us, Lex inside the car, he doesn't bother smiling.

*

It's such a relief to leave him behind in the car park that my mood lifts a little. It's impossible not to be infected by Jess's excitement and Ben's enthusiastic good humour. It suddenly strikes me that I can at last show Calliope to two of the people I love most. As we weave back through the island's heart, Lex makes an enormous effort to be her most sparkling self. Only I would notice the strain beneath the smile, and how tightly she's gripping the wheel. I love her for this – despite everything, she's turning on the old Lex charm, so that Jess is leaning forward in her seat, not wanting to miss a word of rapid-fire chatter, and Ben is laughing easily. Maybe a little bit of it is a habitual desire to enthral everyone she meets, but mainly she's doing this for me. We catch eyes in the rear-view mirror and I mouth, 'Thank you,' at her. She winks back, and for a second it's the nineties again, time shifting and glitching once more.

'Oh, wow,' says Ben, when we get to Calliope. 'This place.'

I smile. I knew he'd get it, that he'd see venerable beauty and atmosphere where others would see huge maintenance costs. I wonder what he'll think of Lex's news about the will. I don't quite believe it myself yet. I can't currently picture a scenario in which I'm allowed to keep it, to come here at all.

Jess and I head out to the garden while Mum shows Ben where he's sleeping, which won't be with me, peculiarly. We've never been under the same roof and not shared a bed. Even just before he moved out, we slept in the same room.

Standing looking out over the view with Jess, I see it totally afresh. It's even more remarkable than it was the first time I saw it. I was an old head on young shoulders in many ways back then, but I was still a teenager and it's a rare one who fully appreciates natural beauty. A hundred and eighty degrees of searing blue is spread out below us, the cleared sky almost merging with the sea. To the east, the mainland's mountains are like airbrushed stage flats, graduated purple-greys fading into the distance. None of it looks quite real.

Everywhere there is evidence of Richard's hand. He'd thought of everything: every texture and colour, every angle, every glimpse of the sea. For the first time in days, I cry for the loss of him. It was him who made everything work here. Not just the upkeep of the place, and paying the bills, though that was him too. It was also the little touches that people usually suspect a woman is behind but were all down to him. The fresh flowers next to each bed, nothing showy, often just a couple of sprigs of silver-green eucalyptus, but thoughtful, and classy. Always classy. Olives in a bowl to pick at, Eleni's homemade tzatziki so fresh it zinged, and a cold drink made for anyone as soon as they got through the door. A memory assails me then, another I'd forgotten: helping him make G and Ts, ice-cubes cracking as the tonic fizz hit them. Guilt that I didn't come again, either alone or with Lex – didn't give him that when he loved it so much here, when he knew how much I loved it too – makes me cry harder.

'You okay, Mum?' Jess sidles up to me and puts her hand through my arm.

'Just missing Richard. There's so much of him here.'

'The whole place is totally amazing. I wish . . .' She tails off.

'I know,' I say, lacing my fingers through hers. 'It's hard to explain.'

I know what she was going to say, but didn't, for my sake. It would have been a reasonable question. Why on earth wouldn't you come here all the time if you could? It's a dream of a place.

'It's even more beautiful than I remembered,' I say. 'As much as I fell for it immediately, I'm not sure I appreciated how special it was. Maybe you can't when you're young.'

'I do,' she says, nudging me. 'Don't lump us all in together.'

'Well, you're exceptional, of course,' I say, smiling, wiping my eyes with the heel of my hand. 'A soon-to-be teenager like no other.'

'Yep, and you know what that means, don't you?'

The phone thing is a long-running joke, but now I've met Cleo it doesn't seem very funny. I wonder where she is right now. She's not here. I know she isn't. There's lightness in the air inside the house.

Jess is still squinting at the view.

'Where are your sunglasses, missus?'

'Inside. I'll get them in a minute.' She pauses. 'So, you were, what, fifteen when you came here?'

I look at her, surprised she's remembered this much. You can see the gold flecks in her brown eyes in the light that's now searingly bright again. They are my eyes, totally different from my mother's china blue. It had always been a source of resentment that my father's genes dominated when he'd never even bothered to meet me. It's the same for Cleo, I suddenly realize. It doesn't make me warm to her, though.

Ben appears in his swimming shorts, looking winter-pale and slightly abashed. 'Are we getting in or what?' he says to Jess. 'Your grandma says the food will be ready in an hour so you'd better get your skates on.'

Jess zooms off and Ben comes to stand by me. 'I can totally see why you didn't want to come here.'

'Oh, shush. You know it's complicated.'

'I'm allowed to say it's idyllic, though?'

'Yes, you're allowed to say that.'

'Lex seems nice. Fun.'

'You'd better not fancy her.' I realize what I've said and blush, but Ben smiles in his laidback way.

'Nah. I always preferred brunettes.'

We stand there not saying anything for a while, and then he rubs his hands together. 'Right, I'm going in before I lose my nerve.' He sets off towards the steps down to the pool.

'I warn you, it's not heated. It's probably still quite chilly.'

He raises a hand without turning and Jess rushes past me, looking younger in her rainbow-coloured swimsuit, her limbs still fleshless, her hips still as narrow as they ever were. Stay like that, I think. Don't grow up.

There was a teacher at my school who was supposed to have had an affair with one of the lower-sixth girls. He taught drama and she was his leading lady. It seemed like a terrible cliché even then – and it was before the summer with Lex and Liam so I could only have been thirteen or fourteen. Rumours flew around school to the extent that I can't believe they didn't reach the staffroom. Everyone wanted to know where and when, what they'd done, how far it had gone.

I remember being more baffled than scandalized. The girl – Suzanne someone – was spectacular as Lady Macbeth, but him? His breath smelt of stale coffee and his skin had the subterranean, cheese-like quality of someone who never gets out enough. I watched her on stage, studied her in the corridors in the days afterwards, and thought, How could you? How *could* you?

What none of us asked was whether it was wrong. We knew it wasn't allowed, that it wasn't supposed to happen, but our minds didn't seem to delve any deeper than that. It wasn't a question of morals for us. It was just . . . rules.

Now, as a grown woman in a new century – as a mother to my own girl – I itch to go back in time and get Lex out of that situation, to get his hands off her child's flesh. Fifteen isn't children, said Papagiorgiou, and although I don't think I agree with him in the context he meant it, it's true that you don't feel like a child when you're that age. No, that's not quite right. *I* felt every inch a child that summer, even as I simultaneously felt wearily old about some things, and especially once everything began to unravel. But Lex never seemed like a child to me. She was everything that was glamorous and effortlessly cool. Her transition into womanhood seemed to be, from where I was looking on with envy, a passage that was entirely smooth and assured.

Until the day our parents married each other, I suppose I had thought she could handle anything. I try to stop my mind going there, but an image of Liam has already sidled in. Across the car park, across all that time, he is just the same. He still makes my skin crawl. And it's not just about Lex, if I'm honest. He was around that night. I don't know what he might have absorbed or guessed at.

I turn away from the pool to look up at the old house. Along her roofline, the glass in the three round windows is ablaze with reflected sun. They flash as I move towards the terrace and at first I think Calliope is sending me a warning, a lighthouse cautioning ships pitching in the deep. But then an idea forms, bulbs switching on in my brain, and I don't think it's that, after all. Or, at least, if it's a warning, it's not for me. I glance back towards the pool as Jess hurls herself into it with a shriek.

Some of the fear that's been building in me since I got here is morphing into something else. Something harder. My hands have tightened into fists.

Then

After the excruciating episode in the attic, I couldn't bear to go out to dinner for Lex's results.

'Aren't you ready yet?' said Mum, when she came up to investigate where I'd got to. 'Everyone's downstairs waiting for you.'

My eyes filled with tears, which I swiped at angrily. 'I'm not coming. I feel sick.'

She came over and put her hand to my forehead. 'You were all right an hour ago. What's going on?'

'Nothing.'

'Well, it doesn't look like nothing, sweetheart. Is it something to do with what you were saying about Liam?'

I shook my head, a single tear rolling down my cheek.

She reached out and caught it with her thumb. 'Oh, love, I know I've been caught up with things, but you can always talk to me, okay?' She paused. 'Lex is –'

'What about her?' It came out sharply. I wanted her to say something critical about Lex, and I couldn't bear it at the same time.

'You're so different, that's all.' She got to her feet. 'Look, we won't be late tonight. Make sure you eat something. There's plenty in the fridge.' She hovered at the door, as if she wanted to say something else, until I turned over to face the wall.

I made sure I was back in bed by the time they returned,

and Lex left quite early the next morning, faithful dog Abigail having called for her by nine. I knew then that she was cross with me because of what had happened in the attic.

I spent the day trying to read, nerves knotting my stomach. Restless as the day wore on, I went up to the attic and searched through the books until I found the old map Lex had told Liam about, the temple above Circe's Pool marked as a thick black cross.

Soon enough, blistering day stretched into sultry evening and the hour of the rehearsal dinner arrived, Penny and Alastair's voices echoing up the stairs a braying reminder that I was being rude to hide in my room. With a last apprehensive look in the mirror, I forced myself to go downstairs.

They were all assembled on the terrace, drinks in hand, some liquid jazz music of Richard's on the old record player. It was Robin I saw first, as handsome as I'd ever seen him: a golden boy who looked like he'd parachuted in from another era. As though he felt my eyes on him, he glanced over and raised his hand. I sent back a grateful smile.

Mum looked pretty and only slightly nervous, and I did a double-take when I saw Abigail. She was wearing a simple black dress that skimmed her hips and made her pale skin luminous rather than sickly. She'd washed and brushed out her hair and it shone warmly against the black, a colour somewhere between bronze and copper under the garden's globe lights. She was standing with Lex, their heads bent together as Lex whispered and gesticulated and Abigail listened, but my relief that Liam wasn't with Lex but standing talking to Richard and Alastair was short-lived. When I went over to join them, thinking Lex was hardly likely to say anything about the attic with Abigail there, she gave me a cold look and angled her body away.

I turned to Abigail, who seemed uncharacteristically pleased with herself, a smirk threatening at the corners of her mouth, no doubt because she'd had Lex to herself all day.

'Hi,' I said pointedly.

Lex said nothing while Abigail's gaze swept over me without really meeting my eye.

'Hello,' she said tonelessly.

'Lex, can I talk to you for a minute?'

She looked me over, expression cold. 'You can say whatever you've got to say in front of Pabs. She knows all about yesterday.'

I took a breath. 'Look, I'm sorry about that. I was asleep when you came in, and then –'

'You were asleep *under* the bed? Oh, come on.'

'Lex told me all about it and, to be honest, the whole thing sounds a bit weird and pervy,' said Abigail.

I rounded on her. 'A couple of days ago, you were all ready to tell Richard about her and Liam. You were writing about how you're always watching Lex and going on to me at the restaurant about how amazing she is. And I'm the weirdo here?'

'Keep your voice down,' Lex hissed.

We moved off down the garden for privacy, Lex wobbling on the plumbago path in wedge heels, which, paired with a bum-skimming stretchy dress, only made her look younger, a try-hard hoping the bouncers wouldn't ask her for ID.

It wasn't like Lex to be a dolly-bird. It was yet another reason for me to despise Liam, who I was convinced was encouraging all this, who was changing Lex before my eyes, moulding her into something she wasn't, some knock-off fantasy babe from a *Loaded* magazine cover.

We ended up at the pool, Lex and Abigail side by side on one lounger and me cross-legged by the deep end, alone. The pump had gone off and the water was dotted with dead insects.

Lex sighed and kicked off her daft shoes. 'Right, let's just forget it, okay? I literally can't be bothered to fall out about this. It's mental that you hid under the bed but then again you are a bit mental so . . .' Her mouth twitched.

Relief seeped through me like balm. 'I actually thought it was Mum and Richard for a minute. The thought of it made me totally freeze. But a bit of me thought it would be a really funny story to tell you too.'

'Ew, yuck,' said Abigail, but Lex was laughing.

'Oh, my God, that would have emotionally scarred you forever. I so wish that had happened.'

And then it was okay again. Or, at least, Lex was okay with me, which was the main thing. I couldn't bear to spoil it again by saying anything about Liam. I felt there was only one choice available to me – either fall out with Lex by trying to stop her and Liam, which would suit Abigail very well, or leave it and be her friend. I couldn't think of another way round it. I comforted myself with the thought that if I kept close to her, that would be enough.

'Listen, I had an idea earlier,' said Lex. She came to sit on the ground, diplomatically halfway between me and Abigail. 'Tomorrow, after the wedding, I thought we could show Pabs Circe's Pool. Take some booze down there, invoke the goddess, that kind of thing.'

Abigail's face fell so dramatically it was comical. But maybe mine did too. Everyone wanted Lex for themselves.

'Oh,' she said, 'I thought you meant just us two.'

Lex rolled her eyes. 'We can't go without Zoë. She's the one who knows all the myth stuff. Anyway, three is better. More witchy. You can't have a coven of two, can you?'

You can, I felt like saying. *We already did, last time we went.*

'But I won't have a white dress on like you two,' Abigail was saying. 'Mine's green.'

'For fuck's sake, Pabs. If you're just going to whinge then forget it.'

'No,' she said, panicked. 'I definitely want to. It sounds really cool. But what did you mean about witches? I thought you said Circe was a goddess.'

'She was known as a witch, too,' I said, as witheringly as I could. 'She knew all about potions and poisons, which was fine until she used them against men. After that they said she was a witch.'

Abigail frowned. 'If it's so special down there, why didn't we go last summer? Or the summer before that?' She was glaring at me, obviously annoyed she'd been excluded, and very obviously trying to remind me of how much longer she'd known Lex. I rolled my eyes.

'I thought it would spoil it if I told anyone,' said Lex. 'That it would, I dunno, drain away its power or something. But it didn't. Zoë felt the magic too.'

'Magic?' Abigail wrinkled her nose.

'Pabs, you're being really annoying. Just trust me. You'll get it when you're there. You'll feel it then. Won't she, Zo?'

She grinned at me, teeth gleaming in the waning light. I wanted to disagree, say that, no, Pabs won't get it because Pabs is a sap but also sneaky, and we're much better on our own, but I didn't quite dare. We'd only just made up and I was on thin ice. A different kind of thin ice from the irritating Abigail, but still fragile enough to fall through. So I didn't say anything. I just nodded.

Dinner wasn't the sit-down affair I'd originally pictured — candles in cut-glass jars and conversation about the theatre — but a buffet that wasn't unlike the one at Nan's funeral, with cling-filmed dishes and curling sandwiches. It meant no one missed us as we stole away, the sun already hidden behind the hills and stars starting to come out in the eastern sky.

'We're going swimming,' Lex breathed into my ear, the fresh-sweet scent of mint-choc ice-cream mingling with the smell of her hair. 'I told Robin and he's keen too. I reckon something could happen tonight if you want it to.'

'What do you mean?' I'd been on my way to get my own bowl of ice-cream when Lex had grabbed me. My appetite vanished.

'You and him. On the beach, in the moonlight, none of the parents around.' She tugged gently at a lock of my hair and started singing under her breath. I realised it was the Robin Beck song off the old Coke advert. *First Time*.

'Piss off, Lex, there's nothing going on,' I said, but I was grinning.

She sang another line, about electricity flowing, a pained expression on her face and her fist to her heart.

I smacked her arm. 'Actually, for your information, and

not that it's going to happen anyway, but it wouldn't be the first time.'

'Bollocks.' She coughed it and I hit her again, slightly harder. Both of us were laughing now.

'Anyway, there's no rush,' she said. 'I hate all that competitive how-far-have-you-gone shit. God, if my dad knew. I think he imagines it's different at a girls' school but they're actually worse. And who needs them anyway? Boys, I mean. Men. They're always sulking. Always pushing for more.'

It took all I had not to ask if she meant Liam. I decided that she must: that this was her way of saying she was fed up and it was over now, whatever it had been, though it hadn't seemed like that at all in the attic. But then, when we set off for the beach and she made no move to pull him away from where he was deep in conversation with Alastair, I thought I might not need to save her after all. Happiness spread warmly through me at the thought. I didn't even care that Abigail was tagging along with us.

From the shoreline, the sea looked like a bolt of black satin, sheened by the moon and almost as unmoving as Calliope's swimming-pool. We hadn't gone to the beach next to the village but the one around the headland, directly below the lighthouse and therefore exposed to the open sea, a deserted little *paralia* the tourists never bothered with, reached by a pale stone path of long, sweeping bends.

Tom had insisted he was not left out of this adventure, threatening to tell the parents we were going swimming in the dark, which would probably have been deemed dangerous and stopped, if he couldn't come along. I had fallen into step with him and Robin on the walk down and the little boy's mood had infected me, a heady blend of excitement and apprehension. I had a bottle of white wine, swiped cold from the fridge, in my hand, but I'd failed to bring a corkscrew. It was an encumbrance once I realized but it wouldn't have occurred to me to ditch it. It was Richard's, and had cost him good money. I was doomed to be a good girl, I thought.

I wedged it upright in the smooth white pebbles of the beach, glass grating as I twisted it in. Robin, seeing it, produced a Swiss Army knife from the pocket of his khakis, holding it up in the dim light with a smile.

'Be prepared,' he said, in a clipped wartime wireless voice, and I thought I couldn't have invented a boy like him in my fondest imaginings. He was a boy from a book. A boy from an era I would probably have suited better, too.

We passed the wine back and forth between us, drinking about half of it. Tom was a little way off, peering with a small torch into the watery clefts between the large boulders that were scattered across half the beach, and Lex was already in the sea – or at least up to her thighs in it, shrieking about how cold it was while Abigail watched her from the safety of the water's edge.

'Shall we go in?' said Robin.

'What about Tom?'

'There's plenty over there to keep him occupied for hours.'

He stood and took off his trousers and shirt without fuss or self-consciousness.

'I won't look if you want to change,' he said and, good as his word, strode off towards the water in his boxer shorts.

Lex and Abigail were still wearing their dresses, although Lex's was hoicked up to keep it from getting lapped by the water. The thought of doing something before she did, however tame in the grand scheme of things, thrilled me. I pulled my dress off over my head and hurried towards the water, keen to get under before Robin turned and glimpsed my simple white underwear: the A-cup bra that was barely a bra at all.

The water wasn't cold, only cool. It had been heated by the sun for almost a whole summer. I was up to my chest, feet slipping on the stones underneath, but Robin was treading water.

'There's a shelf here,' he said. 'It falls off suddenly.' He paused. 'Just in case you don't like deep water.'

'It's okay if you're here,' I said, only daring to because he couldn't see me blush as I spoke in the dark. I pushed off the stones towards him, swimming into a pocket of chillier water and out of it again. Even with him there, the sensation of nothing under me made me suddenly breathless, and I lost my rhythm, splashing a bit and getting him in the face.

'Oi!' He laughed, misunderstanding, and sent a cascade of water over me, the roil from his sweeping arm making me go under for a second, saltwater burning the back of my throat and making me choke.

His arms were lifting me up and clear of the water instantly. In a couple of strokes he'd pulled us back to the lip of the shelf and I could stand again.

'I'm so sorry,' he said. 'I thought you meant to do it.' He turned me to face him and I spun easily, weightless in the water. He smoothed back a strand of hair that had got stuck in my mouth, tucking it behind my ear.

Oh, God, he's going to kiss me, I thought. I was so sure

of it that I glanced self-consciously towards the beach. Lex and Abigail were sitting on the stones, talking. I looked for Tom – the narrow paring of new moon still bright enough to illuminate the white stones – but couldn't see him.

Robin followed my gaze, narrowing his eyes to see better. 'Abs, is Tom there?' he called.

She turned, a cut-out silhouette except for her hair, which flew out, rippling in the pale light. At that moment, a cry went up, which quickly rose into a wail.

'Tom,' Robin said. 'He's hurt himself.' He grabbed my hand. 'Come on, I can't leave you out here on your own.'

We half waded, half swam back to the shoreline. Robin took off towards the rocks where Tom was still crying, though more quietly now.

It was only a cut knee – he'd slipped trying to reach a crab and landed on sharp barnacles – but Robin said it needed disinfecting. I watched their retreating backs as they headed towards the path, my dress stuck to my wet skin, and I had no idea whether I was relieved or disappointed.

'Perfect,' said Lex, when they were out of earshot. 'Now the babysitting is over, I can reveal my surprise.'

She brought out a soft plastic envelope and opened it up to take out her lighter and a green pack of Rizlas. Spreading everything out on a large flat rock, she pulled out a single paper with a flourish. Her fingers were deft in the moonlight, which caught in her rings as she sifted strands of tobacco.

'But you hate roll-ups,' I reminded her. 'You said they go soggy and look inelegant.'

'I'm glad you're taking notes, Zo. And they do, but it's worth it if there's an extra ingredient.' She looked up and grinned.

'Ah, cool,' Abigail breathed. 'You got some weed.'

I sat up ramrod straight. 'Weed? Lex, you promised no more drugs.'

Abigail snorted and Lex gave me a sly look. 'Weed isn't drugs. Not really. I meant pills and stuff. This is totally natural. I was actually going to make space cakes but Eleni got suspicious. Which is ironic.' She laughed.

Abigail grinned. 'Because you bought it off Panikos.'

'Yep.' Lex ran the length of the joint across the tip of her tongue and rolled it gently back and forth between her fingers as though she'd been doing it for a million years. When it was ready, she held it out to Abigail, who took it without hesitation. Her glee at being picked first was embarrassingly plain, especially when Lex flicked the lighter and leant towards her to light it. Abigail's eyes were the brightest I'd ever seen them.

She took an inexpert puff and Lex tutted. 'It's a waste if you're not going to inhale.'

Abigail took another, not much better, then held it out to me, but I shook my head, and took a long slug of wine instead. It was warm now, and tasted sour.

'Come on, Zo, just try it. It's only plants.' Lex had her head on one side, and was doing her best coaxing voice. If she'd chosen to make fun of me, I'd have dug my heels in, but a part of me wanted to try it. And, besides, it felt way less scary than something pharmaceutical.

Determined not to blow it straight out like Abigail, I opened my throat and took it all the way down before letting it out in a long stream. By some miracle, I didn't cough.

'Oh, my God, she's a born pothead,' said Lex, leaning forward to pluck the joint out of my fingers. 'Well done, Zo.'

'My nan smoked like a chimney,' I said, and I was as dizzy from the praise as from anything else, no less susceptible to Lex's approval than Abigail. 'I had a go once, when she'd gone to answer the door.'

Lex laughed, half choking.

Soon I began to feel quite odd. Nice-odd, perhaps – I wasn't sure. It was difficult to tell what was wine and what was weed, and what was just the three of us right there, on that beach, between the lapping water and the cool glint of the moon. I think it was probably all of it. I thought, over and over, as if to brand it into my memory: *All my life I'll remember this night. All my life.*

'Only one whole day to go,' Abigail said at some point.

I was lying back on the beach's white pebbles, aware they were digging into my back but I wasn't feeling any real discomfort. Lex looked up from where she was trying to light a pile of driftwood and dried-out seaweed. 'Huh?'

'Till you're sixteen.'

I tensed, even through the floating haze of what I'd smoked and drunk.

'Are you going to let him, then?'

'Piss off, Pabs.'

Her face fell. 'I think it's romantic.'

'Do you honestly?' I said. It came out sarcastically but I meant it. Robin was the kind of person you could imagine being romantic. But Liam?

Abigail ignored me. She was looking plaintively at Lex. 'Didn't you promise him?'

Lex held her lighter to a small twig, which actually took. It lit the angles of her face. 'It's not the fucking Middle Ages. If I don't want to, I won't.'

I managed not to say anything but inwardly I was jubilant. When Lex suggested we wished for one thing each on the embers of her short-lived fire, I thought that earlier in the day I would have wished for Liam to be hundreds of miles away — for Lex to be saved from him. I think I'd have given all my wishes in perpetuity for that. But, in that moment on the beach, she seemed perfectly safe in her own, apparently unshakeable, confidence.

'You're probably wishing about my brother, aren't you?' said Abigail, interrupting my thoughts. She sneaked a look at Lex and I knew she was trying for laughs.

'Actually, no,' I said simply, and it was the truth.

Certain that nothing bad was going to happen now, I simply wished I could be with Lex forever, that we would always belong to Calliope and each other, and that she would always belong to us.

It's another of those moments I dream of rewinding to. I could have wished to keep Abigail safe from harm, and Lex and me out of trouble. But hindsight is always a wonderful thing.

The worst of it is that if I got another wish, I wouldn't undo it all just to save her. I'd also do it because of the guilt. 'She's nothing but a millstone around our necks,' I exclaimed one morning over breakfast, when the doorbell rang before nine — Abigail had got into the habit of calling round earlier and earlier each day. Everyone had laughed and I'd been pleased with myself for about ten seconds before guilt at being mean sidled in. I had no clue that I'd end up feeling guilty about her forever.

Now

Cleo doesn't come back in time for dinner although, by some unspoken agreement, none of us mentions her absence. Mum has made a *spanakopita*, forgetting that Jess doesn't like spinach. She's never cooked much. Before Richard, in the maisonette, we'd always had meals that were assembled rather than made. And after Richard, well, he did most of the cooking and Mum was happy to let him. He enjoyed it and was good at it, although Eleni prepared the odd treat and left it in the fridge.

Now, the poor *spanakopita* sits forlornly in the middle of the table. The flaky pastry is blackened on the top and the filling is dried out.

'Oh, it's horrible, isn't it?' she says, after a single mouthful, suddenly close to tears. 'Don't eat it. I'm bloody useless.'

She gets up and begins collecting up our plates but Ben reaches out and puts his hand on hers. 'Marilyn, I have to tell you that this is the best *spanakopita* I've ever tasted.'

She stares at him and then her mouth slowly turns up. 'Oh, you. I bet you've never even had it before.'

'That's beside the point.'

She laughs then, and leaves the plates. We all join in, relieved.

'It's actually quite nice, Mum,' I lie. 'But I told you not to go to any trouble. You've got enough to think about without cooking for all of us. We should have had something from the freezer.'

'I know, but I wanted to welcome Ben and Jess properly, like Richard would have done.'

'Well, I reckon we should go down to the village and have pizza,' says Lex. 'My treat. We can show these two the village. Ice-cream for afters.'

Jess looks delighted.

'All right, then,' says Mum, 'but it will not be your treat. I'll be paying. Richard would have wanted that, for our girls.' She smiles at Jess. 'All our girls.'

Cleo's absence hovers in the air again. I know Lex feels it too, from the way she glances at her phone. I catch her eye when she puts it down, but she shakes her head.

The village looks pretty in the twilight. Every day another of the shops or tavernas opens for the season. The dozen or so waterfront moorings have all been taken now, with other yachts having to anchor in the bay. It's always the sailors who kick off the high season here – I remember Richard telling me that.

We eat pizza followed by ice-cream and tiramisu, faces lit by a proper wood-fired oven that could have been in Naples. The Venetians haven't been here for centuries but their influence is still strong, and every third table is occupied by Italians. I'm glad to be among these tourists who don't know us, who don't stare.

As we're getting up to leave, the bill paid, the owner appears from the kitchen and insists we must have a drink on the house, pushing me gently down into my seat when I say, as politely as I can, that we need to go. I've had enough now. I want to get back to the sanctuary of Calliope.

It's when he goes behind the bar to pour the drinks that I notice someone is there, on a stool in the corner, an unlit cigarette between his stubby fingers. Papagiorgiou. He nods when he sees me looking at him, and I glance away as though he's burnt me, my face hot even as my body goes cold.

The digestif in the tiny glasses we're brought, rather than the ouzo I was expecting, is weak and sugary. I throw it down, wishing it was stronger. 'Come on,' I say, as soon as it's gone, getting up and scraping the chair back under the table. 'Jess needs to go to bed.'

'It's not even half nine,' she says crossly, but Ben gets up too, and the others follow, thank God. We're nearly at the door, Lex still apparently unaware of Papagiorgiou's presence, when Robin and Liam appear on the other side. I jolt at the sight of them together, though it's not surprising really, when they're both on their own, both invited to Richard's funeral.

I stay at the back of our small group so I don't have to be near Liam, though I can feel Papagiorgiou's eyes boring into the back of my skull. Jess is chattering on about something to do with a new uniform rule at her school but I can't help tuning in to Robin – who, in a rare faux pas given what's going on tomorrow, is talking again about his campaign.

'Someone from the production team is heading out to the island,' he's saying. 'To scope out locations.' There's a febrile energy coming off him tonight. For the first time, he isn't handsome. He's too thin, the planes of his face too sharp and shadowed in the light from the wood-fired oven.

As I look away from him, I realize that Liam is watching me. Not Lex, but me. At that moment, we start moving outside, and I have no choice but to pass right by him. He smells the same as he ever did, and it's pungent even over the scents of the pizzeria. I think I've got past him when, just as he did once before, he leans in so close that I think he's going to kiss me.

'I remember you, that night,' he says, 'when she went missing. The fucking state of you.'

And then he turns away, gesturing to a waiter at an empty table close to the bar, and no one would know he'd said anything. I stand there, unable to move, but then Jess turns back to me and I make myself smile and follow her out, my legs weak.

'You didn't see him, did you?' I say, under my breath to Lex, as we walk back towards the water, Mum having said she wasn't quite ready for the uphill walk to Calliope yet.

'Liam?'

'Papagiorgiou. He was at the bar in the corner, right by where Liam and Robin will be sitting now. God knows when he came in.'

'Oh, shit. Do you think they'll . . .'

She trails off and I let her because I don't want to imagine that either. We walk on in silence. It's dark now, and a new moon hangs suspended above the bay, its light glancing palely off the hulls and polished chrome of the yachts, and turning Jess's light pink cardigan silver. It reminds me of the night the three of us went to the beach, the night before the wedding. Somewhere in the black, a woman calls for a dog or a child, voice shrill with alarm, and for a second it sounds like she's calling Abigail.

'Any word from Cleo?'

'No, but she hasn't posted anything else,' Lex says, so

softly I lean towards her to catch it. 'I've been texting her and she's read them but hasn't replied. Standard procedure. She'll probably be back at Calliope by now.'

Cleo's absence is becoming unnerving – or, rather, what she might have been up to in it – but at least she's not with the rest of them in the pizzeria. And at least she hasn't met Jess yet. I just know Lex's daughter will be a source of fascination for my girl. She's still young enough to expect adults – and Cleo will seem like an adult to her – to make a fuss of her. Cleo won't, I know, and that will intrigue Jess, luring her in like an ignored cat.

'I do think we need to talk about Liam,' I make myself say to Lex now, grateful for the wine drunk over dinner. The two of us have dropped further back from the others, me having deliberately slowed my pace.

'Really?' She sighs.

'Where's he staying anyway?'

'He said he'd find a room somewhere. Maybe he's sleeping on the bloody floor at Robin's. Christ, seeing those two together was weird.'

'What if they're all in there, discussing it?' I can't help saying. 'Discussing us? Robin seemed to have no idea the other day that Papagiorgiou was so suspicious about us. What if he's telling Robin about all that right now?'

'Don't think about it,' says Lex, flatly, and I'm grateful to her for shutting it down.

'Do you think Liam was expecting to stay at Calliope?'

'I know you're stressed but why do you still hate him so much?'

I turn to her, disbelieving. 'It's because of *you*. You know this.'

'I don't need you to be angry for me. It's ancient history.'

'He was a creep. He threatened me once, you know.' *I think he might have threatened me tonight, too,* is what I don't say. If I did, and it broke through Lex's cool, I might tip into a full-blown panic attack.

She's quiet in the gloom next to me. We're beyond the midpoint of the bay's curve by now and the bars and restaurants have run out, though the lanterns – new LED ones, colder and bluer than the old-style bulbs – continue for another few hundred feet. Without the bustle of the village centre, the scent of the flowers that enjoyed the earlier deluge seems heavier, more potent. The scruffy taverna I remember going to the night she and Liam left me alone to go to Panikos's club night has gone. There's no indication it was ever there.

'I know you don't want to talk about him,' I say. 'You never did then, either. But I think you were groomed, Lex. We'd call him a paedophile now. Cleo definitely would.'

'Oh, for God's sake, it wasn't like that.'

'You were fifteen.'

'Fifteen is not eight. Or twelve.' She gestures ahead, towards Jess, who has linked arms with Mum. The thought of Jess with someone like Liam makes me shudder. 'I turned sixteen that holiday.'

'Turned legal, you mean?' I sound like I'm mocking her, which is the last thing I feel.

'It was different then. The rules were different.'

'It doesn't mean it wasn't abuse.'

'Really? Bit revisionist. I just remember liking the attention.'

'Don't say that. So flippant. You were always like this. It's a defence mechanism. I don't think you were comfortable with it at the time, but he convinced you it was okay, and it was easier to go along with it. That's what grooming is, isn't it?'

She stops and turns to me. 'It was *my* experience. My life. I was in the middle of it, not you. You don't get to say that I was abused, that I was a victim. I do. Me. Only me.'

'Okay. Well, maybe it does have something to do with Abigail, then.'

'What do you mean?'

'If you say you were fine about Liam, that you had it all under control, *liked the attention*, in fact, then she died for nothing. It was my fault. I wrote that note to protect you. God knows what I thought I was going to do that night but, whatever it was, it was all for you. If you're saying you never needed any protection then what I did was even worse.' I take a breath, then say it: 'And he knows something, too, I know he does, and he's in there right now, basically talking to the *police*.'

I'm crying now but she doesn't notice in the dark. I blot away the tears with the cuff of my top. Ben glances back towards us, and I duck my head in case he can make anything out in the dark. I don't want him or Jess to know I'm upset because I'll have to say it's for Richard when quite a lot of it isn't, and that's a lie that makes me feel awful.

'I'm afraid, Lex,' I manage to say. 'I'm really afraid. I feel like something's coming.'

Her face is white in the moonlight as she turns to me. 'What do you mean?'

'Do you remember what we used to say about the magic?'

'At the Pool?'

281

I nod. I don't know what else to say, how to explain it, how it feels like it's seeping out, reaching out, like dark tentacles, over the island and over time, to choke us.

The others have got to the end of the lit road and are ambling slowly back towards us, but I catch her expression before she smooths it into blandness and it's strange to me. I can't read it because I've never seen it on her face before. Except once, I suddenly remember. Back then. I spin through my memories but the answer remains elusive. What it meant then, and what it might mean now.

We begin our ascent, slowly because Mum finds the steep paths hard on her legs now. Just before the last stretch, we round a bend and Jess exclaims.

I look up from my feet.

'Oh, yes, you won't have seen this,' says Mum.

Soft orange lozenges bloom in the darkness around us. They float dreamily across the path and rise slowly from the verges. It's too early for the cicadas so there's no sound, apart from our breathing as we watch, transfixed. In the enveloping dark, there are only these pinpoints of warmth, and for a blissful moment I forget everything.

'But what . . .?' Jess breathes the words.

'Fireflies,' says Mum, softly. 'Aren't they a wonder?'

Lex's phone beeping makes us all jump. An imposition from another time, another world.

'Cleo's back,' she says, face lit eerily by the screen. 'She's up there, waiting for us.'

Then

When I woke on the morning of the wedding, my stomach was queasy with nerves even before I'd properly come to. Or perhaps it was excitement – I'd always had trouble telling them apart.

I'd been dreaming of the beach below the lighthouse, the inky sea overhung by the slender sickle moon. I felt as if I had passed the whole night replaying everything that Lex, Abigail and I had discussed there. I could still see their faces lit by Lex's driftwood fire, how beautiful they'd been. Not just Lex, who always was, but Abigail too. All the jealousy and pettiness had briefly evaporated with the weed. I could see what Lex saw in it now, at least a bit.

Everything's going to be fine, I had whispered aloud, as I got into my little bed after the three of us stumbled up to Calliope around midnight, the lamp on the bedside table giving off a homely glow. *Lex is powerful. Nothing can hurt her. Nothing can hurt us.* As I turned off the lamp, the moon making a ghost of the bridesmaid's dress hanging against the old oak wardrobe, it struck me forcefully that I was happy. A couple of rooms away, the low bass of Lex's dance music went on as she and Abigail bumped around getting ready for bed, and it mingled intoxicatingly with Richard's old piano jazz winding up through the hot perfumed air – he and Mum hadn't gone to bed yet. I didn't even mind that Abigail was sleeping on Lex's floor and I was the odd one out tonight. I was perfectly content.

This heady combination of sensations had lulled me to sleep before I managed to close the shutters, and the intensity of the sun on the whitewashed walls hurt to look at now, as I tried to open my eyes. The light was sharp enough to cut.

I picked up the watch that I hadn't worn since I'd arrived. It was only seven thirty but I knew I wouldn't be able to get back to sleep. Anyway, I liked the mornings when I woke first and had Calliope to myself. I padded silently downstairs, the smooth tiles underfoot wonderfully cool, as was the fridge when I opened it, a soothing breath on my flushed cheeks. It was going to be just as hot as yesterday.

'Here she is, my little nemesis.'

I jumped so hard that my hand knocked against the bottles in the fridge door, making them rattle.

Liam stood there, a nasty smile on his face. Just like at the pool, when I'd been eavesdropping on Penny and Lex, he'd managed to creep up on me without my noticing. He'd already been out by the pool, his skin glowing the same brick-brown that Penny's was, aftershave coming off him in waves because he was hot. Everything about him was too much, not just his smell but the whites of his eyes against the tan, the shine on the waves of his hair. I suppose his sexuality, too – though I couldn't have articulated it like that – the raw threat of him.

'You're really not a fan of me, are you?'

'What do you mean?' I said, shutting the fridge door too hard, so that the bottles rattled again. I turned to face him and he'd moved even closer. It made me want to run from the room but I didn't – *couldn't* – because, whatever was going on between him and Lex, he was an adult, and I found it virtually impossible to disobey adults. Perhaps Lex, for all her bravado, was the same underneath.

'You know exactly what I mean,' he said. 'You can't stand me, but you can't look away either. I've seen the way you watch us. Lex don't notice – she's used to people looking at her – but I do. I thought, This one either thinks I'm not good enough or she wants me for herself.'

My face screwed up in disgust before I could stop myself and his smile turned meaner.

'Oh, so, hang on a minute. You think *you*'re too good for me as well, do you? With where you and your mum come from?' He laughed, and I noticed he'd allowed his accent to become his own, finally. 'You don't fit in here either, sweetheart.'

'I don't think anyone is too good for anyone else,' I said, cringing at how earnest I sounded. 'It's not that at all. It's that she's only fifteen. We're still children.'

'I was working by the time I was fifteen.'

'I just wish you'd leave her alone.'

'Who says she wants to be left alone? You've seen her, how she parades herself about. You think it's for anyone else's benefit? She's showing me her wares.' He laughed.

'I'll tell.'

'You what?'

'I'll tell Richard about the attic. What I heard. He'll sack you. You'll lose your job and you'll never see Lex again.' My blood sang with my own daring.

For a second, I thought I'd got him. But then he smiled again. 'You're not going to do that.'

'I will.'

'No, you won't. Because if you do, I'll fuck all of this up for you.'

I stepped back without meaning to, my back now pressed hard against the fridge. 'What do you mean?'

'I'll sit your mum and Richard down and tell them you've been coming on to me.'

I let out a shocked laugh. 'They'd never believe that.'

'Ha, yeah, maybe not.' He blinked, thinking. 'Okay, then, I'll say you've been stealing stuff from the house, or money from his wallet. I'll think of something. I'm a salesman. I'm a professional fucking liar.' His smile widened to a grin, showing his yellower back teeth. 'Hang on, I've got it. I'll go to Richard and say your *mum* has been trying it on with me, not you. I'll say I don't know what to do about it but I thought he needed to know the truth. That she likes a younger man on the side.'

He reached behind me to open the fridge, forcing me into a horrible sort of embrace, caught between his arm and the door. 'You know Lex's mum cheated on him, don't you? Back in the day. He told me once, when he'd had one too many. Some posh bloke she knew from years before – she'd been engaged to him. Someone from her world.'

I tried to duck under his arm but he moved in closer. Under the aftershave, I could smell cigarettes and last night's drink on him. I could see every tiny black hair pushing its way out of his face. He had to shave every day. I knew that because he never cleared up after himself, leaving flecks all over the bathroom washbasin I had to share with him.

'Mum loves Richard,' I said. 'He knows she'd never do that to him.'

'Does he, though?' he said, musingly. 'I dunno. I think if it happens once, you always worry it'll happen again. You're always half expecting it.'

He swooped in and, for an awful second, I thought he was going to kiss me. Instead he put his mouth to my ear, so that his next words vibrated right through my body. 'Just because you're a frigid little girl don't mean she is.'

And then he was gone, back out into the blinding sun, leaving a trail behind him of something dark and noxious, like poisonous spores. As I stood there, my body starting to tremble, I could feel Calliope seething around me, for me. *Do something*, I muttered. *You have to do something to stop him.*

Really it was a message to myself, but I think a little bit of it was a plea to her, too.

I went back to my room then, not knowing what else to do – getting back into bed and pulling the covers over my head even though it was too hot for it. At ten, I forced myself up and into the shower, because if I didn't I'd make them all late for the chapel. I froze when someone knocked on the door as I was brushing my teeth, my eyes widening in the mirror, but it was only Mum.

She was already dressed in her wedding outfit, the new deep blue dress bringing out her eyes and tan. It was the exact colour of the Ionian Sea. I knew I should ask her how she was feeling, or say she looked nice, but I couldn't bring myself to say anything.

'You're still not ready and you haven't even had any breakfast yet,' she said, bustling inside and coming to stand beside me at the mirror over the sink. She was only an inch taller than me now, even in her little heels. 'You know, just a bit of make-up would look so pretty today,' she said. 'Not much. Just a bit of rouge so you don't look so pale.'

My hackles went up. 'Isn't *rouge* what Victorian prostitutes wore?'

She looked crestfallen, which made me feel even worse.

'Look, I'm not being horrible,' I said, 'but just because you wear make-up doesn't mean I want to.'

'Lex wears it.'

'Well, I'm very sorry I'm not gorgeous like Lex. Not like Lex at all.'

'Oh, love, that's not what I'm saying. You're gorgeous to me.'

'Yeah, thanks. *A face only a mother could love.*' I said it to my own pathetic reflection in the mirror, to my stupid hair, the old phrase dredged up from somewhere, probably one of Nan's. 'Well, maybe I don't like make-up. Maybe I think it looks tarty.'

I expected her to storm off at that, but she reached up to tuck a wayward lock of hair behind my ear. I'd begun to worry in the last couple of days that they stuck out. It had never occurred to me before. I suppose I'd never studied myself much. I probably couldn't have accurately said where the mirrors at home were hung. But that summer, with Lex . . . It was as though once I'd caught sight of myself I couldn't look away, and it wasn't out of vanity. It was to calculate all the ways I fell short.

'You're a funny one,' said Mum. 'When I was your age, I couldn't wait to grow up, leave home. I used to dream about how, when I got a job, I'd be able to buy myself a nice pair of shoes or a handbag. But you, you like being a girl, don't you? You're not in any hurry.'

I couldn't speak. We both watched my face crumple in the mirror. She pulled me into her and I cried hot tears into her shoulder. Wet patches spread on her dress but I couldn't stop. It was an enormous relief to let her hold me, and to let myself go.

'What is it, darling? Has something happened? Was it last night?'

I shook my head, my face pressed into her warm body, which smelt just as it always had. For a moment, I had another of those waves of longing for home, where everything was dull but understandable, utterly known to me and comforting for it.

'Are you sure?' She was rubbing my back and her hand was small but strong. 'Is it Lex? I worry sometimes. Is she . . . kind to you?'

'It's not that. I don't know what it is.'

She wetted a flannel, letting the tap run so the water was cool, then pressed it gently to my red eyes, which were tight and sore with salt.

'People always say, don't they, *Oh, if I had my time again*, and *what it would be to be young again*, all that? I say it myself. But I don't really mean it. It's exhausting being your age. You're not one thing or the other.'

I swallowed loudly because tears were threatening again.

'And, anyway, you'll feel better in a couple of days.'

'What do you mean?'

'Come on, love, I'm your mum. You're due on then, aren't you? Time of the month? You're regular as clock-work, just like me. That's why you're feeling like this.'

She gave me a kiss and let herself out. She was right. With everything else going on, I'd completely lost track. The knowledge made me feel a tiny bit more like myself. The mood-skewering that hormones were capable of, something separate to myself, could be at least partly responsible for why I felt so afraid.

I tested the idea in my head, but it didn't ring quite true – or true enough. The danger I'd felt pressing in before – which had felt so blissfully absent on the beach – was back. The feeling of it reminded me of this horror film that everyone had gone on and on about at school a few years earlier. If you said the murderer's name five times in the mirror, he would appear. It was a bit like that: if I dared to look long enough at my reflection I would see a dark shadow standing behind me, waiting.

Now

When I get down to breakfast, the kitchen is empty. I didn't expect to see any sign of Ben, who relishes a lie-in, but Jess is also absent. On the table is a discarded bowl with two inches of brown milk at the bottom, evidence that she's already had a bowl of the chocolate cereal I bought her in the mini-market.

Mum bustles in from outside at that moment, so distracted she doesn't even greet me. 'Well, I've said to Lex that I won't have her here,' she says, as though we've been in conversation for some time. 'I just . . . I just can't. And Richard would understand that. I'm sorry, but there's no two ways about it.'

'What's happened?'

Mum doesn't hear me, too busy ricocheting around the kitchen, wiping surfaces that are already clean.

Lex comes in from the garden at that moment, raising her eyebrows at me.

'What's going on?' I nod towards Mum as Lex pushes her gently down into a chair.

'It's Cassandra. She's flying in today. Presumably on a broomstick.'

'Oh, God.'

'I can't have her here,' says Mum. 'I'm sorry, Lex, I know she's your mother, and she was Richard's first wife, but she hasn't been here for thirty years. And I don't think I can cope with *her* either.'

I look questioningly at Lex.

Penny, she mouths.

Penny Rutherford. I'd forgotten about the prospect of her coming. I haven't set eyes on Abigail's mother since my last night on the island, which was also a week into the search. Her primary emotion had been fury, seemingly. At the time, I had thought it was directed at me, that she'd somehow picked up on something. A mother's instinct, perhaps.

I understood later that it was nothing to do with me, that there was no motherly intuition. I barely existed in Penny's universe; at most, I was the awkward daughter of Richard's slightly common new wife. It's monstrous but sometimes I think she was probably angry with Abigail for ruining everyone's summer, for causing such a bloody awful *fuss*. But maybe that's unfair.

I look at Mum, whose hand shakes as she reaches for the tea Lex has just put in front of her. Her face is grey.

'Did you get any sleep last night?'

She looks up. 'Not really. I tried it without the pills so I wouldn't feel so groggy in the day.'

'Why don't you go back to bed now, have a nap? There's nothing else you need to do here.'

She lets me accompany her upstairs. I close the shutters, noticing as I do the book on Richard's side of the bed, a receipt from the bakery marking three-quarters of the way through, his half-moon reading glasses on top. John Fowles's *The Magus*. Set on a fictional Greek island, but one also infected by a strange sort of magic. While Mum is taking off her sandals, I touch the glasses briefly, wish he was still here. It's peculiarly comforting to me that he was only rereading it, that he'd got to the end before, years ago. We had discussed it: how many tricks it plays on the reader.

I wipe my eyes and reach down to pull out the cord for the landline by the bed. Mum starts to protest but I shake my head. 'We'll get the phone downstairs, okay? And your mobile.'

'What about Cassandra?'

'I'll deal with her. And Penny. Let me and Lex handle those two.'

'Liam said he'd pop round,' she says, as she turns on her side, pulls the sheet over her. 'You'll wake me up if he does, won't you? I don't want to miss him.'

She always liked him, saw him as an ally because he came from the same background as her and Richard, when no one else here did. I wonder if she'd have viewed him differently if he'd been a posh boy, seen things more clearly if he hadn't made her feel so at ease.

'Do you want a pill?' I say.

'I can't take them in the day. I won't be able to string a sentence together later. If I need something, I'll take one of Richard's diazepam. He had them for his sciatica.'

I close the door softly behind me, pausing on the landing because Calliope's ghosts are whispering, like they used to. My eye falls on a single pink trainer, half inside the little bedroom I used to sleep in, and where Jess is staying now. I peep in but it's empty.

I hurry down the stairs and back into the kitchen, where Lex is standing at the sink drinking water.

'Is Jess outside?'

She shakes her head. 'And I've been out there for ages. I woke up early and couldn't get back to sleep. I've been dozing in the hammock since dawn.' She yawns, then rubs her temples, wincing.

I glance around, something by the well catching in my peripheral vision. The air over there seems to throb and swell but then I blink and there's nothing.

'Is Cleo still in bed?' I say, though I know she isn't. She's gone, too. I just know it.

Last night, as I'd feared, Jess was wide-eyed with curiosity at the sight of . . . I don't even know what relation the two of them are. Step-cousins, I suppose. Jess doesn't have any full first cousins. Ben has a sister who adores her niece but couldn't be less interested in having her own children. And I only have Lex. Not that Lex was ever 'only', even across the span of years when we didn't speak.

Cleo was in the sitting room when we came in the previous night, lying full-length on the squashy old sofa that's been there forever. Having only visited in high summer and spent most of my waking hours outside or in the attic, I don't think I've ever sat on it. She stood to shake Ben and Jess's hands solemnly, her omnipresent phone transferred to her left.

Mum had wanted a cup of tea, in the way that her generation does whenever they get in from anywhere, and Ben was asking about a plug-in mosquito repellent. By the time I got back to the living room with the tea, Jess had sidled over to Cleo, drawn in by her phone's tinny siren song, her little face intent on the screen. I watched as Cleo shifted slightly to make room, and Jess perched on the edge, almost leaning against the older girl. I had been right about the cat thing. I'd known I would be.

'I might go down to Circe's Pool tomorrow, have a look

around,' Cleo had said casually, after they'd watched whatever it was for a couple of minutes. 'I asked Robin about it when I saw him by the harbour earlier, but he'd never heard of it. He was having a drink with another guy who's come out for the funeral. Liam, his name was. He said there's a map here, up in the attic. He remembered it.'

'What's Circe's Pool?' said Jess.

'Oh, nothing,' I said, too fast.

'It can't be nothing.' She looked at me, then back to Cleo.

'It's a pool of water by a cave, below an old church,' she said. 'Circe was a very powerful goddess. I've got a book of myths upstairs I can show you, if you like. We can read about her.'

Jess had nodded, her little face alight with the attention.

'I've no idea where Cleo is,' Lex says now. 'You think she tells me anything? What's wrong besides the obvious, anyway? You've gone very pale.'

I don't answer because I'm already heading for the stairs. I know in my bones that neither of them is here, but I make myself search Calliope's every room. I search just as I once searched for Lex, and again for Abigail. *And one of them never came back*, says a helpful little voice in my head.

Lex catches up with me in the attic. I'm about to open Cleo's enormous rucksack and go through it. For what, I don't know. The missing note? The book with the map in it? Everything is getting mixed up in my head.

'What are you doing?' says Lex. 'Why are you in such a panic?'

Panic, says the same little voice. *Derives from the god Pan*. The heavy book of Greek myths is on the bedside table.

'Cleo said last night that she might go to Circe's Pool today.'

'Oh, Christ. That's all we need. Well, hopefully she won't find it.'

'You think? Cleo? The point is, I think Jess is with her.'

Lex pauses, fishes in her dressing-gown pocket.

'Lex, did you hear me?'

'Yes.' She brings out her phone and holds it up. 'Look, let me ring her.' I wait, Calliope holding its breath with me. 'Straight to voicemail, obviously. Try Jess?'

'She hasn't got a phone yet.'

'Okay, but, look, I know Cleo's been a bit . . . dogged about this, but Jess will be fine if they're together. Cleo will look after her.'

'You're telling me not to worry about my child being in that place after what happened there? Are you serious? Cleo doesn't give a shit about Jess. She doesn't care about anything apart from finding some sort of justice for a girl she'd never heard of until this week.'

'Now, hang on, that's not fair.' Two dark pink spots have appeared high on Lex's cheeks. 'That's *my* child you're talking about.'

'What if she's worked it all out?' I drop my voice. 'Just because she hasn't said anything about the note doesn't mean she hasn't got it. What if she knows it was to do with me? What if she takes it to Robin? For all we know, she's already handed it over to the police.'

'If she has got the note,' Lex's voice is cold, 'then she's more likely to think *I* wrote it, just as you intended back then. And, anyway, if she was going to hand anything over, wouldn't she have taken the diary too? Either way, it's got nothing to do with Jess. This whole crusade of hers is about protecting girls like Jess, isn't it? Think about it. Just stop and breathe and think about it for a second.'

I do as I'm told. Somewhere a sane part of me thinks she's probably right. 'Okay, fine,' I say. 'I'm sorry for what I said. But I still need to find Jess. I don't want her in that place, Lex. It's . . . unpredictable. Do you remember how it was down there that night? You felt it too.'

'Of course I did. Wasn't I the one who told you there was something there to begin with?'

We turn to go back down the stairs and Ben is standing in the doorway, hair on end, eyes still soft with sleep. 'What's going on?'

I search his face for what he might have heard. He rubs his eyes. 'Zo?'

'It's fine. I was just looking for Jess. I think . . .'

'She's gone off exploring with Cleo,' says Lex. 'Little sods didn't think to mention they were going, of course.'

So this is how Penny and Alastair must have felt, I think, as Ben and I get into Richard's car. Except, of course, I can't actually imagine them of all people feeling anything like the way I feel now, with my own child gone.

But it's a short-lived nightmare. Lex's call comes through just as Ben turns left off the road for Circe's Pool. It's lucky: another minute and we'd have had no signal to receive it. I would have had to run those paths again, past the red-painted As on the walls, down through the thick void of silence to the Pool. Somewhere I hoped never to go again, and this time looking for my Jess.

'She's fine,' Lex says, the second I pick up, fingers sweaty on the screen as I try to swipe right. 'They were down in the village. I met them on the hill as they were coming back up. Her tongue is turquoise blue from some revolting bubblegum ice-cream but she's fine. She's with me now, okay? Cleo has gone up to her room so Jess and I are going to play Cluedo.'

Certain catastrophe dissipates into nothing, smoke carried away by a clean sea breeze. Ben turns off the engine and I breathe in the silence. Unclipping my seatbelt, I twist round in my seat, reaching over the gearstick to rest against his chest. He didn't understand why I was so afraid, but he accepted my instinct. I love him for that. His heart, close to my ear, is still racing, as mine must be too.

'What don't I know?' he says, after a while.

'I'll tell you. But not now, okay? I need to do something first.'

He pauses, then nods. 'Okay.'

He turns the engine back on and makes a careful three-point turn. As we drive away, movement in the side mirror catches my eye. But when I turn, leaning out of the open window to look back down the lane, there's nothing that couldn't be attributed to birds disturbing the leaves, heat shimmer disrupting the air. Unless you know the place. The power of it. And I do know it, even after all this time.

Lex is standing outside Calliope's front door when we pull up. I half stumble out the car.

'Is it Jess?'

'No, no. She's in the kitchen. We were about to play Scrabble. She won Cluedo. Miss Scarlet in the –'

'Lex.'

She sighs. 'Penny's just this second arrived. She got to the island last night apparently. She's been sailing round the Aegean since April with husband number two. Come and help me,' she says, looking from me to Ben. 'I cannot deal with this on my own, and I wasn't about to wake up your mum.'

We go via the garden, trying to delay the inevitable. I can hear Penny's voice carrying on the air like a foghorn.

'Ah, here you are,' she says to Lex, when we step inside. 'I thought you'd buggered off.'

I go straight over to Jess, who's at the far end of the table, setting out Scrabble tiles with great precision. I lay a hand on her shoulder just to touch her.

'Who are these people, then?' Penny is saying.

'You must remember Zoë,' Lex says. 'And this is her . . . this is Jess's father Ben.'

'Zoë! Well, you've improved with age, I must say. Where's Marilyn?'

'She's in bed, having a nap,' I say. 'She's not been sleeping much.'

'Not to worry. Just thought I'd walk up on the off-chance. Rupe was getting on my nerves, too. I told him it would be a south-westerly today, but he always thinks he's right. Alastair was the same.'

Cleo is suddenly there, having approached on silent feet. Lex gestures towards her. 'Penny, this is my daughter Cleo. Cleo, this is my . . . this is Penny.'

'I'm her godmother, is what she ought to have said. Good Lord, look at you now. You must have been knee-high when I saw you last. A solemn little thing. Not like your mother at that age at all.'

'Godmother,' says Cleo, slowly. I watch her face change, turn intent. 'So you were Abigail's mother.'

'Leave it, Cleo.' I've never heard Lex's voice so sharp.

Cleo doesn't flinch, just looks at her mother and then, dismissing her, turns to Penny.

As for Penny herself, she's gone pale but is waving her hand dismissively.

'Pabs is not *verboten* as a subject, is she?' She looks around at us. 'Or have I missed something. Alexandra, don't fuss, it's fine. The sky is not going to fall in if her name is mentioned. Besides, it's no good being squeamish when there are people with clipboards in the village who have come all the way from Athens to do just that, on camera. Did Robin mention this programme they're going to make? I think . . .' and here she falters, which makes her look like a different person entirely '. . . well, I'm not sure this reconstruction idea is in terribly good taste actually.' Something unexpected – almost like pain – crosses her face, and I wonder if I've got her wrong all this time.

'They're here already?' Lex is saying.

'Initial scoping out, apparently, then back to film in July. I'll be long gone then, thank God.'

'Reconstructions can be very effective,' says Cleo.

Penny's face still looks uncertain, like it might collapse. 'I know Robin can't leave it alone, but I don't need a bod– I don't need to find anything to know that she's not coming back. I knew that twenty-five years ago and I know it now.'

'But there could be someone out there who knows something, who should be brought to justice,' says Cleo.

'Cleo, I've told you,' hisses Lex. She gathers herself,

which looks like it takes some effort, then turns to Penny. 'Dare I ask when Cassandra is getting here?'

'She'll miss the afternoon hydrofoil. Flight gets in too late.'

'Well, I suppose that's something.'

Penny shoots Lex a reproving look. 'She'll get the early one over to the island tomorrow, in good time for the funeral. She's been terribly upset about Richard actually. You're getting very severe in your old age, darling. Is she a right old battleaxe of a mother?' She directs this at Cleo, who smiles faintly, with only her mouth.

My relief is profound when Penny makes her excuses, for all sorts of reasons. I go upstairs and check on Mum, make sure she's missed the whole thing. Her room is quiet except for a creak from one of the shutters, which I creep over to fasten more securely.

It's peaceful there. Mum is snoring very gently, and I can smell the perfume she's always worn coming from the clothes hanging in the small dressing room she couldn't believe was half hers when we first came. I was embarrassed by the fuss she made about it at the time, and how she washed everything up before it went in the dishwasher. I wished she was more capable of pretending, of *passing*. I wished she would modify her accent, like Liam did when he remembered, like Richard had over time. That she didn't, even though she felt uncomfortable about it sometimes, with types like Penny, was brave and honest. I see that now.

I sink into the easy chair by the window, where Richard used to put on his shoes, and realize how tired I am. The thought jinxes me: I open my eyes I don't know how much later to find Lex standing there, holding out her phone.

My breathing is already fast because I've been dreaming of Athenian prison cells, foetid with heat and daubed in graffiti I couldn't even guess at.

'There's another video,' she whispers, so she doesn't wake Mum. 'Penny's in it. And . . .' she hangs her head '. . . Liam.'

I sit bolt upright. 'What?'

'She must have followed Penny down to the village and found him too.'

Then

Time played its old trick on the day of the wedding, making it simultaneously last three minutes and three weeks. But while the daytime ceremony hurtled past in a happy, uncomplicated blur, allowing me to put aside what Liam had said in the kitchen, the evening's celebration in Calliope's garden stretched on and on, an endless whirl, the sun taking forever to slide into the sea, the Pinkening intensifying until we were dizzy from its pulsing glow. It was as though we'd all fallen under some enchantment. I remembered a strange little English folk tale I'd once found in a library book, in which a girl who refused to marry is cursed to dance until her feet bleed. I thought of Pan there among us, watching approvingly from the sidelines as more wine was opened, and the music was turned up.

It was impossible to settle to anything. Again and again I made circuits, yanking at the loose left shoulder strap of my dress, which kept slipping down. I did it so many times I knew I'd dream of the same action. I didn't much feel like answering questions about school or my new step-family from well-meaning adults I didn't know – and was ready to pretend if anyone tried that I was on an important errand. But no one did try. The status of my bridesmaid dress seemed to grant me immunity from being bothered. Anyway, the only person I wanted to be with was Lex and she was nowhere to be seen. This gnawed at me. I hadn't seen Liam for ages either.

I continued my anxious wanderings, down the plumbago path to circle the swimming-pool, then back up to search the deep velvet shadows of the cypresses, and on into the cool abandoned interiors of Calliope's rooms, filled only with rose-coloured light, until it occurred to me that Mum and Richard wouldn't mind or probably even notice if I shut myself away for a while. If I just *stopped*.

It was as though making that decision persuaded the gods to give me a break because the next person I saw was Liam.

'You seen Lex?' His face was sullen.

My heart lifted. 'Not for a while. I thought she was with you.'

'Haven't seen her since the chapel.'

'Oh.' I tried not to seem too glad at how frustrated he obviously was. They must have fallen out again.

'I need to find her.'

'Why?'

'None of your business.'

I shrugged and headed for the stairs, but he grabbed my arm, yanking me back. His fingers hurt. 'Remember what I said earlier. You tell me if you find her, okay?'

I nodded just to get away, running up first one flight of stairs and then on, to reach the attic. I lay down on the waxed floorboards and closed my eyes, only to open them again because it made my head spin. I'd had four glasses of Richard's champagne and eaten nothing but cake since breakfast. I listened for the ghosts to soothe me but they were an indistinct babble, made excitable by the joy of a wedding, a second chance at love, even if there were to be no babies. I didn't want to admit it, but the place wasn't quite as calming as it had been before Liam's intrusion, grubbiness still hanging in the air.

I breathed in and out slowly until I felt less sick. He didn't know where Lex was and that was a good thing. I'd been convinced they were together somewhere but they weren't. She was probably with Abigail. I latched on to this and wasn't even put out by it. The relief of it, as well as the PMT and the champagne, and everything, made tears suddenly threaten.

I decided to let them come. Perhaps it would count as catharsis – a newly learnt concept that had been in the crossword and which Richard had told me was Greek. As I replayed the various recent episodes, from the club night to the exchange that morning by the fridge, tears ran down my temples and into my hateful hair. I imagined them pooling saltily on the wood, drying to leave a tide-mark of teenage melodrama and masochism, another new word. Of course there was Robin, too, though I couldn't decide how I felt about that: some combination of embarrassment, relief and annoyance with Abigail.

He had approached me as we left the chapel after the ceremony, the heat astonishing after the chill of the old building's interior with its foot-thick stone.

'Zoë, I was hoping to catch you,' he said.

I glanced about, hoping Lex and Abigail were distracted. 'Was Tom's knee okay?'

'Oh, yes. Thank you. But, you see, the thing is, I thought there might have been some confusion last night. Before the knee thing.'

I immediately felt an urge to bolt.

'In the sea,' he went on, red-faced now. 'When we were messing around. Well, I wondered if perhaps . . . Hmm, this was easier in my head.'

'You don't like me that way,' I said. I knew Lex had only been saying it for fun. Almost all of me had known.

'It's more that I can't, really. What I mean to say, is that in another situation . . . Or, rather, that . . . Oh, for God's sake, Rutherford.' He shook his head at his own ineptitude.

I tried to tell myself how old-fogeyish he seemed, like a sensible father already, but that only made me sad, a daft part of me regretful that the possibility was over. I didn't want it now, didn't want anything now, but a ridiculous part of me, thankfully quite small, had thought it might be nice to marry someone like Robin one day.

'Don't worry, honestly,' I said, fiddling with my dress, feeling every bra-less inch of my bare back in it.

'No, well, I've been worried, you see.' He smiled ruefully down at me. 'I thought about it last night when I got to bed and then this morning Abs said . . . Well, I thought I ought to say something before it got any . . . Or went any . . .'

'Your sister said something?'

'Ah. Well, no, not really. Not at all. What I mean is . . .' He came to a halt.

The rest of the wedding party was beginning to pull away in a mass of colour and chatter. It was painfully obvious to me that Abigail had stirred the pot, however much Robin was trying and failing to take it back. Deep irritation swelled inside me just at the moment Lex finally noticed us and gave me a double thumbs-up before disappearing into the throng.

A stray dog I'd seen around before, bright-eyed and cheerful despite his matted coat, approached and cocked his leg against the whitewashed wall of the chapel, the urine a surprisingly vivid yellow. Robin and I watched him as he went on his way, down the curving slope towards the tavernas' bins, the urine snaking after him. I didn't know whether to laugh or cry. I really needed my period to arrive.

'I mean, it's not that you're not absolutely lovely,' Robin started up again. 'You're very intelligent and pretty and . . .'

'Oh, God, please stop,' I said wearily.

'No, but it's true. The real trouble . . .' he paused '. . . well, it's that I have a girlfriend already. Back at home. I haven't told any of the family because I knew my mother would make such a bloody song and dance. Her name's Imogen. We've known each other forever actually – her brother was my best friend at prep school and . . . Well, you don't need to know all that.' He ruffled his lovely gold-streaked hair and sighed. 'Perhaps if things were different then –'

'What's she like?' I interrupted. We'd moved off and around the corner and the view of the bay – the angle and elevation of the incline making it one of the best there was – seemed to mock how pathetically this had turned out. I was inescapably in the perfect location for my first romance. I longed for it now I didn't have to go through with it.

'Ah, well, she's . . .' He stopped to consider.

It was as though he'd never really given it any thought. I hated her briefly then, this Imogen who probably called herself Imo – who had only snared lovely Robin because she'd been born into the same world, just like Lex and Abigail. It struck me that I would probably never belong to it.

'Does she play on the lacrosse team?'

He looked askance at me. 'Oh, um. Well, actually they don't play it at her school. But she does play netball for the county.' He paused, ran a hand through his hair again. 'Wing attack.'

I let out a strangled laugh and broke into a run up the next flight of half-ruined steps. 'Got to go now,' I called over my shoulder. 'Bridesmaid duties and all that. Thanks for the chat but you really mustn't worry. I wasn't expecting anything. Pabs only said I liked you to shit-stir. She's jealous of me and Lex.'

He frowned in confusion but then managed to raise a smile. 'Ah, yes, I see. She's always adored Lex.'

He started to say something else but I had already launched myself out of earshot, vaulting the steps two at a time, the long skirt of my dress balled in one hand so I didn't trip over it. I'd never called her Pabs before because I thought it was horrible. But right then I thought she bloody deserved it.

Thinking about this in the attic, my tears beginning to dry up, I stood off to the side of myself and thought, quite sensibly, that I was just drunk and brimful of hormones I couldn't help. It wasn't a precociously adult voice telling me this. It was someone like the girl I'd been just a few short weeks before, a child with a Blytonian backbone who thought I'd suddenly become quite ridiculous.

'Oh, do buck up, Zoë,' I said aloud. 'You've turned into the most terrible fathead.'

This made me laugh and hiccup. I got up and went over

to the dresser with the mirror that tipped. I looked flushed and wild; pretty, actually. The tiny white flowers in my hair looked good against the brown, as Mum had said they would, if not quite stars in the night sky, then not a million miles away either, unlike the stars. I wasn't certain but I thought my hair was maybe half an inch longer.

I felt almost cheerful then. I didn't have to moon over Robin any more and that would be a weight off. And it wasn't as though he thought I was completely repulsive. He had seemed almost wistful when I ran off. The thought of telling Lex about it lightened my mood further. She would make fun of me, I knew, but also say something strangely comforting. And she was sure to come up with something awful to say about *Imo*. And, best of all, she wouldn't be with Liam while I told her. She hadn't been with him all afternoon.

My thoughts tumbled over each other as I ran back down the stairs. Maybe just the two of us could go to Circe's Pool without Abigail trailing after us. And then maybe Lex would see that, aside from all his other horrible traits, there was no *magic* about Liam. He was appalling in so many ways but maybe it was this that would convince Lex once and for all. I had another idea then. A better one.

I went to my room and found pen and paper. I wrote the note in careful block capitals so it could feasibly have been written by anyone. I did it quickly, without over-thinking it. I'd lose my nerve otherwise, I knew. When it was done, I went into Lex's room to leave it on her bed, but there was so much mess everywhere that I was worried it wouldn't be noticed. I gathered up the worst of it – endless clothes, dog-eared copies of *Mixmag* and three damp towels – and chucked it all into the wardrobe. Then I made the crumpled bed and positioned the note right in the middle of her pillow.

As I ran back out to the garden, I caught sight of Abigail. Irritation flared inside me again. She had changed into a shimmering yellow-green dress that actually looked perfect with her hair, not that I was about to tell her so. But then she started walking in my direction, and I could see that she was really unsteady on her three-inch strappy heels. As I watched, she smacked so hard into one of the wooden supports holding up the terrace pergola that it twisted her whole body round, the strap of her little old-fashioned handbag arcing over her. She didn't appear to notice, and continued determinedly towards me.

'Where's Lex?' she slurred, when she got close enough. Her eyes were glassy, pupils huge. When she blinked, it seemed to take an enormous effort to raise the lids again.

'Didn't that hurt?' I said. There was already a livid mark on her shoulder where she'd made contact with the hard oak. 'How much have you drunk?'

'Where's she?'

'I don't know, I haven't seen her. Look, Robin spoke to me earlier and he told me that you said –'

'I need Lex.'

I rolled my eyes at her rudeness. 'I just said I don't know. I thought she was with you actually.'

'Earlier.' She waved her arm. 'Then she went.'

'Where?'

She shrugged. 'Said she wanted to be alone. Do you think . . .' She tailed off, apparently having lost her train of thought.

'Do I think?'

'Liam.' It came out loudly, just as Richard passed us. I grabbed hold of her wrist, hard, so she wouldn't say anything else, and squeezed. It felt good, though it sounds bad to say it. She didn't seem to notice anyway.

'Hello, girls,' said Richard. He looked bleary and happy, just like Mum when I'd last seen her. Parents don't have a clue what's going on under their noses, I thought. Not a clue.

'Liam, did you say?' He was smiling down at Abigail. 'Do you want him?'

She giggled idiotically and tried to cover her mouth with her other hand but missed.

'No, it's fine,' I said. I gripped her harder, thought about pushing my fingers into her injured shoulder if she carried on and got Lex into trouble.

'Well, if you change your mind, he's over there with Penny,' said Richard. He gestured vaguely, already moving off towards the house. 'I've been sent in for more booze. Better get to it. Have fun, girls.'

When he'd gone, I turned back to Abigail. 'What about Liam? And, for God's sake, don't shout about it this time.'

I saw her eyes weren't glassy because she was hopelessly drunk but because she was near tears. I felt bad then, annoyingly. 'Did you and Lex have a row?'

But it seemed that, if they had, she wasn't interested in sympathy from me. She turned and stumbled towards Calliope without another word.

'She's not in there,' I called after her, but I don't think she heard.

*

It's another moment I wished afterwards I could recall, like a dangerous product, so no one would be hurt. But of course it doesn't work like that. We turn and look longingly at the past, arms outstretched, but the past stares back, impassive, and we're helpless to stop ourselves being pulled further and further away from it.

She had less than two hours to live.

Now

Lex and I go down to the kitchen so we don't wake Mum, Lex holding her phone away from her as though it's radio-active. Outside, I can hear Ben and Jess in the pool. I need to talk to him but that's going to have to wait.

'Come on, then, let's see it,' I say grimly.

The content of the video is not worrying at first. Cleo never appears in these posts of hers; I'd noticed that before. There's no voiceover either. Captions appear at the bottom, the word 'we' used – rather cynically, in my opinion – to lend it an air of professionalism, hinting at an entire team behind it, instead of one girl on a strange crusade.

Looked at objectively, which is not easy, the content is really just Penny being Penny: dismissing what the police did and entirely unaware of the impression that she herself is making – which is not good. Ironically, she's not the kind of mother Cleo might have wished for as a subject in her prurient little interview, and the few comments below it that have already been posted bear this out.

Can't believe she's talking about her daughter.

I would have run away too.

OMG rich people are so brutal.

But then, just as I'm thinking how much worse it could have been, it cuts to Liam. He's captioned as a friend of the family, which makes my hands curl into fists.

'Some friend,' Lex mutters. 'Didn't see him for dust after

Abigail disappeared. He was just *gone*, do you remember?'

I hush her. 'Go back, I missed what he said.'

It's only a couple of lines, but it's enough to make me go completely cold.

'I was there that night, when she went missing,' he says. 'And I know for a fact that certain people knew more than they let on to the police. They still know more. I mean, she didn't just vanish into thin air, did she?' He smiles briefly, before realizing it's inappropriate. It's even more wolfish than it was back then, with those nicotined teeth.

A teaser Cleo has made for her next 'episode' follows, and instead of a static caption it marches across Lex's screen in lower-case Courier as though it's being type-written live.

```
Next time, we speak to a detective who worked on
the case AND reveal a never-before-seen piece
of evidence . . .
```

'Shit,' I say.

'Liam's bullshitting, as ever,' says Lex. 'He doesn't know anything.'

'Maybe he overheard something. When we were talking at your bedroom door that night. Before we left.'

Lex hesitates, then shakes her head. It's not entirely convincing.

'And what about Cleo's piece of fucking evidence?' I say. 'She's talking about the note, isn't she?'

'Not necessarily.'

'Where is she now? Do you even know?'

She gives me a look, half riled and half hurt, just as Cleo comes through the doors to the garden.

She stops when she sees us there. With the sun behind her, she's a statuesque shadow. I can't tell, looking into the light, if I'm imagining the tiny smile on her face.

'You need to leave this alone,' Lex says, holding up her phone. She sounds as rattled as I feel. 'I *told* you that when Penny was here, but you followed her anyway, badgered her for an interview. And Liam – someone you don't even know. What the hell do you think you're doing?'

Cleo says nothing. She goes to the fridge and takes a carafe of cold water from it, calmly pouring herself a glass.

'Cleo, I'm talking to you.' Lex's voice shrills and I reach out to put a hand on her arm but Cleo is already walking past us and heading towards the stairs anyway. I've known her for just a few days but even I can see this sort of approach is useless: Lex's words, like tiny space rocks, exploded into ash by Cleo's formidable atmosphere.

Lex pulls away from me and blunders out into the garden. Instinct, or perhaps old habit, tells me to follow but I stop myself. Instead, I stand and watch the oven clock until three minutes have passed, perhaps like Cleo herself did when she followed Penny.

The attic always felt like mine, right from the start, and it still feels like that now. I try to take some solace from it, Calliope at my back and all around me as I knock on the door, which stands ajar. Through the gap, I can see her sitting motionless in a yoga pose on the floor, right in the middle of a thick band of sunshine.

'Cleo,' I say. And then again, louder. 'Cleo.'

There's a beat and then she opens her eyes. I wonder what I'd have done if she hadn't. An image of me striding over and shaking her hovers tantalizingly.

'Sorry to bother you, but we need to have a little word.' I go over to the old armchair and change my mind at the last second, remembering how the springs splayed even back then so that you felt like you were almost sitting on the floor. I perch on the end of the high bed instead.

'As you know, it's Richard's funeral tomorrow. That's why we're here. I really admire your stance on missing girls, and maybe you're right that not enough was done back then to find Abigail, but I want to ask you to press pause on it for now.'

Press pause. I sound like a manager giving an appraisal. But my voice is steady. It's more than that, actually, and, to my surprise, it's honey, thick and smooth. Assured.

'Your mum has a lot going on at the moment. She adored her father, and she feels bad that she didn't see him enough.' I deliberately lower my voice, as though we're two old comrades, me and Cleo, sharing confidences. 'And of course it's strange for her seeing me again after so long. *I've* found seeing *her* wonderful but it's also . . . disorienting, and she probably feels the same.'

Cleo's face is blank, or beatific, depending on what you think of her, but she's listening, I know she is. Her eyes are focused. Her sandy lashes quiver minutely with it.

'I'll tell you a secret,' I say, dropping my voice a little more. 'Lex wasn't always kind to Abigail back then. We could both have been *kinder*.' I emphasize it, a word that's used as a talisman these days but so often signifies nothing, especially online.

'Both of us feel horribly guilty about that night,' and, here, for the first time, I almost falter, veering so close to the truth that I can smell it. I'm risking Cleo smelling it too. But then I take a breath and Calliope breathes with me and I'm okay again. 'There'd been a little misunderstanding, I can't remember exactly what it was about now, but she was upset –'

'What was it *roughly* about then?' Cleo breaks in. 'If you can't remember exactly.'

I look out of one of the round windows, the middle one, as though I'm casting my mind back. 'Oh, God, it was so long ago. But there'd been some disagreement about Liam, I think, perhaps the night before. We'd been on the beach and –'

'Liam?' She manages to sit up even straighter.

I wave my hand. 'Yes, obviously you've met him now.' I let that land. 'Abigail had a bit of a crush, basically. He was earning good money at Richard's business. He was very good-looking. And, well, he was a man.'

I let this sit, too. Let Cleo think.

'The complicating thing was that he and Lex, well . . .' I tail off.

She forgets herself, leans forward. 'What about them? How old was Liam then?'

'Twenty-nine.'

'You remember that okay.'

I pause, then sigh. 'Well, yes. To be frank, I was worried about it. I was very inexperienced then so I put it down to that a lot of the time. But, I don't know, I always had misgivings. You mustn't tell your mum or anyone I said this, but Liam always made my skin crawl. Maybe it was just me. Your mum and Abigail didn't feel like that. Maybe you didn't either. They flirted with him a bit, you know. Flexed their power, or at least Lex did. But, you know, she had a lot going on that summer. Her exam results were coming out, she had a new stepfamily, whether she liked it or not, and then there was Liam. She was under all kinds of pressure.'

'Pressure,' Cleo repeats. 'Did something happen with Mum and him?'

'I . . . Well, I . . . Not really. Lex liked flirting with him. She never had any intention . . . It used to frustrate him, I think. Well, I *know*. But Abigail . . .'

'He couldn't get anywhere with Mum so he switched to Abigail instead? Because she was an easier target?'

I look down at my hands. 'Well, maybe. I overheard them once. In here actually.'

'Him and Abigail?'

I nod.

'Overheard what?'

'He was saying she was hurting his feelings,' I say. 'That if she really cared about him, like she said, she wouldn't hold back so much.'

Cleo's face has taken on a strange expression. 'They were talking about having sex. He was grooming her to have sex with him even though she was underage.'

I go over to the bedside table, run my finger over the mythology book.

'Anyway,' I say. Cleo has twisted round and is watching me intently. 'There are a lot of memories swirling around. A lot of things being brought back up. Neither of us expected to see him. So it would be really helpful, really kind of you to leave off the posts for now. For your mum. For us. Is that okay?'

She considers this, then nods once. 'He makes my skin crawl, too,' she says.

As I turn and go downstairs, I have no real idea what I've set in motion. There's a sense of redirecting floodwaters without knowing where they might end up: one village saved only for another to drown.

And yet, for the first time in days, I feel light. Even when I walk into the kitchen and find Liam there, drinking tea with Mum, who is still bleary with sleep.

He tips his head on one side to regard me. 'Here she is,' he says. 'Didn't she turn out lovely, Marilyn? In the end.'

While Mum smiles and twitters, gets up to rummage for biscuits, a presence behind me blocks the light and makes me turn. Makes Liam turn, too.

It's Cleo. She regards Liam coolly, then tips her head, just as he did to me, seconds ago. Her heavy plait swings.

'Hey,' she says, with a soft, slow smile so unlike her that my whole body quivers. 'Nice to see you again.'

Then

After Abigail stumbled inside Calliope to find Lex, I left the garden by the side route, breaking into a run – not because there was any clear urgency, but because I felt so jangly and odd. Sure enough, I found Lex up by the lighthouse, smoking. She raised a plucked eyebrow as I bent over, hands clamped to my thighs, panting hard.

'I knew you'd be here,' I said, when I'd got my breath back, triumphant. 'I suppose Abigail didn't think of it.' I nearly said Liam didn't either, but managed to stop myself.

I sat down beside her. Back in the garden, where the wedding party spun on, the sun had already dipped out of sight, leaving only its rosy afterburn. Up there, facing due west and nothing but sea until you clipped Italy's heel, it remained suspended in the sky, like a fat and fiery planet.

Lex's face was glowing just as it had that first night when she'd taken me down to the village. As though she'd been dipped in rose-gold. The effect was even more spectacular against her white dress. She looked somehow more than human.

'Do you know that when they were making the film *Goldfinger*, they covered this woman entirely in gold paint and she suffocated and died?'

Her lips twitched. 'How deep is the hat you pull this weird shit out of?'

'No one has ever found the bottom. It's like the Mariana Trench.'

Lex snorted. 'Actually, that one's an urban myth. No one died from gold paint. Maybe there are a few things you don't know, and I do.' She stopped and a strange look passed over her face.

'Lex, did you fall out with Abigail? She's in a right state.'

'What did she say?' Lex turned to look at me head-on.

'Nothing, really. Just said she couldn't find you. But she was being weird. She was all over the place, actually.'

'She's always upset when it comes to me.'

'True. Is that why you came up here?'

Lex took a final drag of her cigarette, stubbed it out and flicked it over the edge. 'Something like that.'

'Too much pressure.'

'Yep.'

I knew she probably meant from Liam too, but again I held back. I knew for some reason that I didn't count as another source of pressure, not right now. I didn't want to ruin that.

'I guess we're not going to pay a visit to Circe tonight, then?' I kept my voice light.

'Maybe tomorrow. When Pabs won't be a massive liability.'

I laughed, part of me enjoying her criticism, but also disappointed the two of us wouldn't get to go on our own.

We were easy together as we wandered slowly back. As easy as we'd ever been. Having run off the jangling feeling, I didn't sense anything coming now. Not a shift under my feet or an ill-starred constellation above signalling an emergency if I'd only looked up. Nothing.

It wasn't until we reached Calliope that I remembered the daft note I'd written.

The party in the garden felt like it still had a couple of hours left in it. Lex had gone off to scavenge something to eat so I went to check for Liam. When I saw him there, exactly where I'd left him, I didn't know whether to be relieved or disappointed. I couldn't seem to find my way back to my earlier panic, which now felt like days ago. I didn't know why I'd been quite so worried, when Lex seemed to have got bored of him anyway. I realized I was starving, too.

I went and found Lex rooting through the fridge. We piled up a couple of plates with cold meat and salads, hardening bread and dollops of Eleni's tzatziki, and decided to take them up to Lex's room so we didn't have to make polite conversation with anyone.

I fully expected to see the note still on her pillow. I was first into the room precisely because I was planning to sweep it up before Lex saw it. But it wasn't there. Someone had already taken it.

Lex didn't even notice that the bed was made, the floor cleared. She was so used to it being done for her. But even as this thought sparked a twinge of irritation, and I sat down cross-legged on the window seat to eat, another part of my brain was going through possibilities. If Liam had taken the note, he wouldn't be in the garden now. I was sure of that. He could already feel Lex slipping away so he wouldn't have hesitated. Who, then?

It was obvious. No one else would have gone into that room and poked about, combing through Lex's stuff in the hope that some of her shine would rub off. I'd even seen her go into the house, what, forty minutes earlier? Fifty?

I put my fork down, opened my mouth to tell Lex, and closed it again. I couldn't think why I had written it now. It seemed childish at best, and creepy at worst. What had I thought would happen?

I picked up my fork again, and while Lex ate hungrily, shovelling in potato salad and mopping up the mayonnaise with bread, I forced my food down mechanically.

'Let's go outside,' she said, when she had finished, putting her plate on the floor and pushing it under the bed with her bare foot. 'We've been antisocial for long enough.'

In the garden, people turned to us in delight, two girls shimmering white in the dusk, one blonde and one dark. We had been missed after all, or Lex had.

Robin approached me, smiling determinedly, and I knew he wanted to make it all right after the earlier awkwardness. I turned to Lex, wishing I'd told her about it already, knowing she would understand in an instant that she was supposed to drag me off somewhere, or else refuse to leave my side. But she'd gone. I saw a pale flash a little way down the garden, which was now pocketed with gloom. I stood on tiptoe to see over Robin's shoulder though I already knew who'd got her. I'd seen the glint that must have been his watch as he clamped his arm around her narrow shoulders.

Robin was talking to me but I wasn't listening. I was weighing things up. Inside Calliope, the long clock in the hall chimed the hour. Time was ticking on, and Abigail was still gone, following the instructions on my note.

My note.

'Robin, I've got to go,' I said, talking over him.

'Oh. Right, yes, of course. But where?'

I didn't answer. I ran upstairs to my room and pulled off the white dress, letting it pool on the floor and putting on the first pair of shorts and T-shirt I could find. I hesitated at the door, then went back and hung up the dress. I told myself it was because Mum would be hurt otherwise but it was because I was still weighing up whether I should go. Perhaps Abigail had just gone back to the yacht to pass out. How had she got herself into such a state anyway? I kicked a flip-flop so it skittered across the floor.

I tried to work out how long she'd been gone but had no real idea. I was halfway down the stairs when I spotted Tom coming out of the downstairs toilet. 'Hey, have you seen your sister?'

He looked at me, frowning, his mind clearly elsewhere. He had a glass in his hand, a wedding invitation clamped to the top. '*Daphnis nerii*,' he said, indicating its contents. 'Oleander hawkmoth. They're pretty rare.'

I peered closer. The moth's green markings blurred with its distress. 'Have you seen Abigail?' I tried again.

'Pabs? She went to meet Lex.' He headed for the garden.

Not find. *Meet*. She'd found the note. I had to go.

I only thought of the bike when I was halfway down the drive. It seemed heavier than when Lex and I had taken it before, and the chain scraped my legs when I pushed off, streaking them with oil. Resentment and anxiety seethed inside me as the music in the garden faded to nothing. Soon all I could hear was the buzz of the cicadas.

As I pedalled, I went over what I'd written in the note, muttering the words under my breath, and trying to work out what they meant if the wrong person had got it.

Sorry about earlier. I'll make it up to you. Meet me at Circe's Pool tonight, where the magic happens. L.

I'd written it off the cuff, champagne addling my brain. It was pure chance that it might apply as much to Abigail as it did Liam. A hot puff of frustration blew through me as I thought of how Lex habitually treated Abigail – how an apology note would be appropriate almost every day they spent together.

If it wasn't for that, and for the way she flirted with Liam, leading him on, which was a female crime I had had drilled into me since primary school, I wouldn't have been cycling through the dark night on my own. Who knew what reckless local driver might be heading towards me from the opposite direction, like the opening scenes in an episode of *Casualty*, or one of those maths problems I could never do? If X leaves the taverna at 10.23 p.m. and is travelling at 60 m.p.h., and Y leaves home on a bike five minutes earlier and is travelling at 15 m.p.h., where will they collide?

But, no, this wasn't Lex's fault. It wasn't Lex I hated. Or even Abigail. It was him.

Do something, I had pleaded after Liam had cornered me by the fridge. *Do something to stop him.* I don't know who I had been pleading with. Partly myself. Partly Calliope, perhaps. But I knew really that she couldn't help me. She was too benign, too good. Circe's Pool was different. I'd glimpsed something of what it was when Lex and I were there before.

That summer I was on the cusp, becoming a woman but still a little girl in so many ways. That ancient place had got into my blood. It had made me think back to the very beginning of secondary school: to a game we'd played at break; a large group of us, all girls. It was a make-believe game, like the ones we had been playing all through primary school. It was complex and layered, a sprawling epic set in a made-up kingdom, inhabited by queens and white horses and age-old rivalries. But it was the last gasp. It fell apart after a few months, and after that we took up huddles on the edges of the playground, talking about everyday things and avoiding the boys' stray footballs.

Reality had sidled in, the last cobwebs of fantasy swept away. We were Susan choosing not to return to Narnia. But that summer something about Eos had dragged me back to a state halfway between knowing the magic wasn't real and certain that it was.

I didn't just suspect Circe's Pool was haunted — the ancient past clinging as tenaciously as the roots of olive and laurel trees dug into the earth — but potent with something that was as powerful today as it had been at the beginning of Story. I really thought that if I lured Liam there, the place would take care of the rest.

I wasn't brave enough to stop him on my own. But Circe was. She had turned whole armies into swine because they didn't bend to her will. To me, she lived on there, at the Pool, and the years hadn't mellowed her. She would see Liam for what he was and punish him so he never did it again.

Now

I wake at ten to ten with a start. Richard's funeral is set for midday, just over two hours away. Jess had crept into my bed at some point during the night, saying she was having strange dreams. I didn't want to know about their content so instead let her ask me questions about *then*, the two of us whispering into the pitch-dark room until dawn turned it grey. The long-ago summer I described was how it might have been, rather than how it ended, and in those still, liminal hours I half believed in it myself.

Cleo was mentioned only once – just before Jess dropped off – and I managed not to say anything negative or alarmist, only asked that Jess always, *always* told us if she was going somewhere.

'It would probably be easier if I had a phone,' she had said sleepily, inevitably.

When I get downstairs after a two-minute shower, my hair dry-shampooed to save time, Mum is doing surprisingly well. I think she'll likely crash later but, for now, she seems strong. I daren't suggest it, in case she crumbles, but I think the spectre of Cassandra has actually fortified her. Anger that the first wife is descending without warning has taken up some room that would otherwise have been given over to grief.

'Where's Lex?'

Everyone else is accounted for: I'd already seen Cleo

on my way down. We were about to cross on the stairs and ridiculously I stopped dead, hearing Nan in my head, saying it was bad luck. This clearly didn't bother Cleo, who kept coming but gave me a nod like yesterday's. It felt almost friendly by her standards. Conspiratorial. 'Hi, Zoë,' she'd said, and though it was without inflection it was still a greeting.

Now Mum stops bustling around the kitchen briefly. 'Lex? She popped out. She didn't say what for. She seemed . . .'

'What?'

Mum searches for the right word. 'Preoccupied. You know she's been struggling with her eulogy?'

I shake my head. Lex had changed her mind about not speaking, and I'd said she should do it rather than me.

'I didn't ask, but she was trying to write it yesterday, I think. She's brave for saying she'll do it when she's afraid to. I wish I could but I . . . I just can't.'

Her voice wobbles but, with an enormous effort, she manages not to dissolve into tears. 'Anyway, I wonder if she's got herself in a tizz about it.'

I found Lex once before when she'd gone missing, and I'm right this time, too. The walk up to the lighthouse is steeper than I remember and sweat is sticking my blouse to my back by the time I see her.

'God, you're even having a fag, too,' I say.

'Huh?'

She looks up at me and I see there are runnels of white through her make-up, which I decide not to draw attention to. As I'd said to Cleo, Lex was always proud.

'I found you here once before, remember? Are you okay?'

'Not really.' She holds up a notepad covered with crossings-out. 'I'm trying to write something for Dad but everything's coming out as these awful platitudes. I should have just let you do it.'

I sit down beside her. 'Keep it specific and simple. What you remember about him particularly and why you'll miss it. So, you know, the crosswords, checking the weather forecast, the Branston pickle, the perfectly ironed shirts just to sit on the terrace, the insistence on keeping his record player when everyone else was getting CDs.'

'And how he ended up being trendy again, when all the hipsters decided they preferred vinyl.' Lex smiles tremulously.

'Yes, exactly. All the stuff that was wonderfully peculiar to him. It'll make everyone happy to hear it.'

She takes a shaky breath in. 'Thank you. That helps.'

I smile but she doesn't smile back, just keeps on looking at me, and it's the look from before. The one I couldn't quite place. I wonder if Cleo has said something to her, then dismiss the thought.

'What is it? You're starting to unnerve me.' I smile again to lighten it but it doesn't quite work.

'I need to tell you something.'

My hand goes to my chest. 'Is there a new post? It's all gone viral, hasn't it? Is that it?' My words stumble over each other.

'Calm down. It's nothing like that. It's nothing about *now*. It's something I should have told you a long time ago. I think I would have done, too, if we'd . . . stayed close.'

I wait.

'That night, with Abigail. I haven't told you everything that happened.'

I stop, cast my mind back. It's a wrench to do it when there's so much claiming my attention now. 'What did you say to her? I always had a feeling you'd said something horrible – maybe irretrievable – but I didn't want to push you on it. It was still me who wrote the note.'

She holds out her hands, inspects the backs of them. Her nails are all bitten down now. 'Yeah, I did say something pretty awful. I think I said to you at the time that she always brought out the worst in me. Not that that's any excuse.'

'What did you say?'

'She kept on about going to the Pool. You know I'd said the night before that the three of us could go after the wedding?'

I nod. I didn't know Abigail had clung to that idea so hard. I thought she'd just wanted to be with Lex and it didn't really matter where, but if they'd been talking about it before Abigail saw my note maybe that makes my part in it slightly less awful. Or does it? I can't think straight. Anyway, Lex hasn't finished.

'So, she was getting on my nerves. I'd been dealing with Liam, who seemed to be angry all the time after he got back here from London. You always thought he was such a predator, Zo, and maybe he was, but he was also pathetic. I was beginning to see that for myself. And I think he knew it, too, and it made him so *petulant*. I was always having to placate him and stroke his ego, and I suddenly thought, that day, I don't need this hassle. It was like a bloody light bulb going on in my head.'

'But you were with him that night. Before we – we went back to the Pool.'

'Yeah, I know. I was drunk, let myself be persuaded. But I'd decided way before you knocked that it would be the last time. That I wouldn't let him . . .'

'I wish I'd known that,' I say quietly. 'I wish . . .' I tail off because I don't want to say what's dawning on me: that if she'd confided in me that she'd changed her mind about Liam I would never have written that note.

Lex doesn't seem to hear me anyway. I look at her lovely face and I know she's totally immersed in the past, in what she called, with no explanation needed, *then*.

'Anyway, before that I'd been doing quite a good job of avoiding him, but I could *not* shake off Pabs. You know how I could be — how I just needed to be on my own sometimes. You always seemed to know that instinctively. Pabs didn't. I could hear myself getting shorter and shorter with her, and it made me feel bad, but of course that only made me meaner. The guilt, I'm talking about. It made me nastier.

'She just kept banging on about going to the Pool, about how we could go now, just the two of us, and that irritated me as well — the way she was so jealous of you. It was kind of like Liam. All this pressure.'

'Yes, that's exactly how you put it at the time.'

'Well, there you are. I was really feeling it. She'd got this idea in her head about how the Pool would transform her. I think it started off as a way to suck up to me, quite honestly — to be suddenly all keen on the idea of Circe's Pool and being witches down there, channelling the goddess or whatever. She hadn't been fussed until she saw it was a bond between you and me, then suddenly she was really into it. And I think, that night, she'd actually latched on to it in a genuine way. She kept saying we could go in the water and it would be like some sort of pagan baptism or something, especially because the water scared her so much. That she would emerge as a different person, a stronger one. A better one. That it would save her, or something. And when I said no, it was too late, and I was tired and stuff, she got really desperate, saying it had to be tonight. That it was her last chance.'

'God, that sounds odd. She did have this intensity about her, but . . . I mean, I guess she was drunk. I remember seeing her walk into one of those wooden posts holding up the terrace at Calliope and she just kind of bounced off, didn't seem to feel a thing.'

Lex lights another cigarette and I glance surreptitiously at my watch. It's almost eleven. We need to get moving soon but I know Lex has to let this out. It feels enormous to her and I understand that, though I've long known she must have said something really spiteful that night. It was the way she'd followed me when I'd knocked on her bedroom door. The way she hadn't stayed with Liam. So I let her carry on.

She takes in a sharp breath. 'I laughed at her. She'd given this big speech and I just looked at her and laughed. I said, "You think a fucking dip in the water is going to turn you into me?"'

I glance away, like she's dealt me a blow, too. It's because, even across the span of years, I can imagine exactly how I would have felt if she'd said it to me.

'I'm an awful person, aren't I?'

'If you were an awful person you wouldn't have felt so guilty about it all these years. You didn't kill her, Lex.'

334

'And neither did you. So why is it, then, that we feel so awful? Why does it feel like time's run out for us and that when we go down to the house now the police will be waiting?'

My scalp tingles, and a cold internal shudder moves through my body. These are the thoughts I've been having for days, but Lex saying them aloud makes them much too real.

I get to my feet because I can't keep still, and because we've no choice but to face today. 'We have to go,' I say, holding out my hand so I can pull her up. 'You're going to be late for your dad's funeral.'

She laughs, then bursts into violent tears, covering her face with her hands. 'He always said that about himself. He always said, "I'll be late for my own funeral." God, I can hear him now. I wish I'd been nicer to him, phoned him more, *asked* him more.'

'Everyone wishes that. Especially about their parents. Everyone.'

She says something I don't catch. I prise her hands gently away from her face. 'What are you saying? I can't hear.'

She makes an almighty effort to stop crying and stands. It strikes me that we were the same height then and, of course, we still are now.

'It wasn't just what I said to her. It was what I let her do, maybe even encouraged her to do.'

I shake my head, not understanding. 'Come on, we really need to go.'

'No, wait. You need to listen. I gave her drugs, Zoë. Liam's drugs. Not mine. I kept my promise to you, more or less. She wasn't just drunk, although she was that too, but all that stuff about transforming and meeting the goddess. She was *high*. Actually, it was more than that. I think she was probably hallucinating. I've looked it up since.'

'Liam gave her a pill?'

Lex shakes her head. 'Panikos had some new stuff. It was just becoming mainstream then, in the clubs. He had a cousin in Athens who knew about it. Liam had bought some. I told him I wasn't interested but . . .'

'What was it?'

'Ketamine.'

'Were you on it too?'

'No, I told you. I actually meant that promise. But also I was in a weird mood that day. I just wanted everyone to leave me be. I thought in that frame of mind I'd have probably had a bad trip.'

'But you let Abigail have some?'

It's the first pointed, critical thing I've said, and her head snaps up. 'She said it was her choice, that it wasn't up to me what she did. She knew he had it – knew I knew where it was in his room. She kept asking.'

'Why didn't you tell me?'

She opens her hands. 'I would never have told you. You were so . . . good. Innocent. Even if I hadn't made you that promise, it wouldn't have occurred to me to tell you.'

'So, she took some ketamine and you argued about going to the Pool and then you came up here on your own?'

'Basically.'

'And what about when we went back and you were with Liam?'

She hangs her head. 'If I'd thought for a single second that she'd go to the Pool without me I wouldn't have left her. I thought she'd just pass out, to be honest. She was in the garden. She was perfectly safe. There were adults everywhere.'

'You said you looked it up. That it can cause hallucinations.'

'Yes. You can feel disconnected from reality. And . . .' She stops.

'What? Tell me.'

'You don't feel pain properly. It means you can hurt yourself and not realize. There can be . . . It can kind of paralyse your muscles.'

I begin to walk away from her.

'You hate me now, don't you?' she calls after me. 'I know I should have told you before. I just couldn't bear to. I'm so sorry.'

I stop and turn. 'You know what this means, don't you? It's not just that you've allowed me to feel so guilty all these years for writing that note. It's that we're in way more trouble than I was already panicking about. It's bad enough that we lied to the police, and not just by omission. But then I find out you kept her diary and the note without telling me. I said it before, but I don't think you took it in, or maybe didn't want to take it in. Those things are physical evidence. They connect us directly to what happened that night. It's exactly what Papagiorgiou was always after. And now . . .' the pressure in my chest is making it hard to breathe '. . . now you're saying she was on drugs, too. Drugs you gave her.'

'Zoë, please.'

I keep walking and I don't stop.

Then

I left the bike propped against the wall where the path down to the Pool first began to narrow. I was glad to be rid of it, calves burning from all the hills, shoulders stiff from gripping the handlebars.

I had hoped, maybe even half expected, to see Abigail on the way. I didn't think of her as a determined sort of person – it was much easier to picture her having given up, slumped miserably on the verge, writing in her little diary as she wept over faithless Lex. After every bend, my eyes had scanned for her, grateful for the moon that made it possible – that and the flickery dynamo light on the bike. But all I saw was darkness and once, causing me to swerve and almost come off, twin orbs bobbing low in the under-growth, which some last sensible corner of my brain told me were just a cat's eyes.

My journey down to the Pool was different this time, without Lex. What had been thrillingly scary before was now truly unnerving. In the deep bowl of the valley, the dark was thick, like smoke, among the trees. The moon could do little more than gloss the laurel leaves. The glimmer of the stone path under my feet was only faint. The way seemed longer, too. Much longer.

'Are you sure this is right?' I had said to Lex last time.

'It's the only path,' she'd said. 'If you stick to the stones, you can't go wrong.'

You can't go wrong.
You can't go wrong.

I repeated this to myself as I went on. It helped drown out the deep silence, distract me from the wing-beats of black fear in my chest.

I didn't look up at the bell-tower as I neared it, though its silhouette loomed in the top corner of my vision. I thought that if I looked at it directly the bell would definitely start to toll this time. My body was so tightly wound that if it had rung, if anything had skittered across the path ahead of me, if anything had happened at all, I felt sure I would shatter into pieces.

You can't go wrong.
You can't go wrong.

I thought I hated that walk until I reached Circe's Pool. Then I wished it had gone on forever.

It should have been pitch-black down there. It was the lowest part of the valley, buried under the thickest part of the tree canopy. It was half tucked under the hill the church was built on, with a light-swallowing cave next to it. But it wasn't dark. It was as if the Pool was lit from within, pulsing greenly, though that was surely impossible. Either way, it was strong enough for me to spot her little bag on a stone right by the edge.

I ran forward and knelt to open it. I had last seen it at Calliope, when she had slammed into the post and it had swung around her with the force of the impact. The zip stuck at first but I wrenched it open. Inside was the little rabbit diary. Its clasp felt warm, as if she'd only just finished writing in it.

I don't know why it was so important that I got inside

the handbag when what I really needed to find was its owner. Maybe it was to grant myself a few more seconds before I looked up and out across the oddly glowing water, and saw her there.

I opened my mouth to scream, but nothing came out, like those dreams when you're paralysed. When you try to run but your legs won't work. She was floating on the surface, the long ripples of her hair and the skirt of her gold-green dress spread out in the water, like twin algae blooms. The dress shimmered so that she looked as if she might be moving, but her pale body was still. All I could think that the few times I'd touched her, in passing, her limbs had been cool and firm, like dough taken from the fridge.

I couldn't go in. I knew more certainly than I'd ever known anything that I couldn't get into that water. Fear had filled my chest, like a dark, crushing gas. I felt certain I would die if I tried.

So I ran. I ran back the way I'd just come. As I passed the bell-tower, something metallic clunked, high up inside it, and I covered my ears and ran faster. I reached the bike much more quickly than I'd expected and cried aloud at the benign sight of it, though it was obvious now that it had a slow puncture at the back: the tyre was completely flat. Still, I wouldn't leave it behind – and that made a strange kind of sense to me then: if I took the bike, leaving her wasn't so bad.

I don't really remember the journey back. Only my breath coming out in ragged huffs that kept swelling into sobs I had to swallow. And I could smell the Pool, rank and strange. Some of its water must have got onto me, got into my nose. I had one clear thought. I wondered if I'd always smell it. If that would be my invisible punishment.

The party looked and felt the same when I got there, hanging back on its shadowy fringes as I'd imagined Pan doing earlier, in another life altogether. It was as if they'd been turned to stone in my absence and had only just re-animated. The thought of this gave me hope, as though if I hurried now and *made* Lex help me, as I should have done the first time round, there was a chance this could be put right.

They weren't in the garden. I saw that at a glance: fear had quickened my senses, made them as sharp as a wild animal's. But logic also told me that Liam would have wanted to get her somewhere private.

They weren't in her bedroom either. As I ran up to the attic, I realized that would have been too risky: it was where anyone would look for her first. But they weren't in the attic either. I stood there blinking at its emptiness in the moonlight that spilt through the round windows, a trio of cartoon spotlights. My brain spun, possibilities scatter-ing, until I landed on my own neat, narrow bed. It would have been Liam's idea.

The door was closed when I got there. I knocked, not out of politeness but because I didn't want to see. That they weren't inside wasn't a possibility. I knew they were.

I pressed my ear to the door just as she called out.

'Zoë? Give me a second.'

I heard a low rumble that must have been his voice, objecting, and then she was in the doorway, pupils shrink-ing as she peered out at me into the brightly lit hall. I could see nothing behind her but a slice of darkness.

I don't know what my face was doing but the sight of it made her own transform, from smudged to immediate alertness. She opened the door wider to reach through her hand and cup my chin, the contact making the tears start, as if she'd pressed a button. She was still wearing her dress, I noticed, and despite everything else I was glad. It was the entire reason I'd written that note, after all.

'You've got to come,' I managed to push out, trying to keep my voice low. 'To Circe's Pool. It's Abigail.'

'What? You and Abigail are going to Circe's Pool?'

'No, she went already, alone. She went to meet you.'

She shook her head. 'Me? Why would she?'

'You said we would yesterday, on the beach, remember?' I dropped my head. I couldn't look at her. Another half-lie. I could no longer see where one ended and another began.

The door was wrenched right back. Liam stood there, half-naked, his chest bare and the belt of his trousers undone. I looked away.

'You,' he said. 'Fuck's sake. What now?'

But I think he took in the sight of me properly then: the oil from the bike, the streaks of green from blundering through the valley in the dark, from going down on my knees next to the water. My face, too, whatever Lex had seen in it. Tear-stained and sheet-white, I'm sure, but something else as well. Probably it was horror.

He saw that and he was the one to look away. 'The fucking state of you,' he said uncertainly, as he turned back to the dark bedroom, *my* bedroom, his hand going round Lex's wrist to pull her after him. 'You should get cleaned up.'

I reached out and grabbed her other hand. 'Please, Lex,' I whispered, right in her ear so he wouldn't hear. 'It's bad.

It's really bad. You've got to come. I need you.' I didn't dare say more with him there but I shouted the rest of it inside my head, believing Lex would hear me.

She hesitated, and looked back over her shoulder at him, and down at the arm he was still pulling on. I thought I'd lost her. But then she shook him off.

'I'll be back soon, okay?' she said.

'You leave with her now, and that's it.'

She took a deep breath, stepped into the hall and closed the door on him. She reached for my hand, took it in hers. 'Right, let's go. You can explain on the way.'

Now

When I get back to Calliope from the lighthouse, Mum and the others are almost ready to leave for the chapel. I run upstairs to change, glad of the sense of purpose – the necessary prioritization of Richard's celebration. Because that's what Mum wants it to be. 'We're not calling it a funeral any more,' she'd said last night. 'And I think we should all try to wear something blue. For him. It was his favourite colour. Blue for him, and for Greece, which he loved so much.'

When I'm ready, I go outside and find Lex, Cleo and Mum on the terrace. For once, Cleo isn't on her phone. I wonder if Lex has banned it, at least for today. I also wonder if she's had something to do with what Cleo is wearing, which is not one of her oversized T-shirts but a short, skintight dress the vivid lilac-blue of plumbago blooms. Her hair has also been loosed from its plait, and lies in perfect ripples across her shoulders. Most surprising of all is that she's wearing mascara on her pale lashes. I have the urge to ask Lex about it but I can't bring myself to, not yet. I'm still taking in everything she's said, reframing the guilt I've carried for so long.

'Where are Ben and Jess?' I say to Mum, bending down to kiss her cheek. She looks fragile but immaculate in a tailored dress the exact shade of blue in the Greek flag.

'By the pool. Jess is busy saving things from drowning again.'

I don't know if I flinch outwardly but Lex does. I catch it in my peripheral vision.

Jess is leaning out over the water when I get there, her little face a picture of concentration. She has one of Ben's big flip-flops in her hand, which she's using as a life-raft for various insects flailing on the surface. Her dress is almost the same colour as Mum's.

'What's she getting? Bees?'

Ben touches my back. 'You look good. I love the blue idea.'

'Look, Mum.' Jess is holding up the flip-flop for me to see. 'What is it? It's so cool.'

She's saved a rose chafer. Rose for the flower they like best, rather than their colour. I'd asked Richard about them that summer because their small carapaces are so extraordinary: iridescent green and gold, like shot silk. I can't speak for a moment. It's not that I feel panicky, like I have been. Right now I feel sad. Sad for a girl in a gold-green dress who thought she had to slough off everything about her old self in order to be worth anything. To be loved.

'Are you okay?' Jess rests her head against me. 'I miss him too.'

I stroke her hair. 'They're called rose chafers. It was Richard who taught me that.'

We walk down to the chapel. The short ceremony is to take place where Richard and Mum got married. Neither of them was ever religious, and the chapel was deconsecrated sometime in the eighties. They just felt like it was a *proper* place to make their commitment and, now, to say goodbye.

'Seeing the coffin is always the worst,' Mum whispers, clinging to my arm, as we wait in the front pew, repeating what she's said to me already. 'I remember it with my mum. With your nan.'

Cassandra is behind us somewhere, but that doesn't seem to matter any more. 'She can be there if she wants,' Mum said, on the walk down, taken slowly because of the heels she hasn't worn in weeks. 'It doesn't make any difference to me and him, what we had, does it?'

What does matter is who is sitting with Robin. Not just Liam, whom I've had some warning of, but Papagiorgiou, who is sitting on the other side of him, next to Eleni and, I see, with another lurch, Panikos. It's not only unnerving but bizarre seeing them there, in a single pew in the old white chapel. It's like a strange encore for all the players from that summer.

Mum, maybe to distract herself, whispers that Panikos is a successful property developer now. Ever the entrepreneur, he's currently converting a soap factory into holiday apartments, which has angered the heritage brigade. 'But what *would* make them happy?' she says. 'It's been standing empty, going to rack and ruin for forty years. At least he's making use of it.'

While his mother looks exactly as I remember her, Panikos has spread and coarsened. He looks like the wealthy man approaching middle age that he is. His smile is just the same, though. I wonder if he's still running his other business, under the radar.

'Mum,' I begin, then stop.

She leans towards me. 'I know what you're going to say and, no, I didn't invite him. Of course I didn't. I told you,

I always avoided him. People just turn up, here. It's the way they do things.'

I don't look round again because I'm so certain he's waiting to meet my eye, his laser-beam focus hot on the back of my head again. I suspect he's only here to play mind-games with me and Lex, and anger swells at the thought. I think of getting up and asking him to leave, wondering if I've got the nerve, but then everyone is shuffling to their feet because the coffin has arrived.

When Lex gets up and walks to the front, clutching her notepad, her eyes search out mine. I don't hate her. I just can't. I nod at her, like a parent might to a frightened child and she visibly calms. Her eulogy is lovely – to the degree that for a few minutes I can block out the rest and just think of Richard. 'Not a dry eye,' Mum says after, as I knew she would.

Lex catches hold of me as we're leaving, pulls me to a stop. Ahead of us, Mum is between Ben and Jess for the steep walk back up to Calliope. Penny is in a huddle with Cassandra. I can't see Liam or Papagiorgiou anywhere now. I hope they won't show themselves at Calliope, but I suspect they will. Of course the wake is to be held there. There's nowhere else Richard would have wanted for his send-off.

'Did you see him?' Lex whispers. 'How fucking dare he show up? He didn't even know Dad. He came for us.'

'I know. Mum didn't know anything about it. I notice he didn't have any problem sitting with Panikos. He can't not know about all that, surely.'

'He probably turns a blind eye if it suits. I'm telling you, if he turns up at the house . . .'

I take her hand, stroke it. The panic, which had been in abeyance for a while, is creeping back under my skin, but I daren't let it show. Lex feels so brittle with grief and anger that I'm scared she'll snap.

'Come on,' I say. 'Let's go up, get this over with.'

Back at Calliope, we're immediately absorbed in the jobs that need doing: food to get out and uncover. Chilled champagne to pour, as Richard would have liked. No sherry or tepid white wine for him.

Unobserved, I watch Lex's mother when she comes to take a glass, Penny in tow. She looks like a shrink-wrapped version of her daughter, without any of the softness. Her bones are good, but her mouth is sour. She seems to act on Lex like a forcefield wherever she goes; they're always at least twenty feet away from each other. It strikes me that it's not unlike Lex and her own daughter, and at this thought, I look around for Cleo and see a flash of that particular, almost electric, blue at the bottom of the garden.

Cassandra and Penny are heading outside now, clutching two flutes of champagne apiece. Lex approaches, still looking nervy and drawn. She's clutching her own glass, empty, and I wonder how many she's had. I wouldn't blame her for getting drunk. I'm only not because of Jess. Well, mainly her, but also because some low-pitched warning bell is going off at the back of my head, and I can't tell whether it's becoming habitual here or if it's something new that I'll need all my faculties for.

'Did you spot Cassandra?'

'You seem allergic to her.'

'The mean old trouts, her and Penny.' She lets out a

349

humourless laugh. 'Two glasses each. I hope Marilyn's locked up the silver.'

'She'll have her eye on them. I guarantee that later she'll say, "Did you see the pair of them? That's how the rich stay rich."'

'And she'll be right. Look, Zo.' She stops, looks down, twists the silver rings on her fingers.

'What is it?'

'You're being kind today because of Dad, but do you . . . can you forgive me?'

'Not quite yet. But I will.'

She hesitates, then seems to decide. 'If you can forgive me, I think you can also forgive yourself.'

'Maybe. That's not really my main concern at the moment.' I turn to the fridge, then back to her. 'But at least Papagiorgiou didn't turn up.'

'I'll have to say something if he does.'

'That's one of the many things I'm worried about.' I sound lighter about it than I feel. 'Where's Cleo? Have there been any more posts?'

'She's around somewhere. As for the posts, I haven't dared look.' She glances around and pulls out her phone. Confusion crosses her face when she finds the right page almost instantly. She must have kept the window open, to check it regularly.

'What is it?'

'They've gone. She's deleted everything she's posted since we got here.'

'What? Are you sure?' My head whirrs, trying to work out if this is down to me – because of what I said to her.

I look over her shoulder at the grid of colour. The top

left square – the most recent one – is a sunset over a city park. Lex clicks on it. It's dated nine days ago.

'Thank God,' she says, her face clearing slightly, losing some of its pinched look. My own shoulders drop. I decide I can have one glass of champagne, not to celebrate but to let everything go briefly. To think purely about Richard for a while.

Time passes a little more easily. The sky clouds over so that the Pinkening, when it comes, is dulled, new-bruise-like. The heat of the day is sealed in, people fanning themselves with the simple programme Cleo must have helped Mum to make, drinking more and more, until we run out of ice. Even the Greeks are saying it's hot for so early in the season.

'Richard would have approved,' says Mum. 'He loved the heat, for his bad back. Loved a storm too. Do you think we're going to get one?'

I make circuits of the garden, like I did once before, all those years ago. This time, I do it as a grown-up, which means making sure everyone is okay, and has all they need. I pick up dirty glasses and plates and stack the dishwasher in the kitchen. I drank my single glass fast and it's gone to my head. I can't remember eating today.

At some stage, I go outside to check on Mum and see that it's almost dark. There are no stars: there's no wind to blow away the cloud. The atmosphere is expectant and I wander down the garden to hear the sea better. Maybe there will be a storm, the water irritable-sounding. Weaving through it, I can just about hear the music – all Richard's favourites – playing from the house, though some of the guests have gone now, with others looking like they won't be long.

A hand on my shoulder makes me jump but not as hard

as I would've done a few hours earlier. It's Ben. As I turn to him, I see that someone new has just arrived on the terrace above. A group of people I don't recognize from the village part for and then cluster around him. I watch as he shakes hands and slaps backs.

'Jess is fighting it hard but she's almost asleep,' Ben is saying. I make myself concentrate on him. 'I think it's all the sea air. I said she could have a quick nap and then come back down, but she'll be properly out for the count soon.'

'I wish I was out for the count,' I say, but it comes out bitterly and I try to soften it by reaching out to squeeze his hand. 'I'm glad you're here.'

He smiles back at me, pleased. 'You said that yesterday, too. Look, can we have a chat now? I feel like I've hardly seen you.'

I glance back at the terrace and see that Papagiorgiou is looking in our direction, though it's hard to be sure through the gloom. In many ways, I want to say no to Ben, put him off until tomorrow, but that feels like letting Papagiorgiou win. 'Okay, sure,' I say, and lead Ben further into the darkness.

When we stop, he pauses, smiles. 'I suddenly feel unprepared. Ha.'

'Shall I say I'm glad you're here again, to start things off?'

He smiles again, but he's genuinely nervous, I can tell. 'I suppose I'm just feeling particularly aware of things – like how quickly time goes. Your mum said something about it yesterday – about her and Richard – and I know we said we'd give the separation longer but I wondered where you were with it. How you . . . you think it's going.'

'Well, I didn't really want it in the first place.'

'I know I pushed for it, but I think I was only trying to shock you into understanding how serious I was.'

'Are you saying you want to come back?' I toss out the words quite casually but I'm clenched tight inside.

'Yeah, I think I am. You okay with that?'

'Go on, then.'

'Well, that was easy.' His eyes are soft.

'Maybe it can be that easy,' I say. 'But we do need to talk about it properly, back in London, after all this is over.' I swallow. I feel like I'm tempting Fate to say it, but make myself carry on. 'We can't just go back to how it was – how I was – because it went wrong like that, so it would probably go wrong again, eventually, and that would be awful. Awful for Jess, particularly.'

He nods. 'I just wanted to know if it was a definite possibility.'

'Of course it is.' I reach out and take his hand again. 'It was never not a possibility.'

I wish relief would pour in, but it doesn't, or only distantly. Home feels light years away. The notion of us back in London discussing our marriage still seems hypothetical rather than something I'll be allowed to do. I turn towards the terrace, unable to resist it any longer. The bulk of him is still there, his shadow thrown up Calliope's back wall, huge and misshapen.

'How are you actually doing today?' Ben is saying. 'I don't feel like I've been on my own with you for more than a minute to ask. You look . . .'

I make myself turn back to him. 'What? Knackered?'

'Lovely, actually. But, yes, you do look a bit tired now. Tense. Is it Lex?'

353

I turn his hand over and trace a line across his palm, wondering what I dare say. Whether it would make me feel better or worse right now. I make a silent promise. If I get back to London, I'll tell him everything.

But even as I think it, I'm already bargaining with myself. *You don't need to tell him everything. What good would it do? What if he hates you?*

It strikes me suddenly, like a slap, that there are multiple people here, right now, in the garden, who could take Ben aside and tell him instead. Tell him their version. They could tell *Jess*. The thought makes the champagne aftertaste in my mouth sour into acid. Papagiorgiou. Liam. Maybe even Lex, if she was feeling reckless.

'Zoë?' Ben is still waiting for me to say something, face concerned.

'It's fine. I'm just shattered.' London, I think. In London. If I get there, I'll find a way.

'I wondered if it was something to do with Cleo,' Ben says.

'What do you mean?' I say it too fast.

'Well, all this stuff about Abigail, it must be upsetting. I heard her talking to Robin about it, outside the chapel. She's quite fixated, isn't she? It's strange.'

I take in a shaky breath. 'Lex says that's what she's like. She gets obsessions.'

'You've always been a bit . . . funny about all that.'

I will him to stop, but he doesn't.

'It's one of the first things you held back on me about,' he continues. 'Seeing as we've said things need to be different . . .' He tails off but it's not like he needs to spell it out. 'I can still picture you in that pub, the night you saw that girl and thought it was her. It's a cliché, isn't it, blood draining from a face? But yours really did. I thought then that there must be more to it than you were telling me.'

My mind spins as I calculate: how much is enough to satisfy his instincts, and how much is too much, so that he never wants to come back to me at all? And what about what I've lately said to Cleo, in case she's the one to say something to him?

'We were closer than I made out,' I say eventually. 'Me, Abigail and Lex, I mean. We spent quite a lot of time together before . . .'

'I gathered that much.'

'Well, you know what you always say about threes.'

He sighs. 'And she was the one who was left out.'

'Actually, not always. Sometimes it was me. But it was a tricky dynamic, as you know it can be. That night, there'd been a bit of a fall-out. Lex had been sharp with her, I didn't want to know either, and she was out of it.'

'Abigail? You mean drunk.'

'It was . . . it was more than that. Did you see that big guy in the pew with Robin earlier? The smiley one. He's Eleni's son but he was also a dealer back then. Lex dabbled a bit in that stuff and Abigail always copied her. The whole thing terrified me.'

'Oh, shit, so she was out of it, having taken stuff Lex had given her?' I can see his mind working, his headteacher's mind. 'And you were too scared to tell anyone in case it got Lex into trouble.' He's quiet for a while, thinking it through. 'And that's why the big rift. Lex didn't tell the police about the drugs and you wouldn't tell on her. The lie came between you.'

I look down. It's not untrue. That is what happened. It's just that it's not nearly the whole story. For a start, it leaves my part completely out of it. But I nod, even as two tears well over to run down my cheeks.

He wipes them away. 'I said it then, and I'm saying it again now. You were just a kid.'

'I could have done more.'

'People always say that.'

'I made it worse, though.' It comes out in a rush. 'I wrote this note that night.' The urge to confess is overtaking the old instinct to keep quiet.

'A note? To who? Abigail?'

I shake my head. 'But she found it. She misunderstood.'

'These things seem so huge at the time, especially at that age. But whatever happened to her – and surely she must have gone into the sea, intoxicated – was an accident. That's the truth at the bottom of it all, isn't it? There was nothing you could have done to change any of it.'

I am about to answer when a peal of laughter echoes round the darkening garden. It's Lex's laugh, I'm sure it is, but from where Ben and I are standing I can see her just inside the kitchen, her hair bright under the lights. She's not laughing.

'Ben, I need to . . .'

'Go,' he says. 'But remember, there wasn't anything you could have done.'

I can't meet his eye.

'It's all going to be okay,' he says, reaching over to kiss my forehead. 'I'll go and check on Jess.'

I watch him walk away, and as I do, I hear the laugh again, the cool, tinkling sound making me shiver. I follow it to the pool, half convinced that this is another tiny haunting from another time altogether, but then it comes again and I realize it doesn't sound so much like Lex's laugh after all. There's a hollowness in it that I hadn't picked up before.

I hover by the plumbago, trying to see through the blue froth of its foliage to identify who's down there. The lights are on under the water and, once I find a bare patch in the bushes, it's easy to see who's there by its eerie glow. Cleo is talking to someone but I can only see their back. She's dragged one of the loungers close to the water and is half lying on it, stretched out long, her dress riding up around her thighs. I realize two things at once: she's smoking and Cleo doesn't smoke, and the person sitting facing her on another lounger is Liam. As soon as I recognize him, I can smell him, slightly too much, like everything else about him.

She turns her face so I can see it better and goosebumps prickle my arms. She looks so like Lex. The cool light from the pool has refined and sharpened her features but it's not just that. It's the way she's holding herself, the angles of her body, her apparent ease in herself, so that the eye is drawn to the swing of her hair and the sheen of her skin. She laughs again, and pops the cork off a bottle of champagne, holds it out to him. Liam blinks, smiles uncertainly, takes the bottle and puts it to his lips. He doesn't understand either.

Then

'I should change,' Lex said, stopping halfway down the drive to tie the laces of the trainers she'd put on. 'I'm going to ruin this dress.'

I glanced back up at Calliope. No one had seen us on the way out. Liam hadn't come after us either. 'There's no time.'

We started moving again.

'Zoë, I don't get any of this. You're scaring me. By the look of you, I'm guessing you've already been down there. What's going on with Pabs?'

'Don't call her that.'

'Tell me.'

We were walking fast now. I hadn't even mentioned the bike. There was no way I could have carried the weight of both of us with that flat tyre.

'Zoë? If you don't start talking, I'm going back.'

'I wrote a note,' I blurted. 'Abigail found it. It said to meet you there.'

'Not you, too?'

'No, it was written like it was from you.'

She flung out her arms. 'But why?'

'It wasn't even meant for her but she found it first. She was in a right state, looking for you. This was just before I found you up at the lighthouse. Anyway, I told her you weren't inside but she went in anyway. She must have found the note then, assumed it was for her.'

'But who should it have been for?'

I swallowed. 'Liam.'

She turned to me in astonishment. 'Why the hell did you write a note for Liam?'

'I saw him and he was looking for you too. Before Abigail, this was. He was really pissed off.'

Lex shook her head. 'I still don't get it.'

'I overheard you in the attic, remember?' My voice was ratcheting up. 'All that crap about you turning legal at midnight? I thought that if he went down to Circe's Pool expecting to have sex with you and you weren't there he'd be furious. I thought that would be the final straw for him. That he would see it as another prick-tease and then he'd give up and fuck off back to England.'

'Christ, Zoë.'

'I'm sorry.' It came out as a wail. 'I was trying to protect you. He scares me.'

She grabbed my hand. 'It doesn't matter. Everything will be all right. I bet you anything Pabs is down there by the Pool thinking she's having the best trip ever, being all deep and soulful, writing shit poems in her diary.'

'She's in the water.' The words rushed out of me, like I'd thrown them up.

Lex stopped dead. 'But she hates the water. I never thought she'd actually . . .' She searched my face. 'What do you mean, she's in the water?'

I shook my head, hand over my mouth. No more words would come.

'Fuck,' she said. 'Fuck.'

Without conferring, we broke into a run. All I could think of as my feet hit the ground, hard enough to jar, was the way she had been floating, the movement of it that might have been the minute shifting of the water, but might have been her breathing. *Please*, I repeated, as the road rolled out ahead, my gaze trained on the bob of Lex's ponytail, *please let it be her*.

To be back there again so soon was a recurring nightmare. I couldn't have done it for anyone but Lex, even though the whole thing was my fault.

She noticed the bag first, just as I had, but unlike me, she didn't stop. She gathered the bottom of her dress in her hand and ran round the edge of the Pool, pushing through the branches and bushes, which caught in her ponytail and snagged on her dress to reach the bank closest to where she floated.

Lex called her name, over and over, as she went.

Not Pabs. *Abigail*.

I made myself look then, tearing my eyes away from Lex to that strange bloom on the water, the double fan of her spread hair and skirts. Before I could silence it, a little voice in the core of me said she was entirely still now. It also said that I would never know for sure if that had been the case when I'd left her.

I sank to my knees and opened my mouth, not to scream this time, but to be sick. I retched and retched but nothing came out except bile. I lowered my head to my legs and put my arms tight around them, trying to make myself as tiny as possible. Trying to make myself disappear.

I don't know how long I stayed like that, but then Lex was pulling at my arms, prising my hands off my legs. She was soaking wet. Her arms shone like dim radiation from being in the Pool's thick water. Her dress, the skirt filthy now, stuck to her legs, the soaking wet silk making terrible sucking noises as she moved around above me, trying to wrench me into a standing position.

'Come on, come *on*, Zoë. We have to go. We have to go now.'

I yanked my arms away, curled back into my pose. 'We can't,' I croaked. 'We can't leave her.'

'She's . . . gone. I went in and checked.'

'But she was moving before. I think she might have moved. Are you absolutely sure? It's just that people can seem dead sometimes, even be put in a coffin, and then it turns out that they're actually just asleep, or in suspended ani–'

'She's dead, Zoë.' Her voice cut across mine – flat, and much older. 'She's definitely dead.'

We ran like we'd run the first time. Faster. The glow of the Pool pulsed behind us, the place not wanting to give us up yet, long sinuous fingers snaking along the path to snare our ankles, the bells starting to grate against their ropes as they remembered how to ring.

We flew through the dark, not stopping, not looking back. We left her there alone to save ourselves, or so it felt.

Papagiorgiou turned up at Calliope for the first time the following day, just before the Pinkening. I happened to be in the bathroom when he knocked, staring at my own face in the mirror, searching for evidence on its surface of what I'd done.

The small window above the toilet was directly over the front door, and as I climbed on the lid to look out, I sent up a prayer for it to be Abigail, even though I knew it wasn't her timid knock. Even though I knew that was impossible.

The man standing below was broad, his black hair cropped close, a slight thinning visible at the crown. He looked up then, as though he felt my eyes on him, and I pulled back so fast I almost fell, as if he'd burnt me.

He wasn't there long. Richard insisted on sitting with us at the kitchen table, and it was done in eight minutes. I knew that from the kitchen clock, which I watched so I didn't have to look at him — the cool dark gaze that seemed to bore into my skull — so I didn't have to look at Lex either, for fear of us exchanging a glance that would give everything away. It was twenty-one hours since I'd watched Abigail stumble into the house, twenty-one hours since she'd found the note that had lured her down to the Pool.

He was back the next morning, well before eight. Liam had left at dawn without fanfare, headed back to London, and Richard always went out early to buy bread and have a coffee by the harbour. So it was only Mum, Lex and me in the house. We were all in bed when the knock came again, but I was instantly alert at the sound of it. Lex must have been, too — she was already out on the landing when I got there.

'Is it him?' I mouthed at her, as though he could have heard through a solid oak door.

Lex's face was already closing in preparation. 'Remember what we swore,' she said, in a fierce whisper, and I was nodding obediently when I realized Mum was standing at her bedroom door, hair flattened on one side but her eyes sharp.

'Go and let him in,' she said, looking from Lex to me and back again. 'I'll be down in a minute.'

We ended up in the dining room, I'm not sure how. I think Papagiorgiou must have engineered it, although I don't know how he could have known it was the only room at Calliope that no one used because it never got any light, the air always peculiarly still and frigid, like it was underground.

He didn't say anything for a long minute once we were all sitting down, presumably to intimidate us into blurting something out. He was different this time, as if he'd come to some important conclusion since his last visit. My bare right foot was drumming under the table and I had to push down on my knee to stop it.

'Is there any news, then?' Mum said eventually. 'You've already asked the girls what they know.'

He glanced at her dismissively and I prayed again, this time for Richard to hurry up and come back.

'No news,' he said. 'I come back because yesterday, when I ask questions, I think I don't get all the answers.' He gestures at Lex and then me. 'It's more serious now, yes? Abigail is gone another night.'

'We don't know where she is,' said Lex. She was scared, I knew, but she was trying so hard not to show it that she sounded completely cold.

'We wish we did,' I said hurriedly, my eyes flicking to Lex, and then to Mum, who was twisting her wedding ring round and round. I watched it like I'd watched the clock before, to stop me running from the room.

'Someone saw her with you in the garden, at the party.' He pointed at me. 'She looks upset. Then she goes in the house. Did you argue?'

'No,' I said, but it came out as a whisper. '*No*. She

was drunk.' Mum closed her eyes briefly. 'I mean, not that drunk. Just that she'd had some champagne and –'

'She often drank too much,' broke in Lex. 'She did it because she was unhappy, to escape.'

'Unhappy why?' He turned to her, away from me, and I could breathe again.

'She couldn't stand being on that yacht. She was always saying that one day she would just leave.'

'And go where?'

Lex shrugged. It looked too careless. 'I dunno. Get the hydrofoil and fly home, I guess. She said she was going to buy a ticket in preparation. Like a kind of promise to herself, I think. She was always talking about getting away – from the yacht, and from her mother. They didn't get on.'

My insides were clenching at all those past tenses, but he didn't seem to notice. A British policeman would have done. The giveaway finality of it.

'Her mother doesn't tell me this. She reads her diary but there's nothing about leaving, about running away.' He sat back, the chair creaking. 'She writes instead about you two. Especially you.' He nodded at Lex.

'Well, Abigail knew her mother was spying on her,' she said coolly, 'so she wrote about safe things, things that didn't matter. She knew she was being spied on. It wasn't just the sailing that made her so unhappy, that made her want to run away, or . . .'

'Or?'

But Lex clammed up, her face changing so that I could see how she'd looked as a tiny girl.

'We talk about the Arch yesterday,' he said, after a while. 'We talk about the beach you go to the night before the

365

wedding. But what else? What are the things she is not writing in her diary? The *un*safe things?'

Neither of us spoke. I could hear him breathing through his mouth as he waited.

'There's something else we don't talk about yet,' he said eventually. 'Where this diary is now.'

Lex's head snapped up. I saw Papagiorgiou absorb it, too.

'Her mother says it must be with her, wherever she is,' he said. 'But I wonder about this. Maybe someone didn't like what was written in it so they took it. You,' he jabs a finger at Lex, 'say she wrote about safe things. How can you know that?'

'She told us,' I broke in. 'When she said her mum was reading it. That's why she started carrying it everywhere with her. That's why she had it in her handbag.'

'On the wedding night? You saw it?' He was a whisker from smiling in triumph. '*You* took it then.'

'No!' It came out as a screech. Mum and Lex jolted in their seats. 'She always had it with her. Normally she had a bigger bag but at the wedding she was wearing this little handbag, to go with her dress.' I stop, pushing away the image of it abandoned at the edge of the Pool. 'I saw it in the garden, that's all.'

'You saw the diary in the handbag?'

'N-no. It was zipped up. But it would have fitted.' I wiped my hands on my legs. My foot was tapping again.

'You are very . . . observant,' said Papagiorgiou.

I didn't say anything to that. I'd already said way too much.

The questions went on, but he didn't have anything solid and, even in my terror, I understood that we were

366

beginning to go round in circles. He knew it too, and it made him belligerent. He seemed to grow larger and larger in that claustrophobic room. When Richard finally came back, I had to bite down hard on my tongue not to burst into tears of relief.

Within a couple of minutes, he was ushering Papagiorgiou out. 'They're fifteen,' I heard him say, though it wasn't actually true by then. Lex was sixteen. I don't know if he'd forgotten in that moment, or if it just sounded better. More innocent.

We waited for the next day before returning to the Pool. The searches had seemed to go on without pause until then, torchlight strafing the dark once the sun had slid under the sea. But that third morning felt different. Richard came back from the harbour and said the official search parties had been stood down. 'They think she must have gone into the water,' he said, sighing. He meant the sea. They all meant the sea. It was so huge and Eos was so small.

We timed it for midday, which seemed safest. We knew it was a huge risk – that someone might see us – but we had to go. We had to *see*. We weren't thinking straight, I suppose. I think we were almost mad by that point. I remember my stomach cramping and cramping with my period, which had begun that morning, heavier and more agonizing than it had ever been, and ever was again.

I deliberately didn't look when Lex threw the little handbag into the Pool. I'd seen when we arrived that Abigail was no longer visible, the awful relief of it filling me with shame.

When the bag had sunk, Lex came and knelt in front of me and took a pair of nail scissors out of her pocket. She made a mess of it, but eventually managed to break the skin of our palms. The sting as we pushed our hands together and mingled our blood for the oath made me cry out.

'Swear not to tell,' Lex whispered. 'Swear not ever to tell. On Circe, swear it.'

I glanced back at the Pool. The surface was unmoving, unbroken. I had worried about flies but there were none, though the air smelt different. Wrong. And the silence — the silence was terrible. Lead heavy.

Before Papagiorgiou's first visit, I kept asking Lex why we couldn't just confess. After the second, I got it. I watched the blood trickle down my wrist.

'I swear,' I said, and dropped my head.

She pulled me to her and our arms went around each other. She hugged me so hard that it hurt. Her hair was in my mouth and I smelt her scent of oranges. It was just discernible beneath the sweat and fear, the smell of that place.

That was Tuesday. On Wednesday, two detectives from Athens came to Calliope. They asked the same questions Papagiorgiou had, more or less, but didn't seem to care so much about the answers. Theory had solidified almost into fact by then. It was the sea. It had to be the sea.

'The girls need to leave the island soon,' Richard said, when they stood up to go, apparently satisfied, notebooks tucked back inside their jacket pockets. 'They need to get back to the UK for school.'

'Of course,' said the taller one. 'We have your details.'

Mum, Lex and I got the early hydrofoil on Thursday,

the dawn sky peach-streaked above the sheet-glass Ionian waters. We barely talked, not on the crossing, not in the taxi from the port to the airport, and not on the plane. I felt like I didn't let my breath go until I was outside under the grey Heathrow sky.

'Come on,' said Mum. 'We're going home for now. We'll think about moving once Richard gets back.'

I glanced round automatically for Lex, but she wasn't there. She was already in the air on a connecting flight to Edinburgh to stay with Cassandra. Mum's idea, it turned out: a temporary measure while Richard closed up Calliope, while the dust settled. September was approaching fast and I had a new school to start in Surrey. Eos was already taking on the strange and remote dimensions of a dream.

That temporary measure grew into permanence. I didn't speak to Lex again for twenty-five years.

Now

I lurk next to the plumbago for a while, in case they're talking about Abigail, in case Cleo is mining Liam for more information about what I told her, but I can't hear them over the murmur of conversation in the garden and then, as I was half expecting, the distant, low-pitched clatter of thunder. It seems appropriate enough.

I look back at Calliope, my gaze going again to the high round windows. They're dark now, and I wonder if this signifies anything. Perhaps only that Cleo is not up there and is instead down here, talking to Liam, being quite unlike herself.

I make myself move away, back towards the house, but it's a mistake because Mum grabs me, wanting to introduce me to people I either hardly know or have never met. She's drunk now, but if there was ever an excuse, today is it. Eventually I extricate myself without seeming too rude or inconsiderate. I haven't seen Liam or Cleo pass and assume they're still down by the pool. The thunder sounds again, though it's even more indistinct, a low bass roll that must be miles and miles away, over the mainland mountains, probably.

Lex, I think. I want to find Lex. I want her to explain Cleo — want her to say that she sometimes does this: dresses up and tries on a different persona, flexes her sexual muscles, like any young woman has a right to. That this is something Lex has witnessed before, and is unfazed by. I want her to reassure me that I haven't set something awful in motion inside her fearsome daughter.

I have almost reached the stairs when Robin comes out of the downstairs loo. He looks haggard under the hall light. He must have washed his face and run his wet hands back through his hair, dark patches spreading on his blue shirt.

'Robin, I've just got to find Lex and then I'll come back down and we can –'

'Zoë,' he says over me, and I smell the whisky fumes. I've never seen him drunk, not in all these years. Not drinking, beyond a small glass of wine with dinner for politeness' sake, is another way he's always denied himself – not wanting anything that his sister never had.

'I don't think I should have come here,' he says now. 'I didn't think it would remind me so much of that night. Of course I've been here before, for dinner, but . . .' He shakes his head, eyes misting.

'It's the occasion of it,' I say. 'Everyone in the garden. I feel it too.'

'That night,' he says, and his voice breaks slightly. I've never seen him cry either. 'I dismissed her. I *dismissed* her.'

'What do you mean?'

'She was upset. Something had happened, I don't know what, but she was in a dreadful state. She would've told me about it if I'd just taken her aside but I didn't bother. I was sick of it. Sick to bloody death of being the big brother, always left to watch Tom and stick up for her. And she was often upset, Zoë, you know?' He looks pleadingly at me. 'She was so sensitive to everything, so thin-skinned. Everything seemed to hurt her more than it did other people. And I always listened. I always did. Until that night, and that turned out to be the only night that mattered.' He hangs his head. Tears drip off the end of his nose and I put my arms around him.

'It wasn't your fault,' I say, gripping him as he sobs quietly. 'You always made everything so much better for her. It wasn't your fault.'

His breathing quietens and he seems to gather himself, pushing me away gently. 'I'm sorry. It's Richard's day and look at me. I shouldn't have drunk. I never do.' He goes to the front door. 'Will you tell your mum goodbye? I don't want her to see me like this. She already thinks I'm unhealthily obsessed, and she's probably right. I've been pinning everything on the anniversary – the reconstruction and the new posters – but in my heart of hearts I know it's not going to make any difference. She's gone. You must all think I'm pathetic. Mad, even.'

I shake my head. 'I think of her too, all the time.' It comes out tightly, oddly, but he doesn't notice. It's such a relief when the door closes behind him. Guilt weighs down my legs as I go upstairs.

I'm nearly at the landing when a shadow looms over me, almost making me topple backwards. It's Liam and he doesn't move aside. I wonder how long he's been there.

'Was that Robin?' he says, nodding towards the door. 'He's had a few. I saw him heading out and thought I'd walk with him back to the village, make sure he doesn't fall in the sea, drown himself.' His eyes flick up to meet mine and they're glassy. I can smell the booze on him too and, as I do, he lets out a tiny, soft belch, his hand not getting to his mouth in time. 'Lex around? I wanted to say goodbye.'

'No, she's not.'

'Funny being here again. Takes you back. Lex's girl's the spit of her. Don't you think?'

'Not really.'

He leans in, breath hot and rank. 'Still a stuck-up cow, aren't you? Not sure I'd be so up on my high horse, if I were you. Not after what happened back then.'

'And what was that?' I keep my voice low so the tremor isn't so obvious.

'I'm not sure. But like that Papagiorgiou was saying the other day, definitely *something*. You looked haunted that night. No other word for it. Something happened between you and her. You, her and Lex.'

Terror and fury swirl inside me at the idea of them discussing it like this – these men thinking they can air their suspicions about us over coffee and ouzo, decide our fates. Perhaps they can.

I stand aside so he can pass me, my legs trembling under me. 'You're drunk, Liam. Stay away from here. Stay away from Cleo, too.'

He smiles the same smug, twisted smile I remember so well, but he goes, thank God. I follow him to the door and watch him walk unsteadily down the hill until he's swallowed by the dark.

Lex is in her room, lying on the bed. Only a single lamp is burning, a fine blue scarf tossed over it so that the yellow light has turned weird: green and watery, submerged.

'Lex, are you awake?' I say softly.

She turns her head towards me.

I'm suddenly on the verge of tears again. 'It all feels so close. Liam . . .'

She sits up, her face in shadow while mine must be lit by the lamp. 'What about him?'

'He's just left. He knows about that night. About me.'

'He doesn't. He's fishing, hoping you'll blurt something out, like Cleo did.'

'He was with her, by the pool.'

'Circe's Pool?'

'No. In the garden. She was . . . flirting with him. I think. I've never seen her like that.'

Lex shakes her head, as if trying to clear it. 'Cleo doesn't flirt.'

'Well, that's what I thought. It . . . unnerved me. But then –'

'What?' She leans forward. 'There's something else. I still know with you, when you're not telling me something.'

'Well, it's just that I talked to her, to Cleo.'

Lex shakes her head again. 'My head is pounding and I couldn't find anything to take. You're going to have to be clearer. You talked to Cleo about what? Tonight, you mean? She took the posts down, didn't she?'

'Not tonight. Yesterday. I talked to her about Liam.'

'What about Liam? Me and Liam, you mean?' Her voice hardens.

'No. Well, yes, a little bit. But not just that. Also about Abigail and him.'

'*Abigail* and Liam?'

'It was a context thing. I was trying to explain what it was like back then. How you were under pressure from him.'

'But what has that got to do with Abigail?' She cuts across me. 'What context?'

I don't say anything.

'You remember the note?' she says. '*Your* note.'

'What kind of question is that?'

'Well, I know you were trying to protect me, but it was a lie, wasn't it, when you boil it down? And you've lied again, haven't you? You've lied for us, to distract Cleo from working it all out. Like you lied for me with that note.'

Before I can think of anything to say, she's getting up and pulling me after her, down the stairs and outside to the garden. More people have left in the meantime, including Papagiorgiou, thank God, and it's easy to see who remains. The pool light shines from the bottom of the lawn like a milky jewel but it's abandoned when we get there, an empty champagne bottle on its side between two loungers.

Cleo has gone.

Somewhere in the thick canopy of trees above the house, a scops owl begins its eerie call, the long drawn-out *booop-booop* that always sounded more man-made than natural to me, an electronic alarm punctuating the dark, just as it did twenty-five years ago.

'She was here,' I say. 'With Liam. But he left on his own. I watched him walk down the hill with my own eyes.'

'Come on,' says Lex. 'I want to check the attic.'

'I don't think she's inside, Lex.' I don't – can't – explain how I simply know whether Cleo is inside Calliope or not. But Lex is already halfway up the garden.

It's pristine in the attic room, as before. The only sign Cleo is staying there at all is a long white cable snaking across the floorboards, a reminder of her ever-present devices. It takes me a beat to notice that her phone is plugged into it. This throws us both. We stand there looking at it dumbly. My eye lights on the book by the bed. It's the same one as before, the Greek myths, but there's a page marked now, two-thirds of the way through. *Circe*, I think. *She's been reading about Circe*.

I open it and my brain shorts slightly as it tries to take in two things at once. The first is that I'm right about Circe. The second is that the bookmark is a faded piece of squared notepaper covered with the looping capital letters I'd made twenty-five years ago.

Sorry about earlier. I'll make it up to you. Meet me at Circe's Pool tonight, where the magic happens. L.

I hold it up to show Lex. Maybe it's me, or the strange currents that always operated up here, but she seems to sway where she stands.

'Let's check the garden again.'

The note is already damp from my hands. I stuff it into my back pocket and follow her. When we get downstairs, the place has abruptly emptied. Someone has pulled open the dishwasher door a few inches and steam rises from it. Mum and Eleni are sitting on the terrace, alone.

'Everyone goes,' says Eleni, getting to her feet. 'I make coffee but . . .' She gestures at the table, where Mum's coffee sits untouched. She's drinking something deep red from a small glass. It's probably port. She's going to have a terrible hangover.

'Have you seen Cleo?' Lex asks Eleni, but Mum turns.

'Didn't she look like you tonight? God, it took me back.' She begins to cry softly, her face crumpling.

I sit down next to her and hold her hand.

'Eleni, thank you so much,' Lex is saying. 'For everything

all these years, not just tonight. You go home now. You've done enough.' She gestures towards the dishwasher. 'Can we call you a cab? I don't want you walking alone . . .'

But Eleni is shaking her head. 'My Pan waits in his car. I just don't want to leave Marilyn.'

They hug and then she's gone and it's just the three of us. I nip upstairs to check on Jess and Ben, and find that he's fallen asleep on the bed next to her, just as he always did when she was tiny. I close the door softly behind me. The possibility of the three of us being back together in London shimmers in my mind like a mirage in a heat haze.

Lex is rooting through cupboards when I get back downstairs, like I'd seen her before.

'Still can't find the painkillers?'

'No, but I wasn't looking for them. It's your mum's pills. She wants to go to bed.'

I look too, and upstairs in the drawers of the bedside tables in the master bedroom, but there's no sign.

'Mum, are you sure you haven't taken them all?' I say. 'You need to be careful about forgetting what you've already had.'

'Thank you, Zoë,' she says sharply, though she slurs on my name. 'I know what I'm doing. I'm not some druggie. I had five left and, anyway, Richard's back pills have gone too.'

'The diazepam,' Lex says. 'Are you sure?'

'Not you as well. Yes, I'm sure. They were in that smaller box, inside the big one with the plasters and the ointments. I saw them this morning. I took one before the funeral for my nerves.'

I find her some paracetamol in Ben's bag to stave off the

headache that will bear down on her in the night. Upstairs, she falls asleep instantly and I leave the en-suite light on in case she's disoriented in the night.

Lex is smoking on the terrace when I get back to her.

'Any sign of Cleo?'

'Nope. I keep going to text her, then remember she doesn't have her phone. That's unnerving me more than anything, actually.'

I sit down and reach for the cigarettes. 'This is what people do, don't they, in a crisis, even if they don't smoke?' I light one, but it's so revolting I hand it to Lex.

'Is this a crisis?' she says.

'I don't know. I can't think straight.'

'Well, one thing's for certain. It makes no sense that she would be friendly to Liam if you told her that he was some sort of groomer back in the day.'

'No, I know. That completely threw me. So did her dressed like that. I wanted to ask you if she just did that sometimes. Or if . . .'

'I think they're part of the same thing. Dressing like me, being all cosy with Liam, whom she can only despise if I know anything about my daughter at all. And we know now that she found the note.'

The note. There's something my brain is trying to catch at, but it's just out of grasp. I reach into my pocket and pull it out, crumpled now. The L for Lex is slightly bolder than the rest, as though I'd pressed the pen to the paper harder. To my tired eyes, it seems to pulsate, like a speaker vibrating with a bass note.

I hold it up. 'The L,' I say. 'Do you think Cleo could have thought it stood for Liam? Abigail thought it was for her

379

when it was actually for Liam. What if Cleo thinks it was *from* Liam instead of you? That he wrote it to lure Abigail to the Pool.'

A word is circling in my mind, though I tell myself it's ludicrous. Still, it continues to wheel round and round, a dark bird of a word, huge wings of glossy feathers. *Vengeance.*

'Come on.' Lex is on her feet and stubbing out her cigarette. 'I need to check something else.'

We tiptoe back up to the top of Calliope while the rest of the house sleeps on, oblivious. Lex goes straight over to a low cupboard used for storage.

'There was a bag in here of old clothes. That blue dress she squeezed herself into today? That was mine.'

'I don't remember it.'

'Zo, I had a million dresses. You know how Dad spoilt me, even as he told me I should be less spoilt.'

She yanks out a huge plastic laundry bag and starts to rummage through it, pulling out vest tops and cut-offs, bikinis and even a couple of sweatshirts she can't have needed that summer. 'Cleo asked me last night if she could wear an old dress she'd found up here. She said she didn't have anything blue that was suitable. I didn't think anything of it, and then I saw her, and she looked so . . .'

'She looked like you.'

Lex turns. 'Yeah, but not just that.'

Jailbait. A horrible term I haven't thought of in years. Not since that day at the port, when Liam came back.

'There was something else in here,' Lex is saying. 'I buried it at the bottom. I couldn't bear to throw it away, like I couldn't bear to get rid of the diary. It seemed wrong.'

I know then. I can see it in that tiny dressmaker's shop, Liam's eyes inching over it. I can see it glowing out of the gloom next to Circe's Pool. It made her seem like she was floating. I remember it afterwards, too, when we got back to Calliope, traumatized and heartsick and in shock. The thick green tidemark sullying the bottom two feet of the pure white silk. I can't believe she kept it, just like the diary. The thought of it makes me want to scream at her, but I understand the impulse too. I'm not sure I could have destroyed them either. It would have seemed sacrilegious, but also like tempting Fate.

Lex has reached the bottom of the bag, clothes surrounding her, vestiges of the past sparking at me, firefly memories. My own dress is in London, at the back of the wardrobe in a moth-proof bag, only slightly yellowed, taken out and looked at once each August. But Lex's bridesmaid's dress should be here, and it's not. Like Cleo, it's gone.

We take Lex's little car and she drives well: there is no crunching of the gears and she rounds the bends smoothly. Neither of us needs to discuss where we're going. Her face, caught in the streetlights that soon peter out, is totally focused. I think of how slow my progress was that night, on the old bike with its punctured tyre, and how swift ours is now. I try to calculate the time since I last saw Cleo. How long was I talking to the mourners surrounding Mum, and to Robin and Liam? How long putting Mum to bed, and searching in the attic? I don't know, but it seems long enough.

As we begin down the path, Lex lighting the way with Cleo's phone light because it's the most powerful, I list all the places she is more likely to be, to keep a lid on my panic.

We've just missed her and she's now safe in bed.

She's on the beach, looking at the moon.

She's in the village, seeing who else she can talk to.

She's gone to Liam's hotel room.

My insides lurch at the last.

'Lex.' I whisper it, though who or what I don't want to wake, I'd rather not contemplate. 'Should we have gone to where Liam's staying first? Don't you think she'd just go there, if she was going to . . .'

'We'll go there next,' she says grimly. 'If we need to.'

As we hurry along, single file with Lex in front because it's become even more overgrown in the time since we were here before, the phone torch illuminates the wall at our left side in weird, ragged bursts. It deepens the crevices in the dry stone and makes the old painted As seem to loom and dance. When Lex cries out, my heart stops.

Ahead of us on the path is the ghost of a girl who has never stopped haunting me, even when I stayed thousands of miles away from the place she never left.

But then Lex speaks. 'Cleo,' she says, and my blood starts moving again. I squeeze my eyes shut and when I open them, of course it's not Abigail.

It's Cleo.

She stands there in the moonlight, coldly radiant in her column of white, a reincarnated Lex from a quarter of a century ago. But then she moves towards us and there's something fundamentally different about her. It's not just that the dress is so tight that its seams strain, her every curve and muscle visible under the silk, but something unyielding

382

and intractable in her expression that's not Lex at all. And the glow of her can't be a trick of the moonlight because there is no moon. Far above, cloud still blankets the stars. Far away, thunder is still low-rolling, background dread. Perhaps Cleo is simply emitting her own light, some inner source unlocked by the Pool, or maybe by Circe herself.

I lunge forwards, intending to push past Cleo, to make myself go down to that unearthly green water, whatever I might find, but she raises a hand to bar the way. When she circles my wrist, a ring on her third finger pinching me, her skin is as cool as chilled water.

It's Robin who comes the next day, dishevelled and slightly wild-eyed. I had half expected the police. It's almost midday and a soft drizzle has been filtering down since dawn. I know because Lex and I were awake when it started. We never went to bed at all.

He comes into the kitchen, where Lex, Mum and I have been sitting at the table for some time, not quite sure what to do with ourselves, though for different reasons, like survivors of an earthquake waiting for aftershocks. Only Jess has seemed entirely immune to the collective mood this morning. She's reading the mythology book in the sitting room's window seat next to a dozing Ben, the heavy volume resting on a cushion on her stomach. I'm not glad of much, but I'm glad I took that note out of it.

Mum assumes Robin's only here to apologize for getting drunk but I know his face is too strange for that. She gets up and pats his arm. 'You look like I feel, Robin, love. But that's what we do, isn't it? At a funeral, to get through it. You don't have to be perfect all the time, sweetheart.'

She fusses over him, making him sit down at the table and going to the fridge to hunt out leftovers. It's almost unbearable waiting for him to speak. I just want to get it over with.

'I actually came to tell you something,' he says finally. His voice is almost toneless. I wonder if he's in shock.

Lex reaches for my hand under the table.

'It's Liam,' he says, as I knew he would.

'Liam?' Mum closes the fridge door.

'We agreed to meet for coffee this morning but he didn't turn up. He wasn't answering his phone either. So I went to the apartment where he was staying. I knocked but there was no answer and I got worried, you know how I am. I persuaded the woman on Reception to unlock the door, but he wasn't in there. No sign he'd gone to bed at all, actually.'

'Well, he's just checked out early, hasn't he?' says Mum. 'I know he had to go back today. He couldn't stay longer because of work.'

Robin swallows, pulls at his hair. 'But, you see, his things are still there. Well, most of them. His clothes and his wash-bag. His case and his passport. Only his phone and wallet seem to be gone.'

'Well, maybe he's gone off somewhere for a last look before he has to leave. He must have forgotten about the coffee. He was pretty plastered when I last saw him.' Mum looks at me and Lex, as though she's suddenly noticed how silent we are.

'It wasn't just his things that were there,' Robin says. His hands are in his hair again, pulling at it hard. 'One of the posters was on the bed.'

'Posters?'

'The missing posters. Of Abigail. He must have torn it down from somewhere. There was a tear at the top. It was with this old note.' He frowns.

Cleo comes in then. She sits at the far end of the table and begins to scroll on her phone. Behind her, the air above the well shivers slightly.

'I've told the police,' he says. 'I think it might be significant. The note mentions a pool. Circe's Pool. I vaguely remember hearing about it, years and years ago, but I've never been. I think maybe it was Abigail who told me about it. But the note was from Liam.' He takes a shaky breath. 'They're going to search it.'

He steps into the clearing. This ancient place hasn't seen a man in years and it seethes at his intrusion. It heats the big gold watch on his wrist.

It's markedly, illogically, silent here. The hum of insects, the breeze fluttering the olive leaves, the distant sigh of the sea, all of this is absent, as though sound has been switched off, every breath held.

The sudden quiet throws him. Almost literally. He stumbles, then again. He can't seem to stay on his feet. He doesn't think he had that much to drink tonight, and what he had was decent champagne, not spirits, but this doesn't feel like being drunk. More like poison, or bad drugs. His vision is off-kilter, like a faulty camera lens zooming in and out without warning, so that one second everything is blurred and the next he can see every fibrous stitch of every leaf. He can see them *growing*, trembling with the effort of it.

He wishes he hadn't agreed to come, can't think now why he was so determined. He thinks of the bed made up for him back at the apartment: starched white sheets, a sprig of lavender in a narrow vase next to the bed. He opens his eyes, which had closed themselves, and sees that the trees have surrounded him, foliage pressing in on him, branches reaching out to catch at his shirt with bony, needful fingers. His signet ring starts to warm on his finger, growing so hot that he thinks it'll brand him. He works it off but fumbles as he tries to put it into his pocket and watches helpless as it falls, all twenty-four carats of it, into the undergrowth. He gets on his hands and knees to find it but it's gone. The place has taken it and won't give it back.

The whispers start low but even as they grow in volume, he still can't catch the words. 'Fuck this,' he mutters, saying it aloud to prove he has the nerve, but also for the benefit of whoever is there, because he's sure someone *is*. The place answers him by tripping him again. He lands hard and rolls, the seat of his trousers soaked through. As he pushes himself up, he sees how close he is to the edge of the water. It's too small to be a lake, too large to be a pond. The word hovers and then lands on his tongue, which feels too large for his mouth: *pool*. He hears Lex's voice, that posh-bitch drawl: *Circe's Pool*.

She'd told him about this place long ago, showed him where it was on a map, bitten nails pointing it out in some old book. He remembers then: he's come here for her. Not Lex. *Her*. The daughter. He'd given her the keycard to his apartment and she'd taken it but then shaken her head. 'Not there,' she'd said. 'A better place.' And then she'd smiled.

He sways on the edge. It's deep, the water, though he couldn't say how he knows because it isn't clear. He just does. It goes down a long way, deeper than a lung's worth of air. Deeper than two. A girlfriend asked him once why he never learnt to swim. She was a posh girl, too. He always had a weakness for them. He made something up, some near-miss when he was a kid on a sailing holiday that had traumatized him forever. As if. No one could swim where he came from. No one took fucking swimming lessons, much less went sailing.

The shove, when it comes, is entirely shocking and

somehow inevitable. He seems to hang suspended over that lurid water for a long time. *Chartreuse*, he thinks absurdly, as he hits the surface. The name of the liqueur that's the exact same colour.

Memories fall in a steady stream as he descends into the dark, just like people say they do. Playing football on the estate as a kid, the ringing echo of leather bouncing off concrete; his mum's tiny crucifix against her freckled chest; and finally, Lex, turning away from him, rich-girl hair billowing around her head.

The whispers start up again as the pictures fade away. He still can't understand them.

And then,

dark.

———————

When we lift the glass lid covering the well in the ghost-grey minutes before dawn, and I don't think Lex and I could have managed it without Cleo, I hear a sigh. And yet there's no sound at all when we drop in the signet ring, the diary and the dress with its green stains and broken zip. Last of all, nearly forgotten, is the keycard that had allowed Lex and me to do the rest. The poster, torn from a lamp post, and the note pulled out of my back pocket.

Lowering the lid is even harder; not just the enormous weight of it, which tears a muscle in my back, but the fear of glass shattering on stone if we misjudge it.

When it's done, Cleo goes to bed. Lex and I can't. We sit on the terrace and watch as the rain starts to fall.

'Do you think it'll work?' She's turning a packet of cig-arettes over and over.

'I don't know,' I say. 'It might.'

'So many lies.'

'But at least they'll find her now. She won't be missing any more.'

'Zoë?' She reaches out her hand. It's warm when I take it. 'If we get out of this, we won't be apart again, will we?'

I shake my head. The rain keeps falling.

Cleo had said something strange before she went up to bed, after we'd covered the well. 'I didn't push him, you know.' Lex and I had waited for her to explain, but she only shrugged. 'I didn't need to. It was already done. It was her.'

Her. We didn't ask any more.

Around us, Calliope has settled, calm once more. I know then, in my bones, that it will work. We'd lied again, but not for us this time. For Cleo. And, I suppose, for Abigail, too.

Acknowledgements

Huge thanks to my excellent editor Grace Long, whose brilliant editorial solutions, enthusiasm and general thoroughness always make her such a pleasure to work with. Thank you also to the rest of the Michael Joseph team for their fantastic support, in particular Emily Van Blanken, Courtney Barclay, Riana Dixon, Jill Taylor, Maxine Hitchcock, Joel Richardson, Lee Motley, Alice Mottram and Jill Cole. I was lucky enough to have Hazel Orme on copyediting duties once again, so a big thank you to her, too. In my corner on the agenting front, I benefitted from having not one but two brilliant advocates this time. Thank you so much to dear Rebecca Ritchie and Victoria Hobbs at AM Heath.

All the love and thanks to my wonderful family, friends, and fellow writers and colleagues at The Novelry. Special mentions for my great pal Emylia Hall, who was such a top-notch early reader, and for Jeremy Pearce and Claire McGlasson, whose general love and support is so appreciated. Other particular thanks and gratitude must go to Elizabeth Speller for introducing me to the magical Greek island of Paxos, on which my semi-fictitious Eos is based. Thank you so much for the hospitality, local knowledge and unending supply of excellent anecdotes.

He just wanted a decent book to read ...

Not too much to ask, is it? It was in 1935 when Allen Lane, Managing Director of Bodley Head Publishers, stood on a platform at Exeter railway station looking for something good to read on his journey back to London. His choice was limited to popular magazines and poor-quality paperbacks – the same choice faced every day by the vast majority of readers, few of whom could afford hardbacks. Lane's disappointment and subsequent anger at the range of books generally available led him to found a company – and change the world.

'We believed in the existence in this country of a vast reading public for intelligent books at a low price, and staked everything on it'
Sir Allen Lane, 1902–1970, founder of Penguin Books

The quality paperback had arrived – and not just in bookshops. Lane was adamant that his Penguins should appear in chain stores and tobacconists, and should cost no more than a packet of cigarettes.

Reading habits (and cigarette prices) have changed since 1935, but Penguin still believes in publishing the best books for everybody to enjoy. We still believe that good design costs no more than bad design, and we still believe that quality books published passionately and responsibly make the world a better place.

So wherever you see the little bird – whether it's on a piece of prize-winning literary fiction or a celebrity autobiography, political tour de force or historical masterpiece, a serial-killer thriller, reference book, world classic or a piece of pure escapism – you can bet that it represents the very best that the genre has to offer.

Whatever you like to read – trust Penguin.